James Mallory was the captain of the ship. Still, Amanda observed, he lacked discipline. . . .

Mallory came across the cabin and threw himself down beside her. "Now, tell me why you ran from me. A girl such as yourself should be used to a man's amorous ways. Do I seem cruel, is that it?"

As he spoke, he drew her to him, using a strand of her chestnut hair like a tether. He pressed his lips to her forehead, then to the pulse that throbbed wildly in her throat. Before she realized his intentions, his arms engulfed her and drew her into a fierce embrace.

Though she fought to tear his lips from hers, he held her as if in a vise. Somehow, she realized with shock, she lay stretched naked beside him on the crimson coverlet. Uselessly, she howled for him to stop, her cries muffled in her throat as his mouth covered hers once more. His thigh, carelessly thrown across her hips, held her prisoner as perfectly as his embrace.

"You don't understand!" She wailed, "I am not what you think!"

Mallory knew well what Amanda was and was not, and he didn't seem to care. . . .

BY PENELOPE NERI

ZEBRA BOOKS
KENSINGTON PUBLISHING CORP.

ZEBRA BOOKS

are published by

KENSINGTON PUBLISHING CORP.
475 Park Avenue South
New York, N.Y. 10016

Printed in the United States of America

For my husband, Harvey,
With love.

Prologue

Amanda shivered and huddled deeper into the false security of the fragile canoe. The damp chill of the bayou night was a sinister cloak about them, and the sickly light of a moon, shrouded by tattered clouds, revealed a tangle of grotesquely twisted trees and foliage that was no less sinister.

The feeling of impending doom grew as the canoe drifted onward, until the terror choked her throat and paralyzed her limbs. A soft, strangled sob escaped her, and she pressed a clenched fist against her lips to quell the sound.

He turned, a black silhouette against the backdrop of the night, and she saw that his body was no less tense then her own, though he had denied fear.

"Don't Amanda!" he commanded.

His voice was comforting, oh God, yes, so comforting! She nodded mutely, drawing a deep, shuddering breath to calm herself. And then, suddenly, wonderfully, he was pressing her down, down into the canoe, and it was as if meant to be, it felt so right. His lips were sweet and filled with urgency as they covered hers, his arms pressing her the length of his body, and her own, quivering flesh molded willingly to his. No words were said, for none were needed. Desire—savage and hungry, born of their fear, of their need for each other—said it all.

Afterward, he still held her tightly, as if loath to be parted from her by so much as an inch or a second in time. When he finally spoke, his voice was husky, and charged with emotion.

"I love you, Amanda, more than I believed it possible for a man to love a woman! Without you, there is no life for me. I vow, before God, that never will we be parted again; *nothing* will part us!"

"Not even—death?" she whispered, her breath trembling against his cheek.

"Not even death!" he vowed hotly, cradling her in his arms.

A tear trickled down her cheek, and with it came an overwhelming stab of regret. They had wasted so much time! Would there be a tomorrow for the two of them? Or would Death's spidery fingers spin a final web of destiny about them?

Chapter One

"'Tis sorry I am, sir, that ye foind me mistress gone. By t'saints, ye missed herself by not *foive minutes!*"

Amanda's voice, soft with the lilt of her mother's Irish brogue, carried to Aggie in the drawing room.

The man snorted, thrusting the sheaf of overdue notes back inside his seamed pockets. He waggled a finger sternly at her.

"Well, my girl, you do best tell yer Mistress Sommers I do be a-comin' back—and the next time, I'll not leave empty-handed!" He hoisted the handcart's shafts in his meaty fists, and took a step or two down the driveway. "Bloody welsher, she be, just like the father before her!" He flung over his shoulder. "Tell yer mistress I'll be bringing t'constable with me, next time, wench!"

"Oi'll tell her, sir—and I hope you break your blasted leg in the meantime!" Amanda screamed after him, slamming the door at his startled figure.

She leaned against the door, breathing heavily with anger. Gradually, the crimson color in her cheeks faded, and her lips twitched in a gleeful smile. He'd gone. A reprieve—for the time being!

"Amanda Elspeth Sommers! What are ye thinkin' of, hinnie? Take off that cap and apron this instant!"

Amanda startled guiltily at Aggie's scolding. She hurriedly did as bidden, wincing as her nannie continued.

"Are ye oot of your mind, lassie? Do ye think t'delay the inevitable indefinitely, is that it? Och, Mandy, don't I know how it grieves ye! But you've done all a body can do—and all for naught! Now's the time t'put a good face on it, t'give in gracefully, while ye've still your pride—or would ye have your creditors take that, too?"

Knowing Aggie was right did little for Amanda's frayed temper.

"Welsher, indeed!" she stormed. "How *dare* he call my father a welsher!" She flung the white mob cap and frilled apron across the room, and paced angrily.

Her hair, now free of the offending cap, tumbled like a burnished chestnut river about her shoulders and down to her waist. Her dark brown eyes were glistening with unshed tears, and the cream of her cheeks crimsoned again with indignation. She whirled on Aggie before the Scot could make a reply.

"No," Amanda said resignedly, "don't say it, Aggie. My father *was* a welsher, at the end, at least. I know it to be true, though I wish to God I didn't!" she added hotly. "How could he have done it, Aggie, how can anyone love so singlemindedly that grief could drive him to lose it all, and with no thought given to *my* well-being? Did he care nothing for me, is that why? Dear God, Aggie, some part of me hates him for it!"

"Nay, lassie, he loved you well! But he was a weaker soul than yoursel'. Your mother was the strong one, just as ye are. Jessica's death was a terrible blow t'your father, terrible! The liquor an' the dice an' the clubs an' all, the only way he knew t'ease her partin'. He never intended t'leave ye penniless, hinnie, but by t'time he realized the extent of his debts, it was too late!"

Aggie put her arms around Amanda and kissed her forehead.

"Now, nae more of your play-actin'! Ye've put it off long enough. The house *will* be sold—auctioned, to cover the debts—and the furniture, too. Only then can ye get t'creditors off your back. Accept it, Mandy, and go for'ard, not back!"

Amanda smiled bitterly.

"Forward?" She spread her arms out. "Leaving all of this and spending my life as a governess in some dreary house is going forward?" The fire in her eyes extinguished suddenly. Her expression softened. "Very well, Aggie McNab!"

Aggie smiled, and smoothed Amanda's hair. Och, such beauty—and such waste! It was not what she would have chosen for her Amanda, if given a choice, to molder in some great house as governess 'til all that beauty faded. Pah! Privately, she felt it would have been better if Robert Sommers had succumbed to consumption along with his wife, before he'd gambled away the entire estate and ruined his daughter's life. Selfish weakling!

Still, it could have been worse, Aggie had to admit. If not for Mr. Aubrey, the solicitor, having found Amanda the governess's post at Birchwood, the girl would have been literally thrown out on the streets! *Her* Amanda—for as such Aggie thought of her—thrust out into a world that was often cruel and never easy, especially after the protected life she had led. She had needed no domestic skills as the daughter of a wealthy and respected family. Her upbringing had prepared her only for the intricacies of a courtship and the demands of marriage and its responsibilities, and little more. What else could the girl do, but teach? In all probability with her looks, Amanda would have ended up in the filthy stews of London, selling that lovely body for the price of a farthing or two to ward off starvation. Nay, whether the lassie knew it or not, it was better this way!

Amanda gave a last brush to her hair and looked about her. Yes, that was it, she was ready—or at least, ready in body, for never, never would she be ready to leave Christchurch in spirit!

She crossed the room, and perched on the window seat, flinging the leaded, mullioned window wide open to gaze out at the view for the last time.

A rockery curled about the lawn, magenta blossoms spilling down its craggy surface. Towering oaks lined the driveway, forming a green, leafy tunnel to the lanes of Bellbury beyond. To the east rose the spire of the village church, gray-stoned and ancient, pointing a metallic finger toward heaven. Here she had been baptized nearly nineteen years ago. To the west were the whirling sails of the mill, set in patchwork of orderly fields, like a cream-colored giant standing amidst rich brown earth and lush green pasture. Suffolk. Some thought it rural and dull, but not Amanda. She loved it all so!

She turned away, nigh choking with grief. This day

would be forever burned into her mind, along with two others, equally sorrowful. The first, the day of her mother's death, the second, that of her father's, in the crawling damp of the debtor's wing at Newgate gaol. And now, this! In less than two hours the auctioneer's hammer would fall, and Christchurch, the only home she had ever known, would go to the highest bidder.

"Damn!" She thrust Lady Elizabeth's letter into the already bulging portmanteau, and stormed down the stairs without a backward glance, suddenly anxious to be gone, to cut short the bitter pain of parting.

She said her farewells hurriedly, unable to bear it anymore. When it came to Aggie's turn, it was all Amanda could do to hold back the tears.

"Well, my dear sweet lassie, I bid ye farewell, and may God be wi' ye. If ye have need o'me, I'll be at my sister's cottage in Ipswich Town, ye've only t'send word. Hold your head high, hinnie, and guard your temper!" Aggie kissed her fondly.

Then Thomas loaded her two trunks—the only belongings Amanda had—and handed her up onto the perch of the wagon.

With her final farewell wave, the sorry vehicle rumbled along the driveway, carrying her away from Christchurch and all that had gone before.

It was but a short distance to the Latticed Barn, where the public coach could be boarded. The quaint old alehouse was as good as its name, for it did indeed resemble a barn, as pictured on the gaily painted sign swinging above it in the breeze. Latticed windows squinted out onto a street that led to a crossroads at the corner. A duck pond lay on the other side, the noisy animals comically entertaining a group of grubby children with their antics.

Thomas drove the wagon into the side entrance of the alehouse yard, alongside a dray with its team of huge, shaggy horses. Men were unloading the dray and trundling heavy barrels of ale into the gaping cellar beneath the inn.

After taking her luggage down from the wagon, the groom led her inside the inn.

Only rarely had she been inside such a place, yet she could not bring herself to enjoy the experience. She felt ill-at-ease and somehow ashamed, as if her newly impoverished state were a sin, rather than a cruel twist of fate.

"Miss! Miss Amanda?"

"Oh, I'm sorry, Tom! Yes, what did you say? I was daydreaming, I'm afraid!"

"This 'ere's for you, miss. 'Tain't much, but Cook and the maids an' me, we wanted for you to have it, seein' as how you've hit hard times. You and the Missus, afore she died, and your Pa, you was good to us'n. Now we'd like to help you, miss." He hung his head, shame-faced.

Never had Amanda heard Tom make a speech even nearing the length of this one. She looked down at what he had pressed into her hand, tears welling finally as she unwrapped three gold sovereigns from a piece of cloth. She would not hurt him by refusing.

"Oh, Tom!" She flung herself into his arms, burying her head in the leather of his jerkin. He smelled of horses, earth, and good honest sweat, familiar smells that were part and parcel of the niceness of him. "Tom, thank you!" she said finally, lifting her head and sniffing back the tears.

After he left, her aloneness was even more acute. She stood and crossed the saw-dusted floor to peer through the window. A figure she knew well was coming across the village green. She hurried back outside to the street again, and as Meg caught sight of her, Amanda lifted her skirts, and ran to meet her.

The two girls flung their arms about each other, laughing and crying at the same time.

"Oh, Mandy, I thought I'd missed you, I did! I would have been ever so upset not to see you off!" Meg's plump face grew solemn.

"No, Meg, the coach is late—as always. I'm so glad you came to bid me farewell!"

"Well, I couldn't let you leave without saying good-bye, now could I? Not after all the pranks we've shared since we was nippers!" Meg grinned.

Amanda nodded and squeezed Meg's hand affectionately. They strolled back to the inn and stood there chattering for some time.

All too soon there sounded the loud "halloo" of a post horn. The coach careened wildly into the yard, the horses' hooves ringing on the cobbles.

The driver, a stout, red-faced man, leaped down from his perch and tossed the reins to the ostler.

"Wotcha mean, we're late? We made good time 'twixt here an' Ipswich! Post's in the sack, ladies and gents. Me mate'll hand it down to ye. Any more t'board here?"

Amanda stepped forward.

"Yes. I-I'm traveling as far as Birchwood."

"That's hardly pissing distance, me girl! Where's yer sense of adventure? Pretty wench like you'd do well in ole Lunnon Town, she would," he added, winking slyly.

Amanda reddened and glared at him.

"And if all the 'pretty wenches' in 'Lunnon Town' have oafs like you to contend with, I warrant they'll soon all be in Suffolk, good sir!"

She smiled sweetly as his face darkened.

He scowled, rolled his eyes in exasperation at the grinning crowd, and stomped into the tavern.

Amanda knew that the coarse jest had been only that, but she wished she had a companion to travel with. If the driver was an example of what she would have to contend with as an unescorted woman, she shuddered to think what could happen! Gently, Meg teased a smile back into her face.

Soon the driver returned, reeking of ale and wiping smears of what looked suspiciously like pork drippings from his mouth with the back of his sleeve.

Fresh horses had been harnessed into the traces, and the animals were anxious to be off.

Amanda and Meg clung to each other briefly, and then the ostler heaved her two trunks onto the top of the coach.

"Climb aboard, ladies and gents, an' we'll be orf!" cried the driver.

Amanda clambered inside, reluctant to leave go of Meg's hand, for the girl was crying noisily now, all attempts at hiding the tears having failed. The driver's lad slammed the coach doors shut and leaped onto his perch. The driver followed him, his girth rocking the dilapidated coach as he did so.

"*Geeet* up, there!" He roared at his team, cracking the whip across their backs.

With a sickening lurch, the coach shot forward, thundered out of the village and into the Suffolk countryside, leaving a cloud of dust in its wake and a young girl waving frantically, until it was lost from view.

Chapter Two

The road to Birchwood was lóng, hot, and dusty, Amanda soon discovered. Her body ached from the constant thumping over the rutted road. The dark blue traveling gown clung limply to her body, and her face was streaked with grime. Her three companions on the journey were less than friendly, but the driver's frantic pace would not have permitted conversation if they had been. He drove with the fury of someone pursued by the devil, and the four travelers were hard put to hang onto the sides of the coach. The interior was a worn black velvet, the seats hard on both back and buttocks, and though supposedly able to seat six, they were cramped and not a little hot.

After an hour of the wildest driving she had ever seen, the pace slowed somewhat, and Amanda was able to take more leisurely stock of the familiar countryside they were traveling through: mostly farm land with fields of drying hay stretched far on either side of the dirt road. These gave way to a village not unlike Bellbury, to which they clattered over a humpbacked, gray stone bridge. They rumbled through the cobbled streets at a more sedate pace, and Amanda craned her neck out of the coach to see.

Bay-windowed shops bellied out onto the main street: a haberdasher's, a wig-maker's, a bakery—with the yeasty odor of fresh bread wafting out into the morning air. The streets were narrow and winding, running into each other in every direction. Then, as they were leaving the village, she saw the gray walls and wide turrets of a castle with a drawbridge leading over the half-empty moat. This was Colchester.

Amanda turned her attention to studying her fellow travelers. In the seat across from her was a woman of about fifty. She peered at Amanda disapprovingly through a pair of *pince-nez* spectacles that perched on the end of her nose. By her dress and demeanor, Amanda judged her to be a spinster, with a bookish look about her that made one think of schoolmarms, dried and withered and as sour as lemons. God forbid I should end up like that! Amanda prayed fervently.

The traveler to the right was more colorful, though no more companionable. He wore the somber garb and broad hat of a parson. His nose was streaked with little veins, and there was an odor of liquor about him. He turned to stare frequently out of the window, and on one occasion, when he did so, Amanda noticed that he was sneaking little sips of brandy from a tiny flask.

The other man was a huge fellow, who seemed able to sleep through even the most horrendous parts of the journey. He had a belly that rose and fell like some gigantic mountain with every wheezing breath and reverberating snore. His fleshy lower lip wobbled as he slept. He reminded Amanda vividly of Thomas's pig that had won a prize at the last county fair! She giggled at the thought, the sound dying on her lips as the woman opposite gave her a frosty glare.

After two hours, they pulled into an inn to change horses. Amanda rummaged in her reticule for a few coins to buy a mug of ale, for her throat was as parched and dry as the dusty roads they had traveled.

The *King's Arms* was crowded, and the cool flagstones did little to relieve the heat of many perspiring bodies crowded together. The patrons were a diverse company. Burly laborers, arms rippling with muscles, bellied against the bar. Several farmers, ruddy-cheeked and smelling of horses, smoked pipes at the far settle across the crowded room. In the corner lounged a grinning group of young gentlemen, their silk coats and cravats out of place in the simplicity of the old inn.

Amanda sipped her ale, idly watching the dust motes dancing in the mellow sunlight that filtered through the opened window. A shadow fell across the table. She looked up, and her eyes met those of one of the young bloods. His stare was rude, but admiring. Amanda blushed and tried to look down, but could feel his eyes upon her still.

A lazy smile was on the young man's face, and a blond lock of hair fell over his handsome brow. The breeches he wore were expensive, dove-colored and topped by a well-cut coat of black. A huge garnet ring flashed on his hand, the dull-gold band curiously wrought. It was twisted and cut with strange markings, and obviously a foreign piece, she thought.

"Your servant, ma'am! Allow me to present myself." He bowed, his blue eyes taking in every curve and line of her body, "Paul Blake, of Blakespoint, Norfolk, at your service!"

She made a charming picture, albeit she had the

slightly rumpled appearance of someone who had traveled long and hard. Chestnut tendrils of hair escaped from the dark blue hood of her light cloak, and her deep sable eyes glared into his. Her indignation at his bold introduction added a rare fire to her beauty, causing two bright red spots to bloom in her cheeks like scarlet roses.

His eyes wandered to where her cloak fell open, revealing the swell of her breasts thrusting against the fabric of her gown. She followed his glance and visibly stiffened.

"Indeed, Mr. Blake? And having presented yourself, you may render me a further service—that of leaving me be!"

Paul Blake's eyes turned icy. Ignoring the girl's furious glare, he sat himself down on the settle across the table from her, and leaned his elbows upon it. Then slowly and deliberately, he inspected her from head to toe!

If his staring had been insolent before, Amanda thought angrily, now it was positively indecent! The brilliant blue eyes traversed every inch of her body with infuriating slowness, as if their lustful, scorching heat had singed the garments from her, leaving her bared to his inspection. She colored deeply.

"It appears, Mr. Blake, that you are ill-mannered beyond belief!" Amanda rose haughtily. "Good-day, sir! I trust it will not be my misfortune to encounter you again!"

She made to leave, but the young man's hand darted swiftly out and trapped her by the elbow.

"Not so fast, my pretty!" he murmured softly, pulling her down beside him.

Beneath the table, his hand slid down from her elbow to cup her own hand. It would be impossible to attempt to leave without causing a scene! His face was so close to hers she could catch the spicy tang of his cologne and the faint aroma of liquor on his breath. The warmth of his body, pressed side by side and thigh by thigh against her own, radiated heat through her clothing in a manner that caused her breathing to quicken, the blush to deepen even more crimson in her cheeks.

She frantically looked about her for assistance. No one was paying them the slightest heed, save the young man's ne'er-do-well friends at the corner table. They grinned as they caught her eyeing them, and one facetious lout had the gall to raise his tankard to her in salute! Seething, Amanda turned to Paul Blake.

"Let me up, sir!" she hissed softly, "or I will scream to the four winds that you have attempted to force your attentions on me!"

In answer, he boldly released her hand, and instead his fingertips lightly caressed her knee beneath the table.

"Why so coy, my sweet?" he inquired lazily. "A lady would not come here, unescorted. I must presume, in the absence of a chaperone, that you are no lady!" He grinned wolfishly.

Amanda brought back her hand and smacked him hard on the cheek with a resounding crack! Instantly, two red crescents welled where her nails had caught him.

He muffled an oath as she jumped to her feet, his cheek burning with the imprint of her hand.

"Why, you little cat!" He got to his feet as if to pursue her.

Swiftly, Amanda reached out and swooped up the tankard of ale before her, and dashed the dregs into his startled face!

"There, Mr. Blake!" she crowed. "I hope that will cool your ardor! If not, I suggest you try the pigsty for a likely wench; no doubt yourself and the occupants would have much in common."

She turned on her heel and made her way angrily back outside to the coach. How dare he behave in such a fashion, she fumed. It was positively indecent. And yet he was, without a doubt, damn him, the most attractive man she had ever seen!

Mopping at his dripping face, Paul Blake watched her go, a half-smile on his lips. He cursed under his breath, and one hand twisted the garnet ring upon his finger until a welt formed where the antique gold had bitten into the flesh. Turning sharply, he made his way back to his comrades. As he sat down, he received several slaps to his back as the roués baited him good-naturedly.

"Paul, my good man, it seems the famed Blake charm is not up to snuff this day!" jeered one, with a wink at his neighbors.

"Mayhap you are losing your touch, old chap!" snickered the man to Paul's right, adding, "Though 'tis plain the wench has not lost hers!"

The men roared with laughter. Paul sipped his brew sullenly, eyes overbright beneath his blond hair, his knuckles white on the pewter tankard before him. He said nothing in reply to their good-natured banter, seeming almost distant.

"I'll bring him out of his reverie!" promised Brent Darwent, one of the young bloods, nudging his neighbor and winking. Louder, he began, "She wasn't for you, m'boy! Pale, sickly wench, she was—oh, pretty enough, I dare say—but nothing to compare with a *fiery quadroon,* eh?" He laughed, and the others, knowing full well what he was implying, laughed, too.

But their merriment was short-lived. Paul was up and on his feet in a flash, his fist gathering Brent's cravat into a knot beneath his chin until the man was lifted halfway from his chair. Paul Blake's mouth was but inches from that of Darwent, his voice low, but its very lowness menacing.

"Darwent, I would recommend you keep your damn insinuations to yourself, you understand me?" He twisted the cloth tighter, and Brent gasped at the pressure against his windpipe. "For if you do not, my friend, I will not hesitate to call you out—and to take the utmost pleasure in killing you!"

As he said the last words, Blake flung Darwent backward into the chair with such force that it toppled, and the man sprawled onto the sawdust.

The chatter in the tavern ceased, and all heads turned to the scene in the corner. A cut-purse took advantage of the distraction and filled his own pockets from those of the onlookers, almost caught red-handed, as Paul elbowed his way angrily through the crowd to the stables. As suddenly as they had ceased, the various conversations resumed. The young blades ordered a round of brandy, shaking their heads, none of them smiling now.

Outside, as Paul Blake waited for the ostler to bring his mount, the clouds of dust left by the departing coach were just beginning to settle.

"Damn her, that high-tone bitch! She'll not make

fun of me again!" he vowed through clenched teeth, fingering the still-burning welt on his cheek.

He leaped astride his horse, slashed the crop viciously across its head, and, still whipping, thundered away from the inn.

It was late afternoon when the coach pulled up to the enormous gateway of Birchwood.

The mansion was a beautiful Tudor building, with soft, white plastered walls, accented by dark beams here and there. It had an air of age, grace, and gentility that charmed Amanda totally.

The driver's lad helped her down, and after the boy had tossed her trunks to the dirt, the coach careened on its way once again.

A manservant stood by the gateway, a small handcart at his side. Amanda shook out her crumpled gown, and, lifting her reticule, stepped forward with outstretched hand to the man, a pleasant smile on her face.

The groom, somewhat taken aback by her display of friendship, spat on his palms, wiped grimy hands on his equally grimy breeches, and took her own small hand in his huge one, pumping it up and down vigorously in welcome.

"Yer servant, miss! Oi'm Will, groom up at t'house. Pleased ter meet yer!"

He grinned, and when she returned his greeting, hurriedly loaded her two trunks onto the cart. They walked the length of the driveway in amicable silence.

Birchwood was fronted with sweeping lawns, leading to a Palladian-style summerhouse only a few hundred yards from the enormous gates. A small pool with water lilies shimmered in the afternoon sun, and dragonflies dipped and hummed over the still water. The dainty silver birches that gave the house its name flanked either side of the lawn, tossing pale green tops in the playful breeze. The air was heavy, filled with the scent of masses of many colored roses in the flower-beds, and the faint fragrance of honeysuckle wafted from afar.

As they reached the heavy front door, it swung open, and a plump, gray-haired woman in a housekeeper's lace cap and apron came out to meet them.

"Welcome to Birchwood, Miss Sommers. I'm Mrs. Woods. Lady Elizabeth is awaiting you. She expected you'd be tired after your journey, and thought perhaps you'd care to take tea first, and then retire to rest and freshen up for dinner?"

As she spoke, the housekeeper led Amanda through paneled corridors that shone with polish and were full of the fresh scent of beeswax. Finally, she stopped at a door and stood aside as she opened it to allow Amanda to pass.

As Amanda entered the sitting room, a tiny, vivacious woman came forward.

"Miss Sommers, you must be exhausted! Do sit down. We've been expecting you for over an hour, but I expect the coach was late, as always." Her gray eyes were warm and welcoming.

Lady Elizabeth ushered Amanda into a comfortable chair in the snugly furnished sitting room, where, even though it was June, a cheery fire was burning. Velvet-covered chairs flanked the tiny fireplace, their russet tones adding still more warmth to the cozy room.

"I was so distressed to hear of your father's death,

Miss Sommers. I know how it must feel to have lost those you love, and your home as well. Please, don't be embarrassed! I am a woman of the world, and I have great sympathy with your misfortunes. I hope that you and Sarah will be good for each other. I have no doubt of your qualifications, for Mr. Aubrey spoke most highly of you! I hope your time here at Birchwood will be long and pleasant."

"Thank you, Lady Elizabeth! I cannot tell you how comforting it is to find you so understanding. You are most kind! There are many women in your position who would offer me neither consideration nor respect, I know. I am sure I will love it here at Birchwood," Amanda answered solemnly.

Tea was served, brought in by Mrs. Woods. After tea, Effie, the upstairs maid, showed Amanda to her room and helped her to unpack.

Amanda was pleased to be alone at last. Her room was moderately large and comfortable, furnished well with a deep-pink Persian carpet, and cream-colored hangings to the bed. Her window overlooked the front of the grounds, much as her room at Christchurch had done. A wave of longing for her home swept over her, but she forced it aside and turned back to the pleasant room.

Effie had filled a bathtub with hot water and placed it by the bedroom fire. Amanda took off her dusty gown and flung it to the floor, pausing for a minute to look at her reflection in the mirror. Though dirty and tear-streaked still, her face was appealing even in grief. Her body, though rounded and curved exquisitely, was nevertheless petite. Many men had longed to protect that deceptively fragile form. Full lips, almost too wide for the heart-shaped face, puckered up in a mischievous pout.

"Well, Mr. Blake," she announced dramatically to the mirror, "did I wound your pride? I wager many women have longed for you to look at them the way you looked at me! But Amanda Sommers is no plaything, Mr. Blake, and I will never swoon at the feet of any man!" She clutched her heart in a thoroughly theatrical manner, and, giggling, stepped into the tub to bathe.

It was no good, she mused, to spend the rest of her life mourning the might-have-been. Better to take what life offered her gladly, and never to dwell on the past again! There were worse ways to spend her life than as a governess, she knew, though she doubted she would be satisfied with the tedium of such a life forever. If only there was someone she could turn to, some family, however distant, she could call her own. The feeling of being utterly alone in the world was far worse than the loss of her wealth. In truth, she envied the lot of the working folk she knew, like Meg, whose homes, though empty of rich furnishings, were filled with love. But Amanda was a fighter, as her mother had been! Well, then she'd live life to the full, take whatever happiness she could find in both hands, and hang on tight!

She had toweled and dressed when she saw the adjoining nursery door open an inch or two. She continued brushing her hair, pretending not to have noticed anything. The door opened wider, and a little girl stepped shyly into the room.

"You are Miss Sommers, aren't you?" inquired the girl solemnly.

"Why, yes, I am! And you must be Sarah. Am

I right?"

Sarah nodded, a shy smile making her plain face almost pretty. She had none of her mother's vivaciousness, Amanda noted, and seemed small for her eleven years. Sarah was dressed in a bright blue frock that only served to make her pale hair and complexion seem more colorless. But her eyes were a beautiful clear gray and enormous in the slim face, giving her an appealing, doelike appearance.

"Mama said she had invited you to dine downstairs, but that after tonight you might choose whether you would do that, or sup with me up here in the nursery."

"Why, yes, that's a lovely idea! The two of us will dine up here like—like princesses in a tower!" Amanda promised, smiling.

Sarah's pleading expression had not gone unnoticed. The girl was obviously very lonely, Amanda realized, and her heart went out to her. Clearly, Sarah was not allowed the freedom that Amanda had as an only child. But, Amanda thought, I will try to give her many things she has not had before: friendship, new interests, anything to put a sparkle in her pretty gray eyes and a smile on her lips. A measure of contentment came over her at the thought that she might be able to help Sarah. So, the new life was not to be entirely without challenges!

"And, now, Sarah, I must go downstairs to supper, or your Mama will be very cross with me! I'll be up later to wish you good-night," Amanda promised, winking at the girl, who darted back into the nursery with an excited smile on her face.

Amanda hurried down the long staircase to dine. The meal was a pleasant one, and Lord Edward

Compton proved as charming as his wife.

Lord Edward had known Amanda's father, Robert Sommers, quite well, and admired him. Lord Edward had been shocked on learning that the man had gambled away his inheritance and left his daughter so badly off, and only too willing to see the girl come to Birchwood to tutor Sarah, rather than end up in the workhouse, or worse.

A stout but handsome man—his black hair now silvered at the temples—Lord Edward ruled Birchwood with an iron hand—held firmly in check by the velvet one of his wife! A bristling moustache and side whiskers gave him a deceivingly fierce appearance. His admiration of Amanda was obvious, appreciative, but not lecherous.

And it was no wonder he found her attractive, for she looked especially lovely in a gown the color of new copper pennies, cut low in the front and tight-waisted, so that it billowed out in the skirts. Her hair took on a russet hue from the soft candlelight, and the shadows gave an air of delicate mystery to her beauty.

Lord Edward thought, looking at her, that it would not be long before they would be hiring another governess for Sarah and attending the wedding of the lovely young woman seated across the table from him. Penniless she may be, but there'd be some young blood with fortune enough to overlook a dowry and sweep her off her feet, he'd wager!

The months that followed were happy ones for Amanda, though uneventful. The post of governess to the Comptons' only child proved easy, for although not gifted with great beauty, Sarah's disposition was sweet and her mind as sharp and clear as her father's. Lessons went smoothly. Amanda was surprised to find she enjoyed teaching and grateful her father had insisted on her receiving what was, for a woman these days, an excellent education. Sarah soon conjugated French and Latin verbs with equal ease, and showed an amazing aptitude for mathematics, which Amanda privately loathed with a passion!

When school hours were done, Amanda and Sarah went riding about the estate or picking berries in the woods that bordered the Comptons' lands. Soon there was a color and sparkle to Sarah that had not been present before. The Comptons were delighted and treated Amanda more as another daughter than a hired servant.

As September drew to a close, Lord and Lady Compton announced that they would be giving a ball in honor of their fifteenth wedding anniversary. Amanda was invited, and her excitement mounted as the date of the ball drew nearer.

Lady Elizabeth urged Amanda to have her own dressmaker sew her a new gown for the occasion, insisting it was no more than she deserved for creating such a change in Sarah. Amanda, anxious to be a part of the festivities, helped with the preparations, calling on the tradesmen of Colchester to order the decorations and food: huge hams, braces of pheasant, quail, sides of beef. It was to be a splendid affair!

On the evening of the ball, Amanda bathed and dressed with extra care, aided by a giggling and excited Effie. The gown was the height of fashion, cut daringly low in both back and front to set off her cleavage and the smooth whiteness of her back. The waist was tightly girdled with a deep-green sash to emphasize the apple green of the gown's satin fabric. The skirts were caught up here and there in tucks of matching ribbons. Amanda loved it, seeing in it the colors of the trees, the green of the ocean—all the things that she held dear!

She piled her hair on the crown of her head, and, with Effie's eager assistance, dressed it in long loose ringlets, with tendrils of curls framing her brow. Not for her the smelly powdered wigs so fashionable now! Her cheeks were flushed with excitement, her eyes bright and dancing with anticipation; she needed no artificial touches to enhance her beauty.

At the foot of the stairs, Lord Edward took Amanda's arm and led her into the spacious ballroom. The room was alive with light cast by the sparkling crystal chandeliers, and couples were already dancing. The music was provided by a small orchestra, positioned above the ballroom in the old minstrel gallery. Huge silver bowls of roses decorated the laden tables, and their heavy, sweet fragrance mingled with that of the ladies' perfumes.

Several horsehair chaises were placed about the room, where the young girls sat with their chaperones, anxiously eyeing the young men strutting about them in the hopes that they would be asked to dance. The matrons watched their charges sternly, warning them with a glance to be modest and proper in their behavior, while inwardly praying fervently that their daughters would land a handsome "catch"! Tinkling laughter carried from a knot of guests gathered about Lady Elizabeth, and Amanda was pleased to see that her ladyship's face was flushed and happy at the success of the occasion. It appeared to be going famously!

When Lady Elizabeth noticed Amanda, she broke away from her group and, taking Amanda by the arm, introduced her about the room to her friends and acquaintances. Behind their backs, shocked eyebrows were raised that a lowly governess should be treated with such obvious affection and respect, but Amanda noticed none of this. Her dance card was soon filled by the young men, eager to hold this lovely young creature in their arms, obviously caring little for what was considered proper.

Amanda enjoyed dancing, and her lightness of foot made her an excellent partner. It was with admiring eyes and trembling hands that the young men led her to their positions on the marble floor: with racing hearts and stammering tongues that they promenaded her gallantly to the notes of the spinet, flute, and violin: with mournful looks and reproachful sighs that they relinquished her to the succeeding escort.

Amanda felt almost dizzy with excitement! It had been ages since she had attended an affair such as this. The swirling gowns of gold, green, white, and lavender were an ever-changing pattern before her eyes as the elegantly dressed ladies of London swept around her. The men, too, were elegant, in embroidered silk coats and breeches of every hue.

"Amanda!" cried Lady Elizabeth gaily, as Amanda left the ballroom floor after yet another dance. "There's someone here that I would love you to meet!" Turning carefully with the enormous height of her elegantly coiffeured wig, Lady Elizabeth beckoned with her fan to a young man behind her.

Amanda turned around, and gasped in surprise as she saw it was the rude young man from the inn:

Paul Blake!

"Miss Sommers, I am, again, your servant!" Paul said sarcastically. "I believe this dance was mine?"

He took her by the waist and whirled her onto the floor. Unwillingly, Amanda looked up to find him looking down at her! She felt a strange stirring in her body that she had never experienced before and a tingling excitement at the way his eyes seemed to read her mind. She was attracted to him, and there was no doubt that he knew it.

"Well, little spitfire, are your claws sharp tonight?" he whispered in her ear. "And your tongue, madam—is it well-honed?"

He was holding her prisoner against his chest as they danced, his arms so tight she could scarcely breathe! His closeness was having the most powerful effect on her. He wanted to kiss her, she could sense it! It was almost impossible to answer him, and, when she did, her voice was husky and trembling.

"Mr. Blake, you are again impossibly rude! Why, the way you are behaving is—"

"Call me Paul, Amanda—and the way I'm behaving is no more than you should expect, looking as stunning as you do!" His eyes feasted on the swell of her cleavage above the gown.

"Mr. Blake, I will not stay here and permit you to talk to me in this outrageous manner again!" She turned from him, but he grasped her waist and held it so tightly that she winced in pain.

Paul's eyes were cold now and angry. "Don't run from me, Amanda, because, as God is my witness, this time I will follow you, and there will be no escaping me! I don't think the Comptons would care for a scene, do you?"

Some of the other couples were staring openly at them now and, from across the room Lady Elizabeth was eyeing them anxiously. Amanda couldn't make a scene, not tonight! She turned to him, and Paul took her back into his arms with a grin of triumph.

In her heart, she was secretly glad she had relented. This had to be the most wonderful evening of her life.

When Paul left her that night, it was with whispered promises that he would return.

Chapter Three

The next afternoon Paul arrived, dressed casually and mounted on a handsome chestnut stallion. He asked for permission to take Amanda riding, and Lord Compton, delighted to be cast in the role of her father, readily gave his permission.

Amanda was pleased Paul had kept his promise, but at the same time reluctant to leave Sarah. The girl had been acting strangely since Amanda had wakened her that morning, and, try as she might, Amanda could not discover the reason for her behavior. Sarah's normally cheerful face was long and sullen, and her anger seemed directed at the governess.

"Sarah, would you like to play *vingt-et-un* when I come back from riding? And then, perhaps, we could have Cook send up some hot chocolate and some crumpets to toast over the nursery fire, would you like that?"

Sarah shook her head, not even bothering to look up.

Amanda shrugged, and put on the finishing touches to her outfit—a powder-blue riding habit and saucy feathered hat—and hurried to meet Paul, who was waiting below.

They let the horses walk until well away from the house, enjoying the rustling sound of the hooves in the fallen russet leaves and the sharp bite of the wind against their faces.

Through the birch woods was a clear meadow in which to let the horses have their heads. Amanda challenged Paul to race her. Prodding her horse in the flanks and crouching forward in the side-saddle, she took off at break-neck speed across the field, Paul's mount thundering behind her.

"Come on, Tinker, come on, let's show him!" she muttered in her horse's ear as the distance between the two mounts opened up.

Well in front now, she stood in the stirrup and turned briefly to see how far her companion was behind her. Paul was nowhere in sight. Startled that he may have been thrown and injured, she wheeled her mount and cantered back to the copse.

When she reached the trees once again, there was still no sign of him. She dismounted and led Tinker through the thickly wooded bridle path. Wild blackberries snagged at her habit, but she brushed them aside, concern for Paul filling her. She was sure he had been behind her at the start of their race, but then what on earth—?

"Yahooo!" With an Indian whoop, Paul leaped at her from behind a tree, rolling her to the ground and pinning her with his arm against the carpet of leaves.

"Now I have you, my proud beauty!" he teased, laughing at her horrified expression.

"Paul! I thought you had taken a fall! Let me up! This kind of prank isn't funny; it's cruel!" she cried furiously.

"Come now, Amanda, you're enjoying this as much as I am! I didn't mean to frighten you, my pigeon, I just wanted to see how concerned you were about me—and you must admit, you *were* concerned!" His blue eyes held a mocking challenge.

Her riding hat had fallen to the ground and the pins from her hair were lost. She lay beneath him on the fallen leaves, her cheeks pink, chestnut hair streaming over her shoulders.

Paul's eyes flickered over her, noting her huge brown eyes that glowered angrily back into his; eyes that reminded him a little of another's eyes. That pert nose, the riches of her lips!

She flailed against him with clenched fists, but he held her easily at arm's length, grinning at her furious efforts to free herself. Then, suddenly, he crushed her to his chest, forcing his lips upon hers with an urgency that was frightening.

Scared now by the obvious passion Paul was feeling, she redoubled her efforts to escape him, only to find herself held more tightly than before. Part of her loathed him for the fury of his advances, but another, traitorous part of her wanted more, wanted to finally understand that mysterious union of man with woman.

Paul fondled her breasts, and her nipples flowered beneath the velvet of her riding habit. He lingered for a moment, delighting in the firm swell of those lovely curves, before savoring the full sweetness of her lips as she finally responded to him, her lips answering the hunger of his own.

She could feel the pulsing hardness of him against her thigh. The blood sang in her veins, the heady excitement mounted, and the urge to surrender was overwhelming! His hands moved to the buttons of her riding habit, unfastening them expertly and reaching inside to free her breasts from the cotton shift. Taking the taut bud between his lips, he kissed her there. Then, as she moaned softly, desire overcame him, and he was pressing burning, feverish kisses to her throat, her lips, her hair.

"Amanda, my dearest! Oh, God, I want you so much!" he cried, his face shining with sweat, his blond hair damp and curling. "Those eyes, so like *hers!*" he added under his breath.

Amanda was lost to his words in the confusion of her emotions. She didn't want him to stop! The strange sensations he was arousing made her feel wild and restless and toss caution to the winds! But she could not, should not, let him continue!

His hands moved to her thighs, his fingers caressing the rounded, silky flesh higher and higher, then finally between them, until it seemed they were a part of her, and the pleasure was unbearable. Her breathing grew shallow now and throaty, and her cries of delight were like spurs to goad him on. He lifted his body onto hers, but with a sudden, anguished cry, Amanda thrust him away.

"Paul, I—I can't. I want you, too, darling, but it's not right, not yet! Please, give me time, I—"

Paul covered her mouth in a brutal kiss, cutting short her protests.

The startled whinny of Amanda's horse warned that they were not alone in the woods. They scrambled to their feet, hurriedly fastening their clothes only seconds before Lord Compton entered the clearing, mounted on a gray mare. His look told them they still appeared disheveled.

"Thank God, you came along, sir!" Paul cried. "Miss Sommers has taken a nasty spill from that nag of yours. Damned animal bolted and threw her clear over its head before I could grab the reins! Perhaps you could help me get her back to the house, sir, it seems her ankle is a bit twisted."

"Then it's fortunate I decided to join you in your ride," Lord Edward declared.

He dismounted and came across to Amanda, his face showing concern. His eyes met Paul's, who returned his questioning expression boldly. Amanda blushed and seemed unable to meet his eyes.

"Are you sure it's nothing more than a sprain, mi'dear?" Edward asked gently.

Something about the expressions on their faces as he had ridden into the clearing belied Paul's story. He wondered anew if the rumors he had heard about this Blake's reputation abroad had been founded after all? He reached out to help Amanda to her feet.

Her heart was still racing from Paul's lovemaking, and now with guilt that Lord Compton suspected their lie.

She swayed a little as he held her, and finally managed to stammer, "It's nothing, really, Lord Compton! Please, I can walk—"

"Nonsense, child! We'll get you back to the house. Elizabeth will tend to you. Blake, see to the horse, will you?"

Paul nodded, and Edward seated Amanda on his own horse before mounting behind her. He urged the gray mare forward up the bridle path. Paul gathered the horses' reins in one hand, swung himself into the saddle, and, leading Amanda's mount, trotted after them.

As Lord Edward carried her into the house, Blake stopped him.

"I must thank you, sir, for allowing me the honor of escorting Miss Sommers. I trust you will allow me to do so again? I will call upon you later this week, Miss Sommers, to learn how your injury is healing. I only wish I could have foreseen this nasty accident, and have ensured that our ride had a more pleasurable conclusion."

His voice was thick with undertones, and Amanda knew full well the meaning of his last words. The look in his eyes made her squirm with embarrassment, but luckily, Lord Edward obviously suspected nothing, and bade Paul a good-day.

Paul nodded. "Good-day to you too, sir, and to you, my dear Miss Sommers."

With a wave of his hat he led the horse behind to the stables. Lord Edward carried her inside the house.

Elizabeth and Mrs. Woods confined Amanda to bed, clucking over her like concerned mother hens over a favorite chick. They insisted she remain in bed for a few days, at least. Their fussing, though with the best of intentions, made her fret to be up and about again. It was, she thought, just punishment for her part in the falsehood! Paul's easy telling of the lie bothered her a great deal, but, she asked herself, had he not done so with her best interests at heart? They could certainly not have told Lord Edward the real reason for their appearance! No, it had been necessary, she rationalized guiltily. Paul's behavior warranted to preserve her reputation. It was not as if anyone had been harmed by their story.

Amanda was reading in bed on the third morning after the incident, when Sarah, who had avoided Amanda like the plague since the night of the ball, burst in, her face scarlet and tears streaming down her face.

"Miss Sommers, you must come, please! Mr. Blake and Papa are blaming Tinker for your fall. They're talking of having her put down! Please hurry! She wouldn't hurt anyone, you know that!" she sobbed.

Amanda jumped out of bed, gathered a wrapper over her chemise, and hurried down to the stables. Lord Compton and Will, the head groom, were arguing.

"And Oi'm tellin' you, sir, that there 'orse wouldn'ta harmed a fly!" The usually polite groom's face was mottled purple with anger.

"Now, look here, Will," Lord Compton reasoned, "if Tinker's turned unpredictable, there's nothing else to be done! I won't keep a skittish horse in my stables. Miss Sommers could have been killed!" He turned to Paul, his face grim. "Isn't that so?"

"Yes, sir. The mare simply bolted, and with no reason that I could see!" Paul answered, lounging unconcernedly against the stable door.

Amanda stepped forward, her eyes glittering dangerously.

"Excuse me, Lord Edward, but Mr. Blake appears to have forgotten that I challenged him to a race, kicked Tinker into a gallop! Don't you remember, Paul?" Her eyes glared into his, those blue eyes that now were cold as ice.

"Why, yes, now that you mention it, I do recall you

saying something of the sort before the horse broke into a gallop," Paul agreed sulkily. Both Lord Compton and the groom were watching him. "Under the circumstances, sir, perhaps the animal should be given another chance?"

Edward Compton, obviously relieved, nodded, and Will, with an "I told you so!" look on his face, went on about his duties. Lord Compton excused himself and left Amanda and Paul alone, glaring at each other across the stable yard.

Paul walked across to her and faced her angrily.

"You silly little fool! Do you want them to suspect you're not the demure governess they think you are, to know you romped in the woods with me like a common serving wench?" Paul snapped.

"And you'd be willing to see a fine animal shot because of your lies? I despise you, Paul!" she continued furiously. "And, now, if you will excuse me, I must go about my duties as the 'demure governess'!" She flung around, and ran back inside the house.

Once in her room, the anger evaporated, and she threw herself down on the bed to cry. The brief moments they'd spent together in each other's arms came back to her so vividly now! And she would probably never see him again, never be able to tell him she could forgive him anything, if only he would come back and forget their quarrel!

In the weeks that followed, Amanda went about her duties listlessly, with none of the enthusiasm she usually did everything. Sarah, who was again, it seemed, sulking about something, was as moody as before, and the two of them were constantly at each other's throats. Even the servants remarked that the whole house was about as cheerful as a tomb.

Amanda, with none of her usual patience, was furious at Sarah for the slightest fault.

"Not that way, Sarah! How many times must I tell you that in chain stitch the thread must be brought back through the same hole! Now, try again!"

"I won't! I don't like you anymore, and I wish you'd leave Birchwood and never come back!" Her eyes brimming with tears, she flung the needlework sampler across the desk and fled from the schoolroom.

Amanda, shocked at her outburst, ran after her. She found Sarah on the windowseat in the nursery, sobbing as if her heart would break.

Amanda leaned over and put her arms about the girl.

"I'm sorry, Sarah, truly I am! I know I've been awful lately, but I—"

"Please don't marry him, Miss Sommers! You're so sweet, and he's an awful person, he really is!" Her gray eyes were imploring.

"Marry who? You mean, Mr. Blake? Oh, Sarah, don't be silly," she cried, astonished. "I'm not going to marry anyone. Is that why you've been so grumpy?"

"You danced with him at the ball the other night—all of the last dances! I was peeping from the staircase, and I saw you. He likes you, I can tell. And you like him!" she finished accusingly, pulling herself from Amanda's arms.

"Sarah, I did like him very much. But Mr. Blake has not asked me to marry him, and never will. I won't be leaving Birchwood, so, please, don't worry about it, darling!" Had her attraction to Paul been so obvious?

The girl seemed satisfied finally, and let Amanda dry her tears. From then on, lessons at least went well, and the atmosphere in the house became less strained.

But that night, Amanda lay wakeful and thought of Paul. When she finally slept, she dreamed of his handsome face, tousled blond hair, and his bright, blue eyes full of love for her. When she awoke from these dreams, she was ashamed to find her body aroused and taut as a bow string beneath her chemise. It amazed her that she could be capable of such passion. Obviously, Paul had brought to the surface a sensuality in her nature that she would not have believed existed. She did not deny that he had faults, for it was unrealistic to expect perfection in anyone, but she decided that she had been more than attracted to him and would have loved him despite these faults, though it really didn't matter anymore. The quarrel had taken care of that! He would not return.

On the first Sunday in December, Sarah awakened her with excited yells that echoed down the corridors of Birchwood.

"Miss Sommers! It's snowing! Look!"

Amanda wrapped herself quickly in a shawl and hurried to the window beside her charge. Sure enough, soft flakes were drifting down to join the blanket that already covered the lawn. The birch trees were beautiful, tipped with silver like ethereal veiled brides. The window panes were feathered with frost, and their breath made plumes in the air.

After breakfast, Amanda and the Comptons donned fur hoods, muffs, and heavy cloaks, and rode in the drafty coach to St. Ursula's Church. Seated in the family's private pew, Amanda gazed up at the beautiful stained-glass window depicting the Annunciation. Churches always moved her deeply, and she loved the serenity she felt here. The peace of mind she had acquired since losing Christchurch was due at least in part to the quiet moments she had spent in prayer and thought in this very church. She prayed silently that she would find someone special to love. Now that her family was gone, she had no one to call her own.

Several men in the church were moved not nearly so much by the Norman beauty of the structure as they were by that of Amanda! They watched her secretly as she prayed, her silver-fur hood like some huge halo about her face in the light, her eyes lowered under delicately arched brows. Her mouth moved silently, the too-full lower lip even more prominent as she whispered. She had opened her cloak, and below it she wore a lavender fur-trimmed gown, long-sleeved against the cold, with a neckline that reached almost to her ears. Its severity of style only emphasized the curves of her body as she knelt.

After Father Gregory had concluded the service, everyone stayed to chat in the churchyard as usual, despite the cold. Amanda looked up, startled to see Paul standing by the Comptons' coach.

He beckoned to her, a sheepish smile on his face. In his dark-blue cloak, navy breeches, and smartly turned-out boots, he cut a dashing figure against the snow.

She excused herself and, every part of her trembling, walked hesitantly to him. Her feet felt leaden, her heart sounded like a throbbing drum in her ears, and her palms were sticky inside her gloves!

"Amanda," he said softly, "will you walk back to Birchwood with me? I must talk to you!"

She nodded. He took her arm, and he led her

through the church gate and out into the lane. They walked silently for a while, their boots crunching against the crisp snow. Finally, Paul stopped, and turned her to face him.

"Amanda, I'm sorry! I've acted like a rat, and I want you to forgive me, please, dearest? Since our quarrel, I've been unable to stop thinking of you, dreaming of you! I want you so much, Amanda," he murmured, "can you find it in your heart to forget what happened?"

"I—I really want to, Paul! God knows, I've been thinking of you, too. But how could you allow our lie to jeopardize the life of an innocent animal? I can understand the need to tell Lord Compton what you did, but they were ready to shoot poor Tinker because of it! How could you be so heartless?" She turned from him, her mind in turmoil.

Fool! she thought. You've dreamed of this moment, imagined him a million times looking at you the way he is, and you're willing to throw away everything for a quarrel about a horse!

He took her shoulders and turned her to him. "You cannot comprehend how I have regretted agreeing with Lord Compton! Before you were witness to that little scene in the stable yard, I had tried to reason with him—but he was adamant that the animal be put down! I was concerned that he would wonder just what he had interrupted if I seemed too outraged. I admit, I was weak and foolish to let him sway me, but I thought I was doing it for you, my dearest, to protect your good name! I had come to Birchwood only because I had to see you again. I could not wait another day!" He pulled her against him, his arms strong and comforting around her, and covered her face with feverish kisses.

The snow was falling in soft flakes about them, swirling like feathers from an eiderdown, touching everywhere with silver magic. She looked deeply into his eyes. She was sure he was sincere; how could she have ever doubted that he would return to her, that he loved her as she knew, now, she loved him?

"I forgive you, darling," she murmured softly. "I was wrong, too!"

He brought his lips down to hers, and she responded to his kiss with all her being.

Chapter Four

On Christmas Eve, Paul asked her to marry him, and Amanda happily accepted his proposal.

In the weeks since their meeting at the church, Amanda had come to love Paul even more. His constant, passionate advances excited her, and seemed only further proof of his love for her, but she had gently resisted him, and although Paul had sulked at her refusals to allow him to make love to her, he had recovered his good spirits and courted her with resolution. For the first time since leaving Christchurch almost six months ago, the feeling of desolation was gone; all her waking thoughts were of Paul.

Lady Elizabeth was delighted with Amanda's news, and insisted the young couple allow her to give a wedding reception in their honor at Birchwood.

The date for the service was set for the first Saturday in April, and the date seemed to Amanda to glow like a jewel in the calendar of the bright, new year. Amanda and Elizabeth became very close as the wedding day drew nearer.

"You know, Edward predicted this would happen the first night you arrived at Birchwood! Though we shall hate to lose you, I'm so happy for you, my pet!

You've been like another daughter to us both, and your Paul is such a fine young man. What a catch! Since he returned from his travels about Europe, all the mamas have been trying to attract his attention to their daughters, and you've succeeded!" Elizabeth exclaimed proudly.

"He never mentioned Europe to me!" Amanda mused. "But as you say, Lady Elizabeth, he is a fine young man, and I do love him so!" She blushed with the admission.

"There, now, you'll have me in gales of tears!" Elizabeth declared, sniffing. "I've always loved weddings, you know. Why, mine was *the* talk of the town! But not everyone is the same, and if the two of you want a simple, quiet affair, then that's how it shall be," she finished.

"Yes, he—we think it would be best that way."

"And that's how it should be—what the two of you want. You will have this day only once in your life, and it should be perfect."

"Has the dressmaker started on my gown yet?" Amanda asked.

"Why, yes, she's coming to fit you on Wednesday next, at eleven, and then on Thursday, you and I shall travel to London to purchase accessories and to place your wedding announcement in *The Times.*"

Amanda put her arms around the older woman's shoulders.

"Elizabeth, you are the dearest person! I think, next to my mother, you must be the sweetest, kindest woman who ever lived!"

"Nonsense, child!" Lady Elizabeth denied, flushing with pleasure. "You are an adorable girl, and you deserve only the best! Now, run along and see to Sarah's bath, would you? She always spends ages in the tub, and Effie indulges her to the extreme."

Amanda went upstairs reluctantly, for since Paul's proposal and her acceptance, Sarah had become sulky again. Amanda had decided that the little girl was acting badly out of jealousy, for she knew how fond Sarah had been of her before Paul. She had asked Sarah to be her bridesmaid, and both she and Lady Elizabeth were astonished when the girl declared, with hatred in her eyes and in her voice, that she wanted nothing to do with the wedding. Amanda's attempts to talk to her had met with stony silence. And Elizabeth had told Amanda to leave Sarah be and let her solve the conflict in her own time.

As Amanda had expected, Sarah was stiff and uncooperative as she helped her to bathe, and after she had dressed and brushed her hair, she flounced into the nursery, slammed the door, and locked it loudly.

Amanda shrugged, and set about her own bath. In just two weeks, she, Amanda Sommers, would become Paul's bride and Mistress Blake, of Blakespoint, Norfolk!

Amanda loved the name of her future home, and the proud way Paul spoke of his birthplace. His father, he said, had been the son of a chandler, Martin Blake, who had built the family store into a thriving business. Later, Paul senior had married the daughter of a merchant who had a sizable line of ships, plying their trade about Europe, the Americas, and even India. Blakespoint, Paul said, was set upon cliffs overlooking the sea, a wild and beautiful spot! His eyes shone when he talked of the house his father had built, and filled with artwork and exotic curios.

On Wednesday, the dressmaker arrived from Colchester. It would be, Amanda thought, the most beautiful gown ever created! The gentle scooped neckline was heart-shaped, and the skirt billowing and threaded with white ribbons over layer upon layer of gossamer yellow fabric. Yellow silk flowers trimmed the hem, and the sleeves were fitted, coming to a deep flounce at her elbows. She would, she decided, wear her hair piled high, with ringlets falling loose around her shoulders, a wreath of spring flowers to hold the train of her veil in place. During the fitting, through a mouthful of pins, the dressmaker sighed that she wished all the ladies for whom she sewed did such justice to her creations.

The next day, Elizabeth and Amanda clambered aboard the Comptons' coach with overnight bags and ample pillows to cushion them against the notoriously bad road to London.

"Are you nervous, dear, now that the day is getting closer?" Elizabeth asked, settling herself comfortably across from Amanda.

"Yes, a little, I suppose," she confessed. "It's a big step to take, and not a decision to make lightly."

"And of your honeymoon, Amanda, do you know the things a young woman has to know, if she is to be a good wife?" Elizabeth's look was searching.

Amanda blushed, not from modesty, but more from the feeling that she probably knew far more than she was supposed to!

"Elizabeth, I know what you are trying to say, and you need not fear for me. I know all that I should to be a good wife to Paul. My mother and I were very close, and when I asked her questions, as a child and when I grew older, she answered me honestly and without reserve. She was, I believe, very much like you with Sarah, and did not want to raise me as a simpering, witless doll!"

Elizabeth Compton smiled, a wicked gleam in her eyes.

"Then, Amanda, I hope your honeymoon will be half the one that mine was, for I must confess, I remember it with great relish!"

The two women dissolved into giggles, and Amanda was glad that the elder woman was such a dear friend.

They reached London late that night, their bodies stiff and aching from the sixty-mile-long coach ride over the rough and bumpy road that was every bit as bad as its reputation. The Comptons' townhouse in Grosvenor Square was as elegant as the country estate. The two weary travelers were grateful to reach the downy comfort of the enormous feather beds.

The next morning they went by carriage to Madame Dubois's superb salon, and picked out the various accessories Amanda would need for her trousseau.

"*Mais,* Mademoiselle Sommaires, you are enchanting, quite, quite lovely! Per'aps a leetle *petite* in the bosom, but, *oui,* I am old-fashioned, *non?*"

Madame Dubois snapped her fingers, and a young girl came running out from behind a curtain.

"Suzette, *cherie,* bring me the lingerie from my best stock. *Allez, vite, vite!*"

The girl scurried off again, returning seconds later with exquisitely sheer undergarments festooned in her arms.

"For your 'oneymoon, mademoiselle, you would

look positively *magnifique* in this!"

Amanda held up a nightgown of buttercup silk. The neck was low, and ruffled with lace and deep yellow ribbons. The color added luster to the copper lights in her hair, and a reflected glow from the silk added a sheen to her cheeks. The two friends purchased the chemise, delicate shifts, petticoats, and a pair of satin slippers to match Amanda's wedding gown.

Their next stop was at the office of *The Times* in Fleet Street.

As Amanda was helped down from the carriage by a liveried coachman, she noticed a tall, darkly handsome man leaving the doorway of the office. He hesitated when he saw her staring at him, an amused smile at her undisguised appraisal playing on his lips.

"A very good day, to you, señorita, and to you too, señora!" he declared with a grin and a gallant flourish of his hat, before climbing into his own carriage.

They had already composed the announcement, which would appear in the next morning's edition, and Amanda was well-satisfied with the way it read. Soon their errands were finished, and they were free to enjoy the bustle of London.

The narrow thoroughfares were crowded with carriages, wagons, pedlars, and people—people from every station in life. There were the gentry, dressed in the most fashionable clothes, sauntering aloofly along, swinging amber-topped canes, elegant and beautiful ladies at their side with their hooped skirts swaying bell-like as they teetered along the cobbles. On the street corners were beggars, in shocking contrast to the finery of the well-to-do, with their tattered clothes, scraggy arms extended to hold tin cups, begging for alms. "Just a farthing, kind sir, a ha'penny, mi'lady," they wheedled.

Amanda was especially shocked by the condition of the children, especially the chimney-sweep lads. Her heart ached to see them, coming off their shifts with eyes red-rimmed from soot, and their painfully thin bodies covered with running sores.

Hawkers peddled their wares in raucous discord. A pie man strolled the streets, ringing a hand bell to extol his wares, the hot and savory beefsteak pies running with gravy. Another carried baskets of strawberries on both arms, and sang lustily in praise of her dewy, glistening fruits.

A pickpocket darted in front of the carriage, only narrowly escaping the rumbling wheels. The urchin, who could have been no more than six or seven years, grimly clutched a silk purse to his chest. A heavyset gentleman puffed in pursuit. As Amanda watched him pass, the man's embroidered coattails flying and his wig askew, she hoped fervently that the lad would escape him. If caught, he could suffer transportation, imprisonment in the filth of Newgate Gaol, or, worse, be hanged at Tyburn. She shuddered. If not for the Comptons and their generosity, the same fate could have been hers!

That evening she and Lady Elizabeth dined in the candlelit dining room of the townhouse, and the next morning began the tiring journey back to Birchwood.

The days passed quickly until it was Friday once again. The next day would see her Paul's bride.

Paul was invited to dine that evening. After the men had enjoyed their brandy and cigars, the Comptons discreetly excused themselves, and left the couple alone in the drawing room.

They kissed, and then Paul tilted Amanda's chin until he was looking directly into her eyes.

"Amanda, tomorrow, you'll be mine, and mine alone! There will be no refusing me then, my love, for I take what's mine without hesitation—and I guarantee you will enjoy the taking!" he vowed.

Amanda shivered. His words excited her, but the tone of his voice was strange, almost threatening, as it had been often since her return from London.

As he drew her once again into his arms, she felt the hard pressure of a pistol butt against her hip through the cloth of his coat. She drew back, biting her lip nervously.

"Paul, is anything wrong?" she queried.

"Why should there be, Amanda?" he snapped. A look of irritation flitted across his handsome face. He ran his hands through his hair with a quick, nervous movement.

"I don't know! But you seem different this past week, hunted almost. And you are so short with me! Is it the wedding, Paul, have you decided you do not wish to—?"

"I said nothing's wrong, blast it, woman! Now, that's an end to it!" Paul growled, thrusting her from him and staring moodily into the fire.

She tried to force a smile. "Then I believe you, darling! And I'm relieved to hear your reassurance! I had thought perhaps you carried that pistol so often of late because you feared attack from some lady's jealous husband!" She laughed softly. "It was silly of me, I know, but I think, Paul, it's because I love you so very much. I can't believe that tomorrow we will be husband

and wife, and that—you love me!" She lowered her eyes, embarrassed by the confession of her doubts.

Paul's expression softened.

"You're right. I'm sorry, my love, I have been out of sorts with you." He sighed deeply. "It must be prenuptial nerves, but," he added, blue eyes twinkling in the light, "I believe the bull does ever fear the ring through the nose, my dove!" he teased, grinning.

He took her gently in his arms. She ran her fingertip along the line of his jaw. Paul closed his eyes, and pressed that finger to his lips. She thought anew that there could be no man to match him in looks; his hair, so blond, curling over the nape of his neck, his eyes, bright as cornflowers, and his firm lips, that promised such pleasure.

"I understand, Paul. I will try to be a good wife to you."

"Then, until tomorrow, Amanda?"

He left her with a soft, lingering kiss, as she sat by the flickering fire, dreaming of the new life that was to come for both of them.

She stayed there, feet curled under her for almost an hour. Then she snuffed out the guttering candle, and climbed the stairway to her room. She undressed quickly, brushed her hair, and went to look out the window.

The night sky was filled with thousands of stars. The moonlight shone down and lit the blossoms of hundreds of spring flowers that bordered the lawns: daffodils, tulips, hyacinths, all the flowers that would be gathered for her wedding bouquet.

"Good-night, Paul darling," she whispered as she lay down to sleep. "Good-night, my love!"

* * *

She woke with a start as the village clock chimed three times in the distance. Some sixth sense warned her that she was not alone. The room was shadowed. By the door she could make out the silhouette of someone standing there, watching her silently. Her heart hammered loudly.

"Who's there? If you don't answer me, I'll scream!"

"No, miss, please don't! It's only me, Effie! I got t'talk to you. I couldn't make up me mind, see, and then what with the weddin' tomorrow, I thought—"

"Effie, calm down, there's a dear! You're not making sense at all! Now, sit here on the bed and tell me what's bothering you. Have you and Jim had another quarrel?"

Amanda patted the bed, and Effie sat down timidly.

"No, miss, it ain't that. I don't really know how t'tell you, but miss, me and Cook and the others, well, we're real fond of you, Miss Amanda, and we wouldn't like for you to make no mistake." She paused, and eyed Amanda anxiously.

Amanda was becoming impatient, but held back until the maid was ready to continue.

"Well, miss, it was about four years ago, I believe. Miss Sarah would have been six or so then, I think. I'd just been hired, on account of the last maid havin' left, sudden like, and Miss Sarah used to follow me around like a little shadow! Quiet, she was, and lonely, and we got kind of close. Then, one day, when I was polishin' the silver with her watchin' me, she says, all of a sudden, 'Effie, I know why Maudie left Birchwood. She was scared of Mister Blake, just like me!' I looked at her, an' she were tremblin' all over, an' her eyes was so wide! Gawd, Miss, she was scared stiff!

"So, I said, what reason would this Maudie 'a' had for being scared o'him? Well, miss, she told me. It seems she caught Mister Blake and Maud t'gether during one o'the balls—you know Miss Sarah, how she loves to see all the ladies in their pretty dresses?" Effie paused.

Amanda nodded. Her lips felt dry for some reason, and she noticed with surprise that she was stiff and tense.

"Well, Mister Blake, he had Maudie up against the library wall, and he was just slappin' her face with all his might! From Miss Sarah's description, I gather Maud was nigh passin' out, and he was yellin' at her somethin' dreadful. 'Don't you ever refuse me, you slut! You should be flattered by my attentions!' Of course, now, young Sarah don't understand his meanin', but then he turns around, see, and catches her watchin' him! He takes Maudie by the hair, and pushes her bloodied face against Sarah's, and he says if she ever tells *anyone* what she saw him doin', he'll do the same to her—and worse!"

Amanda gasped, the horror of the scene Effie had created hitting her like a slap in the face.

"Don't marry him, miss! He's a nasty piece o'work, if'n you ask me!"

"Oh, come, now, Effie, Sarah could only have been seven years old, at most, then! How can you be sure she didn't fabricate this whole incident just to gain your interest?"

"Because I seed her eyes! The poor little mite was terrified of him!" Effie shivered.

"I don't believe he'd treat anyone that way! To beat a

girl because she refused his advances? Now, Effie, you can't believe it of him! Would *I* marry someone who could be so cruel!" She shook her head in disbelief.

"I'm sorry, miss, but whether you believe me or not, that's 'ow it is! William says he'll run 'im through with a pitchfork if he catches him botherin' us maids!" Effie's face softened. "Oh, I'm sorry, miss, I knows you love 'im! I would have spoken up sooner, but Miss Sarah, she begged me not to. Me an' the other servants knowin' was all right, 'cos who's going t'believe us! But you're different, a lady an' a governess. People'd believe you, and the child's still terrified he'll come after her an' make good his promise!"

"Hush, Effie, I don't want to hear anymore! It's just idle backstairs gossip! I don't believe it, any of it! Now, you'd best go back to bed. We have a busy day ahead of us tomorrow."

The girl scuttled out of the room, surprised by the governess's sudden outburst and visibly upset face.

Amanda paced the carpet, wringing her hands. Paul wasn't capable of such things! He had never ill-treated her for refusing him. In fact, his only fault seemed to be that of an inclination to impulsiveness, but that was one of the things she loved about him! No, he could never be capable of intentional harm to anyone.

She slipped back into bed, satisfied that she was not as bad a judge of character as Effie implied she was. What an outrageous story!

But as she slept, there were no sweet dreams, only a nightmare of herself in a black cage, trying frantically to escape a nameless captor, and Aggie's soft voice urging her to flee, flee before it was too late!

Chapter Five

April 3rd, 1763, dawned fine and clear, the sky a brilliant hue with dainty puffs of clouds.

Amanda dragged herself out of bed, feeling drained and shaky, not at all, she was sure, the way a bride was supposed to feel. The nightmare puzzled her, but she thrust it from her mind. Today was to be the happiest day of her life.

There was a sharp tap on the door, and Lady Elizabeth waltzed in, gaily humming.

"Good morning, Amanda! What a beautiful day! See," she added, throwing open the window and inhaling deeply, "Lucy has been up for hours, selecting only the most perfect blossoms for your bouquet. The tables have been set up in the ballroom, and it's just lovely! Why, Cook's cake is perfection itself—no less than four tiers would satisfy her for your wedding!"

Amanda found herself caught up in Elizabeth's enthusiasm, and smiled at her excitement.

"The dressmaker's girl came with your gown, and I have it all ready in my dressing room," Elizabeth continued. "Now, all that remains is for me to give you this!" She put her hand into the pocket of her morning gown, and pulled out a worn velvet box, her eyes dancing with anticipation.

Amanda took the box from her outstretched hand, and opened it slowly. There on the black velvet shimmered a dainty flower, the petals made of creamy, matched pearls, and the center a large, perfectly cut topaz. Amanda's gasp of delight was more than thanks to Elizabeth.

"I'm so glad you like it, my dear! It was given me by my grandmother, and I feel it suits you perfectly. I want you to have it, to remember me when you're at Blakespoint."

"Oh, Elizabeth, how could I ever forget you! You and Lord Edward have done so much for me—far more than I could ever hope to repay. You—you've been like parents to me these past months!" She bit her lip, suddenly fearful. "Elizabeth, how can I be sure that I really love Paul, that he loves me? Somehow, I'm afraid. I've known him for so little a while!"

"There, there, my pet! You're just going through what every young woman—and man—about to be married goes through, a little pre-nuptial anxiety and uncertainty. Why, everyone feels that way on their wedding day! Everything will be fine, you'll see, and you'll wonder why you ever worried. Now, call Effie for your water to bathe. You don't want to keep Paul waiting at the church!" As she left, she dropped a motherly kiss on Amanda's forehead.

Amanda tossed back her hair and laughed self-consciously. Elizabeth was right. Of course, she was! Amanda felt a silly goose to be so apprehensive!

Effie brought pitchers of hot water and filled the tub. The maid was quiet this morning, but she answered when Amanda spoke to her, and still seemed friendly.

She's ashamed, Amanda thought, of her outburst last night.

Amanda removed her nightgown and stared at herself critically in the mirror. Her breasts and hips were a little fuller now, more womanly, but still as firm and white as marble. Slender thighs tapered to shapely calves and ankles, and her arms were rounded and graceful. She unpinned her hair, and it cascaded in a chestnut cape around her shoulders and down her back, almost reaching the swell of her buttocks. Paul would have no cause for complaint tonight, she hoped.

She bathed slowly, covering herself in a lather of sweet-smelling soap. Then she toweled herself dry, and sprinkled rosewater on her wrists and behind her ears. Mrs. Woods herself brought the breakfast tray, with cinnamon toast, a poached egg, and sausage. Amanda ate greedily, enjoying the quietness of her room and the excellent meal.

Afterward, she dressed in a loose wrapper and went downstairs. The hallway, staircase, and ballroom were festooned with spring flowers and gold ribbons. Huge vases and bowls of the blooms were everywhere, creating brilliant splashes of color against the dark woodgrain of the paneled walls and furniture. Mrs. Woods had truly outdone herself! The tables were elegant with gold linen tablecloths and vases shaped like tiny swans held snowy crocuses and lilies-of-the-valley. The silver dishes and platters shone like dewdrops in the morning sunlight from the windows. On the bride's table was the magnificent cake Elizabeth had spoken of, dark, rich fruitcake covered in marzipan and stiff white icing. On the top tier was a delicate crystal swan, also filled with fresh flowers. The cake was decorated with silver bells, tiny imitation horsehoes, and keys for good luck. It was all breathtaking, and the fragrance of the room she would remember always!

The maids were bustling to and fro, chattering excitedly, polishing things that did not need polishing, wiping crystal glasses that already flashed and sparkled in the light. Delicious smells wafted from the kitchen; roasting pheasant, pasties baking, a suckling pig turning golden on the spit over the kitchen fireplace. In the coolness of the pantry, she knew, would be fruited sherry trifles topped with rich, fresh cream from the Comptons' dairies, and dishes of yellow custard, sprinkled with nutmeg.

The grandfather clock struck ten. Elizabeth and Mrs. Woods shooed Amanda upstairs, clucking over the way she dawdled, and helped her to get dressed.

First, several petticoats were slipped on over her shift, then the yellow gown was put over those. Lady Elizabeth herself brushed and dressed Amanda's hair, and the chestnut glory of it shone like silk. Next, the train of French lace was pinned to her hair and topped with a coronet of fresh lilies-of-the-valley and yellow freesias. She slipped into the white satin slippers and was, at last, ready! She looked unbelievably lovely, the yellow of her gown accenting the darkness of her eyes, the blush in her cheeks, and the full, soft rose of her mouth.

"She's truly the most beautiful bride, isn't she, Mrs. Woods?" sniffed Elizabeth happily, fastening the pearl-and-topaz pendant about Amanda's throat.

"Aye, that she is, mum!" replied Mrs. Woods, with a firm, approving nod, and rare smile.

There was a knock on the door, and, when bidden enter, Lord Edward, who was to give Amanda away, came in. He looked dashing in a dark-brown velvet coat and a waistcoat embroidered in gold.

"Are you ready, my dears?" he inquired.

When Amanda nodded, he took her nervous arm in his left, and his wife's in his right hand and escorted the ladies down the curved staircase.

The maids cooed and aahed over Amanda's appearance, and complimented Lady Elizabeth on the elegance of her lavender gown and high wig with its matching bows. Lucy gave Amanda the bouquet she had made of fresh flowers with ferns and gold ribbons. Amanda thanked her, and then they were outside. Lord Compton handed her into the waiting open carriage, drawn by four matching white horses with white plumes upon their heads.

As they drove slowly through the lanes of Compton, the villagers came out to wave and cheer as if she were a princess, lining the road in small groups as far as St. Ursula's Church.

At the church, a number of elegant carriages were drawn up outside. The coachmen grinned at her, and there were cries of "Good luck, miss!" as she entered the door on Lord Edward's arm. Elizabeth slipped inside ahead of them. Then as the notes of the organ sounded, Amanda approached the altar.

Every head turned to look at her, radiant with happiness. Her hand trembled on Lord Edward's elbow, and he gave her an encouraging smile. The guests, many of them of high society, were struck by the beauty of the young girl.

She reached Paul's side, he, too, handsome in a gold

satin coat and breeches. She looked up at him shyly, and he returned her look with a smile. The light rainbow color from the stained-glass windows played about their heads. It was, Amanda thought, all like some beautiful dream!

Father Gregory, attended by a cherubic altar boy, led in the procession. Sweet Latin chants floated into the air, then died away as the priest raised his hand for the blessing. His rich, vibrant voice filled the church as he presided over the holy service of matrimony, his imposing figure framed by the magnificent altar, covered in white-and-silver cloth, and flanked by tall ivory candles.

Paul took Amanda's hand, and Lord Edward stood aside, a smile on his lips indicating that his prediction regarding the future of this young woman had proved correct. Lady Elizabeth was weeping.

"Dashed emotional woman!" her husband muttered affectionately, patting her hand.

The priest's voice droned as the service continued.

". . . if any of you know cause why these two people should not . . ."

"Yes!" A voice thundered through the church, freezing the words on Father Gregory's lips.

The congregation gasped as one rigid with shock.

A tall, dark man, his footsteps echoing in the awful silence, strode down the aisle, and stopped a few feet away from the bridal couple.

"*Sí,* I know cause! This man—Paul Blake—is a seducer, a cheat, and a damn liar!"

The congregation gasped again, and there was a nervous twitter as many of them stirred anxiously.

Paul swung around to face his accuser, his knuckles

clenched. There was a suspicion of fear in his eyes, coupled with violent anger. His lips narrowed until his mouth was a twisted slit, his face purple with rage. Amanda's face was white, all color drained from it.

"I suspected something like this, de Villarin! Get out of here!" Paul snarled. "You have no right!"

"No right? *Dios!* If I have no right, then may God strike me!"

Father Gregory came between the two men.

"My sons, this is the house of God, and we are here to celebrate the holy service of matrimony! Put aside your—"

"Father, forgive me, but I cannot! My heart is full of hatred for this man—the seducer of my sister, her murderer, and that of the child she conceived by him!"

"My son, God teaches us mercy, even to—"

"No, *Padre,* he showed no mercy to my sister, nor compassion! He—"

A shot rang out as Paul, hands trembling with rage, reached for the weapon concealed in his coat. The explosion echoed like thunder in the church, but the shot found no mark. Scant seconds after the first explosion, the stranger drew his own pistol. His finger jerked on the trigger, and the ball burst from the barrel, exploding into Paul's knee.

The impact hurled Paul back, crashing him headlong against the marble altar and gouging his cheek on the corner, before he reeled to the stone floor, his leg twisted strangely beneath him. A shriek of agony tore from his throat.

Someone screamed in fear.

Father Gregory hurried to kneel at Paul's side, trying to staunch the flow of blood from Paul's cheek with the hem of his robe. Paul's face was contorted with pain, his eyes burning feverishly.

"Leave me be, Father!" he snarled, thrusting away the shocked priest. "I shall kill him!"

Paul tried to haul himself to standing by the priest's vestment, but fell back moaning as the shattered kneecap failed to take his weight. Finally, he slumped senseless to the cold floor. Blood trickled from his wounded cheek, the scarlet river coursing slowly across the gold of his satin lapels.

The dark stranger's eyes closed momentarily as if in prayer, whether for Paul or in penance for himself for what he had done was impossible to tell. He turned to the shocked congregation.

Silhouetted against the stained-glass window, he appeared to them like an avenging angel, towering above them and striking terror in their hearts with a voice like thunder!

"I swear, before God, that all I have said this day is true! This man took my sister's honor. It is only fitting that now I have taken his!" He threw his dueling pistol to the floor, turned on his heels, and strode from the church.

For a few moments there was utter silence, then a murmur began and swelled, until the church was filled with the nervous cries of the shocked congregation. Ladies swooned, their escorts rushing to revive them with faces a little less pale than the women's.

Paul lay across the steps of the nave, his face in agony and waxy from loss of blood, his leg twisted at an unnatural angle. His moans and cries of terrible pain went ignored, as the congregation became transfixed by the tragic figure of Amanda, who had neither moved nor spoken since the Spaniard cast his first accusation. She stood there, stunned and motionless, the bouquet hanging limply in her hands. The stems were crushed in two in her clenched fists. Her mouth moved, but no sound came, and her eyes were staring wide in horror at the crumpled figure of her betrothed.

Lady Elizabeth was scared by her total stillness.

"Amanda, dear, come with me, come with Elizabeth," she said softly, as if to a very young child.

Finally, Amanda looked up, but her eyes remained blank. She allowed herself to be led to the carriage and driven back to Birchwood.

Lord Edward and Father Gregory carried Paul into the vestry and his valet was sent posthaste to summon a surgeon.

The news spread swiftly. The servants knew of the events at the church before Amanda's return. They moved about the house quietly, eyes lowered, as they removed all the decorations and flowers. Elizabeth ordered the food shared among the villagers.

Birchwood lay shrouded in gloom.

Chapter Six

Silently, Elizabeth and Effie undressed Amanda, and, like a puppet, she followed their directions and lay down upon the bed. She shivered beneath the fluffy eiderdown they had tucked about her, though it was warm for April and mellow afternoon sunshine streamed through the opened windows. Her face was leached of all color. Her eyes, though wide open and staring, saw nothing. Elizabeth knew. In them was not even the glitter of unshed tears.

"Gawd, mum, it ain't nat'rel, after all wot's happened! Not even a tear!" whispered Effie anxiously.

"Tears will come, Effie, later. The shock was too much, I think her mind is bruised, like our bodies are bruised by a blow. The healing will take time—and love," Elizabeth explained. Her usually vivacious face seemed older beneath the powder, and there were lines of worry about her lips and eyes. She took Amanda's hand in hers and squeezed it comfortingly. "There, my dear, rest now. I'll have Mrs. Woods bring you some broth later, would you like that?"

There was no reply. Elizabeth leaned over and kissed Amanda's forehead, smoothing her hair neatly about the wan face. She considered the pale form for several minutes.

"Effie, go to the stables and have William ready a horse. Amanda, dear, listen to me. I'm sending William to Ipswich to fetch Mrs. McNab, Aggie. Would that help?"

Relief flooded Elizabeth as Amanda slowly turned her head. Some of the vacant look had gone, though the older woman still felt chilled by the girl's ashen color and stillness. Amanda nodded slightly.

"Yes. Yes, please." Her voice was wooden. She turned back to stare at the ceiling once again.

Effie had not moved. She stood across the room, staring at Amanda and wringing her hands anxiously.

"I done told her, I did!" she muttered, shaking her head.

"What did you say, Effie? I'm sorry, my mind was on other things," Elizabeth apologized.

Effie colored and seemed flustered. "It weren't nothin', mum, just me thinkin' out loud! I'll be off t'tell Will, then?"

"Yes, thank you."

After the maid had gone, Elizabeth drew the draperies, and tiptoed quietly from the darkened room. She found her husband in the study, in the act of pouring a large measure of brandy into a snifter.

"A spot of this for you, m'dear?" He held up the decanter inquiringly.

"Oh, please, Edward!" Accepting her glass gratefully, Elizabeth perched precariously on the edge of a horsehair chaise. "Edward, oh, Edward—what a day!" She sighed. "And I had such hopes for Amanda. It's as if she were my own daughter, I feel for her so! Why, I even introduced the two of them that evening at our ball with the hope that something would come of it!"

Elizabeth sniffed back a tear, dabbing at her eyes with a lace-bordered lavender handkerchief. Edward patted her shoulder awkwardly.

"There, there, m'dear, you must not blame yourself. I'd heard gossip at the club, but you know how it is! These young blades always have a rumor or two flying about, and I didn't put much store in it. Be damned, if I didn't."

Lady Elizabeth nodded understandingly. There was a light tap on the door.

"Come in!" Lord Edward ordered.

Lucy bobbed a curtsy. "There's a gentleman to see you, sir. A Don Miguel de Villarin, he says his name is. Should I show him in, sir?"

Edward eyed his wife inquiringly and nodded. "Thank you, Lucy."

The girl left.

"What could the man want, Edward?" Elizabeth wondered nervously. "Oh, dear, I do hope there's not to be more trouble!"

"Now, now, don't take on, Lizzy, we'll find out soon enough."

They both looked up expectantly as, after a brief interval, Lucy came in, and stood back to allow the visitor to enter. The maid blushed as he shot her an admiring grin and handed her his tricorn. Her blush deepened as he thanked her, and she fled from the room, closing the door behind her.

Don Miguel de Villarin bowed and introduced himself. He appeared taller in the small room than he had at the church, Elizabeth thought, and broader of shoulder, though he was not a stocky man. His crisp, dark hair was tumbled and unruly, and his clothes, though well-cut and expensive, were disheveled and mud-stained, as if he had ridden long and hard. There was something vaguely familiar about him although Elizabeth could not fathom why there should be.

"Well, Don Miguel, how might we be of service to you?" Edward inquired somewhat coldly. The nerve of the chap, to come here after what had happened!

"On the contrary, Lord Compton, I had hoped to be of service to you! You see, señor, I could not return home without at least explaining my actions at the church. I hope that when I have done so, you can in turn relay them to the young lady, who, I understand from your housekeeper, is understandably indisposed at present."

Edward "humphed" agreement. "Very well. Have a seat, sir, and we'll hear you out."

The don declined with a slight shake of his head.

"Thank you, no, señor. I would prefer to stand."

He paced across the study, gazing momentarily out at the lush green of the garden beyond the French windows before continuing.

"Lord Compton, Lady Elizabeth, I had not intended for events to end as they did at the church! My intention was to disrupt the service, yes, and to challenge Paul Blake to a duel, but nothing more." He paused, eyeing them for several seconds before continuing. "But, as you know, Señor Blake left me no choice by drawing his weapon!"

Edward nodded. "We are aware of that! But your desire to challenge Blake, what led up to it? For Miss Sommers's sake, I hope you had good cause!"

Don Miguel de Villarin's jawline tightened perceptibly. The hint of easy good humor in his dark, almost black, eyes was replaced by a look as cold and piercing as jet.

"Of cause, there was ample, señor," he said softly, "for I place no little value on my sister's life! You know, of course, that Blake has a small fleet of merchant ships? Well, I had commissioned him in Barcelona to acquire certain paintings for me in Paris, for which it was agreed he should be paid a buyer's fee. The business was concluded most satisfactorily, and Blake asked if he might winter at my villa in Spain. I saw no reason to refuse him. He had done the business to my liking, and seemed an agreeable man. I told him to pack his bags and come."

Lord and Lady Compton stared fixedly at him, waiting for him to carry on. Miguel rubbed his fingers against his temples, trying to determine how best to do so.

"It was not long before it became obvious that my sister, Maria-Elena, and Paul Blake, fancied themselves in love—or at least, Elena did. Blake seemed increasingly interested in our estates, the gallery, and in particular, Elena's holdings, and I grew suspicious. I believed—rightly, as it turned out—that the Englishman was a fortune hunter. But before I had the chance to have it out with him, Elena came to me and announced her intention to marry Paul Blake! She was only sixteen years old, you understand, and very protected. It was as if Elena was blinded by her love. When I told her my opinion of Blake, she was outraged, and we quarreled bitterly. I told her if she married him, I would cut off all her endowments, that

that man would not gain one penny from the union! Elena vowed that Paul loved her, and that they would marry despite this. I was angered by her stubbornness, her disobedience, and left the villa for a few days. When I returned, I learned that she had informed Blake of what I had said, and that he had also left—supposedly to give Elena and me time to reconcile our differences. The days wore by, and it soon became obvious that Elena was carrying Paul's child. He never returned! I swore to find him, to bring him back to give the child his name."

"But—but you called him a murderer, Don Miguel?" Elizabeth queried.

"And so he is, señora, indirectly! I traveled to Europe searching for him, and finally discovered he had returned to England. But after a few weeks of inquiries, I still had no proof that he was here. It seems no one had seen him or knew where he was, and even his servants at Blakespoint thought him still out of the country. I decided to go to the *Times* office, and advertise for knowledge of his whereabouts. After I advertised, I learned of the impending marriage and redoubled my efforts to quickly find him."

"Now I know where I've seen you before!" Elizabeth exclaimed. "Outside the *Times* office, when Amanda and I were in London for her trousseau. You bade us good-day, did you not?"

"Sí, señora, that is so. I only wish my second meeting with such a charming lady could have been under more pleasurable circumstances." Miguel bowed gallantly.

Elizabeth blushed. "Thank you, sir! But please, continue."

Miguel nodded. "My advertisement brought no

response, until this morning, that is. Then a young man, Jim, his name was, arrived at my hotel." He paused, eyeing the couple inquiringly. "You have no idea what this is leading to, do you?"

Elizabeth and Edward appeared puzzled.

"Should we, Don Miguel?" Edward asked, tugging uncomfortably at his moustache. "Elizabeth, do you know what he's talking about?"

She shook her head.

"Very well, I will explain. You see, the young man brought me—this!"

Miguel de Villarin withdrew a folded square of vellum from his coat, and held it out to the other man.

Edward Compton unfolded the note, and read it hurriedly. Though he recognized the childish scrawl, he obviously could not believe his eyes.

"But this is preposterous!" he exploded finally. "Why would Sarah do such a thing?" He gave it to his wife, who scanned it with widening eyes.

"Jealousy, Edward, and the determination to keep Amanda at Birchwood, whatever the cost!" Elizabeth cried, shaken visibly by the contents of the letter. She had no doubt as to the validity of the signature. "I had no idea how desperate she was, how much it meant to her that Amanda should leave. Why, we should have guessed, the way she has been behaving of late! The poor child!" She returned the note shakily to her husband.

Edward's face was dark with anger. "Poor child, my foot!" he roared. "She's a young hussy that's what! Listen to this, Liz, 'Mr. Blake is an evil man. He has sworn to hurt me if I tell anyone *how* evil!' The imagination of her, the deceit!" He paced furiously in front of the fireplace. "Sarah deserves to be horse-whipped!" he pronounced at length.

"No, señor, please, do not act rashly! Should we not permit the young lady to explain before jumping to conclusions?" Miguel's voice was soft and persuasive.

Edward snorted impatiently. "Very well."

He jangled the bell rope so vigorously to summon Lucy that Elizabeth feared it would be pulled in two.

"Yes, my lord?" Lucy asked nervously, sensing something was awry.

"Would you bid Miss Sarah come here, immediately?" he ordered.

"Yes, sir," Lucy said, hurriedly curtsied and scuttled off.

The silence in the study was so tense it was uncomfortable. Don Miguel wished ruefully that he had simply mounted his horse and ridden off, as had been his first inclination. But no, coming here had been the thing to do, the right thing. He owed Paul Blake's innocent young bride that much. The truth. *Díos!* She had probably not heard much of it from that bastard Englishman!

Lady Elizabeth perched uncomfortably on the edge of the chaise again, still wearing the lavender gown with the gigantic hooped skirts from the morning. She was wringing her hands, and her powdered wig was a trifle askew. Edward Compton was downing another brandy, and Miguel regretted refusing his silent offer of one for himself.

A soft knocking on the door instantly drew everyone's attention. The door opened.

"Yes, Papa?"

Sarah Compton appeared to be about eleven years

old, Miguel thought, though there was wisdom in those enormous gray eyes that belied her youth. The girl's hands were clasped before her, lost within the folds of her white gown, where they toyed nervously with her sash. But her chin was raised defiantly, and her eyes met those of her father without wavering. A wispy serving girl, who was obviously petrified, stood behind Sarah.

"Sarah, I wish to talk to you! Effie, you may go," Edward Compton announced sternly. The maid appeared ready to bolt.

"No, Papa! I think I know what you wish to talk to me about, and Effie is part of it. She wants to stay, do you not, Effie?" Sarah paused.

Effie nodded vigorously, but her expression belied her action.

"As you wish. Now, Sarah, what do you know of this?" Edward handed his daughter the letter.

Sarah took it from him without even a glance.

"I sent it, Papa, to Mr. de Villarin! I saw his advertisement in the *Times,* you see, just after Mama and Miss Sommers returned from the city. I—I copied the address. Oh, Papa, Amanda is such a dear person!" Sarah turned to her mother. "I just *couldn't* let her marry such a—a beast!" Her enormous gray eyes brimmed with tears. "Effie tried to tell Amanda last night what Mr. Blake is really like, but she wouldn't listen, Mama, and I *had* to do something! So when Effie came to my room last night and told me that Miss Sommers still intended to become Mr. Blake's wife, I remembered the advertisement. I did not know what Mr. de Villarin wanted Mr. Blake for, but it was our last chance. Jim, Effie's young man, was persuaded by us to ride posthaste to London with my letter, telling of Mr. Blake's whereabouts. I—I didn't know they would hurt each other, truly I didn't!" With a sob, Sarah flung herself into her mother's arms.

Elizabeth held her close, murmuring consolingly. Edward Compton appeared to have all the wind blown out of his sails.

"But why, Sarah?" he asked bewildered. "Why do you hate this man so? Sarah, you hardly know him!"

Sarah sniffed loudly. "Bec-bec—"

"No, Miss Sarah, I'll tell it, if'n it do be all right? It were not her doin' alone, sir!" Effie looked nervously about her, and Edward nodded.

"Well, yer see, mum, m'lords, Miss Sarah here was quite young when it happened. Mr. Blake was here as a guest, at one o'the balls, an' . . ." Effie quickly told them what Sarah had been witness to, and of the threats that Paul Blake had made against the child. When she had finished, the maid heaved a sigh of relief. "There, 'tis better out in the open! I'll be off by the morrow, mum, as soon as me bags is packed." The maid turned to leave.

"Don't be silly, Effie!" Elizabeth scolded. "There's no need for you to leave us. I'm grateful that Sarah was able to confide in you, though what the two of you did was a foolish, foolish thing!" Elizabeth declared. "Run along now, Sarah, and bathe those red eyes. I'll be up later to talk to you further about this."

After the two girls had gone, Edward coughed uncomfortably.

"Well, Don Miguel, it seems our Mr. Blake is indeed a scoundrel, without question! If you hadn't done so already, I'd be forced to call him out, be damned if I wouldn't! He'll not find it easy to do business in the city after this, mark my words, not if I have my say in it!" Edward declared grimly.

Miguel de Villarin nodded politely. Lines of fatigue had settled about his eyes now, and his face was drawn and gray beneath its tan. A twinge of guilt kept forcing its way unbidden into his mind. Why had he not shot Blake dead? It would have been the more honorable thing to do, rather than wounding him. But, no, he knew he could not have done so, not in cold blood, while Blake's young bride witnessed the deed. *Díos,* he had to get out of here, back to Spain! But first, the rest of his story!

"Now you know how I came to Compton. But there is much, much more. You see, during these weeks of searching for Blake, I received another letter, this one from my steward, Esteban. It had taken almost a year to find me, but the news was as shocking, as painful, as if it had arrived the same day; the day my sister, Elena, torn with shame and grief for Blake's desertion, threw herself and the child within her to their deaths, from the cliffs upon which our villa stands. My desire for revenge burned through me with the searing heat of a white hot blade! When Miss Sarah's messenger arrived this morning, I rode my horse until it dropped, to reach here in time. I could not permit Blake to ruin another young girl's life. The rest you know. And now," Miguel said finally, "I must take my leave. I thank you both for hearing me out. Please tell Miss Sommers she has my deepest regrets. Good-day, Lady Elizabeth, Lord Edward." He strode from the room.

"Well, well!" Edward exclaimed, sinking into a battered leather chair. "This has been an eventful day, to say the least, eh, Lizzy? Thank God, our little Miss Sommers has been spared marriage to that—that cad!"

"Yes, dear," Elizabeth agreed sadly. "I agree with you wholeheartedly! But you are forgetting one very important fact!"

"I am? What's that?" her husband inquired, startled. Good Lord, was there more?

Elizabeth sighed. "Amanda believes she loves him!"

Chapter Seven

Aggie arrived the following evening, her Scottish blood boiling at what had happened.

"Och, ma puir, wee bairn! As if her father dyin' and her inheritance gone were no' enough!"

She ordered the maids about as if she were the lady of the house, but they enjoyed her gentle bossiness, and all felt she was the tonic Amanda—and Birchwood—needed.

Aggie had been living with her sister, Florence, who was Cook at the White Hart Hotel, in Ipswich. She had told Aggie of the gossip she had heard at her work, for many of the wedding guests had passed the night there, and tongues wagged as tongues always will. So Aggie had already prepared for the journey when Will arrived on his lathered horse.

Aggie had approved wholeheartedly of Amanda's position as governess, in lieu of marriage to some nobleman. It was second best, maybe, but a girl who had lost all wealth and position could fare much worse in this day and age, she knew.

She had heard of the Comptons and liked what she'd heard. Birchwood, with its elegant gardens and ivy-covered walls, had been beyond her expectations. It was almost as beautiful as her Scotland!

Lady Elizabeth greeted her, gracious as always, and Aggie liked the woman immediately.

"I'm so thankful you were able to come, Mrs. McNab! Milk or lemon?" Elizabeth offered her a dainty china cup of tea.

"Neither, thank ye, ma'am." She sipped the green Hyson tea with obvious enjoyment. "Miss Amanda will be fine, ye'll see. Ever since she was a bairn, she's taken her knocks and come up smiling. If nothing else, her temper will bring her oot of it! Her dear mother was Irish, ye know," she added, as if Jessica Sommers's birthplace explained everything, "and powerful strong people they are, too—though not, of course, as strong as the Scots!"

Elizabeth averted her head and smiled. "Of course not, Mrs. McNab. Would you like to see Amanda now?"

Aggie was shown to Amanda's room, and her bags taken to the nursery next door. It had been decided she should sleep on a cot in Sarah's room, in case Amanda needed her.

Amanda was staring out of the window, her hair dull, her eyes ringed with purple shadows. She had shrugged on an old morning gown, and it looked as dejected as she.

"What are ye lookin' at, lassie!" Aggie inquired, a broad smile on her face, and her arms outstretched.

"Aggie, dear Aggie, you're a sight for sore eyes!" Amanda flung herself into Aggie's arms and hugged her tightly. "You know, I didn't realize how much I'd missed you," she added sadly.

The older woman patted her gently. Finally, she held

her at arm's length and looked searchingly into her eyes. "And of the young man, hinnie? What of him? I've heard't all. Ye've nae need t'tell me anythin', only what's happenin' inside o'ye?"

Amanda turned away, her head bowed. "I still love him, Aggie! God help me, but I do! I know what Effie said happened, and Elizabeth explained why that—that Spaniard behaved as he did, but I can't believe it! They're all wrong about him, they *must* be! My Paul's not like that. I've thought, these past days, of trying to forget him, but I know I can't. I'm going to London to see him, Aggie. Will you come with me, or must I go alone?" The look on her face was one of grim determination, coupled with sadness.

Aggie shook her head. "You know better than t'ask! I won't tell ye not t'go, Mandy, love. Ye've a loyal heart, and love doesna fly oot the window with adversity. But I'll admit, I think I'd rather see ya parted from him, for he doesna strike me as someone capable of lovin' as deeply as yersel', from all I've heard, and I'll wager ye could end up more hurt than ye are now. But ye have t'find oot for yoursel'. I'll start packin' our bags."

Amanda learned, thanks to Lord Compton's London associates, that Paul had taken lodgings in the city, close to his physician. She also learned that de Villarin's pistol had taken his revenge most cruelly. Paul's shattered leg had been removed from the knee down, for the fragmented bone had quickly become infected. If anything, this news only made Amanda more determined to see him.

Amanda and Aggie decided to take the public coach

to London, refusing Elizabeth's offer of the loan of her own plush vehicle. She was unwilling to presume upon their good will for a journey they had lovingly begged her not to make.

They arrived in the city on a sweltering evening, May 15th, the uncomfortable coach ride having taken its toll.

Their inn, the Ship's Anchor, was on the corner of a narrow, cobbled street, a good enough place, if a little rowdy. Paul's lodgings, Amanda ascertained, were nearby.

They paid the innkeeper and retired to their room, partaking of a light supper of roasted mutton, bread, and thick pea soup. Then they fell into bed and slept soundly, despite the scurrying of rats in the room and the bawdy choruses from the taproom below.

The next morning, Amanda dressed carefully in a light-yellow gown, sprigged with tiny white flowers. The neckline was low, her breasts rising from their lacy fichu like creamy peaches. The pearls and topaz pendant gleamed at the crest of the valley between them. She nodded in satisfaction at her reflection in the greening mirror.

It was close enough to walk to the inn on Weighmaster Street where Paul lodged. Lifting high their skirts from the mud and filth of the gutters, Amanda and Aggie elbowed their way through the crowded streets.

Amanda noticed with surprise that they were nearer the Thames than she had thought, for the masts of many ships in the Pool were cleary visible. Sailors from vessels anchored there were on shore leave, reeling drunk even by daylight. Some were strolling with a painted tart on either arm, or sharing one between two. The street girls looked at Amanda's finery in disgust. Some swept her the deepest of curtsies, and minced: "Good 'morrow, m'lady," and spat as she passed.

Once they heard a cry: "Look out, below!" They leaped off the pavement, narrowly escaping being drenched by the contents of a chamberpot, emptied from the casement above. Amanda grinned at Aggie's totally unladylike reaction to this!

Everywhere was alive, so much alive, it seemed to Amanda, that the narrow, winding streets must burst to contain it all! Wagonloads of fish, barreled and reeking, trundled up from the quayside, bound for Billingsgate market. Sides of beef, hams, and dripping fowl passed to the meat market at Smithfield, stinking of blood. Flowersellers struggled with unwieldy handcarts of amassed blossoms, bound for elegant Kensington or Grosvenor Square, determined to persuade the toffs to buy their wares. Blind beggars, their clothes in tatters and bodies riddled with sores, begged alms on every corner. Grubby urchins fled the flying wheels of coaches and carts that rumbled by. Merchants, clerks, tailors, and prostitutes all rubbed seamy shoulders one against the other, as the city became reborn with the morning. Bow Bells peeled the hour in harmony with the sonorous bonging of Big Ben.

Amanda and a horrified Aggie, who could not believe some of the dreadful sights they had seen, finally arrived at the inn where Paul was lodged. It was named the Figurehead, and a peeling, carved mermaid from the swinging sign above winked lewdly down at them. Although chipped and with faded paint, she was, nevertheless, a landmark to remember.

Amanda inquired of the innkeeper where Paul might be found. He jerked a thumb in the direction of the stairs and mumbled instructions. Heart pounding, Amanda requested Aggie to wait. She scurried eagerly up the stairs, and tapped on the door.

A skinny, ratlike man answered, eyeing her suspiciously.

"Yeah? Whaddya want?" he growled, enjoying the view his shortness afforded him of Amanda's cleavage.

She glared at him. "I'm looking for a Mr. Paul Blake. The innkeeper told me I—"

"Let her in, Charlie! Welcome to my humble abode, Amanda."

She thrust past the man, then stopped in horror at the sight and stench that met her. Paul lay on grayed sheets, in half-light from the tightly closed window. The room stank of stale sweat and the sweet, sickly odor of something rotten. Flies buzzed against the clouded window panes.

Paul's hair, once so blond, clung to his head, dirty and unkempt. His eyes were dark-ringed, but bright with fever. Several days growth of beard was at odds with the unnatural rosy flush to his cheeks. His once-handsome face was marred by a livid, puckered scar across the cheekbone.

Amanda was speechless.

"Well, my dove? Aren't you going to kiss me? Horrible thought, eh?" He laughed bitterly as she recoiled.

"Paul, don't! I know how you feel and—"

"You know nothing, *nothing,* of what I have endured!" he whispered, speech difficult through his parched lips. "Screaming while some butcher hacked off my leg, then again when they cauterized the stump with boiling pitch! And you were going to say you know how I feel? How could you! Your greatest agony in life has been trying to decide which gown to wear!"

She stepped closer, her innocence like that of an angel in the hell of that room. "Paul, I still love you! Let me take care of you, darling," she pleaded. "We can still be married quietly. I don't care that you've lost your leg. You are still the same man!"

"You fool! You really don't see it, do you? My business was founded upon my reputation, my good name. Now de Villarin has taken that from me. Already my orders have dwindled. Soon there'll be nothing, do you see now! And what do I keep you on, my princess," he sneered, "alms for a cripple? Yes, cripple, for that's what I am now!

"I have no vast inheritance to tide me over. I am the lowly son of a chandler's son, who dragged himself up, with all those society snobs looking down their noses at him, to be someone, to build Blakespoint. And now those high-class bastards will take their business elsewhere. Goddamn de Villarin to hell! If it's the last thing I do on this earth, I shall avenge my crippling!"

"But together we can start again, build a new life somewhere else," she pleaded, desperate. "I'll be with you, Paul. Our love will—"

"Love! Ha! I *never* loved you, Amanda! I wanted to bed you, nothing more, to repay you for scorning me that first time at the tavern. But, no, you demanded a ring for your maidenhead. I got to thinking, why not? Your family had a good name, and even if it were a little sullied," he jeered, "I could have used its associations in my business ventures. People understand debtors, you see, they sympathize, knowing if their own notes are called in, they could be in the same predicament. In all, it seemed a good arrangement! You to warm my bed and give me an heir. And, in a few months, when I tired of you, well, there would always be others to amuse me!"

She blanched, close to slapping his face. "You don't mean this. You can't!" she cried. "You're just saying these awful things to turn me away. You don't want me to pity you. But I'll help you, you'll see!"

He shrugged away her comforting hand.

"Don't fool yourself, Amanda! It's over, finished. Get out, do you hear me? *Get out!*" he screamed.

Her fists were clenched, her feet rooted to the floorboards. She wanted to run, but couldn't move!

"Then if you insist upon staying, I'll take what you refused me before!" His fingers darted out and hooked in the filmy cloth of her bodice, wrenching her across the bed and into his arms.

She pulled away, but his mouth was on hers, brutal in its rape of her own, soft mouth. She bit and clawed at him, tearing herself from his grasp. As his hand moved to fondle her breast, she threw him off her with all her strength, lurched him off balance. Freed from his arms, she fled through the door.

Aggie was waiting anxiously in the hallway at the foot of the stairs.

"Miss Amanda, your bodice! Whatever were ye doin'? I thought I had raised ye t'know better! Oh, lassie, he didna hurt ye, did he?" Aggie's distraught face turned concerned.

"No'o," she stammered, "I'm a little shaken that's all.

He—he tried to—! Aggie he's so full of hate! He said terrible, ugly things! That he'd never loved me. Oh God, that he wanted only—!" She could not go on, and covered her face with her hands.

"Hush, now, hush, lassie. Come inside here." Aggie pushed her into a small room off the hallway.

Amanda was choking with grief, the control that she had maintained since the church finally and irrevocably broken.

"Could I have been such a fool? Could I have been so blinded by my love for him that his real self was hidden? No! He told me he loved me; his eyes, the way he looked at me, they all said it! I need him, Aggie! I need him so!" She sobbed quietly, her head on her knees.

Aggie slipped away, and came back minutes later with a man's worn cloak. She wrapped it about the girl's shoulders to conceal the torn bodice. Haltingly, they left the Figurehead, and made their way back to the Ship's Anchor.

Once in their room, Amanda gave way again, her grief like a storm, howling, lashing, wreaking its fury on everyone and everything. At length, she was quiet once more.

Aggie wiped her face, scared at her outburst. Never had she seen the girl broken by anything, not even the death of her father!

By suppertime, Amanda was white-faced but composed. They decided to travel back to Suffolk the next day, for there seemed little sense in draining any further their scant finances on lodgings. After supper, they carried mugs of hot chocolate to their room. Lulled by the sweet brew, Aggie quickly fell asleep. But Amanda paced restlessly to and fro, her mind teeming with questions. The candle guttered, flared up, and died with a sibilant hiss. In the gloom, she was even more depressed.

"Paul, I need you!" she murmured desperately.

Aggie had said she must forget him, but her pride didn't seem to matter anymore. Nothing did, except Paul! Perhaps he had reconsidered sending her away? He'd had ample time to do so since the morning!

Deciding quickly, Amanda grabbed her cloak and left the inn. She drew more than one eager stare from the noisy taproom, but ignored the men's lustful looks, and hurried out into the streets.

The coolness of the breeze was refreshing after the closeness of the room. She pulled the hood over her hair and wrapped the fullness of the cloak tightly about her.

A full moon shone, illuminating the cobbles and throwing the alleys into murkier depths by contrast. There were hundreds of stars, brilliant and cold. The night reminded her of the eve of her supposed wedding day, of the moments she had last spent in Paul's arms. To hear him talk as a heartless blackguard helped little, for her mind and body clung, like traitors, to the memory of his lovemaking. Surely, he would not send her away again? If she had to, she decided, she'd let him take her to his bed, if that was what he needed to convince him of her love!

There was a sharp breeze blowing off the Thames, carrying with it the odor of grain, tar, spices and all the other smells of the wharf, coupled with the tang of the river itself. No lamplight lit this quarter of London town, and those that ventured out by night did so only in the direst emergency, or to use the darkness to conceal their evil deeds. The narrow spaces between the houses were littered and foul-smelling, but from their depths she heard heavy breathing and rustling as the doxies serviced their men, like animals in the shadows.

She hurried on, eager to see Paul, convinced she could persuade him he had underestimated her, that he had misjudged her. A faint scream carried through the darkness, and she gasped and stumbled on the cobbles. She righted herself, and walked on more briskly. The sound of running feet, becoming fainter as they receded, told her that the cry she'd heard belonged to some poor fool who'd lost his purse—or his life—to one of the many gangs of footpads who terrorized the city by night. Her heart was pounding faster now, and she wondered belatedly if perhaps it had been rash to venture out by night, and unescorted. Should she go back?

In a dark alley, two seamen watched the slight figure approach. Though enveloped in the concealing cloak, the step and swing of her walk declared her young and lithe.

First mate Higgins wetted his lips and nudged Bosun Taylor in the ribs. "'Ere's a likely one! Reckon the Cap'n would fancy 'er, Bert?"

The other man grinned, wiping his nose on his sleeve. "Aye, that I'd bet, Alf! Let's get a look at her face, though. Could be she's rigged real fine, but got a face like a bilge bucket!" he chortled.

The slight figure drew nearer.

"You grab 'er from behind, and I'll take her legs, right?"

Taylor nodded, and got into position.

As Amanda drew level with the alley, a burly man in a sailor's stocking cap and garb leaped out at her, lifting her screaming into the air.

"Got 'er, Alf!" His hand moved from her waist to clamp over her mouth and cut off her terrified cries.

Higgins pulled the hood from Amanda's face. "Cor, she's a looker, Bert! Funny she ain't workin' tonight. Don't reckon 'as how she got the French pox, do ye?"

"Nah. Looks clean enough. Smells good, too. And if'n she do be poxed, that be the Cap'n's problem, not ours'n!" He laughed slyly. "We only provides the peaceoffer, see, not t'guarantee!"

Amanda flailed helplessly, pinioned by the short man's hairy arms. The other sailor grabbed her legs, remarking on how fine they were as the rest of her, as he fondled her roughly.

Amanda viciously clamped her teeth into Bert's hand, in a last, desperate bid for freedom. His roar of pain was the last thing she heard, before a splitting blow reeled her into unconsciousness.

Chapter Eight

She woke, her head throbbing with pain, to find herself bobbing up and down in a void of inky, clinging darkness. At first, she thought the blow had played tricks with her mind, but as minutes passed and her head cleared, she realized she was in a small boat being rowed by her captors. She sat up cautiously, the effort sending needles of pain through her cramped, chilly body, and peered over the side.

The Pool of London, where all ships docked when in port, was a forest of indistinct masts and riggings, the bows of great ships looming like eerie sentinels above her, groaning, creaking, as they endlessly tried to escape the heavy weight of anchors. The fog was rolling in like some great, predatory beast, insinuating slimy paws into every nook and cranny. Yellow-brown and malevolent, it gave the ships a disembodied, ghostly appearance. There was heavy silence save for the slight splash of the oars dipping into water, and the soft, sucking sound as they were lifted out.

As they passed a nearby vessel, she could see the silhouettes of huge, furry rats scampering to and from shore along the hawsers, with shrieks that sent shudders through her. Should she leap into the water and seek escape in its murkiness? No! Her mind revolted at the thought, for the filth and the crawling, unseen creeping things that lurked beneath its surface terrified her more than the coarse jests and rude manners of the two oafs that held her captive.

What did they want with her? It must be a mistake! Icy slivers of fear prickled her and froze her stomach. Her body felt chilled and sore. She tried to stretch, but it was useless, for her feet and hands were securely bound with what appeared to be rags.

The taller seaman turned and noticed she was conscious.

"Well, my pretty doxie, are ye ready for me Cap'n's pleasure?" He reached out and chucked her beneath the chin.

She shrank away from the stubby fingers. The man chuckled, patting her buttocks familiarly.

"Aye, the Cap'n'll be pleased wiv ye, lass, for he likes a bit of a fight—adds spice, he do say! Hee! Hee!"

"Leave the wench, Bert, an' let 'er rest!" growled Alf. "She'll be needin' it, for there'll be none t'night—nor in the next few weeks—not wiv our lusty Cap'n!"

The two tars slapped their thighs and hooted at his coarse joke.

Amanda drew herself into a ball. Now that she knew what fate lay in store for her, she yearned for the ropes to be loosened, so that she might try to escape. Better the vermin in the filthy water than the human ones on the ship to which they were bound!

Bert shipped his oars and reached up to grab a rope ladder that seemed to suspend from air, so thick was the fog. He hoisted Amanda over his shoulder as if her weight were nothing, and clambered up the ladder with surprising agility for his girth.

"'Ere we are, me loverly! 'Ome, sweet 'ome for the next few months. Good ole gal she is, too, the *Gypsy Princess.* Ain't none better!" With a grunt, he dumped the girl on the clammy deck.

She lay there, bewildered, until the rags were unfastened, then once again she was hoisted over his shoulder. The other man accompanied them down a narrow gangway and swung open a heavy door that led into a lantern-lit cabin. With a snicker, they dumped her on an ornate bed, and left.

Amanda sat up, wrists and ankles rubbed raw from the knotted rags. She shuffled across to the door, wincing as the blood rushed back into her numb limbs, and tugged hard at the heavy iron handle. It was no use; they'd locked it after them! Desperately she hammered on the timbers until her fists throbbed, but no one came. She crossed the cabin to try the port window. It, too, was securely fastened with wooden slats. Peering through the cloudy panes, she could see nothing but ebony darkness and the feeble glimmer of moonlight beyond.

Perching nervously on the bed, she sighed, exhausted. Was there never to be an end to her misfortunes? Bad enough she had lost everything, including Paul. Now Fate would see her a sea captain's doxie on a voyage, only God knew where. I'll be damned if I let that happen, she determined rebelliously, a plan taking shape in her mind. Yes, it definitely had possibilities! In fact, anything was worth trying, and if she succeeded, she would have, this once at least, mastered her own fate!

She took stock of her surroundings. The cabin was

almost elegantly furnished—in fact, nothing like she had envisioned a sea captain's cabin. A faint odor of tobacco in the air declared the quarters' owner's decided masculinity. A clock ticked loudly on the cabin wall, made in the shape of a ship's wheel, the face set inside.

The brass trim winked in the light from the lantern that hung from a hook above her. A huge desk flanked the starboard side, strewn with charts and a compass. A quill lay in the center—its owner obviously having left in a hurry, for ink had dripped from the nib, making a huge blot on the parchment—and the inkstand stood empty. The four-poster bed upon which she perched, she saw now, was bolted to the deck beneath and draped in crimson cloth, spun richly with gold stitches.

She whirled about, startled, as the clock chimed the hour. Midnight! It was almost three hours since her fateful decision to leave the inn. There was no escape. She was a prisoner, for what purpose she knew, but with what end she dared not imagine.

Her fears were giant moths, ugly, tormenting, beating at her courage until there seemed no way to fie them out but by sleep. She sank back upon the bed, and exhaustion carried her into blissful, pain-free slumber.

Amanda stirred restlessly, dimly hearing that infernal clock strick twice.

"Come, now, wake up, pretty bird!"

A hand shook her, roughly, but not unkindly. She opened her eyes, not knowing at first where she was. Her cheeks were flushed with sleep, her hair tumbled wantonly about her shoulders. Two sea-green eyes twinkled merrily back into her own sleepy ones. She sat up instantly, gasping in shock and clutching her cloak tightly about her as if it were a shield. The man leaned nearer.

"Don't you touch me!" she shrieked. "Get away from me, you—you animal!" All thoughts of her plan were blown to the winds in her shock at waking to find him there! She lashed out with her nails, raking his cheek and drawing blood that blossomed in droplets along the curve of his jaw.

The man growled, grabbed her by both her wrists and swung her across his thighs. Flinging her skirts and petticoats above her waist, with a hand of steel, he paddled her *derrière* soundly.

Amanda screamed lustily, indignant tears burning from behind thick-lashed eyes and flowing down her now scarlet cheeks. Her arms and legs flailed wildly.

"Put me down, sir!" she stormed. "How dare you! I am no child to be treated thus!"

He grasped her firmly about the waist and stood her upright.

"James Mallory pays for pleasure, not pain, vixen! I shall deduct this injury from your purse if you do not compensate me adequately! Shall we start with clearing your debt by a warm, amorous kiss?" Grinning, he hauled her into his arms and brought his lips down on hers. His hands were tight against the small of her back, and she could feel the hardness of his manhood thrusting against her hip. Indeed, his breeches strained under the pressure of his lust! The green eyes had an almost dreamy quality as their lips met. His kiss was tender as his tongue explored her mouth, thrusting, searching, repulsive, but yet—she felt a strange stirring within her! Was she wanton to be aroused by the kiss of a stranger? Nay! Her plan! She could escape this lecherous beast, if she played her part correctly! She returned his kisses with an ardor that stunned him. Then coyly, she pushed him back.

"Why, Captain, so lusty? I thought to give you sport in the pursuit of my virtue, but I see you are not a man to enjoy the thrill of a little *guerre d'amour?*" She sighed, shrugging, and tapped his shoulder, flirting with her dark eyes. "So, I will prepare myself, if you will give me but fifteen minutes alone?" She looked at him in what she hoped was a thoroughly enticing manner, undraping the cloak and letting it fall, seductively slowly, in a velvet puddle at her feet. She delighted inwardly as she saw his face, naked with lust, intake greedily of the voluptuous picture she presented.

He pondered her words only briefly. "Then, madam, I will give you your fifteen minutes—and not a second longer!" With a roguish wink and a lingering kiss to her hand, he left the cabin.

As soon as he had gone, Amanda dashed breathlessly to the desk and picked up the brass quill stand. She weighed it in her palm. It was a fair size, and she supposed the squareness of it would aid her purpose, but was it heavy enough? She glanced around the cabin, but there was nothing else. It would have to do!

She positioned herself behind the door and waited. Her heart drummed loudly in time with the ticking of the clock. Five minutes passed, then ten. Footsteps! They thundered down the stairway! The rogue, he could not even keep his promise! Well, she was ready for him—but not in the manner he expected!

The door opened slowly, and a man entered bearing

a tray. Amanda swung the inkstand over her head in a flashing arc, bringing it down with a resounding thud against the back of the man's skull! He toppled forward into the room with a muffled groan, glass shattering around him.

With a rushing intake of breath, Amanda hopped over the sprawled body and fled the cabin. She pulled up in horror at the foot of the stairway. There, against the railing, lounged a man—a man who looked at her amusedly from bright green eyes!

"Were you expecting someone else, mayhap, wench?" he asked, grinning wider still as he nodded at the unconscious figure in the doorway below. He stepped to the head of the stairs, his broad shoulders blocking out the puny light.

"Why, Sir Geoffrey!" Amanda gasped suddenly, pretending to startle at someone over his shoulder.

The captain whirled about, and, in that split second, Amanda hoisted her skirts and charged up the stairs, passing him at suicide speed as she careened across the decks!

With a whoop of surprise, he was after her!

Which way to run, she wondered breathlessly? There were cables and rigging everywhere, snares of lines, traps of stacked barrels, sailors scurrying about their duties. Such confusion! The seamen gaped open-mouthed as the slender figure dodged and wove with amazing speed in and out of the clutter.

Where on earth was the side of this infernal vessel? Ducking and bobbing, she finally reached it. Black water or not, she was determined to leap over and swim to safety! She yanked off her pattens with trembling hands, and tugged and tore at the delicate fabric of her skirts until they ripped away from her bodice at the waist. Her breath was coming in ragged, gasping pants as she clambered up on the rail, and risked a timid glance over her shoulder.

The captain had sighted her, and was charging across the deck toward her. His face was white with rage as his jeering crew egged him on.

"Go to it, Cap'n, sir! Grab the wench, or it'll be a cold bunk t'night for ye!" Hoots and whistles followed the crude jests.

Incensed, the captain finally reached Amanda, and clutched at her with a powerful hand—too late! She wrenched free, hurdled the side, and pitched into the inky blackness, leaving him a tantalizing spectacle of fluttering petticoats and moonshone hair as she disappeared from view.

The sailors rushed to the side, all jostling to see where the wench had gone. Their Captain ripped off his jerkin, perched straight as an arrow, and dived cleanly after Amanda.

She regretted her hasty decision the minute her scantily clad body hit water! This was not the village pond, nor the beach at Brighton, but the North Sea, colder than any grave and treacherous! She tread water for several minutes before she realized: the ship had set sail while she slept! Gone was the Pool. Even the coastline was not visible on the dimly glimmering horizon. Nothing, nothing as far as the eye could see, but icy water and darkness, the cold of the former seeping through her body and numbing her limbs.

A terrible fear gripped her and panic swept through her body. Terror froze her movements, sending her spluttering beneath the awesome depths. She coughed and fought her way to the surface, the salt water cutting her cries to strangled sobs.

Then a hand grasped her by the band of her petticoats, and she felt herself being tugged toward the looming shadow of the *Gypsy Princess.* Strong arms turned her onto her back, and the captain plowed through the water at home as any merman in the deep! She struggled, then relinquished the fight, letting him tow her back to safety.

The captain roared a command, and line snaked down with a sling attached. Mallory slipped her into the sling and, hanging onto the line himself, they were hoisted aboard the vessel.

Amanda was not so exhausted as totally unmoved by the raucous cheers that greeted her half-dressed reappearance. The rough crew slapped their leader heartily on the back, and he swaggered among them like a proud rooster in a barnyard, Amanda thought mutinously, gritting her teeth. She shivered in her undergarments until his strutting was over, then he hefted her onto his shoulder, thwacked her buttocks and carried her, screaming curses and dripping a trail of water behind them, back to his cabin.

He wasted no time in continuing his attack on her virtue. Quickly he stripped off his streaming shirt and stood before her, naked to the waist, the red-gold hairs on his chest gleaming in the light of the lantern.

Amanda stared at him, horrified, and yet, fascinated—as a rabbit by a weasel is fascinated—as she viewed the tanned limbs and broad, strong chest. His muscles rippled in hard curves beneath the taut flesh.

His jaw was square, made to appear even more so by

the shadows of the lantern light, his high cheekbones emphasizing the slight slant of the green eyes. His nose was not long, but jutted out perfectly to balance the lips of a man who obviously smiled often, judging by the tiny laugh lines at the corners of his mouth. Nothing seemed to match, but when taken as a whole, his face seemed in perfect harmony, even down to the unruly brown hair that curled over his nape.

He approached her then, and wrapped her in a rough linen towel. Her teeth had begun to chatter as she stood in the pool of water that dripped from her body. Leading her beneath the lantern, he began to dry her, his strong hands molding her body beneath the cloth.

She flinched as he touched her, then as his hand, ever bolder, went to a more intimate caress, she slapped it angrily away.

"Keep your hands to yourself!" she gritted through clenched teeth.

He chuckled. "Take off your wet clothes, then, my pigeon. You will catch your death."

"I will not!" she stormed, angry sparks igniting in her eyes.

"Then I will take them off for you."

He took only one step toward her, but she knew he intended to do as he said. The look in his eyes was unwavering.

She nodded assent, defiant still. "Turn your back, then, sir!"

He did so with an amused smile, and she peeled off her remaining wet garments and fastened the towel beneath her armpits. The lantern caught the sheen of her wet hair and cast tawny light on the creamy whiteness of her limbs.

A seaman knocked, then entered, bearing two tankards.

"Here's rum, for ye, sir, and the leddy."

Amanda gasped as the fiery liquor sent heat coursing through her body.

"Warmer now?" the captain inquired.

She nodded without looking at him, and went to perch on the bed.

Mallory came across the cabin and threw himself down beside her.

"Now, love, tell me why you ran from me? A girl such as yourself should be used to a man's amorous ways! Do I seem cruel, is that it? Believe me, my sweet, I will pleasure you gently. A kiss here, like so, and mayhap another here, and here. . . ."

As he spoke, he drew her to him, using a strand of her chestnut hair like a tether. He pressed his lips to her forehead, then to the pulse that throbbed wildly in her throat. Before she realized his intentions, the towel had tumbled to a heap about her waist, and his lips plundered the valley between her breasts. His arms engulfed her, and drew her into a fierce embrace.

Though she fought to tear his lips from hers, he held her as if in a vise. Somehow, she realized with shock, she lay stretched naked beside him on the crimson coverlet. Uselessly, she howled for him to stop, her cries muffled in her throat as his mouth covered hers once more. His thigh, carelessly thrown across her hips, held her prisoner as perfectly as his embrace.

"You don't understand!" She wailed, "I am not what you think!"

The words flooded from her as he gave her breathing

space. Horrified, she watched him slither out of his breeches.

"Hush, now, enough of your teasing!" he commanded her softly. "We must enjoy ourselves before I am forced to leave you for another, more demanding maid—my ship!" His hands cajoled her straining body to be still, but she would not. One leg was free! She jackknifed it with all her strength at what she hoped was his manhood. The kick missed, but instead thudded into Mallory's hard stomach, briefly winding him.

Amanda rolled from the bed. She snatched up the towel, and fastening it as she ran, retreated until the desk stood between them.

He took a step forward, grinning and apparently taking great delight in the cat-and-mouse game. He crossed his arms and slowly and pleasurably his eyes savored her half-naked body.

"Oh, my little tigress! If you only knew what a tempting minx you are, just that way!" He glanced down at his manhood, "See what you've done to me?"

She followed his look and flushed furiously. "Don't you dare come any closer, you—you Bluebeard! If you do, I shall be forced to—to—!"

"To scream? Go ahead! No one will come! You see, I am the captain. On this ship, my word is law! And I warrant you're safer here, than out there, with the men! Didn't you see how they looked at you, my pretty?" His eyes twinkled in the light.

She noticed he was nearer now. When had he stepped forward? The towel began to slip and she clutched it about her desperately. He was right, she realized miserably. She could not run from the cabin, but neither could she stay here and be ravaged by that rutting he-goat! Her mind sought desperately for some words to sway him.

"Captain," she began, striving to appear calm, "I realize I am at your mercy here. It is with this in mind that I beg you, as a man of honor, to return me to my lodgings in London, unmolested."

James Mallory whistled through his teeth. "Fancy words, indeed, but wasted! I cannot return, for we sail as the winds and tides dictate, not I. And, I must confess, I should hate to see you leave so soon!" He laughed wickedly, and took another step forward.

Now only the desk remained between them. He rested one hand lightly on the side farthest from her, and waited for her next move. What was she, he wondered? Some nobleman's by-blow, reared to speak in an educated manner? The mystery whetted his appetite even further!

She stood her ground, though her knees felt weak, and she could hear the pounding of her heart. "Then if you cannot return me, take me with you to your next port-of-call. I will pay you. See, I have this!" She reached up to her throat to show him her pendant. It was gone! The chain must have broken, she realized miserably.

"Are you looking for this?" He leaned over and withdrew the bauble from his pile of clothes. "It was all you left me when you leaped from the rail. A poor exchange for that jewel beneath the towel!" He grinned again, the lantern light sparkling on the pearls and topaz pendant as it swung to and fro from his fist. "How else, I wonder, could you pay me for your berth?" he mused, smiling.

"Why, you rogue! Give it to me, it is mine!" she stormed, her eyes glittering, two red spots of flaming scarlet on her cheeks proof of her fury. But she was not so foolish as to try to snatch it from him!

He realized she had weighed that idea in her mind, and laughingly tossed the jewel flower to the bed.

Her eyes followed its flight, and in that split moment he vaulted across the desk and pinned her to the rough beams of the cabin wall!

He cursed softly as her feet stomped on the arches of his own bare feet, then swept her up in his arms and strode across the cabin. Without ceremony he tumbled her onto the bed and leaped after her, covering her body with his own. He held her arms above her head in one huge fist.

"Now, my little duchess, what was it you said? Ah, yes! Let the 'molestation' commence!"

Above them, the lantern spilled its light in crazy arcs as the ship sailed on.

Chapter Nine

Amanda stirred restlessly and rolled onto her side, sighing deeply. She had sworn not to fall asleep with him beside her, but fatigue had won. She tossed again, and flung a slim arm far to one side.

Mallory lifted it from his chest and kissed the inside of her wrist tenderly, before replacing her hand under the covers. He leaned on one elbow, and looked down at the sleeping girl next to him. A twinge of guilt pricked him, causing a deep frown to furrow his brow. Ah, well, it was over now, done with. How was he to have known she was virgin, when all else pointed to quite the opposite? Oh, she had tried to tell him, but, he cursed himself, he thought she was angling for a higher price for her favors, and refused to listen. By the time he'd realized she spoke the truth, he could not—and hadn't wanted to!—stop.

He groaned as he realized the predicament he could be in. No doubt this Amanda had a giant of a father somewhere, or a brother, who would be only too willing to do battle for her lost honor, or else force him into an unwilling marriage. Gloomily, he decided he would rather duel than marry! As far as he was concerned, marriage held as much appeal as did being hanged from the gibbet at Tyburn, and even less excitement! Still, she was a peach, a jewel, with a beauty the like of which he had never seen before. He traced the outline of her lips, recalling how at the end, she had implored him to stop with those very lips.

Her lashes were dusky crescents over eyes faintly shadowed with sleep, and across one rosy cheek wandered a stray burnished curl. He knew nothing more than that her name was Amanda, and, surprisingly, the name of the one who disturbed her sleep was someone called Paul, and not himself. She had murmured his name often during the night.

Mallory caressed her lovely shoulders, wondering idly who this Paul might be. Not a lover, certainly. A friend? Or, good God! Surely not a husband? He sat up straight then, for the idea seemed plausible. Mayhap her parents had married her against her will to some old, impotent lord, too senile to be a husband in any way but name, and she had fled? He lay back, arms beneath his head, and considered this for some time.

A loud banging on the door signaled his first officer's call to the mess for breakfast.

"Aye, Mr. Emerson, I'll be there shortly," he growled as he rolled out of bed.

He tugged on his boots and perched his tricorn on his head. Before he left the cabin, he rested a lingering glance on Amanda's sleeping form. As he left, he locked the massive door carefully behind him, more for her protection than her imprisonment, and secured the key on his belt.

Amanda's eyes fluttered open, then she closed them instantly as the brilliant light flooding through the port window dazzled them. She stretched lazily, feeling contentment coursing through her like liquid honey. She yawned, her belly growling. Good heavens! Mrs. Woods must have risen late! The clock on the cabin wall showed nigh nine of the clock. The cabin wall! With a gasp, she sat up, pulling the coverlet up to her neck.

The events of the previous night rushed back to her. She clambered from the bed, wound the crimson coverlet about her dragging its weight, and went to the door. Locked again! The remnants of her clothes lay in a pile in one corner. They were still damp, and already bore the musty odor of mildew from their soaking. She hurried across to the cabin's built-in armoire and rummaged in its depths. Her search rewarded, she found a peasant blouse and a rumpled wool skirt stuffed far to the back. She pulled the garments on, wondering bitterly what poor girl's clothes she wore, and just what had happened to their owner? She had a nasty feeling she already knew the answer. That vile, damned James Mallory! How could he have done what he did? It was inhuman. Where was he, anyway? Not that she cared, but she didn't relish the idea of being a prisoner in this small cabin indefinitely. The idea of days spent in its narrow confines and of nights filled with his idea of lovemaking appalled her!

What would Aggie be doing now, she wondered, for with the sunrise she would have wakened and found her gone? A sudden hope filled her. Wouldn't Aggie guess that she had gone to talk to Paul again? Yes, surely she would! And maybe between them, they could find her! The hope died. No one had seen the sailors abduct her—at least, no one who would tell what they had seen. No, she might as well face up to it. She was as good as dead, or, at best, thought dropped off the face of the earth, for the only ones who knew where she was were those aboard!

She plaited her hair furiously into one fat braid, more as a means of venting her anger than any desire to neaten her self, changed and re-made the bed with equally furious movements, imagining with each pounding as she fluffed the pillows that they were that blasted captain's head! Finished, she perched on the coverlet and drummed her fingernails. Her stomach groaned again. At least they could feed her!

She could see the water only a few feet below the port window. It looked blue and inviting this morning. Was it just last night she had leaped into it in her vain escape bid? It seemed ages ago. Another woman, more sensitive perhaps, than she, would have considered taking her own life in its depth, but Amanda dismissed the fleeting thought as quickly as it had come. No, angry and humiliated she may be, but she would not consider dying for the loss of her purity. If anyone should feel guilt or remorse, it should be that—that creature who had taken her so cruelly!

She had known in her heart that the fight was as good as over when he'd tumbled her to the bed. The look in his eyes and the timbre in his voice had been too heated, too full of lust, to make further entreaties worthwhile. Nevertheless, she had bit and clawed until he'd entered her, and she had felt that awful, stabbing pain. After that, thankfully, it had been over in minutes. Though he had seemed greatly pleasured, she had been left feeling miserably disillusioned, and his promises that the next time, she would feel pleasure too, had gone unheeded, for she was determined there would be no next time! Was that all, she wondered, that the long looks and stolen kisses in a courtship led up to ultimately? That brief and unpleasant invasion of her body? She would kill him if he tried to take her again, she vowed!

Someone was pounding at the door. She retreated to the farthest corner of the cabin as the key scraped in the lock. The door swung inward, and a cabin boy of about sixteen years old entered. There was something vaguely familiar about him; then she realized it had been he she'd crowned with the inkstand the previous night, for there was a grimy cloth about his head that served for a bandage.

He looked at her sullenly for a full minute before speaking, the look in his pale blue eyes one of wounded male pride and an intense dislike of her.

"Miss, the Cap'n says if ye wishes, Cookie'll fetch yer something ter eat?" he queried, glowering.

"Tell your Captain I *do* wish it!" she snapped. "And after, I would like a tub of hot, hot water, a scrubbing brush, and a cake of strong soap!" She turned her back on the lad and crossed her arms.

The lad looked horrified. "I can't tell 'im that, miss! He'll 'ave me flogged, he will!"

"Just go, and tell him *I* said so! And be quick!"

The youth fled as if the hounds of hell were after him, and soon another older man entered bearing a tray of steaming food. He was pot-bellied, his bulging middle swathed in a grease spattered apron. A scarf was tied about his head above a single gold earring. He was obviously the cook, but a more incongruous-looking one she had never seen!

"Here's yer grub, missie. Plain fare 'tis, indeed, but a feast alongside o'wot we'll be after eatin' come we reach Morocco." He shoved aside the charts on the desk, and slapped the wooden trencher down on the scarred surface. He put a pewter tankard of ale alongside it. The cook nodded and made to leave.

"Wait! Where is your captain, sir? Please tell him I wish to speak with him immediately!" She sat in the chair at the desk, tearing her glance reluctantly away from the food. Her eyes caught the astonished look on the cook's own face. "Well, what are you waiting for?"

"Nothing, miss! 'Tis just that, the Cap'n, he do be in an all firin' foul temper this mornin'! Likely he'll not take kindly to yer—yer summons, miss!" he explained, shame-faced. "Right riled up, he is!"

"So am I, sir, so am I!" she muttered, standing, her eyes darkening angrily.

What sort of men were these, anyway, that Captain James Mallory could so cow them? Not men at all, mayhap, but mice! She glared at the cook, hands on hips, and he fled almost as hurriedly as the cabin boy before him, and locked the door after him.

The aroma of the food overtook her senses. She sat and snatched up a plump chicken leg, tearing into it with a gusto that would have done credit to Henry VIII. The chicken done with, she licked her fingers and wiped her mouth on her sleeve, and turned her ravenous attention to the hunk of coarse bread and wedge of cheese. The whole she washed down with generous swigs of ale. Replete, she leaned back in the chair and surveyed the cabin.

A few seconds later, she heard the key turning in the lock and the door burst open. Mallory strode in and towered over her. He looked a full six inches taller in his high sea boots and twice as broad as she remembered him. He also seemed ten times as intimidating.

"And by whose permission, madam, are *you* giving the orders on this ship?" he stormed. "Did you forget so soon that I am the master here?"

"How could I, sir, when you have made such efforts to impress the fact upon me!" Amanda retorted hotly, with a meaningful glance at the bed. "I think you owe me an apology, at the very least!"

"You do, do you, madam? Well, I fail to see why? You stroll the alleyways at night like a common trull; is it any wonder that you are taken for one!" His voice lacked conviction.

"Oh, come, now, Captain, enough excuses! I cannot believe that even you can still adhere to that, for I think you found out otherwise, did you not?" She turned away from him, her breasts heaving with indignation.

James Mallory had the grace to grin and look almost apologetic.

"Aye, that I did, my dear! Very well, I admit to the error of my ways! But I will not say I regret them, for to do so would be to deny the very great pleasure you gave me last night, would it not?"

"I *gave* you nothing, Captain, if you recall! And still you have the gall to stand there and gloat over your conquest. Sir, you are no gentleman!"

He shrugged and appeared somewhat chastened by her words, like a naughty schoolboy caught in a lie.

"Yes, you are right! Then, I apologize most heartily. I know I cannot return what I have taken, but I offer you a promise of your safe return on another vessel, at my expense, of course. Does that strike you reasonable, madam?"

She nodded, a little surprised at his easy capitulation. "Yes, under the circumstances. And you will not force yourself on me again?"

He bowed, almost sarcastically. "No madam, my word on it. If not as a gentleman, then as a rogue! Not, that is, unless you, with those beautiful wanton lips, implore me to do so!"

"It will be a cold day in Hades that you hear such from my mouth, sir!" she spat back.

"Well, my little duchess! Your turn of speech reeks strongly of the tavern! Do you blame me for thinking you a waterfront doxie?" He laughed and, striding to the side table, poured himself a generous measure of sherry and the same for Amanda.

She took the glass from his proffered hand with a cold little nod of thanks and tasted it before answering.

"It is only *your* actions that drive me to speak in that manner! Contrary to what you believe, my family owned Christchurch Manor in Suffolk. My father was Sir Robert Sommers. An old family and a respected one," she added proudly.

Mallory nodded. "Aye, indeed. But why do you speak of your father, your home, as in the past?"

"My father died several months ago. In Newgate."

He whispered softly. "I see. The debtors' sector?" His expression showed compassion.

Amanda nodded. "My mother had passed away from consumption. After that, he seemed to have lost all will to live. He tried to drown her memory with liquor, cards, other women—then when he fully realized the depths to which he had sunk and also brought me to, I believe that he simply gave up living." She took a deep sip of the amber liquid and sighed, an expression of sadness on her face.

"Then, madam, how came you to walk the streets at night—and unescorted, too? You could not be unaware of the risks you were taking! Did you not know that thieves and cutthroats lurk in every alleyway?"

"You dare to admonish me, when it was *your* cutthroats that waylaid me? Hypocrite!" she retorted.

"Not at my bidding, woman! They sought to appease me for a wrong they had done and deemed a lusty wench to warm me through the voyage a suitable peace offering."

"Obviously they thought correctly! Your desires seem to tend toward the more animal pleasures!"

"Aye, love, that they do!" he agreed, grinning again, his eyes gleaming almost emerald in the sunlight. "But I ask you again, what were you doing there?"

"I don't see that it is any of your business, sir! But, since you insist, I was going to the inn on Weighmaster Street—the Figurehead. No doubt you know it?" Seeing him nod, she continued. "Paul—he is my betrothed—we had a falling out. I had to talk to him, to make him understand." Her hands were clutching the glass and an angry light shone in her eyes. "And I was almost there when your men set upon me!"

"I see. And your betrothed, will he still wish to marry you when he learns what occurred here last night?"

God's blood, this was even worse than he'd thought! He'd really stirred up a kettle of fish this time—ravaged a maiden of nobility, complete with betrothed, and no way could he get the girl out of the predicament he'd forced her into, that he could see! Not to mention himself! He swore under his breath, tossed off the rest of the sherry and poured himself another.

"I don't know! I wonder if things will ever be the same again. It's not as simple as it sounds, Captain Mallory."

Lord, now she was crying, all the fire fizzled out of her like a damp squib! He tossed her his kerchief, and she blew her nose noisily and at length. He noticed she still looked lovely, even with her hair in that awful braid and tears streaming down her cheeks.

"Come now, it cannot be so terrible." He patted her shoulder awkwardly, and she gave him a smile that somehow rendered him feeling even more guilty.

"Oh yes, it is! You see, I'm not at all sure that Paul is still my betrothed! We had made our arrangements, the wedding breakfast, everything. The service had begun. And as we stood before the altar, this foreigner burst in and everything happened so fast after that!" She briefly told him of de Villarin's untimely entrance and of the shock of it all. "One minute more and I should have been Mistress of Blakespoint and truly Paul's wife, were it not for *him!*" she added bitterly.

"Blakespoint! You mean, your betrothed was Paul Blake, the merchant?"

"Yes! Do you know him?"

"Of him, aye! And a deal more than I care to, madam!" He spoke to her earnestly, his face completely devoid of its teasing expression now. "Miss Sommers, Amanda, believe me when I tell you, you are well rid of him! This de Villarin did you a service, whether you realize it or not. Blake's reputation has a stink that reaches from New Orleans to England, and then more." Paul Blake! Mallory shook his head incredulously.

"How dare you speak of him in that way! Whatever he may have done—if you speak the truth, which I doubt—I love him! And I'll thank you to keep your advice to yourself." She stormed angrily across the cabin, her movements brittle and agitated, and sat on the bed. "If you have nothing else to say, I would like the tub and soap that I requested. I accept your offer to see me returned to England, Captain. And now I would appreciate it if you would leave me alone!"

"Of course, m'lady!" Mallory bowed low and retrieved his tricorn from the desk. "But I regret there will be no bath. You see, for one, we have no tub, and, two, 'tis the maid's night off!" He left the cabin, scowling.

Amanda poured herself another glass of sherry and drank it with unaccustomed speed. What gave him the right to condemn Paul! Whatever he may have done, if anything, it surely could not be any worse than Captain Mallory's assault on her!

She paced the cabin restlessly for some time, the huge locked door seeming a living symbol of her imprisonment. Well, at least he had promised not to touch her, that was something to be grateful for. She may as well go back to sleep. There was nothing else to do in her cell. She stretched out on the crimson coverlet and, clutching a feathered pillow, fell fast asleep in seconds. The decanter of sherry was empty.

Chapter Ten

James Mallory stood at the wheel of his ship, steering her through the whitecaps beyond the prow. The early-morning sunshine glittered across the water as upon shattered glass. A fresh, salty breeze blowing bellied the sails and urged the *Gypsy Princess* swiftly on her course.

It was three weeks since they had set sail. By the morrow they should reach Casablanca and after, fully provisioned and cargoed, depart for the Cape and then on to India.

Since Amanda's statement that her betrothed had been none other than the infamous Paul Blake, he had seriously questioned the wisdom of seeing her returned to England and perhaps to her relationship with that ne'er-do-well. But he could not interfere. It was her life, to do with as she pleased. It would have been easier to let her go her own way if she had been less his type of woman: intelligent, spirited, not to mention beautiful and shapely to boot. Though he had kept to his promise not to lay hands on her again, he was sorely regretting the making of that promise.

Nights were hell on earth as he tossed on a lumpy tick mattress at the foot of his bed. She slept sweetly in his bed and alone! Even beneath the coverlet, her round figure was alluring, with her chestnut hair streaming across the satin pillow and her full lips curved in a slumbering smile. His loins ached with wanting her. Thank God, she would be gone soon and he free from temptation. Still, the idea of handing her over to another's care left him strangely disturbed. Or jealous?

The watch rang the ship's bell. Mallory handed the wheel to the mate's care and went to the rail for a pipe. When he finished, he'd bring Amanda abovedeck for an escorted stroll.

He had explained to her that his men were not to be trusted and that this was the reason for the locked door. Whether or not she believed him, she had nodded and asked only for something to do to while away the hours. Grinning, he remembered the disgust on her face as he silently handed her a pile of his shirts that needed patching or darning and a seaman's sewing kit. Still, she hadn't complained and had repaired them beautifully.

What could have possessed those Compton people to bring the two of them together? From what she said, they had seemed fond of her. Hidden in their estate so far from London? Had they not heard of the rumors that spread after Blake's hasty departure from New Orleans? Or on hearing, maybe, like Amanda, they had chosen to believe them untrue, or at best, highly exaggerated? That would account for their letting the matter proceed to the point of marriage.

He had tried to tell her again only last night of what he'd heard Paul and his mistress had done, but she had covered her ears and refused to listen. Stubborn, hotheaded wench! He could not help but admire her loyalty, though. If ever he allowed himself to love again, he hoped the woman he chose would be equally loyal.

Memories of Margaret washed over him, but the anger that usually accompanied them was gone. He remembered without rancor that night in Richmond, when he had found her with her French lieutenant. Just another memory. His mind was taken over by another vision now, of a slender woman with radiant hair and warm, seductive eyes, a beauty that paled the brilliance of the stars: Amanda. My God, I'm like some moonstruck clod of sixteen, he thought, and, tapping out the bole of his pipe, went below to fetch her.

Together they stood at the rail and surveyed the vastness of the sea.

"It's beautiful, isn't it, James?" Amanda said finally, using his first name for the first time.

He nodded. "Like a woman. Beautiful, restless, wild. And her arms can be just as deadly."

"You sound as if you dislike women, Captain?"

"On the contrary. I find them, some of them, captivating. As yourself, for instance, madam."

"Flattery! I would have thought a sea captain would not squander words on such a pasttime."

"No flattery, Amanda. I speak only what I see to be true."

"And," she teased, "do you find your promise difficult to keep?"

"Aye, that I do, madam!" he groaned, a roguish grin lighting his face.

She turned to leave, her cheeks rosy from his words.

"And you, Mistress Sommers?" he called. "Do you wish me to break it?"

"Nay, Captain!" she whispered hotly, remembering the night he had taken her.

But in answer to his question, he only heard "For shame!" as she left the deck.

The evening meal they took together by lantern light in the cabin as usual. The captain's knowledge and easy wit still amazed her, in such contrast to her first impressions. Lecher he may be, but he could also charm the birds from the trees, she thought, smiling to herself.

He noticed her expression. "Well, I see that not only are you delectable, you also have a sense of humor! Admirable qualities, both. What was it I said that amused you?"

She shrugged and laughed again, finding his good humor infectious. "It was not so much what you said, sir, but rather the manner in which you said it. You interest me."

"High praise indeed! Now *I* am flattered!"

She blushed and shot him a wary glance. "You know well I did not mean it in *that* way!"

"In what way?" he returned, all too innocently, laughing as her blush deepened to a flaming crimson.

"I meant only that you seem so different—at one time cold, cruel, and at others—well, like you are at this moment."

"You mean, burning with desire for you?" His eyes were hungry, wanting.

He handed her a glass of wine, and, as he did so, he let his fingers caress hers gently when she accepted the glass. She could not meet his look, for she knew he would see the confusion in her own eyes. She loved Paul, yes, yes! But how could this man arouse her if that were so?

She had watched Mallory at the wheel for several moments this morning when he had not been aware of it, and it had come as a shock to realize she felt affection for him, a feeling of warmth for his protectiveness and his concern. She knew only too well that he did not have to be this way, that others in his place would have used her and cast her aside, to survive as she might in a strange country.

The meal ended in light conversation, which tonight had an edge to it. Deny it she may, but Mallory's desire was becoming increasingly obvious.

As was their habit on the nights before, Amanda would wrap her cloak about her and she and James would take an evening stroll about the deck.

She started to push back her chair. Swiftly James was behind her, removing it. His breath tickled the fine hairs at the nape of her neck. She shivered. No, not again! She turned, but he had not moved and she was pressed for a moment against his chest.

"Oh, excuse me . . ." Her voice trailed off lamely.

Mallory noticed she lost her composure, and, chuckling, he moved to let her pass.

The stars burned down fiercely, the Plow, the Milky Way, set as they had been for centuries. How could they remain so constant, Amanda wondered, with all the turmoil of life that wheeled below them?

James was smoking a final pipe before sleep. Looking at his face, silhouetted against the shimmering sea, she wondered if he would miss her when she left the *Gypsy Princess,* or if he would find a more willing woman to warm both bed and heart.

He turned and reached to take her elbow and escort

her below. "Shall we to bed?"

She nodded agreement and offered her arm.

As they descended the stairway to the lower deck, a frightened cry rent the air.

"Man overboard, starboard ho!"

All hands rushed to starboard.

"Stay here, Amanda, and wait while I see to this."

James raced down the deck in the direction the crew had taken.

Amanda retraced her footsteps up the stairway once more and leaned over the rail, her eyes scanning the moonlit water for the unlucky tar who'd fallen in. She was so intent on her search that she failed to hear the stealthy footsteps or the creaking of the planks beneath heavy boots.

When she first sensed someone behind her it was too late!

A hand clamped over her mouth, a massive arm gripped her about the ribs and lifted her bodily from the deck.

She flailed at her captor, arching away from his grasp. It was useless! She felt herself dragged down the stairway and across the lower deck, down more stairs and into the fore and aft gangway that was dark as pitch.

"Quite the leddy, aren't ye?" Her captor's voice was coarse, his breath heavy and stinking of rum. His vile hands moved upward to fondle her breasts.

She opened her mouth to scream, eyes wide with fear, but terror choked the breath in her throat, and in that instant his hairy hand clamped over her mouth once more.

"If'n ye scream, it'll be the worse for ye, ye little slut!

Think ye're a fancy piece, don'tcha, struttin' around on that cocky Mallory's arm? I'll shew ya a real man! Let's see if ye can handle this cannon o'mine, me ladyship!"

He grabbed her wrist and twisted it up and behind her back until she whimpered in pain, using it as a lever to force her down onto the planks. He lurched over her, the stink of his rank body reaching her. She tried to get up, but, with a shove, he forced her back, covering her mouth with a slobbering kiss. She struggled to tear her head away, feeling the nausea rise in her throat. Horrified, she realized he was fumbling with his breeches. Little sobs escaped against his mouth, but he would not release her.

"Scared, he! Well, never fear, wench, this ole cannon'll show ya a good tumble. Ye'll know ye've had a man and not some milksop, this time!"

He flung her skirts up and squeezed a soft thigh in each of his huge paws, forcing her to open before him. Then he dropped to his knees between them and reached out and kneaded her breasts through the thin cloth of her blouse. A scream tore from her as she felt him try to enter her. Furiously she tried to push him back, squirming away from his body. He brought his hand back and dealt her a ringing punch across the jaw. The blow stunned her and her vision clouded.

And then, in the darkness, she sensed him change. With a gurgling cry, he fell full weight on her body. Her hand on his back felt something warm and wet, and in the dim light she saw the dull glint of a dagger. Strong arms pulled the dead man off her and his blood spilled on her hand as they moved him.

"Are ye hurt, miss?"

It was Alf, one of the men who had kidnapped her.

Bert was hurrying down the passageway bearing the lantern from the stairs.

Hurriedly she pulled her torn clothes about her and shook her head weakly.

"No, no, just bruises, I think. Thank you, both, so much! He—he was—" she couldn't go on.

"He had a reputation for being a cruel bastard with the ladies. Hated the Captain, too. Didn't figure 'e was up to no good when we see'd him eyein' you these past days. So Bert says, 'Alf,' he says, 'we got her on board, we did, and Cap'n Mallory made it right plain she weren't wot we thought she were, so's we'd best keep an eye out, we had!' So when everyone rushed orf to fish that little bastard out o' the drink—begging pardon, ma'am—the cabin boy, Abner, we decided we'd make sure you was all right."

Alf finished and Bert nodded agreement as he helped Amanda to her feet.

She glanced down at the sprawled body at her feet and shuddered. Even in death he was revolting. She started to shake, her teeth chattering uncontrollably.

James came thundering down the passageway and, in the dim light, his eyes were angry slits.

"What the blazes is going on here! If you've harmed her I'll see you flogged!" he swore. He turned to Amanda just in time to catch her as her knees gave way, and she fainted into his arms. He swept her up and his foot touched the body on the planks. Instantly he realized his error.

"So, it was Thurston! My apologies, I should have known! Canvas the body and pitch it overboard, men. There'll be extra rum for you both, by God!" He carried the girl down the passageway.

"There'll be no prayer said over 'im sir?" asked Bert, nodding doubtfully at the corpse.

"None," said Mallory. "Where he's gone, they're wasted!"

His face was grimmer than either of his men had ever seen before.

Chapter Eleven

James elbowed the cabin door ajar and swept her through it in his arms as if her weight were thistledown.

She was conscious now, but still dazed. The sight of his concerned face and the feel of his strong arms about her was comforting.

He sat her in his captain's chair while he flung back the bedcovers, then lifted her again, and laid her carefully down. He took a cloth and poured water into a basin, then bathed her face.

She had streaks of grime on her cheeks, and the bruise on her jaw was already purpling and angry. He dabbed at it gently until the swelling stopped. All the while he muttered curses under his breath at the dead man who had dared to harm her.

Finally, he set the basin aside and covered her, tucking her in like a small child. She watched him silently. He took a last look to make sure she was comfortable, then started to leave.

Suddenly, words tumbled from her mouth. "Please, don't go. Don't leave me yet!" Her lower lip trembled and her eyes were huge and doelike in the lantern light.

He turned, one hand still on the door. "I think it best you sleep, my dear. You've been sorely frightened, and the blow was no small one."

"I know it. But I can't sleep. I know I can't. Please come and sit by me, just talk to me for a little while. Perhaps then I can put it out of mind." Her eyes implored him to stay.

He closed the door and came to her side.

"Bert and Alf, they were in time? You are all right?" His voice was anxious.

She nodded, her temper flaring with a mercurial suddenness that amazed him, for minutes before she had seemed thoroughly cowed.

"Yes, they were in time, as you put it so tactfully. Do you feel noble, to have saved me from a fate worse than death?" Her voice was bitter. "It would have mattered little. He could have done nothing that you had not already done, could he, James?"

James bit back the angry reply he had ready, realizing the events of the night must have honed her nerves to breaking point.

"Amanda, I've said all I'm prepared to say on this matter." His green eyes were troubled. Could he ever prove to her how he regretted that first night?

"Please, rest now. Tomorrow you'll be bound for England once more. We should reach Casablanca by noon, and I'll book your passage the minute we dock. You won't have to set eyes on me ever again."

The look on her face told him his last remark pleased her. The fire in her eyes dwindled to be replaced by sheer fatigue.

"Very well. I'll sleep now. Good-night."

"Good-night, Amanda. And sweet dreams."

"I fear not, Captain. Not this night." She lay back, her arm cradling her head. Her eyes closed and her lips parted slightly, moist and glistening.

James walked over to the bed and towered over her. Her mouth was as soft and tempting as a ripe strawberry. Impulsively he leaned down and kissed her gently. His arms gathered her to him and he felt her body soften as his lips worked their magic on her senses. He felt her respond, start to return his embrace, and he released her.

"Good-night, again, Miss Sommers." He bowed slightly, and, with a broad grin, quickly left the cabin.

She picked up the satin pillow and flung it with all her might at the closed door. Oh, how infuriating he was! One minute all concern, the next doing his utmost to seduce her. And men always said women were hard to fathom! Rubbish!

She rolled over onto her stomach and tried to forget the brief, but surprisingly pleasant kiss that still tingled on her lips.

James went above and poured a bucket of brine over himself. It was, he decided, a ridiculous means to cool a man's ardor, for after the first rush of icy water, he found himself desiring her more than ever.

The starless night was black as pitch, the *Gypsy Princess* seeming to sail in a void. No breeze flapped the sails, and the moon hid her light behind heavy clouds.

It was a night like this, he recalled, that he had first left England, his homeland, for good, to begin a new life in the colonies. His parents and younger sister lived in Salem, though as a seaman he had traveled the world thrice over, and was at home in many ports.

His father, Richard, always an outspoken man,

had incurred King George's wrath, deploring his foreign policy loudly and publicly. The Mallory family had been forced to flee by night before the King's anger took positive action. Young James had thrilled to the long sea voyage and vowed some day to own his own ship.

His wish had been granted by the damndest twist of fate, and he became captain of the *Princess* for two years. At thirty, he was one of the youngest captains at sea, and proud of it.

When people asked him how he had come by his ship, he would smile and say he had won her in a game of chance. No lie, for the affair had held all the risks and high stakes of such a game.

He had been first officer then, under Captain Hackett, a wily old sea dog only a shade more honest than a pirate. Despite his dubious character, Hackett had known all that could be known of the ocean—her calms, her rages—much as a man knows a wife.

They had been running a cargo of rum into England from the Caribbean, an illegal cargo, for they meant to slip it into some quiet cove on the eastern coast, and avoid paying taxes in London. A government frigate had sighted them just off the Cornish coast, and a customs officer had boarded their ship for search purposes.

For the first time, Captain Hackett had panicked. He was old, at least too old to last long in the rigors of a filthy gaol, and lived in dread of imprisonment away from his beloved sea. In desperation, he clubbed the arrogant young officer with a billy club. He would have killed him if James had not held him back. Mallory had persuaded Hackett to pitch the unconscious man into the sea in full view of his ship so that he might be rescued. He wanted no murder on his head.

But no sooner had the spluttering officer been fished aboard by his men than a cannon roared from their craft! The ball had whistled into the *Gypsy Princess*'s rigging, doing little damage to the ship, but splitting loose a shaft of timber. It fell like a spear, and partially impaled Captain Hackett through the chest.

James had led the British Navy vessel a merry chase up the coast of England for several days. He had finally lost them in a squall off the wild Scottish coast.

Captain Hackett, wounded severely, lasted only two days after docking in New Orleans, enduring the three-month voyage with terrible pain as his constant companion. James left his side only briefly during that time to give orders to his men. After James saw to his captain's burial, he had prepared to find a position on another vessel. Shocked, he learned that Captain Hackett had bequeathed the *Gypsy Princess* to him.

Under his command, the ship had dealt in only honest trade and he soon had a fine reputation and profit to boot.

He tapped out the bole of his pipe, and resigned himself to sleeping in Emerson's, the first officer's cabin. No, he didn't trust himself to sleep at the foot of his bed this night. Not with the memory so fresh in his mind of Amanda's soft body yielding to his kiss.

Dawn crept through the port window with a gray face. Amanda awoke with a start. She moved gingerly, her muscles aching from the exertion of the night before.

Today she would return to England. James had promised. But would he keep his promise? Mayhap not, especially after the way he had kissed her last night. Could she trust him? Though she believed he had done his utmost to keep his promise, it seemed he had little control over his emotions.

What if he decided to keep her on the *Gypsy Princess?* It would be too late to escape if she waited for him to put into port and then discovered the door locked and herself prisoner again. She dare not risk him going back on his word! No, she'd outwit him, just in case. Either way, tonight or with the first tide at latest, she'd be homeward bound. Now, a plan!

First, coin for her passage? Well, she had none. Aye, that was true, but she did have the pearl-and-topaz pendant, valuable enough to persuade any captain to give her berth. A smile lit her face.

She stripped the satin pillowcase from the pillow and stuffed into it the clothes she had worn when she so unexpectedly boarded the ship. Though James was unaware of it, after she had mended his shirts she had also reattached the torn skirt of her yellow-flowered gown to its bodice once more. Her cloak followed the gown. As an afterthought she added one of James's best ruffled shirts for a nightshirt on the voyage. There, the pillowcase bulged like a vagabond's bundle! She hefted it over her shoulder and twirled around the cabin, her eyes sparkling. Soon she would be free of his advances and this dreary confinement! You do not know it, Captain, she thought, but there will soon be another *Gypsy Princess*—and this one no ship!

Cookie was at the door, hammering loudly with a

meaty fist.

She thrust the bundle under the bed, pulling the coverlet to hide it. Then she scrambled back beneath the covers.

"Come in, Cookie."

The man lumbered in with her breakfast tray. He looked at her in an almost fatherly way, his silly smile at odds with the red kerchief around his head and the jangling gold earring.

"Now, how be you this mornin', little leddy? By the saints, 'tis a right good wallop that wretch fetched ye!"

Her fingers went instinctively to the huge black-and-blue swelling on her jaw. She smiled ruefully.

"I believe I'll live, Cookie, thanks to your friends. Another second and—" she shrugged.

He nodded sagely and set the tray down.

"Ain't it true, though! An' if that little bastard—beg'n yer pardon—if that there cabin boy, Abner, hadn't fallen in, Cap'n wouldn't had to have left ye alone. I fair walloped his arse, let me tell you! But watch it, mistress. He be a crafty wretch, and no liking in 'im for you, he hasn't. Cap'n told him last night, off he goes when we dock. Little worm—more bleedin' trouble than he's worf, he is!"

There was a clatter of thunder outside the port window. Amanda started, then jumped as a flash of lightning lit the gloomy cabin. It was not raining and there was no breeze, but she could smell the rain in the air.

"A storm?" she asked, noticing how Cookie, too, sniffed the air.

"Aye. Don't look good neither. Cap'n been readyin'

everything since first light, just in case. Don't know meself which be worse—a storm or that stinkin' Casablanca. Hot as hell, flies, dirt . . ." Grumbling he left the cabin, pausing at the door. "Eat hearty now!"

Amanda grabbed the cheese and a couple of biscuits from the trencher and added them to her bundle. There was no telling how long it would take to find a ship bound for England and she had no intention of going hungry. She finished the thin gruel hurriedly and washed it down with a mug of steaming strong tea.

Then she took a scanty bath with water in the basin and began the painful task of untangling the wild mass of her chestnut hair. James's comb snagged painfully in the tangles, and she muttered curses that would have mortified poor old Aggie.

God, the cabin was close this morning! Perspiration beaded her upper lip and trickled down her neck. She flung open the window wider. The water below was like violet glass, the sky above low-hung with brooding gray clouds.

She braided her hair and secured it in one huge knot above her head. She wished she had fresh clothes to wear, but the peasant skirt and blouse would have to do. She slipped them on. There was nothing left to do now, but wait.

She had decided on how best to escape. When they docked, James no doubt would be fully occupied seeing to all the details of the docking. He'd be too busy to watch her and would probably lock her in the cabin. She had jumped from the railing that first night. It should be even easier to dive the few feet into the harbor from the port window!

She prayed the storm would not set them off schedule. A short swim by daylight, then a swift climb up pilings to the quay would be easy. But by night! She shuddered, remembering all the huge, furry rats she had seen when Bert and Alf had kidnapped her. The idea of the dark, rat-filled water terrified her as nothing else had.

Chapter Twelve

The morning seemed to pass on leaden wings.

Though the past few days she had noticed how hot it was becoming, nothing compared with the heat of this day! The air was so thick and heavy it leeched one's strength, and the sky had only grown darker instead of lighter since dawn. She felt like a caged panther pacing the confines of her cage.

The few tattered books the cabin had to offer were all searfaring manuals and boring with their technical jargon. She almost wished she had some of James's shirts to darn! James. She hadn't seen him all morning, she thought peevishly. Now she realized how much brighter he made the days with his visits and escorting her on strolls about the deck.

Absentmindedly she fiddled with the iron ring of the heavy door. It swung open! Poor Cookie must have forgotten to lock it. Should she go above to see what was going on? Yes! Surely, no one would touch her by daylight, especially with all they had to do with a storm fast approaching?

Amanda slipped from the cabin and ran up the passageway, a flash of lightning with its brilliance bringing her up short momentarily.

The *Gypsy Princess* swarmed with sailors. They reminded her of ants, by the sheer volume of their numbers. Squinting upward, she could see men in the rigging, too, leaning precariously from their positions to adjust the lines. The sky that framed them was black.

She walked hesitantly along the lower deck, but no one took any notice of her, or, if they did, gave no sign of it. What confusion! It amazed her that any of them knew what they were doing. The cannons, as had all other equipment that was not bolted to the deck, had been firmly chained down, so they would not roll and crush the sailors in the storm.

Then she heard James barking orders left and right on the upper deck. He appeared calm and in control as his men leaped to do his bidding. She made her way toward him, weaving in and out of coiled lines and hurrying bodies. The wind was beginning to lift now, for it ruffled her hair as she climbed the stairway to him and huge droplets of rain spattered her nose. Thunder bellowed again. It muffled her voice as she called to him.

A good five minutes had passed when he finally noticed her. His face changed from a look of concentration to one of anger.

"What the blue blazes are *you* doing up here?" He strode to her and practically hurled her out of the way as a crew of men strained at ropes to batten down the hatches.

"I was tired of waiting for you to inform me of what's happening, and thought I'd find out for myself!" She crossly shrugged his hand from her elbow.

"Well, it's not good. Looks as if it'll be quite a storm. We're going to try to outrun it." Distractedly, he eyed his men.

"Can I stay up here and watch?" She had always loved stormy weather.

He looked at her in disbelief. "Can you what? You must be out of your mind, you little fool! Don't you realize just how bad it will be, if we don't outrun this! Where you're standing will be six inches deep in salt water. Men will be washed overboard like pieces of flotsam! Now, get below again—and don't come up until I tell you you may."

"If you can stand it, then I can. I can't bear it down there anymore! It's hot, and there's no air and the cabin smells. I'll take my chances up here."

"You'll do no such thing! Taylor, see this woman back to my cabin and make sure she stays there, or you'll feel the bite of the cat, I'll be damned if you don't—and her too!" He glared at her with his green eyes, daring her to contradict him.

Before she could retort, Bosun Bert Taylor had taken her by the shoulders and forcibly propelled her down in the direction of the cabin.

"Set the top gallants!" She heard James roar as she ducked her head to go below once again.

Bert locked her in with an apologetic smile. Well, here she was again. "Damn!" she muttered, in very unladylike fashion, flouncing across to the port window and pulling it shut against the rain, which was now falling heavily. In a few moments the back of her blouse was soaked with perspiration and the wisps of hair that framed her face curled with the humidity. The gloom in the cabin made it even more oppressive. She stretched out on the bed, determined to sleep, for it seemed the only means left to pass the time. But sleep never came. A few hours later the violent lurching of the ship would not have made it possible even if she'd wished it.

The sea had turned to a foaming gray monster that pitched and plummeted the *Gypsy Princess* as if she were a rag doll shaken in its jaws.

Amanda hung over a basin and retched miserably, while trying to hang onto the bed at the same time. Charts, quills, inkstand slithered to port, then to starboard, then fell in a shambles on the floor of the cabin. She watched the ink run in crazy patterns across the strewn parchment as if drawn on by invisible hands. With a crash, the brass clock was dashed to the floor.

She retched again, the muscles of her stomach screaming. Oh, God, when would it stop! Her mouth tasted foul. There was no water, for the ewer had long since broken. Her throat burned from the spasms. She vowed she'd never board a ship, ever again, if she survived this.

What was happening above her? Cries and shouts carried but faintly down here, and, once in a while, the swift tread of heavy sea boots and nothing more. She hastily said a prayer for their safety on the decks, a vision of what James had said it would be like filling her mind. God help them all!

The cabin door burst open and the cabin boy careened through it as the ship heaved violently again, his eyes wild, his freckled face a greenish hue. His long ginger hair was slicked down like a wet dog from the rain.

"Abner! Come, let me help you!" She staggered toward him, defying gravity, offering him a blanket from the bed.

He snatched it from her without thanks and wound it about him. His pale eyes were full of venom.

"You stay back, you captain's whore. 'Tis all your doing, this! Aye, we all knowed it were bad luck, havin' a woman aboard. Ye'd best watch it, there's talk of throwing ye over, there is!"

She clutched the desk and stared at him open-mouthed.

"What superstitious rot! Abner, you know well the storm's God's doing—or the Devil's—not mine. We may as well be friends since—"

"Friends! Fine friend ye be, wot's cost me me job! Captain's puttin' me off the ship, come we reach Morocco! Nothing but trouble I've had since ye come aboard, and crowned me with that bleedin' great inkstand! Almost got me flogged an' all, up to yer fancy slut's tricks with Thurston—aye, the one wot those bastards Taylor and Higgins done in."

She was speechless. She saw in his vicious state that she'd be able to talk no sense into him and backed as far away as she could. Abner sank down and wedged himself between the bolted-down seachest and the bulkhead and ignored her.

She could smell the stink from the streaming bilges now. Though a wave of nausea engulfed her, her belly was too empty to retch again. She hoped that Abner, the little rat, would get equally sick. It would serve him right!

James reached out desperately to grab Cookie, but the man was gone, his cry lost in the howling wind as he hurtled over the side.

Their bid to outrun the storm had failed, and the

extra sail he'd ordered unfurled to gain speed now worked against him as the wind snarled and clawed them to ribbons.

The ocean was a mass of towering swells, the mere eighty feet of the *Princess* a small challenge to its fury. The storm anchors were useless.

There were cries as lightning hit the tallest of the three masts. It split and plummeted down, killing two more of the crew. The sailors slithered in fear on the streaming deck, clutching at anything, terrified they, too, would be swept overboard into the foaming seas.

James's arm muscles bulged as he fought to control the massive wheel. Lashed into position though the line was, he knew that if he let go, it would snap. Sure enough, the ship keeled, the line twanged free, and the wheel spun crazily out of control, throwing the captain unconscious to the deck.

Alf saw him fall, and lurched across to drag him by his feet down the gangway. Satisfied he was not dead and as safe as anyone aboard this ill-fated ship, Alf scrambled abovedeck again to tell Emerson he now had full command.

The storm continued until nightfall and then at what would have been seven bells—if anyone had rung them—the wind dropped. The rain ceased, too, as did the lightning. The sea was glassy once more.

But the *Gypsy Princess* was a ravaged maiden, her sails tattered, the mainmast gone, her freshwater barrels now cracked and empty. She straddled the becalmed water like a tipsy bawd, too far into her cups to feel shame for her sorry state.

Amanda and Abner were stonily silent as they set the

cabin to rights.

She had her wish and the youth had been sick several times. Her own body felt weak as a kitten's.

Alf had poked his head in to tell her the storm had died down, but she'd guessed as much when the ship had stopped heaving, and resumed an almost normal rocking motion. She opened the window and emptied the broken glass and china into the sea. There were no stars and only the faintest glimmer of a sickly moon peered through the fine mist.

Alf had said he and the captain figured they'd lost over thirty men to the storm, though they'd know more when he assembled the crew for a head count in the morning. The ship was beyond repair without a new mast and rudder, both of which were useless, and, in answer to her fears, he had voiced little hope.

"I don't rightly know, miss! If'n we can hail a passing ship, there's a fair chance of us'n being saved. But Cap'n reckons as how we be pretty far off course, see. Don't rightly know where we be, he don't." His eyes were ringed with exhaustion.

"And provisions?"

"Well, that's not so bad. We didn't lose much food, see, but most of the water be lost. Ye'd best say yer prayers, mistress; it can't hurt none and I believe in the Powers Above, I do. I'll try an' rustle ye up some grub, first chance."

"Tell Cookie not to worry about me, Alf. The crew must come first, and I'm not very hungry," she finished, patting her aching belly and grimacing.

Alf's face had darkened. "Cookie went over, miss. I be runnin' the galley now, seein' as how we'd best ration the vittles—and some o' these rogues ain't t'be trusted!"

"Cookie's dead?"

She sank down onto the bed. She had liked Cookie and his bossy gentleness. Was there no justice in this world? Her temper flared briefly as she remembered the frustration she'd felt after Alf had left.

Abner was lounging sullenly against the cabin wall. He was big for sixteen and sly as a ferret.

She felt uncomfortable, feeling his hostile eyes watching her as she moved about the cabin, and she glared at him several times before he took the hint and helped her again.

When James finally came below, Abner took one look at him and fled. His head bore a rough linen bandage and the pallor of his face was shocking. His shirt was ripped in several places and the leather jerkin brittle with salt water. He looked tired enough to drop.

Her previous anger at him forgotten, she motioned him to lie down and stripped his sodden shirt off, then bundled him over with the blanket. She poured a stiff measure of rum from a cask and held it to his lips, and watched the color flood back into his face. He motioned her away, but she shook her head firmly.

"It's my turn to care for you, Captain."

She checked his wound. It was bleeding still, but not much.

"Come, let's sleep. There's been little enough tonight," he insisted.

She nodded agreement, unrolled the pallet, and prepared to lie down at the foot of the bed.

"No. Lie down here with me."

Amanda looked doubtful, caution springing into her eyes.

"No, I don't think—"

He held open the blanket invitingly, a trace of the old grin on his lips. "Don't worry, my sweet, I haven't the strength to bed you—not even if you were Aphrodite herself!"

She hesitated only a second before scrambling under the covers beside him.

In seconds, he was snoring.

Chapter Thirteen

It was afternoon when Amanda and James awoke. The air was misty and the sky above a sheet of gray, but at least the heavy cloud was entirely gone.

First Officer Emerson entered the cabin at Captain Mallory's bidding and read off a list of the damages. "That's it, sir. A head count of the men shows we lost thirty-five in all. It could have been worse, sir."

"How's the water supply?" Mallory talked as he pulled on fresh clothes. Amanda was too concerned to feel embarrassment.

"Not good. Reckon we've only ten caskets untainted with brine, sir."

"Only ten—among over eighty men! And no telling how long before we're rescued, *if* we're rescued!" he added grimly.

Emerson nodded, pushing back a strand of gray hair from his eyes. "Aye, sir. I've put Higgins in charge of rationing, a mouthful per man every two hours. He's trustworthy and loyal to you, sir."

"I know, I know." Impatiently, Mallory pulled on his boots. "Well, let's see what can be done to improve our lot. Miss Sommers, would you care to come above for a bit?"

If there had been any doubt in her mind that the situation was bad, it was dispelled when she saw the decks. There was a full watch of men on cleanup detail, but they were laboring listlessly, eyes tired, faces drawn under a night's growth of stubble.

The mainmast was shattered about halfway up. In the rigging, men were freeing the torn sails to make way for the spare ones always kept in the hold. Mallory asked Emerson if men were preparing pitch to stop the leaks in the hold, and relief appeared on his face when the older man nodded.

"Aye, sir. We're manning the pumps, too, sir."

"You've done well, Emerson. Good man! Go'n grab some shuteye, I'll take over now."

"Aye, aye, sir."

"And Emerson, could you see Miss Sommers back to the cabin? Ask Abner if he can spare her one of his shirts and a pair of breeches, too—clean ones, mind."

Emerson nodded, and Amanda flashed James a look of gratitude as she followed the first officer down below.

"I'll see to the clothes, Miss Sommers."

He was as good as his word, returning shortly after with both garments and a tray of food to boot.

"Oh, thank you! Now, you go and rest. You look terrible."

Emerson grinned wearily, and did as she bade him.

She tore off her stained and foul-smelling blouse and skirt and hurriedly pulled on the cabin boy's clothes. They fitted her almost perfectly, though the cloth was pulled skin-tight over her bosom and hips. It felt so good to have clean clothes! After so many hours without food, she heartily ate the salt pork, beans and somewhat moldy biscuits. There was a small glass of port wine to wash it down with. Though it did not quench her thirst, she downed it, realizing that every available liquid was precious now.

James's face made her laugh when he finally came to see her. She twirled around, her eyes dancing at his open-mouthed, horrified expression.

"Good God, woman! I can't let you out in those! You look, you look—"

"Like a man?" she asked innocently.

"My Lord, no! They accent—everything!"

She laughed again, knowing what he said to be true.

The rough gray shirt pressed tightly around each thrusting breast and plunged in at her tiny waist. The breeches curved over her hips and ended at her knees, leaving her shapely calves and ankles bare. Chestnut hair billowed over her shoulders and down to her buttocks in shining splendor. Standing with her hands on her hips and looking at him mischievously, she was more provocative than she had ever been in her gown or the blouse and skirt. He felt the heat fill him and a familiar stirring in his loins.

"By God, do something before I forget myself," he murmured huskily.

"What would you have me do, kind sir?" she teased.

"If I told you, wench, you'd slap my face," he growled, grinning.

He turned away from her reluctantly, and went to the desk. Withdrawing a chart from its pigeonhole, he unrolled it, studying it intently.

"Do you know where we are?" Amanda asked, coming to peer over his shoulder.

"Only roughly. By my figuring, we should be here." He jabbed a finger at a point in the ocean, and she gasped.

"But that's miles and miles from Casablanca!"

He nodded. "You see, we were here," he indicated a point not far from the Moroccan coast. "By noon today we would have been over there, if not for the storm." He showed her what the marks on the chart stood for.

"Are you sure there's no land near us?"

James shrugged. "None. We've sighted no gulls or any sign of life nearby. But, see, these little islands here?"

"These? Yes, the Azores."

"I plan to find them. If we drift with the tide we should touch land within a week, at most."

"You mean, there's no way to steer?"

"None, the rudder's had it, I'm afraid. I sent a man over the side to look at it this morning, and he came up certain there was no way to repair it unless we dock."

"Then, we're at the mercy of the sea and the wind?" Amanda asked, the thought chilling her to the marrow.

"Aye, and God's," James said.

They were asleep that evening when the watch woke them. He was a sailor called Reeves, and he pummeled on the door with his bony fists until James leaped out of the bed, tripping over his boots as he did so.

He let Reeves in. "What the devil's going on?"

"A ship, sir! I seed it from the crow!"

"A ship!" He almost forgot his boots in the rush, grabbing a spyglass from the chest and leaving the cabin at a run.

Amanda raced after him, barefooted.

James had the glass to his eye and was scanning the water over the starboard bow. There was a thick mist swirling about the ship, but as her eyes grew accustomed to it, Amanda could barely make out the looming form of a vessel.

"Do you think she sees us, sir?"

"She must have. Our lanterns are in position, are they not?"

"Aye, sir, port and starboard."

"Then assemble the men, Mr. Emerson. I believe we've been rescued!" James's face was one broad grin.

The crew scrambled abovedecks, all men craning their necks to see the ship.

She drifted slowly toward them, wreathed in mist, as if she floated upon it rather than on water. She appeared bigger than the *Gypsy Princess.* The crew seemed to hold its breath as one man. No sound reached them across the water, not even the creaking of tackle or the grinding of her hull as it rose and fell on the waves.

"By the saints, Oi think she's a phantom!" breathed one sailor.

The rest of the men murmured agreement under their breath. Amanda shared their feelings and noticed several sailors cross themselves when they thought no one noticed. She shivered.

"Stand by to grapple, Mr. Emerson." James murmured softly, for the utter silence had woven its eerie spell upon him too.

Emerson quietly sent some men for grappling irons. "So you think she's deserted, sir?"

"Aye, I do. Look, do you see her colors?" Their

voices were low.

"None at all, sir. Grappling iron's ready, sir."

The vessel was so close now that Amanda could read the gilt-painted name on her bows. The *Sea Dragon.* A dragon figurehead reared fiercely from the prow, its nostrils flaring, as if the mist poured from them. There was not a soul on deck nor any lanterns swinging from the yardarms.

Amanda's uneasiness grew as the ship drifted nearer.

Chapter Fourteen

When the *Dragon* was but a few yards off their bow, Captain Mallory ordered the grappling irons flung over her side and secured.

Mallory was convinced the other ship was deserted, herself a casualty of the storm as they were, though she appeared to have weathered it in better shape than they. Still, one didn't look a gift horse in the mouth, and he was not about to sacrifice his men for a superstition. Phantom or not, he intended to board her and take command.

"Emerson, pick some men to go with you and check her out. Please, God, she's not a floating poxhouse!"

He'd encountered one such ship on his voyages, the stench of the bloated bodies carrying a full mile on the breeze.

Emerson had no shortage of volunteers. Arm over arm, they swung across the ropes to the *Sea Dragon*'s rail. The decks were empty of either bodies or living men and silent as the grave. The crew milled about Emerson, suddenly loath to separate and search the vessel despite the promise of booty to be shared from her holds. They were now convinced that spirits held the vessel in thrall. The first officer was of a notion to agree with them.

"Come on, men, let's have at her!"

Reluctantly, Emerson sent two men aft and two forward. The rest he ordered in other directions. But the men made no move to carry out his orders. They wetted their lips nervously, fidgeting with their weapons.

"Let's go, me bullies!" cried one braver soul. But no one made a move to follow him, and he turned back. "Wot are we? Lily-livered cowards?" He spat, disgusted with them.

Suddenly, a hatch flew open and dozens of men swarmed up from the hold brandishing cutlasses, daggers gripped in their teeth! The terrified crew of the *Princess* tried to flee, some leaping overboard in terror. The rest were cut down like stalks of wheat where they stood.

Mallory saw what was happening and bellowed for his men to take up arms. The gunners scrambled to the cannons, but the *Sea Dragon* was too close, the angle wrong!

A sailor thrust a sword into James's hand in the nick of time, as the pirates boarded his vessel. They were gaining her rail as fast and agilely as monkeys.

For the first time he noticed Amanda had followed him. "Get back down below. Hurry now! And do something to yourself, anything! They *must not* know you're a woman. Now go!"

He shoved her headlong down the gangway and whirled to the rail. With a roar he slashed the lines, sending screaming men into the gray void between the vessels.

He spun about at the thud of boots behind them. A

blade whistled past, inches from his ear. He parried the slash, retreated a step, then darted forward and sank his blade into the burly figure. He threw the body away from him, withdrawing his sword. Another attacker was on him instantly!

The crash of steel against steel was deafening. The crew fought like devils, though nigh decimated in number from the storm and the corpses that littered the *Dragon*'s decks.

Bert had a timber clenched in his fists and was flailing it in sweeping arcs. He brained more than one skull under its weight. Alf had just pulled a dripping dagger from the belly of another man, and leaped to attack again.

Cries and screams filled the air, the decks were slippery with gore and the coppery stench of blood was in every nostril.

Mallory had taken on the pirate captain, a huge man with straggly yellow hair and cruel amber eyes.

"So yer think yer a match for Bloody Harry, do yer?" he roared. "Well come on then, yer bastard!"

Bloody Harry's sword lunged at Mallory.

Mallory parried the thrust with his own blade. Thrust, parry, lunge, retreat, they battled across the upper deck. He knew he was exhausted from fighting the storm, but the thought of Amanda at the mercy of these ugly spawn of the devil gave him strength. Blade rang against blade, then suddenly the pirate captain brought his sword crossways in a whistling curve, slashing Mallory's shoulder. Blood spurted from the wound, and the pirate's eyes shone gleefully. Angrily, Mallory returned the cut, but it was parried before his blade could find its mark.

Mallory retreated, only to find the railing at his back. A numbing blow across his knuckles sent his weapon clattering to the deck. He cursed lustily.

The pirate captain lunged forward and tried to throttle him, his forearm held hard across the captain's windpipe. Rasping for air, Mallory summoned his remaining strength and brought his knee up powerfully into the pirate's groin. Bloody Harry reeled away, groaning as the kick found its soft target.

Mallory darted forward and retrieved his weapon.

The other man whirled to fight again, eyes blazing, arms held out on either side. He was a jackal, waiting to spring! Then his amber eyes flickered to something over Mallory's shoulder. Too late, James saw he was surrounded!

The men picked him up bodily and flung him, head first, onto the deck. After the first blinding pain, there was only merciful blackness.

Amanda tore down the gangway and into the cabin, dashing straight to James's sea chest.

She found a seaman's stocking cap and hurriedly pulled it on, stuffing the chestnut mane beneath it. Its shape completely concealed her hair. Then she yanked a gray shirt free and put it on. The garment hung baggily, partially disguising her breasts. A bulky leather vest finished the job.

James's boots were huge, and she quickly discarded all idea of wearing them. Instead, she snatched up his pipe and tapped out the contents into her palms. Spitting into the ashes she smeared the soot over her face, calves, and feet. It was the best she could do to conceal the paleness of her complexion.

Her heart was pounding, ragged breaths choking in her throat. She grabbed James's sword and wielded it clumsily. She'd never used a sword, but didn't doubt she could do some damage with it, however crudely. She whirled around and would have raced abovedecks again, but Abner was blocking the door.

"It won't work, yer know. Any fool can see yer no lad. Look at yer titties!" He laughed nastily.

"Let me pass!"

"No, m'lady, ye're stayin' here! I'm 'anding ya over to them cutthroats—sort of me passport t'freedom, y'are."

"You dirty little—"

"Now that ain't nice, callin' me names while ye're wearin' me own clothes! 'Specially since they's bound to get all tore up wiv them animals pawin' at ye." Spitefully, he laughed again.

She tried to force her way past him, but he stood his ground and her shoves couldn't move him. Damn him! Tears of rage filled her. Damn his black soul! Well, if she had to use the sword on him she would. First, she had one more ace to play.

"I'll give you one more chance, Abner. You let me pass—or I shall kill myself!" She touched the tip of the sword blade to her finger and showed him the crimson trickle that welled instantly. "It's very sharp, Abner, and you couldn't stop me in time, not from over there. Dead, I'm good for neither rape nor ransom. And then you'd have nothing to bargain with, would you?"

Her words hung in the heavy silence. She watched him intently. Had her bluff worked? Yes, for she saw the triumphant look fade from his eyes!

"If I let yer pass there's naught for me to bargain with

anyhow," he argued.

"Just let me go and see how the Captain fares. I'll come back, I promise you!" she swore, lying.

"You'd best be straight with me, or I'll see they kills yer, after they done with yer," Abner snarled.

"Sounds to me you're very sure of yourself, Abner. If my Captain wins, I'll do as well by you!" She squeezed past him and fled up the gangway.

The scene was mass confusion, with bloody corpses on all sides. Dear God, could James have survived this? She leaped barefooted over the sprawled bodies, blood spattering her ankles.

There was a knot of men on the foredeck. Without thought for her own safety, she ran foolishly toward them, brandishing the sword.

"Where is he? What have you done to him?" she screamed recklessly.

The men parted and she saw James sprawled in their midst. One swarthy lout was just about to slit his throat, kneeling with his dagger against James's windpipe.

Bloody Harry had an amused look in his cruel eyes. "Get the little sprat, Garcia!"

The swarthy man stood and lumbered toward her. She held her ground, caution blown to the winds. This man would have killed James! And still might.

"Come on, you foul-smelling old goat! You ape! You dog!" She goaded him, spitting the words through clenched teeth.

As she had hoped, he lunged at her. The leer on his face died as she stepped nimbly aside and he sprawled, face down, on the slippery deck. He reached up and slammed the sword from her hand.

She backed away, her fingers numb from the blow, knowing she must watch not only Garcia, but the others too. They would not honor the dignity of a fight one against one.

Garcia clambered to his feet, his face livid with rage. *"Hijo de puta!"* he cursed. A knife glittered in his grasp.

She saw it leave his grip and dropped instantly to her knees. It twanged over her head and into the rail behind. Like quicksilver another man was behind her. He grabbed her and lifted her, kicking wildly, into the air.

"Slit 'is throat, Jeb!" roared one man.

"Be still, ye bleedin' fool. I don't want ter 'ave ter kill ye," Jeb whispered hoarsely in Amanda's ear.

She didn't, couldn't trust him. Suddenly, he felt her go limp in his arms.

"Cor, the little basket's fainted, 'e has!" Jeb laughed, and relaxed his grip.

As he did so, Amanda squirmed from his grasp and took off down the deck, hurdling bodies and stairs as she went. She didn't stop until she reached the cabin, flung herself inside, and slammed the door shut.

"Quick, help me!" she hissed at Abner. "They're coming!"

He made no move to help her drag the heavy desk to barricade the door.

"For God's sake, please!" she screamed. It wouldn't budge.

"No," Abner said calmly. "Now 'tis my turn to call the tune!"

Her blood turned to ice.

Chapter Fifteen

The door exploded inward and Bloody Harry swaggered into the cabin. He surveyed the pair with amused eyes.

"So. Wot 'ave we here? Two bleedin' little worms, looks like! Ye know what worms is for, lad?" He threatened, gripping Amanda by her shirt and almost lifting her from the planks, "Fer fishin', that's wot!"

The band of men sniggered.

Bloody Harry was so close, his rank breath was full in her face, and tiny drops of spittle sprayed onto her cheeks as he spoke.

"Wanner be shark bait, worm? 'Ow do ye feel about danglin' over the pretty blue ocean, 'til yer eyes bulge an' yer guts curdle?"

She shook her head vigorously.

"So ye don't like fishin', eh? We'll have no more o'yer tricks then, right lad?" He gripped her chin in a huge paw and forced her head back, breathing heavily with rage. But the anger in his eyes extinguished suddenly, and he jerked her head sharply to one side, whistling under his breath. "Cor, mates, look at this shiner 'ere!"

The bruise Thurston had dealt her was now a huge

black shadow the length of her jaw. The pirates grinned.

"Proper li'l scrapper, ain't ye?" Bloody Harry continued, leaving go of her chin and instead yanking hard on her earlobe. She yelped, her mind racing.

"'Twere that bleedin' Captain Mallory wot done it, sir. Don't like me, 'e don't. Fetched me this last night, arter I give 'im lip," she lied.

Bloody Harry grinned wolfishly, showing teeth yellow with rot and many spaces between. "'E did, did 'e, now?"

"'Tis a lie!" Abner yelled furiously. He had been cowed since the pirates entered the cabin, but was fast recovering.

She decided to take the chance before his mouth could give her away. "It ain't sir, on me mother's grave, it ain't! Hates me, 'e does," she whined, nodding at Abner. "Ye little milksop—always was t'Cap'n's pet, ye was!"

"Now, me lads, we'll 'ave none o'that!" Harry reached out and grabbed Amanda by the shirt, for she'd stepped forward as if to attack Abner where he stood. "Wot say we keep this'n 'ere, wot with Barnacle gone—" he nodded at her—"and lock up t'other little twerp?"

The men ayed their agreement.

"Then are ye with us, lad?" Harry peered at Amanda.

"Aye, sir, that I am—t'the death!" she added for effect.

"But that's a lie! I swears it!" Abner's face showed utter panic and beads of sweat dewed the fuzz on his upper lip.

"Shut yer yap, ye slug, else I'll shut it fer ye!"

growled a tall, bearded man.

Abner looked desperately about him. There was no way out! He opened his mouth to speak again. The tall man rabbit-punched him across the back of the neck. Abner folded to the boards.

"Yer name, lad? Wot be it?" Harry asked.

"Jack, sir, that's me name. 'Honest' Jack, some call me." She might as well be in for a penny as a pound!

The men roared approval.

She was safe—for the time being!

"Get yer gear, Jack," Jeb ordered, "and no dallyin', mind."

The gang stomped back down the gangway, Abner's body flopping over the shoulders of the tall man.

She snatched her bundle from under the bed, hurriedly dumped the gown out onto the floor, and raced after them.

She stood by as the bulk of the *Gypsy Princess*'s cargo was carried aboard the other vessel. The bolts of heavy fustian cloth they hurled over the rail in disgust. Finally, the prisoners were assembled. Thank God! James was among them, dazed-looking and bleeding from the shoulders, but able to stand.

With a shock, she realized there were only eight of them left—eight, from a crew that had numbered over ten times that many. Bert and Alf were among the survivors, as were Reeves, a little man they'd called Terrier, and another whose name she didn't know. James, Abner, and herself made up the rest.

Now that she had faced up to the pirates, she had no idea what she would do next! She'd thought only that if she could talk them into letting her move freely among them, she might stand a better chance of being able to help James and his men.

She caught James's eye and he returned her look without expression, but she knew he'd recognized her and was relieved to see she was safe. Some things needed no words.

Now it was her turn to swing across the lines to the *Sea Dragon*'s rail. It didn't look too hard, no harder than when she and Meg had climbed apple trees to steal the fruit. She'd keep that in mind, make it a sort of game. She vowed not even to think of the narrow space between the sides of the two great ships, where she might fall and be crushed by their rolling weight.

She thrust her bundle into her shirt and scrambled up onto the rail. Grasping the ropes firmly in both hands, she let herself drop, swinging her legs up at the same time to hook over the lines. Her knees took most of her weight. She paused, suspended above the gaping void. Perspiration trickled down her face. Gingerly she let go with one hand, sliding her knees forward and grabbing further down the line with her free hand. She'd done it! Now the other hand. Hand over hand, her legs hooked over the ropes, she inched across. Now the rail of the pirate ship was at her feet. She let go with her knees and swung, feeling her wrists screaming at her weight, then boosted herself up and over the rail. A quick scramble to gain balance, and she stood upon the deck. Her face was a broad grin of triumph. Safe! Thankfully, she'd performed well enough to fool her captors. They seemed to notice nothing unusual about her crossing.

Bloody Harry's men herded the prisoners roughly down into the hold. She heard the shriek of chains as they were fettered, then the hatch was closed. Abner had shot her a look of purest hatred as they'd shoved him past her. She didn't care! In a game of survival, only the strongest won—and she intended to win, whatever the cost.

Bloody Harry and the crew kept her busy for the rest of the day, until she thought her back would break from all the fetching and carrying. It seemed as if they were testing her, and those suspicions were confirmed when Jeb said as much.

"Ye doin' right well, me lad. Have ter keep it up, mind, ye've ter prove yerself afore they'll trust ye."

She asked him why he hadn't killed her when he had the chance.

"'Cos I likes a lad wot's got spunk, Jack, and 'Arry's the same. When I see'd yer chargin' across t'deck I says 'Jeb, 'ere's a lad arter yer own heart.' Sorta seemed a shame ter do yer in. Got the makin's of a buccaneer, yer 'ave, with teachin'," he winked slyly and nudged her, "and we's all schoolmasters aboard t'*Dragon.*"

She'd grinned and tried to look grateful. Jeb was proving an invaluable ally, showing her what was expected of her, for he'd accepted her story of this being her first voyage as cabin boy without question, thank God.

By sunset they had left the *Gypsy Princess* far behind. The *Sea Dragon* plowed through the water, leaving a trough of gold-flecked wash in her wake.

Amanda was bone-tired, her nails broken, her hands blistered and bloody from handling the ropes. But she didn't dare to sleep, terrified the cap would fall off if she did, and her identity be revealed. The work they'd given her had been the dirtiest there was and she had no fear that her face would betray her. She could feel how filthy it was without needing a mirror to tell her so.

She ate her victuals in the mess with the rest of the crew. Never had she seen a fiercer-looking mob. Most of them were bearded with shaggy manes of dirty, crooked hair. They wore rough linen shirts under leather vests, or just the vests over powerful naked chests. Some had loose white linen breeches to the knees and were barefoot as she was, while the others tucked them into sea boots. She had seen no man yet who did not bear a scar on some part of his body, or one that carried no weapon. They wore daggers or cutlasses as casually as other men wore handkerchiefs!

Their talk was coarse and seemed only of the fights they'd been in or the women they'd had. She'd almost given herself away by looking squeamish as one man described vividly his raping of a young, virgin, native girl on some island they'd looted.

"Wot'sa matter, lad? Never straddled a wench, 'aven't yer? By the saints, Jack, me word on it, next place we 'it, I'll find yer a ripe one—wot's never bin plucked, like! Me an' Quince 'ere, we'll even hold 'er down fer ye, providin' ye shares her arterward." Riggs hooted, slapping her across the back.

She shuddered, fear crawling up from inside her belly and spreading through her limbs like maggots. If they but knew!

Chapter Sixteen

The days wore on. She lost track of time and never knew which day dawned with the rising sun. She was about her labors long before its orb crested the horizon, slopping stews, soups, salt pork and beans from galley to mess in a huge cauldron that made her close to fainting from its weight.

She had swabbed decks, holystoned them too, done everything that was asked of her. She didn't dare refuse a command, didn't dare do anything that would draw attention to her! The threat of Abner talking hung over her head like a guillotine.

There was an added threat now, too. Garcia. He watched her with beady, malevolent eyes, hoping, she knew, that she'd make some mistake and give him an excuse to harm her. He'd yet to miss a chance and her flanks throbbed and her ears rang from his kicks and cuffs. He loathed her for making a fool of him when he'd lunged at her on the *Princess*'s decks. The men ribbed him about it constantly, when they thought her out of earshot, and he snarled back in angry Spanish. Soon, she knew, he'd find some reason to use on her the cat-o'-nine tails he carried.

She sighed deeply, wearied beyond belief though the

sun was barely up. Which devil was worse? The one in the hold or the one on the decks? Either way, she knew her luck couldn't last forever.

She feared Bloody Harry, too, though he was not as overtly cruel as Garcia. He tended to treat her as he'd no doubt treated Barnacle—the *Dragon*'s boy who'd been killed in the skirmish—with belligerence and curses. He was dangerous when angered, but so hopelessly sotted with rum most of the time that he noticed little.

It was Garcia who really ran the ship, and he would force allegiance from the crew if it came to a true struggle for the position of leader. She'd wondered if she could turn the men against each other, start them at each other's throats, but she discarded the idea. What could she gain by it?

Her only hope lay when they reached port, wherever that was. Perhaps then she could escape and bring someone to rescue the others—or free them herself. No, she'd never be able to do that! The keys to the prisoner's shackles hung on Garcia's belt, with no hope of parting them from him that she could see.

The sky overhead was a brilliant azure, a depth of color she had never seen in England. The blue of the ocean mirrored its hue, stretching on either side of the ship as far as the eye could see, darkening to violet where it met the horizon.

She craned her eyes above to where Jeb crawled among the rigging like a spider in a web. The sunlight dazzled her, flashing off the bleached-white flapping sails. No gulls wheeled above, a sure sign if there had been that land was not far off.

"Eh, Jack, ye deaf or wot?"

Amanda still gazed upward, the name meaning nothing.

"Jack, you piss bucket, git back ter work," roared Quince.

With a shock, she realized he meant her, and fell to it again.

It was around sunset when Amanda heard the order given to drop anchor. Surprised, she hung about the men trying to appear to be working, but intent on eavesdropping. Several casks of rum had been stacked on the deck and she heard Garcia give the command to break them open for the crew after they'd manned the Capstan.

"Eh, *estupido,* over here!" Garcia was after her again.

"Aye, aye, sir!"

"Go down to the galley and get victuals for the prisoners. *De prisa!*"

Hurriedly she did as he ordered. That was strange. This was the first time they had let her near the *Gypsy Princess*'s crew. Something had to have happened, or was about to happen.

The cook was grumbling as he handed her a single trencher of dried hunks of bread and a pitcher of water.

"Is this it, then?" she asked hesitantly.

"Aye. Wot yer expect—pheasant and plum puddin'?" he growled.

"Nah, just funnin'," she continued. "Why'd we drop anchor?"

"'Cos we're almost 'ome, lad! Cap'n decided we'd 'ave a little 'ome-comin' party, like."

"Oh, I see."

Well, she thought as she carried the trencher to the hatch, that explained at least some of the strange goings-on.

She clambered down the rope ladder into the dark hold. The bulkheads were leaking and smelled foul, puddles of stagnant water everywhere. The light from the hatches cast shadows like prison bars across the timbers.

James and his men were fettered to iron rings set in the wall for that purpose. Their chains forced them into a constant, bent-over sitting position that she knew had to be agony, especially after so many days.

"James?" She peered into the gloom.

His chains scraped against wood as he tried to stand. "Blast it! I can't see you! Come over here."

She did so and tried to hide from him with a smile her shock at his appearance. His face was hidden by a beard, but what she could see of it was deathly pale, his eyes so dark-ringed, they appeared to be only black holes. His spirits seemed surprisingly good. She darted a meaningful glance at Abner, then back at James.

"No, he's not said a word, yet. He couldn't, he's had the fever. We lost Terrier last night from it, too," James explained.

"Then that's why they had me bring your food?"

"Aye, they won't want to risk catching it by coming down here. I've been going crazy worrying about you, Amanda. Do they suspect you?" He insisted as she shook her head. "Are you sure?"

"So far I've been lucky. James, I've been trying to find a way to free you, but they're always watching me, everything I do!" She handed out the meager rations as she talked. "I'll keep trying, though, believe me," she promised.

"I know you will. Don't worry about us. Right Alf?"

"Aye, Cap'n. We've bin worse off afore this." His voice wasn't convincing.

"Your friend Abner here told us in no uncertain terms what he thinks of the act you pulled on him!" James's face bore a trace of a grin.

"Arr, 'tis a grand life, t'be a cabin boy!" Amanda smiled. "But not wot I'd call easy, gov'na."

He smiled back at her heavy cockney twang. "You're wasted, Amanda. You should be in Drury Lane! Seriously, I think we can pull through. They're talking of selling us into slavery in Morocco. If we can't escape now, we can try then. Promise me if the chance comes for you, you'll take it without thought for us?"

She nodded. The lie was worth it to set his mind at rest.

"I'd best go now, James. Mayhap they'll send me again?"

He nodded, and took her hand and kissed it. "Be careful, sweet. I'll take care of your friend here."

Abner, who was chained next to him, looked up malevolently. He was squatting on his haunches, apparently in a vain attempt to ease his position. "That's wot ye think, yer bloody—"

"Hey, Jack, wot's keepin' yer down there?' Jeb roared into the gloom.

"He's settin' 'em free, 'e is!" screamed Abner suddenly at the top of his lungs. "Yer precious cabin boy's settin' 'em free!"

"He's wot?" Jeb scrambled down the ladder.

Abner lurched sideways from his haunched position and knocked Amanda's feet from under her as he rolled, tripping her with the length of his taut chains.

She fell half-across him onto the slimy boards, scrambling to regain her footing.

Abner's hands clutched wildly for the stocking cap and tore it from her head. "Yer see, ye bleedin' fools! Yer cabin boy's a blasted whore!"

Jeb gaped in disbelief as she stood finally, seeing even in the shadows the wild mass of hair falling about her shoulders.

"Ye done it now, yer 'ave, whoever ye are! Ye've really gone an' done it!" Jeb's face, so familiar to her, was totally unrecognizable in his fury.

He lashed out with his booted foot at Abner, his kick forcing a scream from the lad's throat. Abner's revelation had not brought the freedom he expected.

Jeb's fingers caught in Amanda's hair, twined tight in its mass and wrenched. His friendly gray eyes were cold as slate now, any hope she'd harbored of him helping her, if the need arose, dashed by their chilly stare.

"So. Ye've made a fool o' me too, 'ave yer? Well, ye'll not be laughin' long, wench!"

He pulled her to the swinging rungs of the rope ladder. Her scalp screamed beneath his fingers. The pain, oh God, she couldn't stand it!

James tore at the chains that bound him, knowing in his heart there was no way to help her. Hopeless rage filled him, ripped at his guts, and spewed forth as an inhuman roar that filled the hold.

Bert and Alf strained to free themselves, too, as Jeb hauled Amanda up the ladder by her hair.

He threw her over the edge of the hatchway and she sprawled on the deck, tears streaking her dirty cheeks.

Her poor, traitorous hair fell in tangles over her ravaged face. Her skull was afire. She reached up weakly to cradle her hurt. Oh, God, help me, please God! she prayed silently. Every nerve in her body was taut as bowstrings.

Jeb crawled from the hold after her. She groveled at his feet, her spirit broken by her fear. She hung on to his boots.

"Don't hurt me again, please, Jeb!" Her words were almost incoherent.

A circle of men surrounded the pair now, their excited shouts of surprise bringing still more men to push and shove to the front to see what was happening.

"Jesus y Maria!" breathed one. "A woman!"

The eyes of the crowd echoed his words and the glances exchanged were full of anticipation.

A hush fell on the scene as Garcia arrived. The men parted like the Red Sea to let him through.

Chapter Seventeen

Never in her nineteen years had she felt such consummate terror. Garcia's squat body towered over where she lay. And all about her, on every side, stood circle upon circle of men, each pair of hungry eyes fixed hotly on her. Her flesh crawled. She got slowly to her knees, biting her lip 'til it bled to stem her whimpers. Then she rose to standing.

Aloft in the rigging a lone gull wheeled off into the sunset. Its lonely mew was like an epitaph.

She lifted her eyes to Garcia's, then quickly away, unable to be bold, to be brave anymore. Her look was riveted instead on the "cat" that dangled from his hands. She couldn't draw her eyes away!

"An English whore!" He spat, disgust written on his face. "And a dirty one at that! We'll have your friend take care of it, *sí?* Jeb! Bring water, now!"

Jeb lowered a bucket over the rail and brought it back, slopping in his haste. He looked at Garcia questioningly.

"Douse her, *amigo*. Let's see what's under the filth."

A silence grew among the crowd of men, and a flutter of expectancy coursed visibly through them. Every man leaned forward as a man instead of a hundred.

Jeb dashed the water over Amanda's slight form. She gasped. The sodden shirt clung to her like a second skin, outlining all, even to the tips of her thrusting breasts beneath the leather vest.

"Now, señorita, you will remove your jacket, *sí?*"

The crew's quick intake of breath caused his cruel smile to broaden. Terrified, she did as bidden. The men hooted as her figure was revealed through the plastered-down shirt.

"Like a bleedin' mermaid!" breathed one man, for her long hair, streaming wet, clung in strands over her body like seaweed. "Never see'd a mermaid with a tail like this'n, though!" He leered.

Amanda scanned the men's faces, desperate to find even one that showed compassion. There was none. They all bore a look, the same look, that she knew only too well. She couldn't stand here this way any longer! Her knees felt ready to buckle beneath her. She hesitantly moved to cross her arms over her breasts.

"No, *muchacha,* you will not move unless I tell you, you understand?" Garcia sidled around her, slapping the cat o' nine tails against his other palm as he went. Then he flicked the whip at her in one swift turn of his wrist.

The knots stung her back. She arched forward, her breasts thrusting in a way that caused the pirate crew to howl for more.

Garcia sidled around her again, agonizingly slowly. She tried to follow his movements with her eyes. He paused directly in front of her. She did not even see the "cat" move in his grasp, but felt the pain as it bit into her breasts. She screamed and started to run.

Jeb thundered after Amanda, whirled her about by her arm, and dragged her back to Garcia with a snicker.

"Don't make it harder on yourself, *muchacha,*" Garcia said so softly that only she could hear him. "We have a score to settle, you and I, *sí?* The sooner you obey, the sooner you shall die—and that will be the easy part, I promise you!" His voice purred with pleasure.

"Shall we ask the señorita to dance for us, *amigos?*" he asked in a louder voice, an amused smile on his fleshy lips as the men roared: "Aye!"

The cords of the cat sang through the air and cracked across her naked calves. "Dance, *señorita, por favor!*" Garcia sneered as she leaped forward.

With faltering steps she started to sway to and fro. One step, two steps—she couldn't go on! The whip slashed threateningly down across the deck. Terrified, she moved again.

"Around, *pequeña,* show us your treasures!" laughed Garcia.

She turned this way and that, a mockery of a dance.

Someone had a mandolin, and started to play a lilting Spanish lovesong. She forced her body to obey. The music quickened, and the circle of men widened to give over the upper deck entirely for her dance. And still Garcia leered, his glances from her to the whip the only spurs needed to goad her to obey.

Her hair sprayed wildly in all directions as she whirled. The men clapped in rhythm to the mandolin's hurrying notes. She would dance until she dropped dead on the deck! Then they could do with her as they wished. Nothing would matter, but the dance!

She crooned the melody as she turned this way and then that, circling the men with eyes that saw none of them, with a mind that had locked them out completely. They ceased to exist. She danced proudly, her hands upon her hips, fitting her movements to the Spanish style of the melody.

Above her, the sky darkened from its rosy hue to the deeper tones of twilight. A man lit lanterns on the yardarms, and her leaping shadow partnered her as she swayed. The light caught the ship's dragon figurehead, and its scales and fangs glinted blood red. The stink of grog filled the air.

The pirates savored her body as they watched and there were none that did not feel the heat course through their loins.

Garcia's smile was catlike in its pleasure at her debasement. The revenge he had planned was sweet, *sí*, sweeter with a woman as its object.

"That *puta* will beg for death before I grant her its release," he swore under his breath.

Quince licked his lips greedily as Amanda hovered past him. God's blood! He'd been a fool not to notice those ripe breasts beneath her boy's garb! He leaned forward, reached out a greedy hand to cup those breasts. Then he hauled her unresisting body into his arms and tumbled her to the deck. The rest of the crew yowled with excitement.

Amanda didn't move. She lay absolutely still as Quince straddled her body. His breathing was heavy as he tugged the gray shirt from her belt, his hands unsteady with lust.

"Enough, dog! The wench is mine!" Garcia flung Quince backward angrily.

"Nay, Garcia, mine first! Ye can 'ave after." Quince turned away from Garcia, and lunged for Amanda once more.

Garcia's hand darted to his boot and the stiletto concealed there. It shimmered through the air, and Quince dropped forward, dead. The Spaniard retrieved his bloody weapon and wiped it on his shirt, giving Quince's body a careless kick.

"*Amigos,* the wench is mine—for this night. Tomorrow, she is yours!"

He dragged Amanda to her feet and down the stairway to his cabin.

A hundred pairs of jealous eyes followed him.

Amanda dimly realized that they were alone, the dance over. Garcia was saying something. What was it? She struggled to make her mind obey, to clear her head.

When had he brought her here? It was as if she was coming out of a deep coma. Her head throbbed. She didn't want to face reality, better to return to the sleep. She rolled sideways onto the bunk, feeling the curtain that had covered her mind start to enfold her again.

No! He was forcing something to her lips, his hand on her throat squeezing the muscles until she winced and opened her mouth to cry out. The fiery liquid trickled over her tongue, dribbled down her chin. Weakly, her hands fluttered to push the tankard away. Its rim hard against her mouth, he tilted it again. She felt it course through her again, the rum bringing life into her icy feet, the heat of it spreading through her limbs.

She choked. "Enough, enough!" she said weakly, shaking her head.

"So, you are back, eh?" Garcia set the tankard down on a small table, upon which a crucifix glinted dull gold in the puny light.

There was an overpowering smell of garlic in the tiny cabin. She looked about her dazedly. The table and the narrow bunk upon which she sat were its only furnishings. He saw she was recovering and slammed the door behind him. His smile stretched eerily from one ear to the other earringed one.

"I want you to know what is happening to you, *pequeña.* You dared to make a laughingstock of me, Garcia! Now we shall see who laughs!"

He came toward her slowly, his elegant boots soundless, his flabby body surprisingly graceful. He reached out and ran a finger across her cheek, a sigh breaking from behind his misshapen teeth that seemed to hiss around the room like a live animal.

She willed herself to be still, but inside she trembled as a reed before the wind.

"You are lovely, *pequeña!*" he purred. "It will be a pity to destroy such beauty."

His hand stroked her face, moist palms clinging to her flesh. A shudder of revulsion passed through her.

"Don't," she whispered weakly.

"What's the matter, eh?" He breathed into her ear, his meaty hand pressing her against him. "Do I not make you burn with passion like your *capitán* in the hold?"

The keys at his belt were hard through the cloth of her shirt. Her fear was a fanning breeze to the dying embers of her courage.

"What will happen to him?" Her words trembled on the silence.

"He—all of them—will die, of course," Garcia answered softly, "and with exquisite slowness! You are dying too, at this very moment, *pequeña."*

She turned smoothly to him, letting his arms encompass her. "Then I have nothing to lose, señor."

Her voice would have warned him if he knew her better. It held a deadness, an empty timbre like dead leaves, a rustle in the gloom. She willed her hand to caress his thigh, slowly, languorously. Garcia's expression was one of ecstasy. His face was raised, his eyes closed, his hands tangled in her hair.

Stealthily she slid her hand down, down carefully to his boot and to the stiletto.

"You are very strong, señor, never have I seen such strength!"

Her voice caressed and flattered him as her hand wormed its way up behind his back. Garcia ground himself harder against her, savoring her submission and the feel of her soft breasts crushed against his chest.

There was a different fear in Amanda now, fear for her immortal soul.

The Spaniard started as he realized, too late, her intent. With a curious feeling of unreality and detachment, she thrust the narrow blade into his back, sinking it into the soft flesh to the hilt.

His face registered disbelief, then realization. The dim light of death was in his eyes. A gurgle started low in his bowels and spewed forth from his mouth as a river of frothy blood. He dropped soundlessly to her feet, the look of disbelief at his own mortality still in his dark eyes. He was, she knew, quite dead.

She knelt over him and unfastened the huge ring of keys from his belt, panting as she maneuvered the heavy body.

As an afterthought, she pulled the stiletto from him, panicky as the unwieldy flesh resisted her momentarily. She wiped the bloody blade on Garcia's own chest and thrust it inside her shirt.

The door groaned slightly as she opened it. She peered out into the gangway, seeing no one in the darkness. Garcia's cabin was on the upper deck. To reach the hold, she must first traverse the open upper-deck area and then lift the hatch and climb down to the hold.

She slipped from the doorway and closed it softly behind her, then made her way through the shadows and up the stairs. Cautiously, she crossed the deck, hugging to the confusion of coiled ropes and barrels for cover.

A concertina was wailing, the coarse voices of the crew lifted in a bawdy sea chanty. They were gathered about the mast on the upper deck, most of them sprawling drunkenly as they sang. Then she saw Abner. He was lashed to the mast, his head sagging forward, apparently unconscious, for she could see his belly heaving and knew he was not dead. A slim, curly-haired Spaniard she'd known as Delgado was idly flicking daggers into the deck. Two more of the knives glinted on either side of Abner's bowed head.

She circled the men warily, scarcely breathing, praying no one would find Garcia—not yet! Above her the watch slept in his lookout. The beating of her heart, she was sure, had to be audible. She hurriedly retrieved the pendant from her bundle in the galley and skirted back up and across the deck. The hatch groaned as she struggled to raise it. Then she found the rope ladder with her feet and climbed down.

She silenced the five men with a finger to her lips, and hurriedly tried each key until they all stood free beside her, muffling groans as the blood rushed back into their numb limbs.

"Blessed God, you did it!" James held her briefly to him. "What's happening aloft?"

Words tumbled swiftly from her lips as she told him. "We must escape. They plan to kill you all!"

"I know. Did you see Abner?"

She nodded. Oh, how she longed to hide from reality in James's protecting arms! But they must hurry.

James was quietly giving orders to his men. They nodded agreement. He took the stiletto from Amanda and handed it to Bert.

"Off you go, Bert!" The man touched his head in salute, and climbed up from the hold.

"Amanda, go with Alf and do as he says. We're going over the side. If what they told you is true, we can't be far from land. We have to risk it, love. We're safer in the sea than on board."

"What about you?"

"Don't worry about me, sweet, the captain is always the last to leave a doomed vessel! Now go on," he urged. His eyes lighted with an eagerness that scared her.

"What do you mean?" She cried over her shoulder, for Alf was already propelling her to the rope ladder.

"Just go, you'll see! And Amanda—"

She paused halfway up the ladder.

"I'm sorry for what happened, that first night. Forgive me?"

"It was a mistake. I forgave you long ago," she whispered as she climbed up.

"One more thing," he called softly. "I love you, Amanda."

She smiled, and the moonlight touched her hair. And then she crawled through the hatch after Alf.

They moved in silence, she dogging Alf's shadow in a bent-over sprint. Her foot touched something soft and yielding in the gloom. The starboard-watchman's body sprawled at her toes, Garcia's stiletto sticking from his back. Bert had obviously wasted no time.

Alf helped her to climb the rail and mounted it beside her. She let herself drop into the water.

The sound of their dives seemed alarmingly loud, but there were no cries from above them. Alf swam to her and led the way. She kicked out and swam after him to join Bert.

When they turned and trod water, she saw two more shadows drop into the ocean, a faint glimmer of moonlight silvering the spray their dives threw into the air. Reeves and the other man struck out for open sea.

The water was cool, not cold enough to numb the limbs, and very calm.

"Where's James?" she queried anxiously, spluttering as the salt water licked at her chin.

"Don't 'e fret. The Cap'n's got t'get a little revenge, now ain't he?" gasped Bert. "We'd best start swimmin' as ordered or he'll bawl our arses out for disobeyin' 'im!"

He started swimming slowly, weakened from the imprisonment. The others followed him.

Alf turned on his back to look at the *Sea Dragon.* Tongues of fire were dancing over her decks! Men were running everywhere, little black ants against the deep violet sky. Their cries carried on the wind.

The *Sea Dragon* exploded into a ball of fire!

"Be Jesus! The bloody ship! He's blown 'er up. Swim, lads, the wash'll kill us. *Swim!*"

Frantically, they struck out for open sea. Amanda saw the flames, the showers of sparks, the huge, splintered timbers creating impossibly graceful arcs in the air, and knew without question that no one could have escaped the inferno of the *Dragon*'s shell. The surrounding sea was littered with burning debris.

She and Alf grabbed a timber, its ends shattered and black, and let it carry them onward.

Bert was less lucky. A door smashed down, plunging him below the water. He disappeared and was seen no more.

They turned to look at the remnants of the vessel. Most of the foredeck was gone, along with all rigging and the figurehead. The gaping holes were smoking, flames licking at the carcass left them.

And then, as they watched, there was a second, gut-ripping explosion. The *Dragon* reared violently, enveloped with smoke. Then the sea was a storm of debris once more.

Amanda sensed rather than saw the huge timber that

smashed into them, for all her attention was on fighting the heavy swells the explosion had caused.

As the timber smashed between them, the three of them received the full weight of its impact.

The sea's greedy embrace sucked them below the foaming, thrashing surface.

Chapter Eighteen

Paul came toward her, his face bright and eager with love, such love, for her. He came swiftly, arms outstretched, as if floating over the golden wheat and the nodding, scarlet poppies. His blond hair was dazzling in the liquid light.

She reached out her arms and ran, too, her white gown billowing like a cloud about her, chestnut hair streaming behind her in the scented breeze. Her heart sang with joy. *His, his forever, never to be parted again, never to be alone!*

Her arms enfolded him, and then he suddenly faded in her embrace as if the light had dissolved him.

"No," she screamed aloud. "You can't leave me alone again!" But only the wheat murmured a reply.

The light was dazzling. From its haze ran another, taller figure, leaping, hurrying, over the stalks. There was strength in this face, compassion, love for her mirrored in his green eyes.

She began to run toward him as she had done to Paul, and stopped, confused. Still he came on. Only a few yards separated them now. He was smiling, his lips moving. She couldn't hear the words for the rustling of the wheat.

"Yes, James, what did you say? I can't hear you!" she cried. She concentrated on his lips.

"I love you, Amanda."

The stalks whispered among themselves. "Does she love him, does she, does she?"

Why wouldn't they stop? The words of the wheat echoed through her mind like a million soft sighs.

"No, James, don't say it! I don't love you!"

He stopped short, the smile fading. He stumbled, stood again, faced her over the quivering stalks of wheat. His face showed bewilderment.

Then two pistol shots rang out, the sounds tearing at her eardrums, throbbing over and over, until she covered her ears with her hands. Smoke, smoke everywhere! Where was he? Panicking, choking, lungs bursting, she fought the smoke. Wisp by wisp it wafted away!

Now it was dark, the dark of a moonless, starless night. Then a single lantern hung suspended in the air, its gloomy glow a huge butterfly of light. A thing stood in the light, a mangled, twisted thing that had been James. It held its head under its arm, and the gray, pale lips were moving, "You killed me, Amanda. You did this, you!" The sad, awful green eyes reproached her.

Suddenly, the severed neck of the thing spouted fountains, rivers, oceans of blood, flooding her, drowning her. She was swimming in blood!

And she screamed and screamed and drowned.

Her fingers were numb. Not with cold. No, she was burning hot. The numbness came from fear, fear that she'd lose her grip on the edges of the door beneath her, fear that she'd sink forever into the endless sea.

Her hair trailed off the door and on top of the glassy

blue it fanned out, twisting and flowing like Medusa's locks. Her lips were cracked, her flesh singed and blistered from the hot sun that shimmered down, relentless, on her spread-eagled body. It was the same sun that had taunted her, tortured her, these past two days. Or was it three?

Her body craved water, while surrounding it was a form of it that was undrinkable. Her tongue felt huge, furry, alien. She believed it might try to choke her if she slept again. If only she had a knife, she could rip it from her mouth, the twisted, traitorous furry thing! It had killed James with its treacherous words, and she sensed, she knew, that she would be next. She must not sleep! She slept!

There were rats on the door, looking at her, waiting, watching. Their eyes were red with blood, their bodies the size of cats. Her own eyes were wide with terror, the pupils huge, dilated black pools. The rodents surrounded her, giving her room to grovel, to beg for mercy. One of their names she knew. Garcia. He was the rat with the cruellest eyes, with yellow teeth, with the longest, yellowest teeth she had ever seen.

She lunged wildly at the rats, forgetting her fear of falling from the door. She had to kill them, or they'd devour her!

There, only one was left now; all the rest had fallen into the water. She giggled hysterically, then stopped, horrified. Garcia was coming after her, mincing across the door on dainty clawed feet!

She raised her fist, crashed it down again and again until the rat lay still. Her eyes blurred, focused again. She felt unspeakable horror as she looked at where the rat had lain. She'd made a terrible mistake; it was a man! There was blood beneath him in a pool. His blood.

She opened her eyes and tried to lift herself from the bunk. A gentle hand forced her down. The same gentle hand supported her neck and dripped precious, life-giving, glorious fresh water into her mouth. She sank back. She sat up again, forced the flask to her lips, and help it tight to stop those hands from taking it. Then she retched and vomited.

Hands washed her clean, and covered her in a rough blanket. She flung the roughness from her blistered body, raved with the fever that racked her, tossed wildly with the delusions that tortured her. There was no peace for her.

Fernando turned to his father-in-law, his dark eyes full of pity and concern. "We must return. This girl will die if we don't."

Julio Rios growled, disgusted. "A pirate's whore!" He spat. "Let her die, my son. For Juan's sake."

Fernando said nthing. He knew the story only too well, knew how Bloody Harry had hanged Julio's only son before his eyes. But the girl could have had no part of it. She must not be sacrificed for an old man's bitterness.

"I must insist, señor. I will tell Sebastiano to turn around." He left the cabin.

The *Bernadetta* tacked and came about, the little vessel bobbing on the blue water like a cork. The nets were hung up once more. The crew knew there would be no fishing, not today. Soon they were heading back to Blanes.

Fernando pressed wet cloths to Amanda's head. She looked ashen beneath the cruel, opened blisters that covered her face. If he could not see the deep rise and fall of her breasts he would have thought her dead. He grinned. And to think they had thought her a boy, spying her from the *Bernadetta*'s deck sprawled across the blasted remnants of that door. He'd been about to tell Sebastiano to pull away, thinking her another mutilated and probably bloated corpse amid the *Sea Dragon*'s debris of timbers and bodies. They'd passed several shark-eaten remnants of men in the past two days, he recalled, feeling green again. His father-in-law had gloated each time.

But, when he, Fernando, had seen the girl's fist pound weakly against the door that had served her as a raft, he had put aside Miranda's father's protests, and dived over and fished her aboard. He could not bring himself to let her die, pirate's whore or not. They carried her onto the stone quay on that same door.

A crowd of women waited by the jetty, their faces fearful. If their men had returned so soon, with their nets empty, it bespoke some terrible tragedy. Their fear turned to avid curiosity. They watched with bright black eyes as the men carried the girl ashore.

They would have followed the procession to Fernando and Miranda's cottage if that bad-tempered Julio had not angrily bade them leave and mind their own business!

Miranda was in immediate control. She flicked the long, blue-black braid over her shoulders and smoothed her colorful skirt over her hips.

"Well, my husband," she asked, "why are you not hurrying to fetch the physician, eh? Go, and be quick!"

Fernando smiled and saddled the village's only horse, his horse. It was his one remaining luxury. He cantered out of Blanes.

Miranda went back into the cottage to tend to her patient. She bathed her gently from head to toe, clucking at the blisters that covered the exposed flesh, then again at the light weals on her breasts and calves. If she *was* the pirate's woman, they had not treated her kindly.

Finally, she brushed out the wealth of matted chestnut hair and plaited it neatly in two braids. A wave of compassion filled her. *Pobrecita,* whoever you are, she thought, you are too young to have endured so much! Miranda felt far older than her own twenty years, especially since her recent marriage.

She covered Amanda with a light coverlet and left her in the cottage's only room. First, Miranda would fetch wood, and then start the fire for supper. As an afterthought, she took the jeweled flower-pendant from her apron pocket and went and tucked it into the girl's closed fist. It might have some meaning for her and give her some comfort to know it was there.

The fish stew was bubbling over the coals when Fernando returned. He was alone.

"The physician says he will come soon. He has a woman in labor to care for first. A difficult birthing. He hopes to be here tomorrow, *querida.*"

"Tomorrow! *Aiee!* I hope she will last that long! She is very bad. Tell me, how did you find her?"

Fernando explained. "And when we saw the figurehead we knew what had happened," he finished, wolfing down spoonfuls of the savory stew as he talked. "Your father thinks I am a fool, that I should have left her, but I couldn't do it."

Miranda rumpled his hair. "Softhearted, yes, but no fool. And Father only acts that way because he is so bitter, my love. If he thought you a fool, would he have given you the *Magdalena* for my dowry?" she asked sternly.

"I suppose not, but he probably thinks me a fool for turning fisherman, anyway. And you, Miranda, how do you feel?"

"Very proud, my husband! You're doing what you wish to do, and not what your arrogant brother insists you should do. I'm so happy—and all I want is to make you happy too!"

"You have, already, *querida mia!* Come, come over here!"

She came across the cottage to him, and he took her about the hips and laid his head on her belly.

"I feel him kicking!" he exclaimed.

She laughed, rubbing her flat stomach.

"Kicking indeed! Señor, I believe you are listening to your own belly groaning, after all you have eaten tonight! It is too soon for the baby to kick, anyhow. And, also, how do you know it will be a 'he'?" she teased.

He growled and embraced her playfully. "With such a lusty husband, how could you give me anything but sons?"

Miranda laughed. "Now, Fernando, behave yourself! We have a guest!"

As if she had heard them, Amanda whimpered, then

rolled restlessly from side to side, murmuring a string of words slurred with fever. Miranda hurriedly went to her and touched her forehead.

"She is burning, Fernando. I pray to God the physician comes soon!"

But by midnight the fever had risen still further and no physician had arrived.

Chapter Nineteen

She lay on the narrow precipice that separates life from death. One move, one quiver, could have sent her hurtling into the abyss that yawned below. But Miranda would not let her fall.

When the physician came he shook his head.

"You are wasting your time, my dear. You cannot save her." His brown eyes were mournful.

"But her injuries, you said they are not so great, señor! Why won't she live?"

"Because she doesn't want to. She is willing herself to let go of life. I've seen it before—many times. We physicians can only help to heal the body. If the mind is bent on its destruction, there is little we can do."

"Well, I can, señor!" Miranda had sworn, softly. "I will not let her die. Such waste! She must have been very lovely before this, no?"

The physician left, leaving no hope for the girl, but a stern warning that Miranda should not tire herself, to be careful of the child within her.

Miranda went to the huge bed that her brother-in-law had given them as a wedding gift, and perched on the edge of it. Then she folded back the coverlet and gently smeared the ointment from a crock on the girl's sunburned face. How could anyone sleep so long and so deeply, she wondered. The nuns at the convent above Blanes, Our Lady of Mercy, had given her the ointment and promised to pray for the girl. She, Miranda, with God's help, was sure she could do the rest.

Miranda's long fingers, tanned and strong, moved with gentleness over the girl's body. The burns were healing, the lash marks fading. If only she would wake up! Four days of tormented tossing and turning, mumbling, and screaming had passed. Her words were English, and Miranda understood none of them, but she sensed the terror behind them. She calmed Amanda in soft, lilting Spanish, kissed her cheeks and brow as if she were a child, held her hand and willed her to live. Afterward, for a while, she would sleep, still and peaceful, until the dreadful delirium started once more.

A week passed since Amanda was brought to their cottage.

Fernando and Miranda spread blankets over the stone-flagged floor and slept on them next to the fire. He said nothing about the inconvenience or the discomfort, knowing Miranda had made a pact with herself to see the girl live. He loved his wife deeply. It was a small price, an aching back every morning, to pay for her happiness.

Julio Rios had handed over the *Magdalena* entirely to him now and his days were long and grueling as captain of the little fishing boat that was sister to the *Bernadetta*. But at the end of every day Miranda would be on the quay, waiting for him, her hair lifting in the breeze, her shawl tight about her shoulders, and a welcoming smile on her lips.

Sometimes a twinge of guilt pricked him. He could have given her so much! Was it right to ask her to settle for so little? He looked about the cottage's single room, neat, swept clean. A string of onions hanging from the low-beamed ceiling gave off their pungent odor. Miranda could make any place a home!

Now she was spooning broth into the girl's mouth. *Madre de Dios,* but he was a lucky man, to have such a woman! All the arguing and anger that had accompanied the announcement of his decision to marry her had been well worth it. Even if his brother had not come around immediately, *Mamacita,* his little mother, had given her blessing. But then his brother had relented, and agreed to meet Miranda, and been as taken with her as the old lady had. And he, Fernando, was the happiest man alive!

"Fernando, come!" Miranda's excited cry brought him quickly to his feet.

The girl was awake, her eyes clear and seeing for the first time. She said something, her expression puzzled.

"She's wondering what happened, where she is!" exclaimed Miranda excitedly. She patted Amanda's hand. "You are safe, *pequeña,* and with friends. Rest, now."

Amanda felt the gentle touch that had soothed her through the past week. She sank back onto the feather pillow. Miranda's voice cajoled her to sleep, as the girl continued smoothing her hair. The strange words she used were like a soft lullaby. Amanda slept deeply and without the terrible dreams.

Miranda's face wore an expression of delighted triumph.

* * *

When Amanda woke again, sunlight was streaming into the cottage. Birds were singing in the tree by the window and beyond their song, the soft splashing of the waves against the shore reached her ears. Where was she? Who were these people? She didn't understand their rapid language, but their kindness needed no translation.

The black-haired Spanish girl came across the room. "*Bueno,* you are feeling better, no? Come, eat, we have to build up your strength. You are a bag of bones!" She laughed and Amanda smiled back.

"Where am I?" Amanda asked again.

Miranda gave her a spoonful of gruel, thick with cream and sweetened with honey.

"I'm sorry, I don't understand you. But I am Miranda." She said in Spanish and pointed to herself.

Amanda nodded. She understood that much. She copied Miranda's own actions, and told her her name.

Delighted, Miranda repeated it, her smile broadening as Amanda nodded vigorously. "So, we are friends, no?"

She clasped Amanda's hand and kissed it, and Amanda laid the girl's brown hand against her cheek.

"*Gracias!*" she said. It was the only Spanish word she knew, apart from "buenos días."

Miranda nodded. "It was nothing. I am glad that we could help."

Much later, when Fernando came home, the sky was dark outside the cottage.

He shared Miranda's excitement, embarrassment reddening his face when this Amanda repeated her thanks over and over again. He knew no English, but had learned a smattering of French.

"Mademoiselle," he began, *"nous avons . . ."* He told her how she had come to their cottage.

Excitedly Amanda answered him in French, the schoolgirl French her tutor had taught her so long ago.

Fernando grinned and relaxed. Now they could communicate!

Amanda explained haltingly how she had dressed as a boy, how she had escaped from the *Sea Dragon*—all of it, even to her killing of Garcia. But nothing about James. Her voice broke when she described the Spaniard's death.

"May God forgive me!" she finished finally.

Fernando frowned. "You had little choice, mademoiselle. He would have done terrible things to you and killed you, finally. You were meant to survive, that is why Fate brought you to the fishing grounds, why you were not killed by the explosion. You must not torture yourself with guilt, mademoiselle! Put it behind you, *oui?"*

She had to, if only to keep her sanity. The promise she had made herself, to take whatever happiness life gave her and hang on tight, would carry her through this. Now she must concentrate on the business of living again. Survive, she would. Whether she would find happiness ever again, she did not know. But she could try.

By the following morning her condition had improved even more. She opened her eyes, squinting against the sunlight, the glare hurting after the nothing-gray of that seemingly endless sleep.

Everything was a blur at first, then gradually she made out the figure of the young woman, Miranda, against lacy curtains that billowed around her head and shoulders like hair.

Amanda shook her head to clear the fuzzy feeling in it. The effort sent stabs of pain down the back of her head that ebbed to a dull throb. She moaned, and the sound caused the vision at the window to turn and come toward her.

Miranda murmured something softly in Spanish that Amanda didn't understand, but her meaning was clear, for then Miranda pointed to her own head and made signs of pain.

Amanda shook her head gingerly and tried to sit up. With a motion of her hands, the girl gently insisted she lie still, and left the room with a swish of her skirt.

Amanda closed her eyes once more. Then the memory of the *Sea Dragon*'s explosion and the knowledge of James's death bombarded her again. The hopelessness she felt was boundless, the grief awful in its choking agony. Tears flowed down her cheeks, streaming across her throat onto the pillow.

He had loved her, and had tried to make up to her for what had happened that first night. She wanted to tell him so many things left unsaid, and now he was gone.

She dozed fretfully for a while. When she awoke the Spanish girl was standing over her again, dark eyes full of warmth and compassion. She had a bowl of soup in her hands and set it on the sill. She helped Amanda to sit up a little, plumping the pillow.

Miranda sat on the bed and began to spoon the warm, chowdery liquid into her, chattering away as she did so. Her earrings flashed gold in the sunlight, jiggling as she laughed. Amanda could not understand her, but liked her warmth and good nature anyway.

Then she began to mime how her husband had fished Amanda out of the water and dragged her into the boat. She even told comically how Fernando had thought she was a boy and his embarrassment at finding she was not!

Amanda found herself smiling as Miranda laughed delightedly at the story's conclusion.

When she awoke again it was twilight and the room was shadowed with lavender light. The sound of the sea carried now, and the rhythm of the sound was a lullaby, the gentle sigh as the waves kissed sandy lips a tender refrain she enjoyed. She lay back, pleased to find her head less painful, though her arms and legs, back and hips were still miserably sore and aching. The burning feeling in her eyes had lessened too, and the salve the girl had applied to her face, hands, and neck had eased the rawness considerably. It was, she decided, time to get back on her feet, since she was never one to enjoy lying in bed all day.

She made her intentions clear, and stubbornly sat on the side of the bed in the borrowed shift. Miranda fetched her a dark-red skirt and cream-colored peasant blouse, which she declared proudly she had embroidered and sewn herself.

Amanda showed her delight and slipped the garments on. Her body was painfully thin and her hair, she knew, was salt-stiff and in need of washing.

Miranda helped her to do so and then carefully toweled it dry, exclaiming at its length and heaviness and her enjoyment of the rich colors as the setting sun tinged each strand with chestnut and copper lights.

Every day she grew a little stronger. After breakfast,

a meal she enjoyed with gusto now that her strength was returning, Amanda decided to take a stroll around the village and seashore.

The air had a balmy feeling and was very warm. The sky and ocean were unbelievably bluer than they had ever been in England. Trees—palm trees she believed—grew close to the sand, sticky dates strewn at their trunks like myriad insects. It was strange to see them, so lush and fronded, springing from the seemingly infertile sand and rocks. She fingered the textured trunks curiously, then sat in their shade and let the almost-white sand run through her fingers—like the sand in the hourglass her father had kept in his study.

My life is like that, she reflected, running relentlessly away with no form or plan, spilling through the days, the weeks, and soon years, with the same careless ease. She sighed and squinted against the light out to the horizon. If only James had not . . . Tears welled in her eyes and flowed over her cheeks like rivers. A lump in her throat refused to be swallowed and her chest ached with longing for him and for his affection and the protective haven of his arms. It felt as if the agony would never go away.

She walked, barefoot, letting the playful waves cover her bruised toes with tickling ripples. There was the stone wharf where, Miranda had described, they had carried her, half dead, onto land.

An old fisherman sat there now, mending nets and lobster pots, a battered woven hat on his head and fraying breeches at his knees. She could feel his eyes on her as she approached, and knew that beneath the shadowed brim they would be dark eyes, made bright with curiosity.

"Buenos días, señor."

The old man smiled a toothless smile, removing his clay pipe, and inclined his head politely. His whole face seemed to be nose and chin under the hat.

"Buenos días, señorita."

He jerked a thumb toward the sea and mumbled a few words, then, seeing she didn't understand him, made signs of someone who felt hot. Then she understood that his remark had been of the coming closeness of the day. She nodded agreement and he smiled in satisfaction.

Several children had gathered at his feet now, and watched her with wonder. One braver than the rest clambered onto the beached boat, where the old man was laboring, and fingered her hair and chattered like a little parrot until the old man cuffed him away with a sharp scolding. The boy grinned and leaped off across the sand, the others swarming after him, laughing and giggling as they went.

But the women that she met would neither speak to her nor even meet her eyes.

That evening she asked Fernando why they treated her in that cold fashion. Incredulous, Amanda discovered that most of the village believed she had been a doxie for the pirates' pleasure. Miranda laughingly agreed to enlighten the villagers at the first opportunity. Fernando, reddening from having to relate the latter information, asked Amanda what she intended to do now.

"I don't know. I believe I should return to England, but the thought holds little appeal. There's Aggie though, and the Comptons, bless them, but I would be forced to a very dismal life there. Part of me yearns to see the colonies I've heard so much about. Perhaps I could earn enough here somewhere to buy passage on a ship."

Her voice trailed off doubtfully. Her head was pounding again, and she felt very tired and achy.

Miranda had suddenly started to chatter excitedly again and the young man translated.

"Miranda says that she has the pendant that belongs to you. It was still around your neck when you were brought ashore, and she put it away for safekeeping."

Amanda smiled with relief. She would at least have a little security, for the piece was probably worth a great deal. But it had been given in love and she was loath to part with it, unless she needed the money desperately.

The days drifted by and with them a feeling of restlessness growing inside her. Fernando and Miranda had been more than kind, but the cottage was not big enough for three and Amanda missed her privacy. Also, Fernando and Miranda needed theirs, for their love for each other was very obvious. She had given them back their bed and slept instead on a blanket by the cooking fire, but the sounds of the couple's lusty lovemaking each night left her yearning for her privacy more than ever.

Often she would borrow Miranda's shawl from its hook and walk out into the night and gaze up at the heavens. A pumpkin-colored moon floated in a sky of dark blue and the waves were crested with silver foam. It was only at night she could give way completely to her grief. The shrill squeaks of the bats hanging in the trees neither alarmed her nor frightened her but seemed more to be companions in her melancholy.

Since Fernando had discovered she could speak French, they had conversed some, though his command of the language, he admitted, was wretched. It was to him she went finally to broach the subject of leaving. Fernando explained in turn to Miranda, and the two were lovingly insistent she stay until she had definite plans. But Amanda remained firm in her resolution to leave despite their pleading, and Fernando reluctantly agreed to see what could be done.

Impatiently she waited, doing her own inquiring among the villagers for alternate lodging. No one would take her in. She was still under suspicion.

Fernando was leaving one morning—foregoing his fishing for once—dressed in elegant breeches and shirt with a flat-topped sombrero and embroidered waistcoat. He mounted his horse and rode off.

He returned the next morning before *siesta,* beaming with excitement. He explained to the two women, over crisply fried fish and steaming saffron rice, that his mother and brother had expressed their concern for the English *señorita* and had invited her to stay at their home indefinitely. His brother, having just returned from Barcelona that same morning, would arrive the following day to escort her there. Amanda was greatly relieved, though a little nervous, and thanked him deeply for his family's generosity.

The next day dawned cloudy and overcast, with, Julio swore, a definite promise of rain before afternoon in the yellow-tinged clouds. He bade her farewell gruffly, Fernando translating and apologized for his ill manners from the first day. Then Fernando and the older man cast off the lines, and the *Bernadetta* and the *Magdalena* skimmed across the water, headed for open sea.

Amanda turned back to the cottage, deeply grateful to the couple and touched by the concern Fernando had expressed for her well-being as they bade her farewell. They would not be too far away, and a message could always be brought if she wanted to see them, so her doubts were allayed.

Amanda swept the floor of the single room where all of the living was done in the cottage, and set the bed to rights. Before Miranda left for the beach to scrub the clothes on the rocks, she chided Amanda to rest for the journey. But Amanda finished quickly and decided that she would bathe before Fernando's brother came for her. It would be well to look presentable and try to create a good impression.

She gathered up a fresh supply of clothes—Miranda's again—and a sliver of soap, and clambered up a narrow trail that bordered the convent.

Chapter Twenty

There was a pool that bubbled in a rocky hollow before tumbling down to join the sea. It was cool and shaded there, surrounded by pines and bushes.

Amanda slipped off her clothes and waded into the icy water. Oh, it was refreshing! She lay back and floated, noting amusedly that her nipples had hardened. The light that filtered through the branches dazzled her eyes. Turning over, she swam lazily around the pool, every fiber of her body tinglingly alive from the water's caress. Then she soaped herself thoroughly from head to foot, while seated on a smooth rock, before plunging back into the water. Afterward she lay back again and reveled in the dappled light that played over her body, unaware that the sun was rapidly fading.

Suddenly, a rumble of thunder clattered through the hollow, followed by a flash of lightning and huge raindrops. Startled from her daydream, she let out a shriek and waded quickly from the water, pulling the fresh blouse over her dripping body. A second blue-white flash outlined the trees and she clutched up her skirt and ran wildly for cover, the rain now falling in sheets. She huddled beneath a tree, frantically trying to don a now-sodden skirt. Water streamed from her hair and the blouse clothed her like a second skin.

Then a splintering crack sounded as lightning struck the tree beneath which she stood. She looked up, eyes wide with horror, realizing too late the folly of her shelter. The top of the tree was ablaze and ready to fall, but she stood as if rooted to the spot, paralyzed with fear!

In the same instant that the blazing boughs began their rapid descent, two arms reached out and tore her from the ground, flinging her across a saddle and holding her, struggling and half-naked, while the horse careened wildly through the trees to the clearing just above the village. There, her rescuer dismounted and dragged her roughly to her feet, a torrent of Spanish pouring forth from his lips, each word as sharp and angry as a blow!

She raised her hands as if to ward off the harsh sounds, pleading between huge, shuddering breaths for him to stop.

"Ah! So you are the English miss I am to take into my home! What a fool to seek refuge beneath a tree in such a violent storm! The branch missed you by inches—you would have been killed!"

She lifted her head angrily and glared at him beneath a curtain of streaming hair, furious at his tone of voice, surprised, too, that he now spoke in English. Her eyes were as stormy as the weather, the lashes wet with the rain that still fell.

"Fool, am I? Then, sir, I will not presume on your hospitality! You may consider your offer refused. I will seek other accommodations!"

She swung around and flounced away through the

mud, until, with a horrified gasp, she recalled that she was naked from the waist down! With a squeal of embarrassment she flung her arms down to cover the dark triangle between her thighs, her face blushing scarlet to the hairline at the realization he could not have helped but see.

In exasperation, he discarded the hat he wore, and strode across to her, removing his cape as he did so and wrapping her roughly with it.

She pulled the garment tightly around her and ventured a timid smile, her eyes meeting his face for the first time. But the smile faded and she gaped at him, horrified, the color draining from her face until she was a chalky white.

"You!" she whispered finally, her voice as dead as dry leaves in autumn. "You!"

She swayed slightly and would have fallen if the man had not reached out and steadied her. In her mind she saw him as she had seen him last, a smoking pistol in his grip and the same hard set to his jaw as he stared pitilessly down at Paul's writhing body in the little church.

He shook her slightly, a puzzled frown on his tanned brow, the anger fleeing his face and concern taking its place.

"Señorita! What is wrong! What have I done that you stare at me that way? Have we met before?"

And then he recognized her and he, too, was for a moment returned to the English village, and the wet, bedraggled creature she was now was replaced in his mind's eye by a vision of innocence betrayed, clothed gloriously in yellow, and rigid with shock, a bouquet of spring flowers falling, crushed, from between her fists.

He regained his composure first and lifted her, still stunned, onto his stallion. He mounted behind her and urged the horse into a brisk canter, his arms supporting her tense frame from falling. The rough track was awash with mud and the horse slipped more than once on the downward journey.

Miguel's mind was teeming with questions. That this girl should be here, in Spain; that of all the English women, Blake's betrothed should be the one to whom he had offered his hospitality! It was incredible! And if not for those eyes, those still hauntingly beautiful eyes, he would not have recognized her in the gaunt figure that rode before him. Undoubtedly she hated him. Her tone and the stiffness of her body said so. All the anger toward Blake and his guilt over his own shabby treatment of the affair surged back into his body. He kneed the horse roughly, pressing him into a gallop, forcing a startled gasp from Amanda as she swayed for an instant at the violent change of pace.

Soon they were at Miranda's cottage. The girl hurried through the puddles to greet them, a shawl held over her head against the rain. Her welcoming smile faded as she noted the grimness of her brother-in-law's face and the pallor of Amanda's.

"Miguel! What happened? You look terrible!"

"This little idiot chose to shelter beneath a tree—in this!" He gestured angrily at the storm outside as they hurried into the warmth of the cottage. "I was lucky enough to pluck her away as the tree was struck, and my concern overcame my tongue. I'm sure the señorita is just a little shaken, that is all." He stopped and warmed his hands over the blazing fire.

Miranda, glimpsing Amanda's surprising lack of

clothing beneath Miguel's cloak, ushered her into a corner of the room, clucking at her sodden hair and attire. She wrapped a towel around her and left her to dry herself, then hurried back to Miguel, a determined set to her jaw. He was in the process of tasting the simmering stew over the fire, and started guiltily at her fast return, before grinning and handing her the spoon.

She snatched it from him and flung it back into the pot, standing accusingly before him, hands on hips.

"Why, Miguel, is the señorita unclothed? If you have ill treated her, I will see Fernando knows of it!" she whispered angrily.

"Now, Miranda, there is no need to be angry! She was bathing in the pool by the convent when the storm struck. Never fear, her virtue is, to my knowledge, unscathed!" He grinned wickedly.

Miranda snorted in disgust and shrugged her shoulders.

"Very well, Miguel. I believe you. But do not think your haughtiness of manner and your feigned dislike of women deceive me! You are your brother's brother and he is *mucho hombre,* much man. I would not leave any sister of mine alone with you!" She glared at him, then the glare faded to a smile and a bewitching giggle. "Come, we will eat and forget the storm and your unfortunate first meeting with the English lady. Let's start again."

He nodded doubtfully. He was willing to try, but was she, Amanda, he wondered, willing to let him?

The three of them waited out the storm in uneasy silence, broken now and then by Miranda's half-hearted attempts at conversation.

Finally she gave up and went about her chores in the

cottage, leaving the other two to sit and stare morosely into the fire.

Amanda, now clothed and dry, sat by the hearth, her head on her knees, staring stonily into the glowing coals as if seeking the answer to some mystery there.

Miguel sprawled uncomfortably in the only chair, his fingers drumming an irritated rhythm on the arm from time to time, his darkly handsome face set in a ferocious scowl.

It was puzzling, Miranda thought, that such a little thing could have caused such great hostility between them, but she deemed it wiser to remain silent than pursue the matter further. She would meet Fernando at the wharf very soon and maybe he would be able to explain it.

The stew was served and eaten in the same manner, each of them accepting their steaming platter from her with thanks, but neither glancing at the other during the meal. Consequently, her own appetite suffered and she felt irritation welling up inside her as she believed a mother must feel when pushed to the brink by sulky children.

It was with relief that she noticed the storm had died down to a steady rain. Miguel followed her gaze and jumped restlessly to his feet.

"Señorita Sommers, I will ask you once again. Do you wish to travel to Villa Hermosa with me? The decision is yours. Whatever you decide, I shall be leaving soon. If you wish to accompany me, please hurry yourself. There is quite a way to travel to my home, and we have already delayed long enough."

He pulled his cloak around his shoulders, though it was still steaming from the heat of the fire, and strode from the cottage to the two tethered horses outside.

Amanda stood up, her mind already decided on going with him. Fernando had said that the invitation had been issued by his mother and perhaps she would need be involved with him for only as long as it took to reach this Villa Hermosa. God, what a bear! Little wonder Fernando had spoken so little of him. But he'd find she would give him short shrift if he tried to use his domineering ways with her! The day has come, she decided firmly, slipping on Miranda's old cloak, when I will be my own woman, and seek my own way in life. And, Don Miguel, she seethed, I will not forgive you for what you have done to my life!

Outside, the rain fell steadily, the ground puddled and miry. Offshore, the sea was enveloped in a fine mist and there was no hope of the weather improving, if the gloomy, slate gray of the sky were anything to go by. Gulls huddled on shore, too, their presence itself prophecy of worse weather to come.

Amanda embraced Miranda fondly and thanked her in the little Spanish she had learned. Miranda's eyes were brimming with tears, though a sweet smile was, as always, on her lips. Amanda felt tears sting her own eyes and turned swiflty to where Miguel waited to hand her up onto the prancing bay mare.

After a brief farewell, Miguel kneed his stallion into a brisk trot and forged ahead, followed by a seemingly meeker Amanda, who inwardly seethed at his cavalier behavior and was, in fact, very far from feeling meek!

By mid-afternoon they had traveled over half the distance and Amanda's flanks were numb from the unaccustomed rhythm. But her pride would not allow her to ask de Villarin for a brief respite, so she gritted her teeth and winced with every hoofbeat.

Her companion rode ahead of her, effortlessly erect in the saddle, horse and rider as one. From time to time he turned, hoping probably, Amanda thought nastily, that she had been swallowed up in some huge pothole, and would henceforth be no bother to him. When he did turn, she smiled sweetly at him, the smile fading to a groan the second he turned away.

The track was sandy and littered with rocks. In places it measured only four feet in breadth, the mountains rearing up like a wall to her left and a sheer shelf of cliff plunging to the restless Mediterranean on her right. Never being overfond of high places—especially when viewed from the back of a spirited horse—at times her heart was in her mouth, and she wished fervently that she was back in safe, very flat Suffolk. There the highest hills were mere molehills compared to this!

But soon the treacherous mountain paths gave way to wooded slopes, and earth ochre-colored and shadowed with the plentiful *piñons* that were everywhere. The rain had stopped and the late-afternoon sun was winking between the trees, dappling with feeble light the two cloaked figures that rode the twisting path.

With the sun's return, sparrows were making use of the rain puddles for a joyful bath, hopping and fluttering, fighting and chirruping with noisy gusto. Soon the soggy cloaks were slung across their saddles. The damp locks of Amanda's hair that had escaped the hood had dried to curling tendrils around her forehead and cheeks.

They emerged from the woods at the crest of a gentle

slope that dipped white-sanded skirts into a blue sea. A tiny village lay in the lap of this slope, the elfin-sized cottages clustered together quaintly, their white walls rose-tinted in the last rays of the sun.

Miguel wheeled his horse and cantered back to her, reining his mount in at her side.

"There," he said, pointing proudly across a small valley to the hillside beyond, "is Villa Hermosa. My home, señorita, and yours, too, for as long as you wish it to be so."

She felt surprised at the warmth in his voice and the gentleness of him now. But he had not finished. His dark, almost black eyes flickered to her face, and she read a look of apprehension in them.

"I know, señorita, that you despise me for maiming your *novio*. But I was angry, very angry, at the manner in which Blake treated my sister. Revenge drove me to deal with him in that way. I've given it much thought, señorita, and I believe I have done you a service, however indirectly. For being the kind of person he is, he would undoubtedly have made you an unworthy husband."

Until the last sentence he had spoken, she had almost been convinced of his sincerity, empathized with his grief for his sister and the dark hatred that had driven him to fire that crippling shot. But that he should attempt to rationalize it by endowing the action with such a worthy motive was unforgivable! Red spots of anger bloomed in her cheeks and her hands clenched on the reins.

"Oh, come, sir! Pray do not attempt to lay your guilt at my feet! At least be a man and accept the responsibility for your own actions. Where I choose to grant my affection and the worthiness—or lack of it—of the receiver of those affections is my concern, not yours! I loved Paul Blake dearly—even after I heard your 'accusation.' And, if he had not wished to spare me, I would have married him despite the injuries he bore. But," she added, her voice breaking as she remembered the hurt and squalor of their last meeting in that stinking room at the Figurehead, "he would not marry me, and I am forced to accept his decision. Now that part of my life is over and I wish to dwell on it no more. I will accept your mother's hospitality with gratitude, but only for as long as it takes me to find a means of making my own way in life. I would appreciate it if you, Don Miguel, would leave me to pursue my own course and keep your solicitousness for those who ask for it!"

She sat her mount calmly, meeting his stunned scowl with a boldness that was almost brazen.

He returned her look for a few moments that seemed to last an eternity. Finally he spoke, and his voice was so soft she wondered afterward if she had imagined the words.

"This is a man's world, Señorita Sommers. You would be wise to accept assistance when offered, for a woman cannot, however determined, exist at this time without a man's protection. You have courage and great aspirations, but despite this, you are a very foolish young woman!"

He clicked to his mount and started down the slope, leaving her no choice but to follow him.

The village and sea were bathed in liquid gold, the sun a fiery globe that was half-cupped by the horizon's rosy hand. They passed a little church, whose stained-glass windows were ablaze with the light of many candles from within and the reflection of the setting sun from without. The grassy square was deserted, the children no doubt still at their *siesta.* The smells from the cooking pots were mouth-watering, and Amanda's stomach growled traitorously as the fragrant aromas assailed her nostrils.

They began the climb up to the villa, the horses straining as they approached their stable. And then she saw it, washed with light, white walls cool and regal behind the dark green of the trees. Villa Hermosa! Twin turrets leaped skyward at either end, giving an almost castlelike appearance to the gracefully built house. There were black wrought-iron balconies fronting the upper casements and exotic vines trailing there, leaving splashes of purple and lavender where they wandered. The lower-story windows were lit from within by the seductive warmth of many candles.

As they clattered up to the carved door, a wizened old man whose face was burned to a rich mahogany and whose back was bent with age, hurried from behind the house somewhere to take their mounts.

Miguel slid from his horse and came to assist her down from her own. His arms reached up to clasp her waist and for a second their eyes met, and she thought she read a glimmer of male appreciation there that was swiftly masked by polite indifference. And then, wonderfully, she was down from that hard saddle, and he was leading the way through the door while she followed, considerably slower, her back, buttocks, and legs agonizingly sore and stiff.

A plump maid met them and took Amanda's damp cloak from her. She asked if the señorita wished her to unpack her bags. Amanda, at a loss for words, hesitated; Miguel smoothly intervened.

"Thank you, Bonita, but there will be no need. The señorita's trunks and personal belongings were lost at sea. Señorita Elena's belongings are to be brought out and made available to her until she has purchased more of her own. Will you see to it, please?"

The maid nodded eagerly and motioned for Amanda to follow her, her ample figure already leading the way up the huge, curving staircase.

At the foot of the stairs Amanda paused and turned to her host.

"Thank you, señor. And when will I have the pleasure of meeting your mother, Señora de Villarin?"

"Tonight, at supper, señorita. And, now, if you will excuse me . . . ?"

He bowed stiffly and left her staring after him. Slowly she climbed the stairs behind the buxom maid.

Chapter Twenty-One

Her room was very pleasant, and Amanda warmed to the care that had obviously gone into making it so for her. There were flowers on the dressing table, and the bed had been turned down in readiness. Light from a pair of candelabra revealed pale yellow draperies and yellow-and-white velvet chairs. The carpet was a Moorish weave, of stylized flowers in chocolate and butter yellow. A welcoming, feminine room, Amanda thought.

A pitcher of steaming water was somehow already on the dressing table, and she filled the porcelain bowl and splashed her face, removing every vestige of grime from the long ride.

When she had finished washing, she shook out her hair from the single coil and brushed it briskly with a dainty brush from the dresser, until it gleamed copper in the candlelight.

Then she removed her wrinkled blouse and skirt and lay down in her shift, stretching luxuriously on the crisp sheets.

She was almost asleep when a light tap on the door signaled Bonita's return. She murmured for the girl to enter and drowsily saw her do so, carrying something in her arms. A few seconds later, she was lost in blissful sleep.

When she awoke, crickets were singing below her balcony and stars were darting hot points of light through the blackness of night. She slipped out of the bed and went to the window. Below, the sea was glittering as it caught the haloed moonlight, the iridescent glint of silver making each ripple seem to hold a myriad of silver fishes.

Someone had snuffed the candles as she slept and the room lay in heavy shadow.

Bonita came in then, carrying a taper, and relit the twin candelabra. She chattered cheerfully in Spanish, and was delighted when Amanda showed a little understanding. Then she crossed over to the carved armoire and flung open the door. Amanda understood that those were Don Miguel's sister's clothes and that she was to use them.

Nodding her thanks, she burrowed inside and selected a deep-pink gown with a modest but becoming neckline, and sleeves that fell in pleats of lace at the elbows. The skirt was tucked at the hem, each tuck set off with a pair of tiny white silk roses. It fit quite well, although a little large in the bosom, but the color became her.

Bonita sat her down and swiftly caught her hair up on top of her head with an ivory comb. Cleverly using every strand of the heavy hair, she entwined it this way and that into a high crown of curls, wisps of which were artfully dampened and twisted into sweetheart curls over her ears and nape. The effect was stunning and very, very feminine. Bonita stepped back to admire her handiwork, well pleased with herself. Then, with a small gasp of triumph, she snatched a rosebud from the vase and set it with a pin into the elegant coiffure. It was a perfect finishing touch, the creamy petals accenting the rose of the gown and the blossom's own fragrance enveloping Amanda in sweet perfume.

Amanda smiled her thanks at the delighted maid and Bonita, smiling too, pointed to a tiny ormolu clock that indicated she should go downstairs to dine.

A little nervous, she descended the stairs, noticing the portraits that adorned the walls, some of the faces reminding her of Fernando and others of the stern good looks of Miguel. Obviously the de Villarin forebears! The rich, dark paneling on the walls showed that love and care had been lavished upon it. A magnificently chased pair of silver-handled swords were crossed over a shield bearing the family coat-of-arms in the entrance hall, and there were fat, waxy candles or sconces in every alcove to light the way. She followed the maid's pointed directions and swept through a long corridor that led to the dining room.

Miguel was standing with his back to the door in conversation with someone so that his height and broadness of shoulder hid her view entirely. He heard her footsteps and turned, crossed to her side, and took her elbow, leading her with a firm hand to meet his mother. The first thing that struck Amanda was the incredible frailness of the old lady, followed by a feeling of surprise that she resembled Miguel so greatly, or, rather, that he resembled her.

Below the severely upswept whiteness of her hair, her eyes were black and piercing as jet. The skin of her face had the velvety-soft quality that comes to women who have lived well and to a good age, but she had the tiny figure of a very young girl. Her hands held a silver-topped cane at arm's length. She met Amanda's appraisal with an even franker one of her own.

Finally, Doña Francesca stood and crossed to Amanda, slowly, but with a proudness of carriage befitting a queen. Obviously her appraisal of the girl had had an approving outcome, for she held out her hand in welcome and smiled, her dark eyes twinkling.

"Welcome, my dear, to Villa Hermosa. My son and I are delighted to be able to help you. What a terrible ordeal you must have suffered! Fernando has told me of your capture and escape from those awful pirates. You must recover, eat, rest, and not think of leaving us for a great while. I lost my daughter two years ago—I do not know if Miguel has told you—and your presence here will be so welcome! This old house hasn't heard a young girl's laughter for too long."

Amanda took the outstretched hand and clasped it warmly between her own hands as she thanked the older woman. So, she doesn't know, she thought, that I was betrothed to her son's sworn enemy.

They dined beneath a crystal chandelier, and Amanda was hard put to resist gobbling down the food, she was so famished. Never had her appetite been so voracious!

The Doña's English was almost as good as her son's, except for minor errors that Miguel seemed to find amusing, though Amanda thought it more polite to ignore them and found him rude to the extreme.

Course after course appeared before her. Fish, peppers stuffed with herbs and savory meats, delicately seasoned chicken, chunks of beef coated with a rich sauce, and a full-bodied red or white wine to complement each course! Before long, her head spun from the wine and the rich food. Even Miguel seemed softer and more approachable than before. Why, his face was rather attractive; dark eyes against tanned flesh, and crisp, curling black hair that shone blue in the candlelight. If only he would smile more often, an extremely attractive man . . .

But why were they staring at her? Had she? She had! She had voiced her last opinion aloud! A nervous giggle burst unbidden from her lips. I must be drunk, she thought wonderingly. What will they think of me? She stood shakily and tried to excuse herself and retire, but the words were slurred and, try as she might, they would not come out correctly! She felt the blood rush to her face as she blushed with shame, still endeavoring to leave.

But it was not to be. The day's events and the wine would not let it. She saw the room reel and right itself, and reel again, and it was not until she felt those strong arms lift and carry her along the corridor that she realized it had been she who had reeled and not the room!

Miguel carried her up the stairs effortlessly and, as she looked up at him and tried to protest, he smiled down at her mockingly.

"And so, *pequeña,* you are able to take care of yourself, are you? Ha! The wine took better care than you! Remember, lovely one, that you must be careful with whom you partake of spirits, for there are men who would take advantage of your state at this moment. Perhaps even kiss you passionately—like this!" And he lifted her head to his mouth and pressed a hard lingering kiss on her lips that bruised and excited them at the same time through the heady lethargy she felt.

Then he dropped her unceremoniously onto the bed and strode back to the door, pausing.

"I will send your maid to help you retire, señorita. Sleep well."

His laugh rang out as he closed the door behind him.

Chapter Twenty-Two

Miguel poured himself a glass of wine, kicked off his boots, and sprawled across the bed. He rested his head on one arm, the other hand holding the glass, swirling the wine in it around and around. He grinned. Red wine, red as the lips of the English miss when he'd finished kissing her. *Díos,* he'd enjoyed it!

How furious she would be when she awakes tomorrow and remembers—if she remembers. She has a temper as volatile as any Spanish *cantina* wench he'd met! He felt the heat course through his loins. And the face and body of an angel, were it not for those wanton, wicked lips. She'd never know how he'd ached to tumble her down on the wet grass and take her this afternoon. The blouse had been slicked to her breasts, its hem ending above a tantalizing spectacle that had made his pulse quicken. Miguel, you blackguard! he chided himself with mock severity, you rush off to aid a fair maiden in distress and you, the gallant knight, think only of bedding her!

He took another sip. Pity his damned feelings had held him back! But she was not the sort of woman one took casually, like plucking a peach. She was to be treated with respect, courted, married, and *then* bedded. Just as Maria-Elena should have been. Poor little Elena. His last glimpse of her had been through the casement, her oval face and dark eyes pleading with him to stay, not to bring Blake back against his will and force him to marry her.

Miguel wondered for the thousandth time if he had turned back, done as she bade him, if everything would have been different, if his sister would still be alive. He'd wanted only to see that the child bore its father's name, nothing more. He would not even have insisted on Paul staying, though divorce was, of course, out of the question. Until he'd heard Elena had killed herself, that is. Then his fury had demanded a duel, Paul's death, under the pretext of honor. But what it really had been, he knew, was revenge. Blake had forced the decision he'd made by drawing first. Then he'd lost all control. He pushed the uneasy thoughts from his mind, turning instead to Fernando.

Miranda had made Fernando a good wife, and would soon make their child an excellent mother. What perversity had made him refuse Fernando's request to allow their marriage at first? Did he fear Miranda was a fortune hunter, as Paul had been? He believed that concern had been at the back of his refusal. But Miranda, he knew now, wanted only Fernando's happiness, not wealth. Miguel shook his head and laughed. Fernando, his brother, a fisherman! It was not the occupation that amused him, more the idea of Fernando choosing one so difficult, so tiring. Fernando had never enjoyed hard work before.

Consuela rapped on the door and came in at his

command, bearing a tray of coffee.

"Thank you, Consuela. You're looking lovely tonight."

She blushed. *"Gracias,* Señor Miguel. It is good to have you home again."

"And good to be home. Especially with such pretty flowers as you to fill it!"

She nodded her head, accepting his compliment and smiling back impishly. "You have not changed these past two years, señor," she declared firmly, wagging her finger at him, "you are still a wicked man!"

She left the room, her plump buttocks jiggling seductively beneath her skirts.

Díos, but he wanted a woman! Caro! She'd be more than happy to see him after so long, and he could attend to some business too. He'd ride into Barcelona in the morning. But tonight, he grinned, Miguel, you'll just have to burn!

Miguel asked Manuel, the gardener, to ready his stallion. Manuel bustled about, still not believing his luck in living long enough to see his Miguelito return. But, *gracias a Dios,* he had, and with a lovely señorita, too! Since Don Carlos de Villarin's death, Manuel had always had time for Miguelito, to listen to his problems and give him advice when he asked for it. He felt as if Miguel was the son old Josefina, his wife, had never given him, and looked out for his interests accordingly.

Miguel returned his love, concern written on his face as Manuel leaned for support for a second against the horse.

"Are you ill, Manuel?"

"No, no, Miguelito, it is only the *vino.* I am testing

the villa's grapes a little too often of late, and these old bones are so dry, they soak it up like a sponge!"

Miguel smelled the wine on the old man's breath and laughed. "Easy, *viejo,* save some for me, eh?"

With a wave, he set off down the slope, a small traveling bag lashed to his saddle. He was humming softly to himself as he clattered through the village and up again onto the Barcelona Road.

Was Amanda Sommers as pure as she was lovely, he wondered? *Díos,* that she was beautiful there was no doubt, with that rich, russet hair and skin like moist rose petals! If there was one thing in England he had loved, it was the dewy freshness of the women's complexions.

The horse knew the way well and he let him set his own pace, while he drifted into thought. Envisioning Amanda again as he had come upon her beneath the tree made him smile. The sight of her had sent his blood racing! It was fortunate she felt only loathing for him, he mused, for he knew if she were more worldly, more inviting, more like Caro or the other many women he had bedded in the past, he would be sorely tempted!

He changed from a hum to whistling a bawdy melody. *Díos!* This English woman had stirred him more than he cared to admit! He chuckled to himself, remembering the ride from Blanes to the Villa, and how he had watched Amanda secretly. Several times he had seen her face screwed up in suffering as her flanks were bumped again and again on the unaccustomed saddle. Stubborn wench! And yet he had to admit grudgingly, she had uttered not one word of complaint, not whined for him to slow down as many women would have. It must be the stiff upper lip the British maintained, though he doubted it were her lips that had been stiff!

By mid-morning the sun was high, and horse and rider were in need of rest. He tethered the stallion to a bush and hung over a stream to slake his thirst, soaking his kerchief and mopping his sweating face and neck. Then he sprawled under a tree, fanning himself with the broad-brimmed black sombrero.

Though eager to see the latest cargo for the Barcelona Gallery, he almost wished he did not have to go. It was more amusing to watch the señorita flush with anger or retort caustically to his taunts! If only that damned incident with Blake hadn't come between them, he would have perhaps courted her. He admired intelligence in a woman and spirit, and she possessed both. Not to mention beauty.

It was mid-afternoon when he clattered onto the cobbled streets of Barcelona. The tall buildings mushroomed up close together, forming narrow alleyways. All shutters were closed against the heat of the afternoon, and, apart from a few mangy stray dogs that nosed the dust and gutters for food, the streets were deserted. The sun cast sharp black shadows everywhere, and the reflected heat from the white walls left a shimmering heat haze. The city dozed as perceptibly as her occupants.

He went to an inn by the quayside, convenient for his business the following morning, and he woke the innkeeper with a few hearty knocks on the door. He kept up the pounding even when cursed vividly and, at length, from the casement above. Finally the man opened the door and let him in. His grumbling and irritation dispersed magically when he saw who his guest was and the gold of the coin that Miguel waved temptingly before his greedy eyes.

Señor Cristobal booted a bleary-eyed groom into the alley to take the señor's horse to the stable and then showed the Don into a small but clean room overlooking the wharf. Then he left to continue his *siesta.*

Miguel did likewise. He woke as the city was coming back to life. Below in the street, servants and housewives scurried to cook the evening fare. The sky was a deep lavender, and it reminded him of the last afternoon he had bedded Caro, over two years ago, and their passionate farewell.

He dressed in clean breeches and yet another ruffled shirt, pulling a fawn waistcoat and jacket over them. Luckily, Bonita's packing was excellent and the clothes had suffered little in the traveling bag. Then he tugged on the black boots again and went below.

The inn was very different in the evening. The taproom was full of brawling, carousing men. Sailors were attempting to pinch the buttocks of a tavern wench in one corner, and she was teasingly trying to prevent them, finally bringing her metal tray down on one lusty tar's head with a resounding clang. There was a small knot of merchants at another trestle table, but a brief glance assured him that the man he sought was not among them.

Miguel sat in a corner and ordered brandy. The wench who had crowned the sailor brought it to him, her smile and the calculated sway of her buttocks inviting him to pinch—and more. But he good-naturedly gave her a hefty tip, and she flounced away, disappointed.

When he had finished, he went out into the crowded streets to stroll with the others of Barcelona, a tradition known as *paseo.*

The teeming crowds of humanity fascinated him, and it was with enjoyment he renewed the greetings of old friends and acquaintances. The children were fresh scrubbed and cleanly dressed, their hair wetted and plastered down tidily, or else brushed into perfect ringlets. Young ladies were modestly clothed, their *mantillas* pulled discreetly over their blue-black hair, carefully attended by *duennas,* or with a Mama or Papa hovering very close at hand. Young men would signal frantically to attract their attention, while trying to maintain the strictest secrecy. But Love finds a way, and more than once Miguel saw notes exchange hands feverishly and secret smiles meet across the courtyards.

He was observing one particularly dewy-eyed young couple trying to touch hands in the throng that moved like a meandering river, when a man walking quickly in the other direction almost collided with him. Instead of apologizing for almost throwing him to the cobbles, the man gaped at him, popeyed and open-mouthed, before hurrying off with a muffled oath. The stench of his unwashed body lingered behind him, and Miguel stared after him until the man ducked into an alleyway and was lost from view. Miguel shrugged and walked on.

An excited crowd had gathered in the plaza, and he joined them to see what the amusement was. A young man sat on the statue's base, strumming a guitar. In the center, a young gypsy girl was swirling to the rhythm of a peasant dance. Her hair hung loose and black to her waist, where it was lost in flying skirts of bright reds and yellows. Her legs were long and slender and almost totally revealed beneath the flurry of petticoats. Her teeth flashed white in the torchlight and her earrings, too, captured the light and gleamed gold. When she had finished, her head raised triumphantly, her breasts heaving from exertion, the young man moved among the crowd, his hat upturned to collect the coins the willing crowed offered.

Then a younger lad, very slender and dressed in a richly embroidered *bolero* and tight breeches, joined her. Together they moved to the rippling chords, dancing almost back to back, each glancing haughtily over their shoulders at the other as they circled the courtyard. The music grew wilder still, and their feet stamped and their hands clapped ever faster. The girl's hair wildly tossed this way and that and the lad's eyes burned deeply into hers, until finally the last chord finished on an echoing sob. The crowd went wild and cried appreciatively: *"Olé!"* as the pair took a well-earned bow.

Caro would have to look to her laurels, he thought, as he wandered back to the inn to dine, for the girl had danced well.

The next day he breakfasted in his room, then strode down to the quayside, in search of the ship that bore his cargo. Many ships were anchored at quayside and still more offshore, awaiting their turn to dock and unload.

He grabbed an urchin by the shirt and spun him around. "Whoa, *muchacho!* Would you like to earn a few *pesos?"*

"Sí, señor!" The lad's eyes shone.

"Very well! Inquire for me the whereabouts of a merchantman, a French one. Her name's *L'Aigle d'Or*. Hurry now, and I'll double it!"

The boy nodded and fled along the quayside, darting in and out of trunks, barrels, and bales of various goods.

Sailors, stripped to the waist, toiled at loading the waiting wagons, their bodies glistening with sweat. There were a few doxies leaving the ships, faces haggard in the cruel light of morning. Some of the men hooted and whistled at them, but they stayed aloof and picked their way delicately among the clutter, their gaudy finery brassy by daylight.

Soon the boy sped back, his eyes already on Miguel's hand, anticipating the coins he would receive.

"She's out there, señor. Look, the big ship with the golden eagle. One of the sailors said she'll be dockside this afternoon. Did I do good, señor, did I?"

Miguel ruffled the boy's hair and laughed.

"Here's your money, *hijo*. And yes, you did well. Now be off with you!"

It was an easy task to hire a fisherman to row him out to the ship. The watch hailed them as they neared her.

"Ahoy! Who goes?"

"Don Miguel de Villarin! I have business with your captain and request permission to board."

The watch passed down the message and, shortly, a Jacob's ladder was flung over the port railing, and Miguel clambered up it onto the ship. The mate directed him to the elegant cabin.

Captain Alexandre was delighted to see him and bade him be seated.

"*Mon ami,* the cognac of *la belle France* is *magnifique,* as always. Will you have some?" He offered the decanter with an elegant flourish.

Always a dandy, today Alexandre had outdone himself. His breeches were a pale lavender and his coat of the same hue, embroidered all over with silver threads. The waistcoat over the ruffled pink shirt was striped with purple, lavender, and silver, and the captain's wig was elaborately powdered and styled, and topped by a huge plumed hat.

Miguel's eyes ached from looking at him. The heady scent of the cologne Alexandre used was a little overpowering in the close cabin. But he was, nevertheless, an excellent captain and a good friend, and Miguel cared little for appearances, as long as the man behind them was a worthy one.

"Well, Alexandre," he said finally, savoring the fine French brandy and helping himself to a *bonbon* from a silver dish. "Let me see them!"

"Oh, but you are anxious, *mon ami!* And for what? A few paltry paintings! Come, some more cognac, *oui?"* But his eyes were smiling, for he knew well his friend's lack of patience when it came to his art purchases. Miguel was as impatient as a child with a new toy!

Finally, he opened his heavily locked armoire and drew out two rectangular objects wrapped in velvet. He propped them on the table, and removed the coverings.

Miguel strode forward eagerly. The Rembrandt was as fine as he had imagined! Its colors glowed richly in the dim light. This artist's work had undergone an upswing of popularity lately, and the painting would fetch a good price in the colonies. But the delicate pastoral watercolor by Lorraine he intended to keep for his own private collection in the Villa Hermosa tower.

"And how much did you get them for, Alexandre?" He lounged back in the chair and propped up his legs on the table.

Alexandre pursed his lips and named a figure.

"Monstrous, you rogue!" Miguel roared.

"Mais, mon ami, you know very well that these paintings—"

"—are worth much less!"

"But with the commission for my own labors! *Monsieur,* you rob me of my commission if you agree to less!"

"Rot, Alexandre, and you know it! I'll give you . . ."

He named a considerably lower figure and Alexandre, weakening as he knew he would, finally agreed on an amount that was profitable to himself and agreeable to Miguel. Miguel promised to have the letters of credit drawn up by his bank and sent to the captain. Alexandre in his turn would arrange to deliver the paintings to the de Villarin Gallery the next morning.

After the paintings had been returned to their safe hiding place, he bade the Frenchman farewell and had the fisherman row him back to the quayside.

As promised, Alexandre delivered the paintings to the gallery the next day and Miguel instructed his manager on the hanging of the Rembrandt and the handling of his accounts.

And, now, he was free to visit Caro!

Chapter Twenty-Three

Caro's balcony jutted out over the narrow, winding street, as did those of all her neighbors. The black curls of the intricate ironwork were attractive against the old white walls, and their starkness softened by trailing ivy that twined among the railings.

As he glanced upward, the door to the balcony flew open, and a figure dressed in severe black-and-white hurled out and collided with a metallic twang against the iron. A torrent of curses followed the maid, words he had rarely heard and even less rarely used himself! The voice was shrill and penetrating, and he recognized it well. He winced as the voice railed on and on and finally ended with an explosive: *"Madre de Dios!"*

He pulled the bell handle and listened to it jangling deep within the house. Then the heavy plodding of feet sounded, followed by the grating of wood as the door was opened a crack.

"Sí, señor?" asked the voice in a monotone. Dark, melancholy eyes looked at him without interest.

"So, Rosa, you do not remember me, eh? Ah, well, *adios!"* He turned as if to leave, knowing full well the maid would not let him.

"Señor Miguel? Bienvenido, señor! Come, come, inside, I am sorry, señor, but—"

"—but *la señorita* Caro is furious with you, and has, once again, ground your spectacles into the carpet, am I right?" He laughed and pinched the plump cheeks, rewarded by a nearsighted smile.

"Sí," Rosa confirmed dolefully.

"And tomorrow Señorita Caro will be ashamed, desolate, and have them repaired until the next time, saying 'Aiee, Rosa, you are the cleverest, the best maid' she has ever had, no?"

"Sí," Rosa chuckled, still doleful.

He chuckled, and sat down in a high-backed chair, his legs stretched out comfortably in front of him, while Rosa hurried off to fetch her mistress.

Caro arrived several long moments later, entering as her profession demanded, theatrically, and fanning herself. Her blue-black hair was piled into hundreds of artfully elegant curls on top of her head, loose tendrils adding a wanton, gypsy look to her face. Her dark eyes were diamond hard, but, with her seductive smile, their hardness passed as brilliance. The emerald gown she wore clung to her curves, the neckline plunging to the valley of her breasts where a white carnation, pinned there, obstructed the tantalizing view. Her slender wrists and fingers were a-glitter with flashing jewels.

She feigned surprise, and smiled a warm welcome, the black beauty spot at her mouth rising almost to her high cheekbones as she did so.

"Miguelito! Querido mio, I have missed you so, darling! When did you return? What?" she replied, astonished at the date he gave. "And in all this time you did not come to see Caro! Shame, Miguel, you are a

horrible man. You vowed you loved me!"

"You know very well I did nothing of the sort," he chided, knowing she knew it too and playing the game. "I believe we agreed that our—involvement—with each other would be on a different level?" He broke off and grinned again, enjoying the pouting expression on her face, although he knew she was not in the least perturbed.

"Sí," she agreed, sighing deeply. "It is only my body that you love!"

"Sí," he agreed, sighing just as deeply.

He stood and crossed to her, taking her hand and kissing the tip of each finger tenderly, gazing into her eyes. She moved into his arms, molding herself to him as the ivy molded to the railing. She pushed him away gently as his fingers trailed across her back, tracing circles there. "Not here, silly! Come!"

Miguel followed her upstairs to the boudoir, a room he had known well. A low whistle came involuntarily from his lips. Since the last time, the entire room had been redecorated in white: hangings, walls, the canopied bed, the armoire—everything! Even the masses of blossoms in the vases were white, with no greenery showing to detract from the effect. It was like stepping into another world.

She said his name softly, and he turned, gasping at the picture she presented. Raven hair streamed to her waist, black rivers of sparkling jet falling over a girdled wrapper, also white. She seemed to glow like a jewel in the starkness of the room, her lips more crimson, her eyes blacker, and those long, slender glimpses of flesh glowing with a golden, tawny warmth.

He went to her then, unable to restrain himself—and

not wanting to—and grasped her by the hair, pulling her head back and smothering her bared throat with feverish kisses, where the pulse throbbed wildly. He released her and loosened the girdle at her waist, then pulled the garment down from her shoulders, drinking in and savoring the full voluptuousness of her now-naked body.

Caro stayed motionless, a faintly mocking smile on her lips, anticipation glittering in her eyes. Ah, this Miguel, he remembered, he had not forgotten how to please her! What a man! She stepped gracefully to him, one hand twined in his dark hair, the other burrowing inside his shirt to caress the dark mat of his chest.

He lifted her and carried her to the white vastness of the bed, tearing off the coverlet and laying her down on the silken sheets as if she were a fragile orchid. He lay beside her and mouthed the taut peaks of her breasts, his loins pounding. Her nails raked his back, spurring his passion onward. He trailed his tongue down to the soft plains of her belly, Caro writhing upward to his kisses in spasms of passion. He reached down and caressed the curves of her legs until at last he could bear it no more, could wait no longer.

Miguel entered her roughly, with a savage lunge that told the extent of his desire for her. She responded with a cry that spoke of equal passion. He slowed after a while, moving tenderly and deeply, all the while his mouth locked to hers.

She read the look in his eyes. There was grief there, mingled with the desire, self-reproach, pain.

"Love me fiercely, Miguel, wildly! It's been so long!" she cried.

He needed no second urging, his body driving with a

will of its own, the pleasure immense, filling him throughout long after she cried out her own ecstasy. Finally, savagely, he was spent. Shuddering, he fell back to where her arms awaited him.

When they awoke, there was noise in the street below and the aromas of different dishes cooking in many kitchens.

Caro shivered, though the room was warm, the film of moisture that covered her now felt cold and clammy. Miguel drew her close, and brushed a kiss against the coolness of her breast, fighting to regain sleep, to recapture the mood of before.

It was the hour of *paseo,* the time when all the people dressed in their finery and took a stroll in the coolness of the evening, before dining at ten o'clock. Dark shadows crawled across the room as the orange sun forfeited the earth to the moon's winning hand. The scent of flowers was heavy and cloying in the air, and somewhere a foolish bird warbled a last, mistaken trill.

A sharp tap on the door shattered the dream he had lost himself to. Caro was out of bed and across the room in a single lithe move, taking with her the last vestige of magic.

He groaned in disappointment and sat up, smoothing the black commas of tousled hair into rakish order and yawning with the satisfaction of a well-fed cat.

Rosa burst into the room, clucking her disapproval. "Señorita Carlotta, you will never, never be ready in time! Señor Rafael is waiting below, the carriage too, and he is most angry, señorita! He says that this could be your biggest night, that everyone of note will be there—and no Caro! *Aieee!*"

Caro was already dressed, the tight costume with its

masses of scarlet ruffles beneath a black overdress brilliant against the room. She poked Miguel in the ribs with a long fingernail and motioned to the hooks at her back. He groaned and sat up to fasten it for her, then pressed a kiss to her shoulder, seeming to want to say something, but at a loss for words.

"What?" she asked, surprised. There was, for once, a hint of softness in her eyes.

"Thank you, Caro." He smiled.

She shrugged and looked at him with understanding. "Caro knows you, Miguel. We are friends, and friends help each other, no?"

He nodded, marveling at how well she had read him and his innermost thoughts.

"Vaya con Díos, Miguelito! And don't make it so long, *querido,* before you come again! I am glad I helped your hurt a little, whatever it is, but you must help too, eh? *Adios!"*

And then she was gone and only her perfume remained.

He relaxed again, seeing her in his mind as he had first seen her, at Don Carlos de Alicante's ball. She had danced the *flamenco* with the proudness of a queen, and the fire of a kind that can only become great. The guests had been left speechless, drained wholly after her performance, by the throbbing of her castanets and the staccato plea of her heels against the flagstones of the courtyard, an embodiment of the violent passions of love and, its twin head, hate. He had wanted her then, his senses lost in the sight of her, black hair held in a single, heavy coil at her nape, the tall comb flashing in the light of the torches. She, her spirit sensing his desire, had danced only for him, asking not for a love that burns with steady constancy through time, but for the savage fires of passion joined with passion. Now, only the full, throbbing notes of a guitar were needed to recall that first night he had wanted her.

Well, he must leave, return to his villa. For now, he thought, grinning.

Rosa brought water and he bathed leisurely, then dressed, and left, riding through the maze of narrow, shadowed streets more at peace with himself than he had been since leaving on his search for the Englishman.

Chapter Twenty-Four

Miguel was strangely anxious to be off, despite the more-than-pleasant interval with Caro. The next morning saw him mounted, dressed again in the dark breeches and ruffled shirt, the watercolor bound in cloth across his saddle, heading back out of Barcelona.

This time his pace was not as leisurely, and he kept the horse at a steady gait. By noon he was back at the stream where he had quenched his thirst on the outward journey.

He did the same this time, then settled beneath the tree to eat the victuals the tavern wench had prepared. The stallion snuffled at the ripe cheese and tossed its head in disgust, turning instead to the sparse grass. Miguel tore away hunks of the crusty bread, munching them along with bites of tangy cheese. The whole he swigged down with a small *bota* of red wine. The tavern girl had done him proud, and he vowed to pay her closer attention on his next trip to the city. Sated, finally, he stretched out for a short *siesta* before continuing home.

The sun was high above, a white octopus of heat that extended blistering tentacles in all directions. The sky was brilliant and cloudless, a seemingly endless canopy of blue. In seconds, he was dozing.

He awoke when he heard the stallion's shrill whinny of greeting, and another horse answer. Still bleary-eyed, he struggled to a sitting position, then jumped to his feet hurriedly. Three riders were coming along the track, and one stood in the saddle to point in his direction!

Swiftly he unbound the traveling bag and took out his pistol, loading it carefully despite the need for haste. He glanced about him for a hiding place, but apart from the tree and a few bushes, there was no cover. Instead, he stretched out on the ground again, the pistol in his grip concealed by his black sombrero. To a casual observer, he was just a weary traveler resting in the shade. But the dark eyes were not quite closed, nor the well-muscled body totally relaxed.

The three riders reined in their mounts a few yards from him. Their leader, a paunchy man whose hooked nose seemed to dominate his face, stepped from his horse and stood, hands on hips, just in front of Miguel.

"Hey, *amigo!* Wake up, you have guests!" He looked back at his companions and grinned, little pig eyes almost lost in his heavy jowls. "You see! I told you! The bastard is asleep. I'll finish him quickly and be done with it, eh?" The others grunted agreement.

The fat man pulled a knife from his belt and waddled toward the apparently sleeping figure.

Miguel waited, scarce breathing, every muscle in his body tensed and ready to spring. From beneath half-closed eyelids he saw the booted foot of the man about two feet away from his head. He felt the slight change of position as the lout prepared to plunge the dagger into his chest and simultaneously rolled to his right.

The heavier man, finding no target, lurched off balance. In a split second Miguel had him, one arm hard against his throat, the other, pointing the nose of the pistol at his massive belly.

"One move from you, *amigo,* and you will have a second navel! Tell your companions to dismount and throw down their weapons, if they value your filthy hide!"

In a shaking voice, his hostage did as bidden, wetting his fleshy lips in fear. He was right to be afraid, for his companions merely grinned, the older of the two withdrawing a pistol from his shirt and pointing it at the two by the tree.

"It is of little account what happens to him, señor. He is nothing!" He sneered. The muscle in his arm flexed as he slowly squeezed the trigger.

Miguel saw the movement and fired first, still retaining his grip on his hostage's throat. The other man toppled from his horse, but not before discharging his pistol. De Villarin felt the man before him sag. The last rider wheeled his horse and careened off back toward Barcelona, lost in a cloud of dust.

Blood flowed from a huge gouge in the fat man's belly, staining the grimy jerkin. He checked for a pulse and found it barely throbbing. The man was dying. His tiny eyes flickered open and his lips formed a feverish prayer.

There was nothing Miguel could do. He reached for the *bota* of red wine and drained the last few drops into the dying man's mouth.

"De Villarin, help me, *por Díos!*" His head lolled lifelessly to one side.

The other rider was dead also. Miguel thanked God

that there had been only three of them. He left the bodies where they lay and fastened his bag once more. But before he did so, he reloaded the pistol, and thrust it inside his shirt. Luckily, he had escaped, this time. The next time he might not be so fortunate. Next time? Why did he assume there would be one? The nagging question in his mind was suddenly clear. The fat man had addressed him by name! Surely, no ordinary highwaymen were on such familiar terms with their victims?

Then something, shining in the sunlight, caught his eye. His face was dark with rage as he plucked it from the dead man's hand.

Chapter Twenty-Five

When Amanda awoke the next morning it was with a headache that would have done credit to a giant. She stumbled to the mirror, shuddering at the reflection it threw back.

Quickly, she glanced at the clock. Already it was past seven! She groaned. On top of disgracing herself last night before the de Villarins, now she would be late for breakfast to boot! Her stomach rebeled at the thought of food, but she knew she'd have to put in an appearance, at least, for politeness. No doubt the insufferable Don Miguel would be there to gloat over her behavior!

She grabbed the brush on the dressing table and furiously tugged it through her hair until it shone. There was no time to do anything further with it or do more than splash her face and hands with water from the basin.

The armoire presented an enormous choice of gowns. Deciding swiftly, she took out a pristine white morning gown, and tugged at the tasseled bell rope to summon Bonita to fasten the numerous buttons on the dress. In a short while she was ready.

With a last glance in the mirror, she pinched her

cheeks to give them color, and hurried down the staircase to the terrace, where, Bonita informed her, the de Villarins took their morning meal on fine days such as this.

The gardener, Manuel, had proved that a rocky mountainside could bear even the most fragile of blossoms. Gardenias, creamy white and waxy, nodded serene heads in the breeze. Lime trees grew in tubs at intervals along the terrace wall, where they formed a living windbreak on inclement days and offered shade on hotter ones.

She peered over the edge of the little wall, surprised at how high up Villa Hermosa stood. The village below looked like a child's toy, little clusters of homes like bees around a flower of green that was the plaza. Then, several cottages, spaced farther apart, led the way to the white sand and rocks, and beyond, the lapis lazuli blue of the Mediterranean, which even at this early hour shimmered under a dizzying heat haze. Beyond, to the east, rose the mountains, ochre from the sandy earth and olive from hardy spruce and *piñons* that dotted the rugged, craggy slopes. The view took her breath away.

Doña Francesca was seated on a wicker garden chair on the stone-flagged terrace. Her white hair was elegantly swept up over the fine black eyes and, in the severity of her black mourning gown, she was imposing indeed.

Amanda saw, however, with a wave of relief, that she was smiling.

"*Buenos días,* my child! Did you sleep well? Good! Come, sit down by me." She indicated the chair next to her with a wave of her cane. "Tell me, how do you like it here? Do you think you could learn to love Villa Hermosa?"

"It's beautiful, Doña Francesca, and, yes, I'm sure I could! I've never seen such a view! You must be very proud of your home!"

"Indeed. One of the main reasons it was built up here, on the mountains, was to warn our ancestors of the arrival of the dreaded English ships, Señorita Sommers." She laughed.

"Really? I hope that I am not invading too, señora."

"Certainly not. It is our pleasure to have you, my dear, and I hope you will feel free to stay as long as you wish." She looked up as Rita, the housekeeper, came toward them bearing a tray. "Tea or coffee?" Doña Francesca offered.

Amanda chose the coffee, hoping it would clear her head. There was no sign of Don Miguel, and for that she was glad.

As if the old lady had read her thoughts she said, "My son sends you his apologies for not being here on your first morning, but he had to go to Barcelona on business. His gallery is one of his favorite ventures, you know."

Amanda nodded politely and the doña chatted on. Thankfully, she made no mention of Amanda's outrageous behavior the previous night, and Amanda heaved a sigh of relief.

"Tell me, Señorita Sommers—Amanda—why did you come here?"

She looked up, astonished. "I thought Fernando had told you of my capture by pirates, señora?" What did the woman mean?

"Then you would have us believe that Paul Blake's

betrothed would come to Spain simply as a result of a chain of coincidences?" The doña pursed her lips, and her eyes were piercing as they fastened on Amanda's face.

"I'm sorry, señora. I did not realize that you knew who I was. Your son didn't say he had told you, and I decided better not to bring it up, to open old wounds."

"My son did not tell me, Amanda. He probably believes I'm a senile old woman, but I miss very little, believe me! He mentioned your name when he told me what he had done to Señor Blake, that is all. He was most upset when he returned from England. I doubt he even recalls telling me. But I remembered. Are you here to harm my son, señorita?"

She still spoke in a friendly tone, but Amanda was not deceived. Underneath the lightness of her voice, she could sense the old lady's fear.

"Doña Francesca, please, don't worry. I know it seems incredible, but I had no idea that Don Miguel was Fernando's brother, not until we faced each other in Blanes. Believe me, I did not even know onto what shore they dragged me when they rescued me from the sea, let alone plot to gain entry to your home! I admit, I have no liking for your son, señora, but I did not connive to enter your house to get revenge! If you wish, I will leave immediately."

She rose, wiped her mouth with her napkin, and started to cross the terrace. She didn't know where she would go, only that she must leave. She would not stay where she wasn't wanted!

"No! Come here, child." The señora's voice quavered as the order rang out.

Amanda stopped, but didn't turn back to face her.

This thing with Paul dogged her every move, damn him! What was she thinking? It hit her suddenly that she hadn't thought of Paul in weeks! That the longing for him was fading. No, she loved him! If not, all the pain, all the ordeals she had been through, had been for nothing!

"Yes, Señora de Villarin?" she asked coldly.

"Please, Señorita Sommers, please, don't leave! I had to ask you, as a mother who cares for her child. Can you understand that? Miguel torments himself with what he did to Paul Blake, that shot, fired in anger so the man would suffer. He feels guilt enough, señorita! I thought, perhaps, if you still bore some love for the man, that you might wish to harm Miguel. Do you still love Paul Blake?" she added quietly. Her hand on the silver-topped cane trembled slightly.

Her question hung heavily in the silence.

Amanda turned to her. "Doña Francesca, I don't know anymore! I thought I did, but now I wonder if I saw him only as an escape from my loneliness." The hopeless quality of her voice held sincerity. "Whether I do or not, I plan no reprisal, no revenge, on any member of your family. I swear it!"

"Then forgive me for asking, Amanda. May I call you that? Please, let's have more coffee—and no more of this unpleasantness. I believe you. Life has a way of being stranger than say, fairy tales, at times. Am I forgiven?"

Amanda hesitated. Yes, the doña was sincere; she had believed Amanda.

"Yes, of course. Please, tell me more about Villa Hermosa." She reached out and clasped the older woman's hand. Her caress was returned unhesitatingly.

Amanda and Doña Francesca spent a pleasant day touring the magnificent house and grounds. The beautiful, glowing paneled walls, covered with tapestries and portraits, reminded her, with longing, of Christchurch. By *siesta* that afternoon she and Doña Francesca had dissolved any residue of ill feeling between them and replaced it with a fast-growing friendship that was not marred by the difference in either age or country. They had even agreed to help each other with their different languages.

She left the old lady at the door of her room, and went to her room to lie down. The sound of the sea on the rocks below carried to her, and unwillingly she thought of Maria-Elena, Miguel's younger sister, who had leaped from those very rocks to her death.

There could have been no doubt in Elena's mind that she loved Paul. She had not been able to bear to live without him, Amanda thought sadly. Did Amanda love Paul, had they ever loved each other in the way that she'd seen Fernando and Miranda love? Her thoughts were confused when she finally fell asleep.

She had just awoken when she heard the echo of a door slamming far off and rapid, booted footsteps in the hallway.

Hurriedly Amanda got up and pulled a loose wrap over her shift.

Doña Francesca was already dressed and standing on the last step of the curved stairway, trembling violently. Excited voices reached Amanda as she hurried down to see what was happening.

Miguel stood in the doorway, still dressed in his traveling clothes, and across the chest of his white shirt was a dark smear of blood. Something had angered him terribly, for his fists were clenched until the knuckles showed white and his dark eyes were smoldering. The shirt was sodden with sweat across the back, his boots covered with dust.

"Hijo, are you hurt?" Doña Francesca's voice was trembling.

"No, *Mamacita,* please, don't be alarmed. Let's go in here." He led his mother into the study and sat her down.

Amanda settled Doña Francesca gently with a footstool at her feet. Miguel poured himself a glass of sherry and quaffed it in a single, short movement. Amanda could feel the hostility and rage in him as if it were alive. Now Miguel was talking, his anger evident as he did so.

"Three men on horseback waylaid me as I rode home. They intended to kill me. I was forced to kill one of them to escape." He gestured to the rust-colored stain on his shirt. "This is their blood, not mine. Have no fear, *Mamacita.'*

"The rogues!" the old lady exclaimed. "Your picture, it is safe?"

"Sí. They seemed intent only on killing me, but perhaps they intended to rob me afterward. That may have been the case. What puzzles me is that they addressed me by name." He looked intently at Amanda.

"Perhaps," Amanda ventured, "in Barcelona someone saw that you had money and they planned to ambush you? That would be plausible, would it not?"

Miguel nodded. "A little too plausible, señorita! Convincing, too, were it not for this. I pulled it from the finger of the man who tried to kill me, after I had killed him."

She gasped at what Miguel held up between his fingers. It gleamed gold in the afternoon light through the window, a dull, antique gold set about a blood-red garnet. A ring—Paul's ring.

The look on his face chilled her.

Chapter Twenty-Six

"Just what are you implying?" Amanda asked quietly.

Doña Francesca looked wildly from one to the other. Her eyes were full of pain and disillusionment as they rested finally on Amanda.

The look tore at her heart. Miguel, she could see, was barely able to contain his fury, but he fought it with rigid control until Bonita answered his summons.

"Please take Doña Francesca to her room, Bonita, and see that she is made comfortable. And no one is to disturb us in here. Señorita Sommers and I have some business to attend to."

His jaw was set in a hard line, his eyes unwavering and scorching as he said her name. Bonita nodded, her senses warning her of the explosive tension in the room. The old lady protested, but then did as Bonita insisted, resting a fearful glance on her son's face.

"Miguel, I beg you—"

"Please, *Mamacita,* go for now. I will talk with you later."

Amanda defiantly faced him across the room. How dare he imply that she had anything to do with the attempt on his life!

"Well," he asked, "do you have any more plausible

explanations?" His voice held sarcasm.

"Just because the man who attacked you wore a ring similar to Paul's, you immediately jump to the conclusion that I'm plotting to murder you!" Two crimson roses bloomed in her cheeks, and she paced the floor, indignation and rage filling her.

"Not similar—the same!"

"Nonsense! There must be many like it, m'lord!"

"On the contrary, there *is* only one such ring. You see, it bears the de Villarin crest, cut here, into the gold." He held it up. "It was given to Blake by Elena—before he left her."

His words were like a slap in the face.

"I—I see. But I know nothing of what happened to you today. I swear it!" she finished hotly.

"And you came here entirely by chance! Do you expect me to believe that lie too?"

"I don't care what you believe, damn you!" she shouted, her eyes blazing. "As God is my witness, everything happened as Fernando told you. If you don't believe me, then think what you wish. For the second time today, one of your family has called me a liar!"

She turned, and would have left the room. Miguel's grip on her arm flung her around to face him.

"Where the devil do you think you're going?" His brown, almost black, eyes smoldered as he glared at her.

"I'm leaving Villa Hermosa, and where I go is none of your business!" She pulled at the doorknob. He strode between her and the door and kicked it shut behind him.

"You are going nowhere until I say you may,

Señorita Sommers. Or should I call you Blake's whore!"

"What!" She flung herself at him, clawing and scratching like a madwoman. "Damn you! Damn you!" she shrieked.

He took her wrists and held them with a grip of iron to her sides. His face was inches away from hers, unrelenting.

"Does the truth hurt so much, my little spy?"

His expression changed slightly as he looked down at her flushed face, her hair falling about her shoulders like liquid silk, her wrapper open to her waist framing soft, thrusting breasts. Rage, mingled with desire, sent his blood pounding with the urge to take her.

She struggled to free herself, writhing, spitting, squirming like a cornered alleycat in his grasp, her chestnut tresses tangling about them as they struggled.

He forced her down on the flowered carpet, her lovely body heaving as she fought him off, her legs thrashing wildly, scrabbling to stand. The wrapper lay far to one side where it had fallen in the struggle.

"Did you fight Paul for your honor, Amanda?" Miguel asked cruelly. His lips crushed her own soft lips in a savage kiss as she sprawled beneath him, leaving her breathless and seething.

"Paul was more of a gentleman than you will ever be, Don Miguel!" She spat the words.

"Then tell your 'gentleman' this, when—and if—I return you to him!"

He took her shift in his hands and pulled. The cloth screamed as it rent in two. Her honey-soft skin trembled as he touched her naked body. Her breasts surged traitorously under his mouth, the tips swelling between his teeth with a will of their own. She was on fire, afire with rage and a savage, peculiar desire to have him take her, to take her and give him no pleasure in the taking.

Swiftly he thrust the shift above her hips, exposing her to his glance. His eyes held hers as he tugged off his own shirt and breeches. Broad, tanned shoulders bore her down, overcoming her wild efforts to resist him. Arms of steel gathered her up into another embrace, then he covered her mouth in a fierce kiss and plunged into her.

His passion was like a storm, a whirlwind, lifting her into its vortex, spinning her wildly, furiously. Mercilessly he rode her, on and on, until it seemed it would last forever. Her nails clawed into his back, her cries begged him to stop, yet her body demanded he continue with an urgency that terrified her. Down, he thrust her, down into the soft fiber of the Turkish carpet, his lips continuing to assault her tingling breasts, arousing a response she yearned desperately to refuse him.

After what seemed like forever, he stood, towering over her where she lay, still quivering, beneath him. Only a scrap of her shift remained, clasped in her fist. He quickly dressed, then knelt beside her, noticing the brightness of her eyes, the stunned disbelief at her own torn passions in her eyes.

The heated anger had gone from his face, driven out by his savage taking of her. But the cold fury in his eyes still terrified her. He thrust the golden ring into her hand and clamped her trembling fingers about it. He grinned mockingly.

"No wonder Blake wanted you, *pequeña!* The face

and body of an angel, and a passion in those cold, English veins that would outburn Vesuvius! The ring's your thirty pieces of silver, Amanda. And make no plans about leaving Villa Hermosa. You are staying for as long as it takes me to find Paul Blake and kill him, as I should have done before! There'll be no little Judas to warn him this time."

After he left, she pulled on the wrapper hurriedly and peered around the door. The long corridor was silent and empty, the faint sounds of dishes clattering reached her ears as she sped through the hallway and back up to her room.

Closing the door behind her, she leaned upon it and waited until her chest had stopped heaving, until her limbs had ceased their shaking. The mirror threw back a reflection of herself that she scarcely knew. A wild mass of tumbled hair, eyes that shone overbrightly beneath dark, stormy brows and lashes, lips turned deep crimson from his bruising kisses. She even looked like a Jezebel now, after what he'd done to her, she thought bitterly. There had been none of the gentleness of James's lovemaking that first time nor the tenderness that followed. Only savage, animal coupling, hatred, lust. She had to leave! No power on earth could force her to stay.

Furious tears fell as she tugged on Miranda's blouse and skirt and flung the wrapper and shredded shift far out of sight. Then she took the ring and hurled it from the open casement, down, way down, to the rocks below. Thirty pieces of silver! She seethed.

She slipped from the room and to the front door at the foot of the stairs. There was no one about. She squeezed through the few inches she'd opened, terrified the hinges would groan and give her away.

The sky was darkening above, streaked with pinks and oranges, the pines black silhouettes against its fiery hues. She ran down the driveway, looking back only once at the villa. Candles had been lit in the salon. They appeared warm, cozy, welcoming. But not for her.

The massive wrought-iron gate towered before her, intricately twisted into the de Villarin coat-of-arms. She clutched the ring of the gate, tugged at it, tried with both hands to wrest the double gates apart. They rattled loudly, but did not open. Minutes passed, and still she refused to admit she had failed.

"I believe you need this," Miguel said, urging his horse forward from the shadow of the pines.

He looked down at her mockingly, a huge black key brandished in his fist.

"I said you will not leave unless I wish it, Señorita Sommers. And I do not wish it—yet." He extended an arm. "Will you accept a ride back to the house?" His voice was acid with sarcasm.

She stormed past his outstretched hand, her angry movements causing the horse to rear slightly, and fled back to the villa.

Chapter Twenty-Seven

Miguel was scowling as he surveyed the strewn pile of papers across the desk. Damn! He hated this part of the business. If given a choice he'd leave all this to Esteban, his steward, and devote his own time to collecting paintings for the gallery.

He cursed again and flung the quill down, ink splattering as he did so. What the devil was wrong with him? he wondered, running a hand through his crisp, black hair. He couldn't put his mind to anything anymore, it seemed, not since that damned afternoon he'd taken Amanda Sommers here, on this very rug. God, the feel of that satiny flesh beneath him, those graceful arms and slender legs! He knew he'd made his anger an excuse to take her, knew he'd wanted her from the first, but it had been even far sweeter than he'd expected. What would it be like, he wondered idly, to have her come to him warm, willing, and eager? He would never know.

He felt anger surge through him at the thought of her and Blake together. Well, he'd deal with Blake soon enough, then the woman could go where she wished. Only then would he be rid of the whole shoddy business.

He glanced at the clock. Good, in a short while Esteban would be here. Perhaps then Miguel could take his mind off that damned woman.

"Come in, *amigo!*" Miguel reached forward and shook the other man's hand.

Esteban looked at Miguel's littered desk and laughed. "Not having much luck, are you? Here are the books for the almond orchards. Why don't you give me the rest of the accounts and I'll go over them for you?" He was fair for a Spaniard, with wise gray eyes that missed little. "Eh, what's wrong, Miguel?" he asked shrewdly.

Miguel briefly explained to him what had happened on his return from Barcelona.

"I think you're right," Esteban said finally after Miguel had finished. "It was no chance attack. Coupled with the ring, there's just too much to point to it being deliberate."

"Wait, there's more." Miguel described the girl's unbelievable story and subsequent arrival at Villa Hermosa. His anger resurfaced as he did so, and his words were heated.

Esteban whistled, his eyes narrowing. "I don't blame you for not believing her. That is *some* story."

Miguel nodded. "So you see, he has sent his little spy here, to my very house! Damned nerve—he takes me for a fool."

"Then he will learn otherwise, eh? Do you want me to ride into Barcelona and find out what I can about your attackers? You can't go; they know you. It'd be too risky."

Miguel nodded. *"Sí,* that sounds good. But be

careful, good friends are hard to find." He grinned.

Esteban laughed. "The señorita, she is pretty?" he asked suddenly.

"Why do you ask?" Miguel looked wary.

"Because, my friend, it is unlikely you'd issue orders that she is not to leave the villa grounds—unless her charms are such that they demand imprisonment." He caught the guilty look in Miguel's eyes and laughed again. "Manuel told me you had ordered the gates locked at all times."

"Yes, but for my peace of mind, only," Miguel insisted. "The attack on me was so soon after she arrived here—she *had* to have slipped away to warn Blake that I was planning on leaving the villa. I can't risk her warning him again."

"No, I suppose not. But I ask you again, is she pretty?"

"Does the sun set every evening? Yes, you damned rascal, she's pretty. If you like wide, innocent brown eyes, skin like milk and roses, chestnut hair that traps the light like spun gold or fiery fingers! She's pretty—but I wouldn't trust her one inch from my sight!"

"Then it's lucky she's so easy on the eyes, eh? That close, you might otherwise end up blind!" Esteban snorted at the scowl Miguel shot him. "She's in your blood, *sí?"*

"Sí, like a fever that cannot be quenched. Tell me, did you ever feel that way about a woman?"

"Once."

"And how did you put out the fire?" Miguel asked eagerly.

"I married her, señor!" Esteban chuckled at the horrified expression on his friend's face. "Come, tell me about these men. What did they look like?"

Amanda wandered the corridors of Villa Hermosa, restless and seething. Arrogant, that's what he was, arrogant and an animal to boot! How dare he imprison her here like a—a concubine in some sultan's harem! And then to expect her to dine with Doña Francesca and himself as if the situation were entirely normal. Blast him, it was absolutely ridiculous! Color flooded her cheeks.

She retraced her footsteps to her room and sat down at the dressing table. She began to pin up her hair, stopped, flung the pins down. No! She'd take her meals up here from now on, and if he didn't like it he could go hang. Prisoners, after all, were under no obligation to please their gaolers.

She removed her gown and lay on the bed in her cotton shift. Devil take you, de Villarin! she fumed. Even her body had betrayed her for his touch, had rebeled against her vow to remain unmoved and aloof from his savage lovemaking. She was not deceived by his words or his anger. He'd used the situation to give himself an excuse to take her. She'd seen the desire flare up in his eyes like fire. Hypocrite! He was no better than other men, for all his talk of honor.

"Señorita Sommers?" The tapping on the door continued.

"Come in, Bonita."

"Bueno, you are awake and rested. If you will sit here, señorita, I shall do your hair, yes?"

She replaced the scattered pins in their box, casting a sidelong glance at Amanda.

"No, thank you. I shall not be down for dinner—or

any other meal from now on. I'm staying here. You know that your Don Miguel is holding me here against my will, do you not?"

The maid's downcast eyes confirmed that she did.

"Sí," Bonita admitted. "And it is none of my business, señorita, but Don Miguel, he will be very angry when I tell him you refuse to dine with him and the *Doña.* Perhaps I could tell him you are feeling ill?" she finished eagerly.

"There's no need. I'm not afraid of his anger! Just tell him that I refuse to share a table at which he is seated."

Bonita's expression was horrified. "Very well, if you are sure that is what you wish. . . ." she said doubtfully.

After the maid left, Amanda smiled triumphantly. There, she'd show him she was not chattel to be ordered about at whim!

She snuggled under the coverlet, imagining Miguel's face when Bonita told him. His black eyes would flash; his jaw would harden with displeasure. But she would not go down, no matter *what* threats he commanded Bonita to make. A little laugh burst from her lips. *Touché,* Don Miguel. The thought had no sooner entered her head when the door burst inward.

Amanda scrabbled to a sitting position so quickly that she cracked her head on the bedpost. Miguel loomed over her. He was grinning as she tried to cover herself.

"So, you refuse to join me, do you? Well, it seems I must persuade you otherwise."

"You will not," Amanda said firmly, far more firmly than she felt. She'd not expectd him to respond to her message in person.

"I will stay here then, and have a tray sent up from

the kitchen."

Her eyes widened with alarm as he reached down and scooped her into his arms.

"What are you doing? Put me down immediately!" she shrieked.

"What I am doing is taking you down to dinner. And no, I will not put you down." Purposefully he strode across the room, out into the corridor and started down the staircase.

"But I'm not dressed," she wailed.

"Sí, Amanda, that is true." His eyes danced wickedly, his lips curved in a wide smile. "But how lucky for me, *no?* Good food, ancient wines, and a feast for the eyes, too. Ah, Amanda, the gods are smiling on this poor mortal!" They were almost at the foot of the stairs.

She kicked her legs and tried to squirm from his grasp, but he held her even tighter. The white shift was riding up her thighs now. "Very well!" she agreed angrily. "Take your hands off me and I will get dressed and come down." She'd barricade the door, this time. That would show him.

"Sorry, *pequeña,* I don't trust you. You'll go up the same way you came down."

He turned about and carried her back to the top of the stairs like a sack of potatoes. Inside her room he let her down and closed the door behind them. Her bluff had been called, damn him!

She dragged a gown from the armoire, inwardly furious. The humiliation of it, of having to dress in front of that beast, on top of everything else!

"Don't bother with the gown, sweet. It will be a waste of our precious time if I have to take it off you." He came behind her and tugged the garment from her hands. His arms reached around her and cupped her breasts, weighing them in his tanned hands. His thumbs brushed against the nipples until they flowered beneath his touch. Firm lips nuzzled the fine hairs at the nape of her neck, sending shivers the length of her spine where it pressed against the broadness of his chest.

"Stop it! You told me to dress for dinner, and I will do so!" She thrust forward, trying to throw him off balance, but his hands continued to cup her, and she could not.

She wriggled sideways. Miguel turned her smoothly to face him. She opened her mouth to curse him. His own mouth covered hers in a lingering kiss, with lips that tasted vaguely of sweet, heady wines. The scent of him was masculine, a mixture of sandalwood, the wine, his own scent. She closed her eyes, lost wholly to his kiss for several seconds before she realized what she had done. She pushed him away guiltily.

"How dare you! You said we would go downstairs, and we will!"

"We will not! I'm afraid my appetite has flown—to be replaced by, shall we say, a different appetite?"

He pulled her suddenly back into his arms, ignoring her fists as they pummeled at his chest as if they were merely the harmless fluttering of butterfly wings. He held her head between his palms and kissed her soundly again.

Amanda felt her limbs grow weak and heavy under his embrace. The will to fight him was still there, but ebbing as surely as the tides. How could his kiss arouse her so when she hated him with all of her being?

Quivering, she stood like a lovely marble statue as he unfastened the straps of her shift and pulled it from her. Her hands fluttered to cover her nakedness. Softly, he commanded her to be still.

God, she was a vision before him, that narrow waist, those proud, rose-tipped breasts aroused from his kisses! Her hair was a river of burnished light, her lips full and parted as she watched him fearfully from wide, sable eyes. He dropped to the bed and pulled her onto his knees. His kisses left a brand upon her breasts, seared her as surely as a torch as they traversed the soft slope of her belly.

"Please, Miguel, please!" she moaned softly, desperately.

"'Please stop,' *querida*—or 'please, Miguel, go on?'" He paused, a teasing expression on his face.

"Yes—no, I don't know anymore!" she wailed.

She sighed deeply as he pressed her down onto the bed. His caresses were creating sensations she never knew existed, throbbing pulses that made her blood sing, her flesh tingle, her heart beat wildly. She sensed that there was more to this pleasure, wanted to discover that ecstasy she had dreamed of, but never experienced.

Miguel entered her. She gasped and strove to push him away, one last show of resistance that she knew was only a token resistance. He moved gently at first, each thrust building the pleasure within her. Her hands reached up, tangled in the crisp, dark curls of his hair, drawing him near. His cheek was against her own.

Now her cries were of pleasure. He moved deeper, gathering her to him and holding her possessively against the dark mat of his chest. His kisses were ardent, hungry, arousing her until she felt she would explode from the heat radiating through her. She throbbed, yearning for release.

It came like a dam bursting through its banks, flooding her with the tumultuous ecstasy of its release. She cried out, a long joyous cry that brought Miguel to his own fulfillment.

He shuddered and lay beside her, playing with one long strand of her hair, pressing kisses to her shoulder. The shadows in the room lengthened, the sky deepened to a deep, inky-blue. The moon rose in silver splendor.

Miguel laughed softly as the last light fell on her rosy-flushed face and half-closed eyes.

"Do you still wish to go down?"

She shook her head dreamily and yawned with satisfaction. Then she snuggled deeper into the curve of his body.

"A pity," he said with mock sadness. "I had hoped to give you cause to fight me, with the same conclusion in mind."

"Again?" Her eyes opened suddenly, wide velvet pools of surprise.

"Again, *mi pequeña estrellita,* my little star," he murmured.

She sat up then, instantly wide awake. The totally unexpected tenderness angered her somehow. He seemed to have forgotten their situation, captive and lusting gaoler, to be treating her as if she had willingly succumbed to his lovemaking! How dare he!

She crawled from the bed, winding a sheet about her, and went to the casement and stared out, unseeing, confusion filling her.

"Come back to bed, *querida.* The night is cool—and

I alone can warm you!" Miguel said, teasing laughter in his voice.

"You flatter your prowess, Don Miguel!" she flung back at him haughtily.

She saw his teeth flash white in the shadows as he grinned.

"You seemed—content—my sweet!" Miguel responded, yawning lazily.

"Content! Not so!" she lied. "Your embraces leave me cold, Miguel. Your touch revolts me! I *pretended* pleasure, m'lord, to hasten the end, for I would *die* rather than sleep the night with you!" Her voice was triumphant, mocking.

"Then do so!" he roared. He knew she lied for he knew well a woman's ways in passion, but her brazen denial of her pleasure—when even now her eyes still bore that heavy-lidded, sated look—infuriated him. "Do so—for I will take you again and again, as many times as I wish, dead or alive!" Damn her, he would break her spirit, somehow. "Perhaps my touch would not revolt you, Amanda, if you imagined I were Paul!"

He was rewarded for his killing remark by a shocked and furious gasp.

Chapter Twenty-Eight

"Doña Francesca, please! I have to talk to you!" Amanda hurried after the doña.

This was the first chance in two weeks that she'd had to talk to Miguel's mother without his presence. Two weeks of hurt, reproachful looks from the older woman across the table that were like thorns in her heart. She had liked the doña very much those first few hours before her son had put a stop to the friendship with his accusations. She had to convince her that she was telling the truth.

Doña Francesca turned, an anxious expression on her face. She looked about her fearfully. "My son will be angry with you, señorita. He has forbidden you to speak to me, no? For myself, I do not care, but I fear what he will do to you!"

"But I have to convince you, señora, that all those things he accuses me of are not true! When did I have the opportunity to sneak out, to tell Paul's men of Miguel's plans to ride to Barcelona? I had arrived only the previous afternoon!" She sighed. "Come, Doña Francesca, do you believe what Miguel has told you?"

"At first, I must be honest, Amanda, with what we had talked about that morning, I did wonder if what he had implied could be true. But, now, no. I do believe you. Why would you *need* to fabricate such a story to reach Villa Hermosa, to pretend drowning? No, Fernando told me of your injuries, the burns, even the marks of the pirate's lash. You would not, could not, have gone to such lengths to gain access to my house.

"Señorita—Amanda—Miguel would not believe you, whatever he discovered to the contrary. He does not want to. His anger at you feeds his desire for revenge on Paul Blake. He must keep that anger burning, my dear, because he intends to kill the man, and my Miguelito is not one to kill in cold blood." She sighed and sank down into a chair, her hand on her chest. "It is all so upsetting, Amanda. I feel for you, too. Yes, Bonita has told me that he has—forced his attentions on you. I cannot tell you how I have begged him to leave you alone, to let you return to England. But he seems driven, driven by a demon inside him that will not let him rest!"

"Doña Francesca, perhaps you should lie down for a little while? You are so pale!" Amanda murmured, her voice concerned.

"Come with me to my room then, child. I must tell you how it was before, with Miguel. He was not always so stern, so cold."

In the doña's room, Amanda settled the tiny woman in the vast bed, plumping up the pillows and fussing over her until the doña waved her back. The huge, dark furniture made her appear even frailer, Amanda thought.

"You know, Miguelito, he is a good son, a fine brother. After my husband's death, he took over all the estates, all the work his father had done before him. It was a heavy burden for any man, and he was only a lad of sixteen. He would work at the accounts for hours, something he loathes, searching for ways to keep the de Villarins from ruin. Yes, for while his father was ill those several years, the businesses *were* floundering, and we had no Esteban Soreno to advise us then. Yes, Miguel hated it, but he did it! He was the don, head of the village and of this house, not only in name but also where it counts—in their respect and in their love. He tried to be a father, too, for Fernando and for Maria-Elena. I think his fear that he would fail drove him to be sterner with them than he might otherwise have been, especially with Elena. You have met Fernando, my happy-go-lucky son! He listened or he did not, as the mood took him or as he wished. But Elena! She worshiped Miguel, tried to please him in every way. She did not complain when he turned away her suitors—and she had many, for she was a lovely girl. Fortune hunters, he called them, and I expect some of them were. But then Señor Blake came here, and Elena fell under his spell."

Amanda nodded, patting Doña Francesca's hand. "Don't go on, it is making you upset!" Her voice shook. She knew the spell that Elena had fallen under.

The older woman's face was tinged blue about the lips, and her hands trembled even more than usual.

"Rest now, please. We can talk some other time."

"No, Amanda, I have to tell it all now. You must understand *why* Miguel is the way he is, then perhaps you can forgive him.

"It was not long before we noticed the way Elena looked at Paul, the way her dark eyes would light up every time he spoke to her, or when he entered a room.

A fool could have seen she loved him! Then Miguel came upon the two of them, kissing, on the terrace. He was furious, *aiee,* I have never seen him more angered!"

Amanda nodded, saying nothing. The doña seemed to have a need to unburden herself, as if the pain of her memories festered like a wound, and that the telling would drain and cleanse it, as nothing else had.

"Elena and Miguel quarreled bitterly. She told him of her love for Paul, that he had asked her to marry him. Miguel swore that if she married Paul, he would see that not one penny of her inheritance from her father—money that Miguel himself had recouped after our losses—would ever fall into Paul's hands! That the two of them would be cast out to live on whatever Paul possessed and not a whit more. For the first time Elena defied him, and said that she didn't care, that Paul loved her, and that was all she wanted from life. Miguel stormed from the house in a rage, and, as always, when he is angry, off to Barcelona.

"After he had cooled down somewhat, he returned, and told Elena that he had been wrong, that she should have all that was due her, even if she married Blake. You see, his tempers are short lived with those he loves. But it was too late! Elena had told Paul everything—and he had left. Oh, yes, he promised to return, saying he would leave only for a short while to give Miguel time to come to his senses and make peace with Elena. What we did not know was that Elena was carrying his child. *Aiee,* how she must have trusted him to return to her.

"When Miguel discovered Elena's condition, he realized that Paul had only used her, his sister, an innocent child of sixteen, who had believed herself in love and loved in return. He swore that he would bring Paul back to marry Elena, to give their child a name, if nothing more. He left to find him. Shortly after, my daughter threw herself from the terrace to the rocks below. It took a great while for the letter to reach Miguel, telling of her death. I—I believe it was only a short while before he learned of Paul Blake's plans to marry you! The rest you already know."

"Thank you, Doña Francesca. I am glad you have told me everything. I'll call Consuela to see to you. Try to sleep, now."

Amanda turned to leave, pondering what she had heard, her face serious. It had explained so much.

"Señorita Sommers!" Doña Francesca's voice shook. "Can you ever forgive him?"

"I—I will try, I promise you. Sleep well."

The doña did not come down to dinner that evening, so Amanda and Miguel dined alone, glaring at each other across the massive expanse of table in stony silence.

When he finally spoke, the silence had been so great that she dropped her fork in surprise.

"I have a little outing planned, just the two of us!" He winked wickedly.

She ignored his expression and shrugged. "Am I supposed to say 'thank you, m'lord?'" she snapped. "It is only since I came to Villa Hermosa that I have found freedom to be a reward, rather than a due. I don't think I care to participate in your 'outing'!"

"Well whatever you'd *rather* do, *mi inglesa,"* he said sarcastically, "you are coming riding with me. There's a bay, a little cove not far along the coast that I think you'd enjoy. Be ready by nine, or else I shall be forced to come and assist you to dress—again!"

His meaning was not lost on Amanda, and she shot him a murderous glance that would have withered most men. Crimson color flooded her cheeks.

"Then I hope the horse throws you!" she seethed.

"I doubt it," he rejoined, grinning again in that exasperating way. "He is much better trained than you, my little filly. Should I escort you to your room?" His dark eyes twinkled.

"No, I think I can find it by myself," Amanda retorted. "It *is* the one with the bars and the chains, is it not?" She pushed back her chair hurriedly and fled—though during the brisk walk up to her room, she listened twice to see if he was following her. Good, she was safe! She locked the door, undressed, and brushed out her hair.

In the shadows, she lay thinking about what the doña had told her. She could not lie to a friend, could not promise to forgive her son. She had said she would try. But *nothing* would make her forgive the way he treated her, taking her at his will and against her wishes. Nor would she forgive him for the way he'd forced such violent responses from her own body, as if it and that damned man were collaborating against her! No, never! And tomorrow he planned to have her ride to some deserted spot with him, alone, and there to take her again, no doubt. Well, enough time had passed. She'd done little enough to get herself out of this situation, now it was time to try again!

The hallway was deserted as she peered into it over the balustrade. Voices carried to her from the study, Miguel's and another. He was talking to Esteban Soreno, his steward. So she could not make her exit via the main door. The kitchen entrance was out of the question, too, with the servants busy clearing the dishes from dinner. There was only one other way.

She turned back into the room, crossed it, and flung open the casement. Far below the light from the full moon above touched the waves with silver. The tide was going out, leaving a narrow ribbon of white sand between the rocks and the sea. If she did it fast enough, she could climb down, round the cliff upon which Villa Hermosa stood, find a track up into the village, and be gone before the tide came in. Then, freedom!

It would take courage and the surefootedness of a goat. The courage, she had, the surefootedness, she didn't know, but was determined to find out. It was a different prospect to climbing trees, or even hanging from a rope where the water might have cushioned her fall, as the climb from the *Gypsy Princess* to the *Sea Dragon* had been. She gulped, almost deciding against it. Then she remembered how Miguel had been so cocksure that there was no way in which she could avoid the dreaded ride.

"Ha! That is what you think, *Señor Burro!* You may ride, but you will ride alone," she whispered gleefully.

Determination goading her, she quickly selected one of Elena's divided riding skirts, a dark-blue one of velvet, high boots to protect her against the sharper rocks, and a long-sleeved lilac blouse, the darkest she could find. She didn't think anyone would see her, for only the rear of the house perched on the cliff top, while the rest was fronted by the grounds and the mountain-side, but she wouldn't take any chances. Finally, she drew on the pearls-and-topaz pendant, kissing it for good luck.

Here we go, Amanda, she breathed softly, it is now or never. She opened the casement and stepped through it onto the wrought-iron balcony, testing the trailing vines that wove in between the rungs. They were not strong enough! The vines tore in her hands when she pulled. She stepped back inside the room, searching for something, anything, that would serve as a rope.

Sheets! Frantically she flung back the coverlet and hauled the top and bottom sheets from the bed. Then, she replaced the coverlet tidily. If Bonita came in, she would believe her in some other part of the villa. She ripped the sheets into wide, long strips, knotting them securely as Jeb had taught her as cabin boy aboard the *Sea Dragon.* She grinned, remembering how Aggie had always said that no knowledge was ever wasted. How right she had been! Knotting the very end of her makeshift rope tightly about the widest paling of the balcony, she fed the rope down over the edge, then, after closing the casement behind her, she clambered over the balcony rail.

Miguel's face wore a strange mixture of expressions as Esteban entered the study, almost gloating, partially afraid, as if he could not decide which mood held him. His fists clenched and unclenched constantly.

Esteban noted his friend's expression, but said nothing regarding it. "Did you tell her?" he queried.

"Yes—she fell for it—but not without a display of temper, as usual," he grinned ruefully.

"Well, as I told you, the men that attacked you are here, in the village. I ate their dust all the way from Barcelona!" Esteban smiled and smacked his lips as

Miguel handed him a full measure of brandy. "This will no doubt wash it away, though!"

"You are sure they suspect nothing?"

"No. Señor Cristobal recognized them by your description immediately. Seems they questioned him pretty thoroughly about how often you had stayed there, and so on. So I oiled his tongue with a coin or two, and he sent his stableboy to find them and pass on the message as if it came directly from him."

"*Bueno.* What did you have him say?" Miguel asked, drinking deeply from his own brandy glass.

"Just what I told you this morning. That he'd heard they were after you and he had it on good authority that you intended to go riding tomorrow morning, alone and unarmed, and that if they paid the price, he could tell them where and when."

"So, the trap is set, for both our quarry." A shadow crossed Miguel's face.

"You're hoping she is innocent, aren't you?" Esteban had read Miguel's look correctly.

"*Sí,* I suppose so. No! Damn it, I don't care either way. That temper—she'd make Shakespeare's Kate look like a lamb! She's Paul's woman—and he's welcome to her."

Esteban knew him well. Miguel's words failed to convince him. "Then I'll get back to the *cantina* in the village. How about you?"

"I'll watch the walls and the gate."

"The walls! Miguel, she's a girl, not a spider! Those walls are of solid rock and close to ten feet high! Her only escape is through the gate, which you've left unlocked. Why bother with patroling the walls?"

Miguel snorted. "If you knew her, Esteban, you'd

not question my plans. She's a lady, in some ways, but in others she has all the wiles and tricks of a street urchin. No, I'll watch the walls, too—or risk kicking myself in the morning."

Esteban slapped his back, laughing. "Very well. I hope the night ends as you wish it, one way or another. *Buen suerte!*"

"And to you, too. Good luck, *amigo!*"

After the steward left, Miguel went to the heavy draperies and pulled them apart slightly. The moonlit courtyard was empty, and beyond by the gates there were only shadows.

He drew his father's pair of silver-handled pistols from their rack above the fireplace, and loaded them with care. His body felt heavy with dread as he tamped down the powder firmly. Then he donned his darkest cape, and slipped out of the doorway and into the night.

Chapter Twenty-Nine

Amanda smiled as she clambered, arm over arm, down the knotted sheets. It had been easy, far, far, easier than she would have believed possible. Her heart was in her mouth for a few seconds as she finished the worst part—where the rope hung down over the drawing-room window—but, luckily, it was dark inside and empty, and her spirits soared.

There was an incline next, where it looked as if the winds had eroded the rocky edge. She left the rope dangling and scuttled backward down the slope like a crab. Now came the hard part. A rocky wall of vertical cliff yawned at her heels.

She backed over the edge cautiously, holding on tightly with her hands, while feeling the way with her feet. Only when she was sure her toeholds were secure did she move her hands. The boots were too big, but necessary with the razor-sharp edges of the rocks. She wished fervently she had gloves to protect her scratched palms.

She moved her right foot down, reached, found a toehold and burrowed in. Now the left foot. Good! She repeated the process, going down cautiously at the speed of a snail. It was hard work, the exertion making her pant. She glanced down at the waves beating against the rocks below, throwing silver spray up into the night. She looked away hurriedly. Don't look down, she told herself, never look down. She inched across, searching desperately for any niche that would hold her weight, resting every few steps, spread-eagle, with the rocks against her cheek, to catch her breath. The wild pounding of her heart was like a drum in her ears. The wind blew gusts of cold air that chilled her despite her heavy clothing, rippling her hair this way and that like a flowing pennant. Its strands kept whipping across her face. Damn! Why hadn't she thought to pin it up?

A rock and a shower of dirt bounced down from above her, loosened by her climb. It plummeted to the beach below. She could not hear it hit the ground and for that she was glad.

Grim determination egged her on, and the thought of Miguel de Villarin taking her against her will, of keeping her a prisoner for his lust, was all the spur she needed to goad her into continuing. Halfway! It was too late to go back, too late to do anything but grit her teeth and finish what she'd started. And her prize would be freedom, freedom from Miguel, the pirates, even James, and memory, perhaps.

She lifted her hand from the rock and shifted it downward. Her left foot followed, then her right hand. Suddenly, the wind swirled her hair across her face, blinding her. She tossed her head, trying to free her eyes, and that one jerky movement cost her her balance! Her fingers slipped free of one of their holds, her feet of their niches.

A scream tore from her, lost in the wind as she swung

violently by one arm. Panic froze her. Her back-flung eyes saw the sea beneath, the teethlike rocks that would impale her if she fell. The muscles in her shoulder tore under her weight, sending spasms of agony through her. She whimpered, fighting back tears, refusing to admit she could not hold on, that she was going to fall.

Her fingers started to slide from their knobbly grip. She could feel it slipping away beneath them as if time had slowed the momentum. And then her fingers clawed air, clutched wildly at the empty night air. For an instant she hung suspended, then she was dropping with terrifying speed. A shrill cry rent from her lungs as she hurtled down.

Miguel paced restlessly, hugging the shadows of the wall that encircled the villa gardens on three sides.

For seven hours he had kept his vigil, feeling relief and concern wash over him alternately. He had misjudged her, falsely accused her, apart from the physical assaults he'd been driven to in the name of revenge. And all the time she had sworn she was innocent, and he had refused to listen. He cursed himself bitterly and at length.

"Nothing, eh, *hijo?*" Manuel's grip on his shoulder startled him.

He shook his head. "No, not yet, my old friend."

The gardener's teeth flashed white in the darkness. "You look relieved, Miguelito?"

Miguel shrugged. *"Sí y no.* I had hoped to put an end to all of this tonight. Now it seems it must continue at least until tomorrow."

"Sí. But why torture yourself any longer? Señorita Elena is gone. All of this cannot bring her back, eh?" He patted Miguel on the shoulder in a fatherly fashion,

and took another puff on his clay pipe.

"Blake has sworn to kill me, Manuel. When one of us is dead, then it will be over. Listen, did you hear something?"

The old man cocked his ears and listened intently. "An owl, Miguelito, just an owl. Come back to the house. It will be morning soon." Manuel shuffled off back down the shadow of the wall, humming as he went.

Dawn found Miguel still standing by the gate when Esteban rode up on his black mare. Miguel swung open the gates and he clattered through.

Their eyes met. "Nothing?" Esteban asked.

"Nothing," Miguel answered. His voice was full of fatigue, but held a certain satisfaction.

"Then you will let the girl go?"

"I suppose so. But I will personally see her on to an England-bound ship, and not leave her side until the vessel lifts anchor!" He laughed. "And you?"

"The men spent the night carousing. They were very drunk by the small hours. They didn't appear to be waiting for anyone, though. Paul wasn't with them."

"Damn! I thought it might be too much to hope for. He's hired them to do his dirty work. We can talk over breakfast." He smiled. "And I shall finally introduce you to my little volcano of an English miss!"

His step was light as he ushered Esteban before him into the house.

Rita, the housekeeper, had set breakfast on the small table in the salon. The smell of hot sweet rolls and coffee filled the room. A bowl of colorful fresh fruits was the only centerpiece on the sky-blue damask cloth.

Rita came behind them pouring fragrant coffee into

their cups, clucking at the early hour of the meal.

The draperies had been drawn, and birds were singing in the purple-flowered vines at the windows, the sky outside still streaks of pinks and oranges and violet.

Miguel's spirits were obviously high this morning for some reason, Esteban thought, and he believed he knew what it was. "Well, what time does the delectable Señorita Sommers raise her pretty head from the pillow and join us?"

"Soon, my friend. Be patient. And don't forget you are a married man!"

"My little Destina would not let me forget, señor! Not with her belly out again. I swear she grows more with each child. This one must be a giant." He laughed. "Judging by the number of *dragées* she insists she must have every day!"

"Sugar plums? Another girl for you, Esteban, to add to your harem!"

"*Por Díos,* I hope not. Six women in one family is enough for any poor soul to contend with, Miguel."

Miguel grinned. "And think of the dowries in years to come, *amigo,* five, perhaps six! Your pockets will be empty, I wager."

He finished his coffee, and rose to pull the bell rope.

Bonita answered his summons. "*Sí,* Don Miguel?" She was relieved to see the don in such good humor, and flashed him a warm smile.

"Tell the señorita she must get up. The sun is high already. And, Bonita—tell her the don said, 'Please.'"

He winked at Esteban, and Bonita laughed delightedly and hurried off.

"How long before the little one arrives?"

"Three more months. An eternity of aching backs and ups and downs of temper that leave me weak! *Aiee,* poor Destina, she waddles like a duck and cackles like a goose."

"Shame, Esteban, when I saw her last she glowed like a jewel, like a blossoming peach."

"Sí, but what good is a peach when you cannot pluck it, *amigo?"* He rolled his eyes and groaned.

Miguel feigned shock. "Esteban, you rogue, I believe after the child is delivered I must send you away on business—or else your impatience will reward you with reason for a seventh dowry!"

The men roared with laughter. Bonita hovered by the door, wringing her hands nervously.

"Well, Bonita, what did she say?"

"Don Miguel, I did not give her your message. I—"

"Well, out with it, Bonita." Esteban laughed. "Did she bid you tell the señor to go to Hades before she'd breakfast with us?"

"No, señor Esteban. I did not tell her because—because she is not there! She has vanished. I searched the entire house, even awoke your Lady Mother, Señor. The señorita has gone." She stopped, a fearful expression in her eyes.

Miguel charged from the room and leaped up the stairway two or three treads at a time, and burst through Amanda's door with a force that threw it crashing against the wall. Esteban was right behind him.

"How did she do it?" Miguel wondered incredulously. "I did not leave the wall or the gate—not once!" His face was black with rage.

"I believe your answer is here, Miguel." Esteban had

stepped out onto the balcony and pointed to the knotted sheet secured to the rail. He yanked up the entire length of the makeshift rope and whistled softly. "By all the saints, Miguel, this rope could never have reached all the way to the beach. She must have climbed the rest of the way down! Miguel, I had doubted you, but I swear, to attempt it, she must be *some* woman!"

Miguel said nothing. The look on his face caused the astonishment to fade from Esteban's own face, too.

"Do you think she made it, señor?"

Miguel shrugged. "I don't know. But I intend to find out."

Esteban could not mistake the coldness in his voice. If the señorita had survived, Esteban did not want to be there when they faced each other!

Chapter Thirty

Amanda moved her legs gingerly, an inch or two at a time. One sudden move could send her hurtling from the narrow shelf to her death. Thank God, at least she was alive! She could hardly move her right arm with its torn muscles. It lay wedged beneath her, fuzzy with pain and with pins and needles. Her hip and side felt badly bruised from the shock of the impact, but miracle of miracles! it didn't feel as if anything was broken.

She wondered how long it would be before they found her? Yes, she knew Miguel would come, if only to make quite sure she was dead. It might be morning before anyone noticed her disappearance. She'd planned it all too well, she thought ruefully. How many hours could she stay here, without moving or falling asleep? Her mouth was dry and tasted foul with fear. She peered down below without turning her head. Dear God, it was a long way down! She could feel the panic turn her limbs to water. Perspiration started above her upper lip and on her palms. How could she prevent herself from sleeping? Her aching body yearned for rest.

She started to yell, "Help! Somebody, help!" No one answered her cries, but she kept on until her throat felt hoarse. Then she started to sing: lullabies, sea chanties she'd learned aboard ship, anything that would keep her mind alert. It worked for a while, until she'd exhausted her repertoire and boredom crept into the game, a dangerous companion to sleep.

She started counting the stars, stopped when she realized the monotony was exactly the reason some people counted sheep to aid their slumber. Instead, she tried naming the constellations. There was the Big Dipper, there the Little Dipper, the Plough, the North Star. It reminded her of James. Poor, dear James! Why was it one only realized the worth of someone after they'd gone? She supposed death had a way of stripping the sham and the trappings of life away, leaving only the things that held true worth unchanged. And those were all that mattered. She admitted to herself for the first time that perhaps she hadn't really loved Paul. Infatuation, that's what it had been. And he was a solution to her loneliness, nothing more. Then what he had said that last time at the Figurehead Tavern had been no lie!

She saw it all with terrible clarity now. What a fool she'd been! None of the terrible things that had happened to her would have occurred were it not that her pride had been deaf to what he'd said. Tears trickled from her eyes. All of it, her kidnapping, everything, had been her own stupid fault.

She was still awake somehow when dawn arrived in all its glory. The few times she'd started to doze her fear had wakened her more thoroughly than any songs or counting. It had been a long, terrifying night. Her hopes soared. If she could just hold on for an hour or two more—Bonita would find her missing when she brought her water to bathe. Just two more hours!

It was less than that when she looked up and saw Esteban and Miguel peering down over the edge of the cliff.

"Are you hurt?" the steward yelled.

"I'm only bruised, but I can't turn, there's no room!" she yelled back. She closed her eyes. Thank God!

The two men were arguing above her. The wind carried their words away.

Soon a rope snaked down across her body and dangled below her almost to the beach. It swayed back and forth and there was Miguel, climbing carefully down to her. She saw his expression as he reached her, cold fury in the black eyes, his lips set in a hard line.

She saw he had the end of another line looped about his shoulder. He climbed over her and helped her to turn, and then to sit up. Somehow she wasn't frightened with him beside her. The blood rushing to her numbed arm was painful, but she could move it slightly, although the muscles hurt.

He looped the rope around her waist and knotted it firmly, balancing precariously half on and half off the ledge, his own rope his only support.

"Can you hang on?"

She nodded mutely, and he yelled to Esteban to start pulling.

She was half tugged, half pushed up the cliff face, Miguel climbing up behind her until they reappeared over the edge.

Esteban helped her to scramble over the incline, showing her a track that led around to the side of the house and onto even ground. She hadn't even seen it last night, but she knew she would not have used it anyway. It led back only to the grounds of Villa Hermosa with the imprisoning, vine-covered walls on all three sides.

Shakily, she sank to the ground, murmuring her thanks to the fair-haired man. He grunted something and would not meet her eyes. Even his posture told her that he did not like her.

"What are you sitting there for?" Miguel came across the courtyard, scowling. He wasn't even breathing heavily from the climb. "Did you forget we have an appointment at nine?"

"An appointment?" Her brows creased in puzzlement. "I'm so tired, señor, my mind's not clear yet. What are you talking about?"

"To go riding, remember? I'll see you at the stables. And don't be late." His voice brooked no refusal. He strode off, coiling the ropes as he went.

Stunned, she gaped after him, an angry retort freezing on her lips. The callousness of him! Didn't he realize what she'd been through?

She stood up shakily and dusted her skirts off with quivering hands. A reaction had set in and her insides felt trembly and weak. She turned to face Esteban.

"Is he so angry that I tried to escape? Does he feel I should enjoy my imprisonment and not try to leave?" The color flooded her cheeks suddenly, and she stamped her foot in her anger. "What is wrong with that man?" she fumed.

"He's in love with you, señorita," Esteban said suddenly as they entered the main door. "He's in love, and yet he hates you. Is it any wonder he's so angry?"

She stopped short, facing the man. "You must be mad! He only has loathing for me. He believes Paul Blake and I are conspiring to murder him!" She laughed.

"Aren't you, señorita?" Esteban asked softly.

The laughter died on her lips.

Chapter Thirty-One

Bonita brought her water to bathe, and Amanda did so, soaking luxuriously in the hot tub for over an hour. Its heat took away some of the bruised, achy feeling from her hip, which had already turned black and blue, but nothing could ease the pain in her shoulder—and not the one in her heart! Why couldn't that arrogant beast let her rest, just this once? She needed to be alone to think, to reflect on what she had realized about Paul and herself during that long, lonely night.

"Señorita Sommers, Don Miguel is almost ready! You had best hurry, he is in a very bad temper, señorita, and already Consuela is helping him on with his boots!"

Amanda stood wearily and stepped from the slipper-shaped tub into the soft towel that Bonita held ready. Her body was rosy pink from the water, her face flushed. Her upswept hair had escaped its pins in places, and the freed wisps were damp and curling.

Something had happened to her during the night, Bonita thought, for the señorita seemed less of a young girl and more the woman now. It was not a physical change, but rather a subtle, fragile difference in expression and in her eyes.

Amanda toweled herself, then stood and allowed Bonita to pull a shift over her head, raising her injured arm with a moan of pain as she did so. A dark-green skirt followed, then a *bolero* over a green-embroidered beige blouse. She left her hair as it was, not caring what she looked like, pulling on a broad-brimmed hat to shield her eyes from the sun. The little maid had borrowed a pair of Doña Francesca's knee-high riding boots for Amanda, and the smaller size fit perfectly.

Amanda hurried downstairs to the stables, her mind in turmoil. If she told Miguel that she had realized she didn't love Paul, had never really loved him, would he believe her and let her go? She doubted it, but she could lose nothing by trying—or rather, nothing that he had not taken already! Amanda shivered. He had crippled one man, killed yet another, with less thought than killing a rat. She must be very careful with this cold rage in him now. She felt instinctively that it was far more dangerous than his heated temper of before.

Miguel was standing by the stables, conversing with old Manuel. That he was fond of the old man was obvious.

The don wore a full-sleeved white shirt tucked into black breeches, and boots. She noticed, with surprise, a glint of silver in the cuff of the boot. A knife? Then she saw a slight bulge at his chest beneath the white shirt. A pistol, too? He obviously intended to take no chance of being waylaid again!

Miguel looked up as he heard her approach, a mocking smile on his lips.

"I was just about to come and get you, but I see you are as impatient as I to be off!"

He assisted her up onto the back of the bay mare she

had ridden from Blanes. His choice of mount would have pleased her at another time, for the horse was daintily made, showing its Arab lineage, and very spirited. But with her aching body, she would have much preferred some docile hack! His own stallion was a magnificent animal, the darkness of the rider contrasted well with the silvery ghost-gray of the steed.

They held the horses to a walk until they reached the seashore. It was a fine, cloudless day, very hot, and the sea a smooth sheet of turquoise marble. The horses' nostrils flared as they caught the salty tang in the air, and Amanda could feel her mount straining to run.

The mare needed little urging, and stretched out in a beautiful swift stride at the slightest touch. Miguel and his stallion thundered beside her across the sand. Crouched forward over his stallion's mane, his dark hair almost buried in the gray silk of it, he was as handsome as a god, she thought. From deep within her, she felt a trickle of fear mingled with yearning.

Her hat had come unpinned and rested on its cord across her shoulders when they finally slowed to a walk. Her face had been whipped by the wind until her cheeks were as bright as cherries. Miguel felt a stab of desire course through him. Damn her! Even this morning, even with what would soon happen, he wanted her!

"Come, señorita, there's a special place I would like to show you."

She looked at him quizzically. His voice sounded different, softer. Should she try to talk to him now? The chance was gone! He had already ridden on.

He led the way along the beach to where the rocks were so high and cluttered that they had to ride upward a little and through a tiny thicket of pines to avoid them. They came out to a lovely, quiet cove. The mountains towered behind as a backdrop, giving way at their base to dry grasses the color of corn. Here and there, a crimson wildflower tossed a wanton head among the gold. From the grass, the sand stretched white, soft, and unblemished to an azure sea. The silence was broken only by the restless washing of the waves upon the sand.

Miguel saw that Amanda was entranced by the place as he had been on discovering it for the first time, and he felt peculiar pleasure at her reaction. It was a pity he'd had to bring her here under such circumstances, but he had chosen this place for the confrontation for a reason: it had only one way in, and the same way out. When Paul's men came, as he knew they would, he could not fail to see them, hear them, riding up the beach. Now it was just a matter of waiting.

Amanda dismounted awkwardly, trying not to use her injured arm any more than was absolutely necessary. That blasted Miguel, he couldn't even help her down, damn him! Instead, he stared moodily at the horizon, seeing nothing of her difficulty—or pretending not to.

She sat down angrily and tore off her hat. Suddenly, tears of self-pity filled her, spilled onto her cheeks. Heaving sobs racked her body.

"Díos! Stop that infernal racket!" Miguel growled.

He strode angrily to the girl, and roughly patted her shoulders. Women's tears irritated him as nothing else could, made him feel guilty for causing them, and consequently weakened. Was this another of her ruses?

"Here, dry your eyes. I'm not impressed," he said

coldly, tossing her the kerchief from his throat.

"The last person I'd try to impress would be you, Don Miguel!" she said hotly, glaring at him through the watery mist. The kerchief was sodden. "Tears are wasted on the heartless!" She flung back his kerchief and faced him angrily. "I wanted only to tell you that I realized, up there on the cliffs last night, that I didn't love Paul, that I'd never really loved him. I think I convinced myself that I did because, at that time, I needed to have someone to love. But I don't suppose that what I say will make any difference, not to you!"

"Well, well, how convenient your emotions are! You change your colors like a chameleon, my dear! But you're right, it won't make any difference. I'm not letting you go!"

"It won't make any difference because you won't let it!" Amanda cried. "It's just as your mother said—you have to stay angry at me until you've killed Paul. You're too much of a coward to do so in cold blood!" She turned her back to him, tossing her head defiantly at her outraged captor's face.

He was behind her in two swift strides, flinging her about by her injured arm to face him.

She yelped sharply in pain, and brought her other hand back and dealt him a hard slap across the face. The stinging blow sounded even louder in the quietness of the cove. His face bore the imprint of her fingers even above its tan, and his black eyes smoldered.

Fury filled him. She dared, she, Paul's woman, dared to call *him* a coward, when even now he waited for Blake's paid assassins, alone! *Díos,* he'd punish her for her words in the way he knew she hated most. When her body betrayed her yet again, she'd be sorry she'd taunted him!

"Take off those clothes, Amanda, and be quick—I haven't much time," he commanded harshly.

A trickle of fear, a quiver of excitement, filled her.

"No!" she whispered, "never again!" She swung around suddenly and started racing up toward the pines and their tethered mounts. Miguel's heavy footsteps pounded the wet sand behind her. Her heart hammered wildly with apprehension. Just a few more yards, just a few more, and she would fling herself astride the mare and gallop out of his life! Yes!

She almost made it, but then he brought her down with a flying leap, rolling her above him as they fell to break her fall. His fingers plucked the pins from her hair, letting it tumble about them in wild, chestnut disarray. He held her helpless by her injured arm, and quickly removed every inch of her clothes, tossing them to the four winds in his haste. His own followed.

Her eyes widened as he stood naked before her, the silver medallion of St. Christopher shining in the dark hair upon his chest, every part of him golden-tanned and well-muscled.

Her lips were slightly parted and moist, her breathing ragged with fear. She lay naked at his feet, her hands shielding her soft breasts from his scorching eyes, her thighs pressed trembling together.

He dropped to her side, lifted her, carried her into the sea.

When the water reached his chest he halted and stood her before him. His eyes lingeringly traversed her face: the wide pools of her fear-filled sable eyes, the creamy splendor of her satin cheeks, the soft and glistening curve of her tempting mouth. Hungrily he crushed her to him, covering that mouth with his own in a sweet and savage kiss.

Above them, in the azure sky, the sun climbed higher into the heavens, until a shimmering haze of heat danced upon the sparkling water, a heat that was rivaled only by the heady, throbbing heat in Amanda's veins, as the lapping water and Miguel's teasing tongue upon her breasts combined, and drove her to fever pitch. She couldn't stand it! The strange, tingling sensation spread outward from her breasts to her belly, to her loins. She feebly tried to force his lips from her body, but somehow the action ended with her fingers twined in his crisp, dark hair, and she, moaning softly. Damn him! She didn't want him to stop—ever!

His hands were everywhere, caressing, bewitching, until she begged him, pleaded with him to take her, while at the same time, her small, clenched fists beat wildly at his chest to demand he free her.

She drew a sharp breath and gasped as he entered her, opening her gently and filling her with his hardness. Slowly he withdrew and thrust inward once again. He repeated the delicious torture again and again, until her body arched forward to hold him fast within her.

"Now, Miguel!" she pleaded, desperately. "Now!"

He pressed a kiss to her mouth, trailed tongue and lips down the length of her throat and to her breasts once more, where the waves cupped them.

"Patience, *querida,*" he soothed huskily, "you are not ready. Soon, my dearest, soon . . ."

She was moaning now, pleading with him again and again. Her passion had reached its peak, and pride was vaniquished, desire her conqueror.

Miguel clasped her waist and drew her tightly to him, driving himself against her harder and harder and deeper with every thrust. Then he felt her body pulse, and little cries of ecstasy broke from her lips. Her eyes closed as she relaxed in his arms, the wealth of her hair fanning out and floating above the water, twisting this way and that in the sea's caress. Seconds later, he found his own release, and they rested, entwined.

Later, he gathered her into his arms once more, and waded to the water's edge. Side by side, they lay, sated and exhausted in the wet and silken sand, letting the ripples wash over their sun-kissed bodies.

A single rider was coming through the trees.

Miguel reached for his pistol, hurriedly shrugging on his shirt and stuffing it into his breeches as he did so. His eyes squinted against the sunlight as the horse pranced through the pine thicket and came toward him. His muscles tensed; his hand was ready on the weapon.

"Get back there, in the caves," he ordered Amanda quietly.

Startled, she did as bidden.

"Hola, Miguelito! It is only I, Esteban!" The rider drew nearer, slid from his horse, and strolled, grinning, toward Miguel.

Miguel's hand dropped again to his side, and he replaced the pistol on the rock and returned to tucking in his shirt.

"Well, what happened?" he asked, his eyes narrowing.

"They took off back to Barcelona, *amigo.* I followed them up to the wooded spot—you know, by the bend in the road leading down from the villa?"

Miguel nodded.

"Well, they tethered the horses there, and watched as you and the señorita rode by. Then, there was much excited talking and arguing—" he paused and nodded at Amanda "—about her!"

Amanda came forward at this, pushing wet strands of hair from her eyes. "I told you both, señores, I know nothing—"

"I believe you, señorita!" Esteban interrupted excitedly. "For there was one of them that knew you, though it was clear that the rest did not. And this one said, Miguel, my friend, he said he thought *they should let Blake know that the Sommers woman was with de Villarin, here in Spain!*"

Miguel's head jerked upward as the import of what Esteban had said sunk in. "Then you mean, they didn't—?"

His question hung in the breeze as he turned to face Amanda. Never had she seen anyone appear so crushed, she thought gleefully, flashing him a look of utter triumph. She couldn't help it, not after what he'd done to her again and again, turning even her body and its desires against her. It was all she could do not to yell "I told you so" right in his arrogant face!

Instead, she leaned haughtily down and dusted off her hat.

"May we return to the villa now, señores?" she asked sweetly. "I believe I have some packing to do!"

She marched aloofly across to her mount, swung easily into the saddle, and trotted off. The two men followed her silently.

As they mounted their horses, Esteban looked

keenly at Miguel.

"I'm sorry, my friend. It seems the morning was wasted."

"Not entirely, Esteban, not entirely!" Miguel grinned, shame-faced, his look following Amanda as her mare cantered away from them.

"I thought as much!" Esteban roared, slapping the don heartily across the back. His laughter continued as Miguel's face reddened.

"So you hate her, do you, you rogue? You're a bad liar, Miguel!"

The steward wheeled his horse and rode after Amanda.

Chapter Thirty-Two

"You have my deepest apologies, Señorita Amanda," Miguel said stiffly.

He was not accustomed to having to account for his actions. Never had he felt so humbled as he did before this slip of a girl! Amanda was unimpressed. Her eyes sparked fire.

"Not accepted, Don Miguel—just as you refused to accept *my* word that I had nothing to do with your attack! I have only one thing left that I wish to say to you—" she paused.

"Yes, señorita?"

"The Devil take you, de Villarin!" she exploded, and stormed up the stairs.

In her room she dropped wearily to the bed and sank into a deep, sound sleep for the first time in many weeks.

It was afternoon of the next day before she awoke, her face showing disbelief when Bonita told her she had slept the whole twenty-four hours.

"Who changed my clothes!" she said suddenly, looking down at the clean, sweet-smelling night gown she was wearing. "It wasn't—?" Suspicion filled her eyes.

"It was I, *señorita.* I bathed you and brushed your hair, too. You were very tired, and did not even stir as I moved you." She smiled. "Will you get up now? The señora is taking luncheon on the terrace. She asked me to tell you, if you awoke, that she would like very much for you to join her. *Sí?* Good. Let me help you to dress."

Bonita left Amanda at the terrace. Doña Francesca's face broke into a delighted smile.

"So, you are feeling better, no? Child, you don't know how happy I am that you and Miguel have solved some of your differences. Perhaps now the two of you can be friends, *sí?*" Her sloe-black eyes twinkled. "Or if not friends, then at least cordial enemies!"

Amanda smiled politely, but said nothing.

"Let's eat now. You must be hungry after so long a sleep. Rita, give Señorita Sommers a large serving. We must not have her English friends thinking we did not feed her at Villa Hermosa." The older woman laughed as Amanda's expression became startled. "Yes, my dear, Miguel is taking you to Barcelona very soon, and he will see you safely aboard a ship bound for England, with a reputable *capitán* to ensure you are well cared for."

Amanda hurried around the table and soundly kissed Doña Francesca until she begged for mercy.

She couldn't believe it. Finally she would be going home! Her appetite turned voracious and she finished the heaped platter with amazing speed.

"I wanted to ask you, Amanda, if you would do something for me?"

"Yes, anything. I feel lighter than air. I feel wonderful! Ask and it shall be yours!"

Doña Francesca laughed. "I hope you will agree as readily after I tell you. I want you to stay here for two more weeks before you depart for Barcelona."

Amanda's face dropped. "Another two weeks! But I—"

"Not for Miguel; for me, Amanda! I miss Elena's laughter, having a young girl about the house. Please, would you stay, for my sake?" Her hand trembled with emotion. "I would like to consider you my friend. The little time we have we can use to get to know each other with no unpleasantness—this time." She beamed as Amanda slowly nodded.

Amanda and Miguel avoided each other like the plague for the next week. They spoke only when forced to, and then were barely civil. If Doña Francesca noticed their behavior, she said nothing of it. And the two women were fast becoming friends.

Amanda found the doña spirited and intelligent and her wit as sharp as her own. She described in her turn how she had masqueraded as a cabin boy, and the doña laughed until tears rolled down her cheeks at Amanda's gamin smile and false cockney accent. They were still laughing when Don Miguel came into the drawing room.

"Good evening, *Mamacita,* Señorita Sommers." He barely looked at her. "I hear there is a ship bound for England in Barcelona at this moment. Tomorrow we shall travel to the city and I will see to your passage. Will that be satisfactory?"

"I—I suppose so," Amanda said doubtfully, glancing up Doña Francesca. The doña's lips were tightly pursed, and disappointment was written on her face. "Couldn't we go in another week, say?"

"I'm afraid not. I have some unfinished business to attend to there, if you recall. I can combine it with the pleasure of seeing you safely out of the country." He stormed from the room as suddenly as he had entered.

"I'm sorry, Amanda. He's like a bear these days." The doña said apologetically. "I think he's confused and—perhaps a little in love, too!" She smiled.

"Francesca, you sound like Esteban. I can't see why you both imagine Miguel is in love with me. His behavior indicates he hates me!"

"I'm not sure that Miguel realizes it himself, my dear! It has never happened before, and, I admit, I was beginning to wonder if it ever would. Do you care for him—at all?"

Amanda thought briefly of the feelings he stirred in her with his lovemaking. But that was only desire. She didn't even like the brute, let alone love him!

"No, I'm afraid not!" she said vehemently.

Doña Francesca smiled. "Then it will be easy to tell him no, that you will not leave tomorrow, that you will stay the extra week that you promised me, will it not?" The smile deepened.

Amanda saw she had been tricked and laughed delightedly. "You and I are very much alike, Francesca. Devious and deliciously wicked! Yes, I'll do as you say!"

The doña and Amanda dissolved into giggles at the thought of Miguel's scowling face when they would tell him.

The evening air was heavy as Miguel, Doña Francesca, and Amanda sat at dinner the following Sunday. After Rita had filled their glasses, the old lady proposed a toast to Amanda's safe journey the next week. Reluctantly, Miguel had agreed to postpone her departure, though not without a heated argument. The three raised their glasses.

"To your safe return, my dear, and to happiness and peace of mind for us all," the doña said.

Amanda and Miguel murmured polite agreement and the three glasses touched. As they did so a flash of lightning lit the room, followed by an ominous roll of thunder. Not long after, the storm broke and rain lashed against the casements. Quickly, the maids hurried to shutter the windows. Miguel ordered the fire lit in the sitting room and they carried their glasses with them and sat down cozily to wait out the storm.

The room was richly furnished in shades of blue and gold. The furniture was solid and comfortable. Black wrought-iron sconces curled out at intervals along the paneled walls, but these were not lit. Instead, two candelabra and the flickering fire provided the only lighting. A highly polished low table held a silver bowl of orange-and-yellow flowers.

The paintings on the walls were old and very good: one small da Vinci portrait and two charming Renaissance rural scenes. In all, Amanda thought, her favorite of all the rooms in the villa.

She settled herself in a deep stuffed chair next to the fireplace, her legs tucked up beneath her. Miguel's mother seated herself opposite, while he sprawled across the chaise, restlessly drumming his fingers on the table from time to time.

Blast! Miguel thought, eyeing the foul weather through the one unshuttered window. He'd planned to ride into Barcelona this evening and find some sympathy—and no little pleasure—in Caro's arms. But the storm had put an end to his plans. He eyed Amanda over the rim of his glass with speculation in his eyes. Why did she deny the pleasure he knew he gave her? Women! They were all so perverse, so contrary. Somehow though, Caro's feline grace and charms failed to stir in him the same lustful, blood-pulsing desire that this English señorita inflamed. What was it? Her eyes? That glorious hair? That ripe, wanton mouth that made a man yearn to crush it beneath his own lips? He sighed. No, what he enjoyed most was that undauntable fire that coursed her veins: the feeling that however many times a man might take her, make her his woman, there was a small part of her that remained unconquerable, an enigma, a mystery. It was the mystery that excited him! Would she ever be wholly one man's, relinquishing all, for his love? He met her casual glance in his direction with a suggestive wink. His eyes traversed her throat and rested on her breasts where the aqua-colored silk of her gown ended in frothy lace.

She read his thoughts and colored deeply. Miguel chuckled softly to himself as she shot him a look that spoke volumes as to her opinion of his boldness.

"More wine, Amanda?" He rose and filled her glass before she could answer him, his fingers entrapping hers for a second before she withdrew them as if his were red hot.

"*Gracias,* Don Miguel!" she said coldly.

Doña Francesca could not have helped but see, though she made no sign of having done so. Amanda shuddered as the storm howled against the windows, rattling the frames. It was as if a wild animal sought entry.

Doña Francesca rose somewhat shakily. "I'm sorry, children, but I think I shall retire and leave you young people alone." She paused and looked long and thoughtfully at Amanda. "It was a long day, and I'm a little fatigued."

Amanda noticed her lips had a bluish tinge. "I'll help you upstairs, and then we'll summon Bianca to get you to bed."

When Amanda returned to the sitting room, Miguel was drinking yet another glass of wine. His eyes held a look she knew only too well.

"Sit next to me, *querida mia,"* he said in a teasing tone, "we'll pretend your chaperone is sleeping." He patted the chaise next to him, and grinned.

"You think of nothing else, do you, sir? We will not pretend anything. I'm going to my room." She swept haughtily to the door and pulled up short.

Miguel was standing now, one booted foot trapping the hem of her gown.

She tugged at it furiously, enraged when he refused to budge. "You're drunk," she accused, trying to turn and face him.

"And you, *mi estrellita,* are the wine that has made me so!" He laughed and lunged for her waist, a devilish smile on his face. "One kiss, and I will free you from this drunken lout's embrace," he cajoled.

"Not one," Amanda vowed, "not one kiss, nor anything else, willingly." She turned her face away from his.

"Why, look!" Miguel said suddenly, glancing over his shoulder, "over there in the corner!"

Her head snapped around to see, and her mouth met his in a resounding kiss.

She gasped and flung herself back, but he grasped her by the shoulders and practically lifted her from the floor and kissed her again, this time with more passion than she would have believed possible in a single kiss. The fire and candlelight softened his features, and for an instant she saw a glimpse of the other Miguel, the one his mother had spoken of. His kisses melted her as fire melted ice. Damn him.

"Tell me, Mandy, swear to me that you did not enjoy that kiss, and I will become a monk," he declared roguishly.

She chose to avoid the issue. "Don't *ever* call me 'Mandy' again! Only those I love have ever done so, and you, señor, certainly do not fit that category."

"You're hedging, *Mandy,"* he teased, "swear to me, now, that my kiss left you unmoved, and I will keep my vow."

"It bored me! And you are an insufferable, arrogant, lecherous—" No word was low enough to describe him!

"And you, my dear, are a little liar! Let me try it again. Perhaps my lips need practice." He took a step toward her, grinning. His hair appeared almost blue in the light.

She was saved from his next kiss by the timely entrance of Bianca, and the maid's appearance was so distraught that even Miguel was instantly sobered.

"La señora! *Aiee,* she is very bad, Don Miguel—and in such pain!" She wrung her hands, tears streaming down her old cheeks.

Miguel was past her, leaping up the stairs in his haste. Amanda followed as fast as her skirts would allow.

Doña Francesca was like a piece of delicate parchment, so pale and translucent was her skin. Her lips bore a pronounced bluish tinge now and, Amanda thought, she had never seen Francesca appear so totally dwarfed by the massive, four-poster bed. The doña clutched one hand to her chest and clawed at it weakly, her expression one of agony. Amanda felt her forehead. It was cool and clammy. She turned swiftly to Miguel.

"Is there a physician in the village?"

"Dear Mother of God, I hope so! I'll find him, wherever he is." He strode over to the bed. *"Mamacita,* I must go for the physician. Amanda will stay with you, never fear." Concern etched furrows in the tan of his face.

Her magnificent, sloe-black eyes were clouded with pain. "No, *hijo, por favor,* do not leave me! I would have you both here, beside me. I fear I have not long left."

"Nonsense, *madre mia,* I will ride like the wind, and soon you will feel well enough to dance the *sardana!"* His look belied the lightness of his words.

"It's too late, *hijo.* Stay with me. I am not afraid to die, but—" Her voice broke as another spasm of pain wracked her tiny frame. Her hand closed convulsively on Miguel's and would not free him.

"Señor Miguel," Bonita said softly, "Manuel is here, outside in the hallway. Bianca told him about the señora. He says he will go."

"Let me do it, Miguelito, for her." Manuel entered

the room, indicating the doña. His dark eyes were shadowed with worry.

"No, *viejo,* not on such a night as this! You have not ridden in years. I'll not have you break your neck in this storm."

Miguel's softly spoken words had no effect.

Manuel pulled himself upright and replied firmly, "Doña Francesca needs you here. It is your place, Miguel. Do you forget who made a man of you, after Don Carlos died?" His voice was stern. "Then listen to me now. I will go." His jaw jutted defiantly.

Miguel shrugged, exasperated. "You are our dearest friend, Manuel. God be with you, and take my stallion. He's the swiftest and most sure-footed in the stable. If anyone can save your old neck, he can!" He turned to Bonita. "Fetch Manuel my heaviest cloak and a hat. We'll not have you, *viejo,* using penumonia as an excuse to sample still more of the villa's wine!"

Manuel laughed, cast a concerned look at the tiny figure on the bed, and hurried out after Bonita.

Chapter Thirty-Three

"Miguel, how can it take so long?" Amanda paced restlessly. "It must be over an hour since Manuel left, and the ride down to the village is not more than fifteen minutes at most!"

"Patience, Manuel will not let us down. He thinks of the de Villarins as his own family, you understand? Perhaps the physician was in another of the villages and he has ridden on." His calm words rang false when coupled with his knotted fists and tense frame.

"Miguel, let me go into the village! I cannot stand seeing Francesca in such pain," Amanda begged. Her sable-dark eyes glistened with tears.

"No. I forbid it. We will wait a little longer."

He could not risk Amanda careening down that twisting road in this weather. And so they waited. Another quarter of an hour ticked by, underlined by the chiming of a distant clock, until Amanda felt she would go crazy with worry. Finally, she could stand it no longer.

"Miguel, I'm going to my room to change from this gown. It's stifling with the storm."

He nodded and she swiftly hurried along the corridor.

She did not change the aqua gown. Instead, she removed the unwieldy hoops that supported it, threw Elena's burgundy cloak around her shoulders and raced breathlessly down, through the house, and out to the stables.

She led the bay mare into the driving rain and heaved the saddle over the horse's back, cinching it tight. Then she gathered the reins in one hand and leaped astride her mount, hitching her voluminous skirts about her hips as she did so. It would be easier than side-saddle, and less dangerous. She dug her heels into the horse's flanks and galloped up to the double gates. They stood open and the metal rang with the vibration as she thundered through them.

The village below was enveloped in the darkness and the rain, the road, a blind trap in the night.

She slowed to a trot, letting her mare pick the way, for the steed must know it well. Tree branches whipped at her as she rode; the storm still howled above. Her cloak was sodden in minutes.

Thunder cracked, and the horse broke into a canter. It was foolhardy to attempt such a speed in daylight, when the potholes and tree roots could be readily seen. By night and in foul weather it was treacherous. Undaunted, Amanda rode on recklessly, the wet cape flapping behind her like batwings.

She had traveled only half way when a horse careened toward her out of the dark like a spectre, its gray body looming suddenly before her own rearing mount. Miguel's horse!

“Halloo, Manuel!” she cried eagerly. Then she saw it was riderless, its eyes white and rolling with terror. She let it thunder past, her anxious eyes scanning the wet darkness about her. Had the old man been thrown?

She made the last curve without any sign of Manuel, and clattered around the corner past the shoemaker’s, almost colliding with another rider.

“Whoa! Señorita, are you from the villa?” The man threw back his hat and she recognized the physician who had tended her in Blanes.

“Yes, señor. You must hurry, Doña Francesca is very bad, I think it is her heart!”

“Then I will waste no more time.” He urged his mount forward toward the track leading to the villa.

“Wait one second, señor. Manuel, where is he?”

“Manuel? Why I haven’t seen that old rogue in many months! Try the *cantina,* señorita!” He kneed his mount forward.

“But how did you know about the señora?” Amanda cried after him.

“From the priest, Father Juliano!” The physician shouted over his shoulder, and was gone.

Puzzled, Amanda rode down the narrow street, her horse’s hooves ringing on the cobbles. At the church, she dismounted and tied her horse to the palings that surrounded the graveyard.

She beat upon the massive door with her fists, hearing the sound echo hollowly within the church. “Father, please open the door! Father Juliano!”

Finally the door swung open, creaking loudly. The tall priest stood aside to allow her to enter. “It was not locked, my child. The House of God is never locked,” he chided her gently.

"Father, did you send the physician to the villa? And where is Manuel? His horse passed me as I rode down, alone."

The priest nodded. "Sit down, my dear. I'm afraid I have some bad news. You see, Manuel is dead." He took her hand, and squeezed it to comfort her.

"But how? The physician said nothing of this!" Her eyes were huge and dilated with shock.

"I saw no point in delaying him. There was no doubt in my mind that Manuel was dead, you see, and Doña Francesca has greater need of the señor's services. The old man was shot, señorita! He managed to cling to his mount until he reached here, then fell to my feet as I was leaving after the evening services." His face was deeply sorrowful.

Amanda's own was chalky white. "Dead? I can't believe it! Let me see him—I *must* see him, Father." She grabbed the man's arm and shook it in her urgency.

"He is in the vestry, señorita. Please, it is not a pretty sight! He is at peace now, you can gain nothing by—"

Unhearing, she thrust past him, mounted the altar steps, and ran across to the vestry. The door stood open, a single candle burning within.

A figure lay across the table, quite still beneath a rough woolen blanket.

She crossed the room in two steps and pulled back the cover. Manuel's lifeless eyes stared up at her and beyond to some point that she could never see in this life. His eyes reflected the light twofold as if twin candles had replaced his soul. There was a gaping cavity just below his ear where the pistol ball had entered, dark blood still welling from the wound and spilling onto Miguel's cloak.

"My God!" She fought back the nausea as the priest led her away. "Who did this? Who?"

Father Juliano shook his head and shrugged. "I do not know, my child. I heard the shot even above the thunder, then shortly after the horse came careening through the village, as I told you. Manuel fell at my feet. He was already dying then. There was much blood everywhere, and he had trouble speaking, but finally I understood. His last words were to send help, that the doña was gravely ill. Then he died in my arms. I went to the physician's house, then returned to carry his body in here."

Amanda nodded numbly. She felt cold and shivery. "Father, will you come with me to Villa Hermosa? I hope and pray that you will not be needed, but—"

Father Juliano hurriedly fetched his things in a battered reticule. Amanda untied her horse and clambered astride, the priest mounting awkwardly behind her.

They were a strange pair riding up the mountain to the villa in the rain. Everywhere was pitch black, with neither stars nor moon to light the way. At intervals, the lightning forked the sky with jagged scars of white brilliance. The incline was slick with mud, but despite her heavy burden the hardy mare never faltered.

When they reached the courtyard the villa was ablaze with light. Amanda urged Father Juliano to hurry inside, and went to stable the mare herself.

Minutes later, sick with dread, she staggered to the door. Bonita flung it open at her pounding. The maid's eyes were swollen and tear-filled.

“Doña Francesca, will she—?”

“No, señorita. La Señora, she died, just a few minutes ago. *Gracias a Díos,* you brought the priest in time! *Aiee,* this is a dark, dark night for us all.”

Amanda sagged against the door, tears filling her own eyes.

Chapter Thirty-Four

A week had passed since Doña Francesca was laid to rest in the churchyard, her vault strewn with the flowers that had been her favorites—the sweet gardenias. Not far away lay Manuel, his own resting place also covered with the flowers he had tended so carefully while living.

"Well, Miranda, I shall miss you!" Amanda said, giving her a fierce hug. "Thank you and Fernando for everything, and write to me after you have that beautiful baby!"

"Sí, I promise. You take care, and don't let that Miguel bother you; his bark is far worse than his bite," she added in a whisper, with a broad smile.

The two women embraced, then Fernando handed Amanda into the coach with the de Villarin crest in gilt on the door. *"Adios,* Amanda. I wish we could have known you in happier times. Especially now that your Spanish is better than my French." A fleeting smile crossed his face, then his dark eyes clouded again. *"Vaya con Dios!"*

Amanda smiled, and turned to watch Miguel striding from between the graves to the coach.

"Are we ready? Then let's be off!"

He swung himself onto his horse, Esteban riding at his side, and the coach rolled its way out of the village.

"The don, he is taking it very hard, no?" Bonita said from her seat opposite.

Amanda nodded, lost to her own thoughts. At last, she was homeward bound. Now that it was finally happening, she was not as eager to leave as she had thought she would be. Miguel had told her two days ago that he would wait no longer to confront Paul.

"Miguel," she had said, "why not leave things as they are? It has been several weeks since his men tried to kill you. Perhaps he has given up?" She had meant only to help him find some peace of mind, for the loss of the two closest to him at one time was a heavy burden to carry.

But he had looked at her, his eyes burning with vengeance. "No, Amanda, I will not rest until I have found him! Do you think it an accident that Manuel was murdered, wearing my cloak and my hat? There was no one who would wish to kill that harmless old man—unless they believed he was me! I was a fool to let him go! Do not fear though, for I shall avenge him, I swear, as my name is Miguel de Villarin, I will do so!"

His words had made her shiver, she remembered. Then she recalled the night his mother had died, and a very different Miguel.

After that first shock of grief, she had run upstairs to him. He was sitting alone by her own bedside in the dark, his face buried in his hands. He had looked up as she entered, bearing a lit candle, disbelief written on his face.

"You came back?"

"Of course! I loved your mother too, you know,

Miguel. That is why I rode into the village against your orders. I couldn't stand watching her, doing nothing to help her! Do you really think I could have left her that way?" Her voice was low and full of compassion.

He had not answered for several moments. "Amanda, thank you," he said finally.

She laughed softly. *"De nada, señor*. But you cannot sit here in the dark, alone, you know."

"I'm not alone, Mandy."

There had been such warmth in his voice that the breath had caught in her throat. They had spent the night together, losing themselves in such bittersweet passion that the memory of it alone sent her heart racing. The grief they both shared had united them for that night, and they had found some measure of peace when dawn burst through the window.

She felt very different about leaving now, not even sure that she wanted to return to England at all, and to the life of a governess in someone else's house, caring for someone else's children. She'd felt a pang of jealousy seeing Miranda blooming and heavy with child. Still, it would be lovely to see Aggie again, and to tell her that she was well. Poor Aggie, she must have been frantic on finding her gone that morning four, or was it five? months ago. By now, the letter Amanda had sent should have reached her.

They were already a few miles from the villa when she saw that the rocky, sandy soil had given way to the fertile land that nourished the de Villarin orchards. Almond trees bordered the road, a veritable ocean of dainty white blossoms as far as the eye could see. Men and women were working in the fields, woven sombreros of huge proportions shading them from the sun. The young girls were like flowers in their colorful blouses and skirts, with kerchiefs over their heads. The matrons were dressed entirely in black like enormous, bright-eyed crows.

Miguel rode alongside the coach on his stallion, deep in conversation with Esteban.

Soon they left the almond groves behind. The sun rose higher in the brilliant blue of a sky, unmarred by even a solitary cloud. The heat of the air became almost tangible, hazing the horizon until distant objects seemed to shimmer in its spell.

Amanda squealed delightedly as a new sight caught her eyes. Orange trees, row upon row, stretched as far as the eye could see, luscious fruit hanging ripe in their boughs like Japanese lanterns. She'd rarely seen oranges in England, let alone tried the exotic fruit.

"Pepe! Please, stop." She hung out of the coach until it halted, then clambered swiftly to the ground before either of the men could dismount to assist her.

"It's so beautiful, Miguel, this country of yours, so wonderfully alive, different. Even the air is different," she cried, inhaling deeply and whirling about.

"Here, taste this, Señorita Amanda. We are very proud of the de Villarin orange groves." As he spoke, Esteban peeled the fruit with his knife and handed it to her.

Amanda bit into it greedily, laughing as the juice sprayed in all directions with its tangy, sweet fragrance.

"Delicious, absolutely delicious," she mumbled, her mouth full. "Is it true that this fruit can prevent scurvy, that soon they'll be a common item in the galley aboard ships on long sea voyages?"

Esteban laughed. "You're well informed. It's not

been proven yet, but some believe so." His eyes twinkled. "For the sake of the poor sailors and the de Villarin purses, I hope it's so, hm, Miguel?"

She had devoured several oranges and filled her skirts with more of the strange fruit before the coach was allowed to continue.

It was past noon when the coach halted once more. Bonita grumbled as she dismounted, for she had refused to stretch her legs since the beginning of the journey and was becoming stiff.

"That Pepe, he's always staring at me so!" she complained to Amanda, but her smug little smile told Amanda that she found his attentions most agreeable.

Bonita produced a basket and cloth and the party sat down to eat a picnic lunch. Fragrant pink slices of ham, sardines, tomatoes, and onions appeared from the small basket. A loaf of bread and a dewy bunch of purple grapes followed, and, finally, a leather *bota* of red wine. They ate heartily, then stretched out for the inevitable *siesta* until mid-afternoon, when the day would lose some of its intense heat.

When they were ready to continue, Amanda was surprised to see Miguel tie his stallion's reins to the rear of the coach and clamber inside next to her.

"So, you are enjoying your first sights of Spain, eh? Well, I promise you, there is much more, and I intend that you shall see all there is to see before I hand you over to Captain Alexandre." He smiled grimly.

"You make it sound more of a threat than a promise, Miguel," Amanda observed.

"I'm sorry, I hadn't meant to! However, I think I should tell you now that I mean to make our presence in Barcelona very, very public."

"How so?" she asked, eyeing him keenly.

"It will be the surest way to find Blake. We'll let him come to us!"

"And the most dangerous!" She shivered. "He could strike at any time that way, and we would be unprepared."

"On the contrary, Pepe and Esteban will cover our every move from a distance. To my knowledge, Blake and his henchman know neither of them, and they'll be able to protect us unnoticed until I can arrange a meeting with Blake. He'll no doubt be burning to discover why you are here with me! You will be the cheese in my trap, but a very carefully guarded cheese. Don't look so scared!"

His plan sent shivers of fear the length of her spine, the memory of Manuel's death mask clouding her mind. She had wanted to marry the monster that had done that to an old man! She shivered again.

"I think tomorrow we'll find something that takes your fancy in the marketplace. I'd like you to have a memento of your months in Spain." His voice held a bantering quality.

"I think, señor, I have all the mementos I need, in here," she said pointedly, tapping her brow.

He grinned and continued, "and then in the afternoon we shall go to the *corrida,* the bullfight. It is a very colorful spectacle."

"And a barbaric one, too, I've heard!"

He shrugged. "You will be able to decide that after you have seen it. It is a test of skill and bravery, the agility and intelligence of a single man against the superior strength and unique beauty of a powerful animal—the bull."

"Then little wonder you seem to enjoy it, as you and that particular creature have much in common!" She retorted hotly.

"Why, *gracias, querida,* I had no idea my prowess was so great!" He chuckled at her reddening cheeks, slumped back in his seat, and tilted his hat over his eyes.

The rat was sleeping! Amanda sulkily turned to watch the countryside, fuming. Was there no taunt, no remark acid enough to pierce his thick-skinned hide!

The lush fields gave way to dry, rocky countryside. Here and there a struggling, gnarled olive tree fought for life amid the poor soil.

She commented on the starkness of the terrain, and Bonita informed her that it had been a battleground before, many of them fought against the English.

"Some of my people have no love for the English until today, señorita," she finished quietly.

"And you, Bonita?"

"Oh, señorita, I did not mean you! *Gracias a Díos,* I am fortunate enough to be able to judge people by their actions and not by their country or race. I find you *muy simpatica!*"

The coach was forced to pull over to the side a little later, to make way for a large number of people on foot. They were chanting in Latin as they walked, some barefoot, the older marchers leaning heavily on staffs. There was great joy and piety on their faces, though many had bleeding, blistered feet bound in rags. Miguel had awoken, and, in answer to her question, told her that the people were pilgrims.

"They are going to pay homage to the Virgin of Montserrat. We call her the Rose of April, the Dark

One of the Mountains. She is the patron saint of Catalonia, as this area is called."

The road the pilgrims traveled seemed a hard one to Amanda. Towering above them were weird formations of rocks that looked forbidding and impenetrable, and she could see neither the monastery nor the shrine through the clouds at the mountain's peak that Miguel had said was up there.

The first thing that struck her as they entered Barcelona was its people. It seemed as if every nation and race could be found by scanning the myriad faces as they passed through the winding streets. Many had the sculptured features and dark complexions that spoke of the Moorish blood that flowed, however diluted, in their veins. Others were fairer-skinned, their hair and eyes lighter, from the northern Spanish regions bordering France, and hundred upon hundred had the look of fierce pride coupled with good humor that was Catalonian.

The coach halted in front of an inn that boasted an air of respectability many they passed had lacked. The innkeeper, Señor Cristobal, who obviously knew Miguel and Esteban, hurried out to greet them. Pepe and the ostler took the coach and team to the stables, and a boy came out to carry the single reticule and bag Amanda and Bonita had brought.

The inn was cool compared to the streets, and dark, now that the light outside was rapidly fading. Strings of garlic and sausage festooned the walls.

The *patrón* seated them at a heavy scrubbed table and platters were slapped down before them. Then he ladled heaping quantities of *mariscos*—shellfish—from a huge black pot onto each platter, with great chunks of thickly buttered bread and tankards of ale to wash it all down.

When they had eaten, they were taken to their rooms by the innkeeper's daughter, up a flight of gloomy stairs.

Amanda's room was spartan compared to the one she had enjoyed at Villa Hermosa. There was only a bed, a rough chair, and a table, and, of course, a statue of the Virgin in one corner. The view from the window did little to make up for the plainness of the room. Another building loomed up across the alley, and below were the roofs of the inn's kitchens and stables some twelve feet below. Still, it was fresh swept and the bedcovers were at least clean.

Bonita came in to help her undress, and, after, Amanda quickly dropped off to sleep.

Chapter Thirty-Five

Amanda dressed the next morning in a deep-blue gown that had been Elena's. Bonita had altered it for her, and Amanda was pleased with the way the color complimented the golden tan of her skin. The maid swept up her hair into a burnished knot, and into this fastened an ivory *mantilla* comb, studded with pearls. It had been Francesca's. Amanda had felt surprise mingled with gratitude when Miguel told her that he thought his mother would have liked her to have it. The white lace *mantilla* hung down exotically when fastened over the comb, and she was well pleased with her appearance when she sallied downstairs, Bonita in attendance.

Miguel had never looked more handsome and, she noticed, with a twinge of jealousy, that the tavern wenches seemed to think so, too. They fluttered around him like cooing doves, fingering the silk of his light-blue shirt and using their admiration of the cloth to touch the muscled chest beneath. He seemed to be enjoying himself enormously and his slow-spreading grin infuriated her even more than usual.

Miguel took her arm and they wandered out onto the plaza that fronted the inn.

There was a market in the square, stalls almost

covering the flagstones. They browsed for a while, enjoying the novelty. There was a flower stall covered with crimson, pink, and white carnations, magenta peonies, and roses, their sweet fragrances heady in the warmth. These perfumes mingled with the less pleasant odors from the fish stall, where all types of fish shone, scaly and glassy-eyed, on the wooden surface.

An old woman was extolling the virtues of her wares, little reed cages that held finches that were hopping and trilling sweetly. Farther away, a peddler hawked his pots and pans, sharpening knives on a whetstone in return for a good purchase.

Amanda was particularly pleased by a stall that offered bolts of cloth and lace trimmings. The richly colored silks and satins billowed like ribbons in the breeze, their brilliant colors a sharp contrast to the funereal black crepe alongside them.

Amanda turned to show her finds to Bonita, who followed the couple at a discreet distance, and her eyes fell on a shabby, unkempt figure who was in heated argument with one of the stall holders. They seemed to be haggling over the price of some item, but it was not this that held her attention, rather the feeling she had seen him before. Stringy hair, almost cadaverous face, very short—Paul's valet! The same man who'd opened the door to her at the Figurehead Inn! Charlie, Paul had called him!

She grabbed Miguel's arm and nodded in the man's direction. "Over there, no, the short one! He's one of Paul's men," she hissed excitedly.

Miguel followed her gesture. "Are you sure?" Then his eyes narrowed with realization. "By God, yes! It makes sense—I saw him before, on one of my business trips here—we collided, he almost knocked me to the ground, then took off like a madman. I think I'd like to ask this rogue a few questions. Bonita, attend the señorita," he ordered crisply.

Miguel strolled casually across the square, and Amanda realized for the first time that Esteban had been with them. He shadowed Miguel from about twenty feet away without seeming in the slightest part interested in his friend's doings. Pepe appeared from nowhere and took her and Bonita's elbow. Over her shoulder, as Pepe hurried them back to the inn, Amanda saw that Charlie had turned and noticed Miguel's casual advance.

The Englishman took off at a run through the stalls, sending an old woman's numerous woven baskets and hats rolling onto the stones. Miguel dodged and weaved around the obstacles, and was soon lost to Amanda's view.

The man, despite his short lead, gained in the market square, was now only a little in front. Miguel could hear his hoarse, ragged breathing as he ran. The maze of narrow streets was like a rabbit warren, the white houses claustrophobic in their closeness.

Miguel felt the sweat pouring down his back and face as he charged after his prey. They were, he knew by the odors in the air and the unkemptness of the alleyways, nearing the poor district that led to the waterfront. Old women stared disinterestedly at them as they raced past.

Suddenly, Miguel came out onto the wharf with its clutter of cargo and timbers. He saw the man dive back into another alleyway and made to follow, just as a wagonload of fish stopped directly across the mouth of the alley.

Roaring at the driver to move his wagon, Miguel stood helplessly while the old man labored to clamber back onto the seat.

Impatiently he stepped back a few paces, then ran, and leaped onto the cart, slithered over the slippery load of fish and was back in pursuit! Esteban almost collided with him on one street. They combed the alleys together.

But despite backtracking in every direction, the man was nowhere to be seen. Cursing, they made their way back to the marketplace.

She awoke drowsily from her *siesta,* stretching every limb with contentment. There was a light tap on the door.

"Come in, Bonita!" She rolled over onto her stomach and watched the dust motes in the sunlight from the window.

A firm hand thwacked her rear, and she flung around, knowing instantly that it was Miguel and with that realization pulling the covers up to her chin.

"How dare you simply walk in here, without even announcing yourself!"

His eyes traversed her slender curves beneath the single sheet and he grinned lazily. "Don't you think it's a little too late for all that indignation? Come *pequeña,* we have only a few days left together, let's make the most of that little time!" He pressed her back down onto the bed, and soon stood naked before her widening eyes. His lean, hard body was as at home without clothes as with. The darkly curling hairs of his chest tapered to a V above his hard belly, and within that rich pelt the medal of St. Christopher gleamed on a silver chain. Crisp, ebony curls of hair molded to his fine head, and in his jet-black, sensual eyes his desire burned like flame.

He took her passionately, but without haste, turning her protests aside with caresses and lingering kisses that encompassed every inch of her body until it, too, kindled and burned like a flame. She gloried in the feel of his arms about her, holding her tight, his whispered words in her ears telling of his desire for her and of the pleasure she would receive.

For the first time, she returned his kisses, drinking deeply of the sweet soft-hardness of his lips, then fiercely pressing her body to his as her own passion soared to incredible heights. When they finally found release it was as one, their bodies crushed fiercely together, lips upon lips, thigh against thigh, arms entwined in a tangle of ecstasy.

It was dusk when they awoke, and the sky was beginning to grow violet. Somewhere she could hear a guitar playing softly. The melody trembled, soared, throbbed with melancholy, and, after the moments she and Miguel had shared, it made her feel like crying. She didn't want to leave him, not now, not ever!

"Miguel, what song is that?"

He opened one eye and looked at her sleepily. "A love song. What else could be so sad, *querida?* Music is life to the people of Catalonia. Esteban plays well, does he not?" He lay back and closed his eyes.

She poked him in the ribs, until he opened them again. "Miguel, wake up and talk to me!"

"How can I when this poor body is exhausted from pleasuring you, mistress?" he teased. "If I awaken fully you may have to suffer the consequences!" Grumbling, he sat up, his hair tousled and his eyes heavy-lidded with sleep.

"Perhaps I would not mind the consequences over much, señor," she admitted, shyly reaching out to caress his chest. Her bare breasts brushed against his arm as she did so.

"Careful, *pequeña,* you are playing with fire! Now, why did you wake me up? For this?" He playfully bit her shoulder and growled.

"No. That man, Paul's man, did you catch him?"

"Not a chance, though we scoured the whole town! But never fear, now that we've been spotted, Blake will make some move. Promise me that you'll not go anywhere alone, not even with Bonita? Pepe, Esteban, or I *must* accompany you, or you could be in trouble."

She nodded. "I promise. But I don't see why *I* should be so protected? It's you Paul is after, not me!"

"Before, yes," Miguel replied grimly, "but I would wager he believes you and I are in league against him somehow, now that he knows you are here. His mind is warped, twisted. Only a pistol ball can cure him now, as one would put down a rabid dog."

He got up and dressed swiftly. "Come on, lazy one, you will be late for dinner."

After they had finished the simple meal, they walked the streets in the evening air, along with the hundreds of other folk enjoying their *paseo.* It was a warm, sultry evening with a crescent moon floating in the velvet darkness, attended by a shower of white-hot stars. The scent of flowers was everywhere.

Tonight the plaza by the cathedral was filled with people, and after Miguel and Amanda had thrust their way to the front, they saw there was dancing in the square. Torches cast giant shadows over the cobbles, and to one side a small band of musicians sat upon the rim of the fountain plucking mandolins and guitars.

Circles formed, then more circles, the smaller ones turning to and fro within the larger. It was a dizzying spectacle. Three steps right, three left, arms above the head, to the side, then left again. On and on they whirled, the girls' dresses flying with a flurry of petticoats, the young men handsome and arrogant.

"Would you like to try it, Amanda? Come, then, we will show these people how to dance the *sardana.*" Miguel flung his elaborate coat to Bonita, and led Amanda into the innermost circle.

Slowly he showed her the steps and she imitated him, enjoying herself enormously. The music grew faster and faster, tiny drums throbbing, flutes wailing. Faces flashed by, blurred and unrecognizable, but she was lost to the rhythm. Swaying, turning, the circles moved swiftly, but with the precision of the interlocking cogs of a clock.

Finally the music ceased. New dancers joined the circles. Miguel led Amanda back to Bonita, pausing to speak to an old man as he did so. He caught up with her, his dark eyes flashing with merriment.

"The old man says you dance with the abandon of a true Catalan! I did not tell him," he added in a low voice, "that you make love with the same abandon!"

Chapter Thirty-Six

She was dreaming, dreaming the same dream that had haunted her those first weeks in Spain. She saw the *Sea Dragon* explode, saw the tongues of leaping flame encompass the vessel. The smell of smoke was everywhere, stinging her throat, her nostrils, choking her. . . .

Amanda sat up, terror gripping her. It was real! There was smoke everywhere, filling the room, and licking at the door were flames, real flames. *My God, the room's on fire!* she realized with a surge of panic.

Coughing, she staggered to the floor, beating on it with her fists. The heat blistered her hands. Jagged red tongues reached for her chemise.

She reeled away, her eyes smarting and watering. Cries for help peeled from her lips, choked on the rawness and tightness of her lungs. She staggered blindly through the smoke, somehow reached the window, and flung it open. The fresh air revived her, but sent the flames leaping to twice their former size, crackling and laughing as they engulged the bed in their awful embrace.

She could hear Miguel screaming something from the passageway behind the door that was a torch.

Frantically she tried to hear what he said, but his voice was lost in the roar of the flames. She climbed out onto the windowsill, close to losing consciousness. The roof of the kitchen looked so small—if she missed it and fell to the cobbles! . . . She was sobbing as the flames raced toward her. Then she saw him, Miguel, climbing up onto the kitchen rooftop from below, his arms reaching up. He was telling her to jump, jump into his arms. The wall that the bed had been against burst into flames now. Her only chance was to do as he said!

She poised, standing, hanging on to the top of the windowframe for balance. A crowd had gathered, light moons of ghoulish faces turned upward to see her fall. Then one grinning face broke away from the crowd, and in that instant she knew who had set fire to the room, knew who had tried to burn her alive! The face had been Paul's. She leaped from the sill.

A white-faced Miguel and a trembling Bonita forced brandy between her lips in the street below. She choked and came to, her throat raw from the smoke.

A chain of people passed wooden buckets of water one to another, and Amanda realized with horror that there was a gaping black hole where her room had been, and half the one next to it—Miguel's room—before the fire was under control.

The innkeeper was wringing his hands and crying unashamedly at the loss. Esteban paid him off handsomely, and he ceased his crocodile tears and showed them to alternative rooms on the other side of the building.

"All of my things—they're gone!" Amanda wailed suddenly, "my topaz pendant, Elena's gown, all of it." She sat up in the bed.

Miguel looked uncomfortable, glancing sideways at Esteban. He nodded, and the steward withdrew the jeweled flower from his vest. "Your damned bauble is safe, *querida,* though I think you worry more about its safety than your own. Here you are." He put the chain over her head, and grinned innocently.

Instantly suspicious, she eyed him intently. "Are the de Villarins so bad off you have stooped to thievery?" she snapped.

"Oh, well, since you've such a nasty, suspicious little mind, I may as well show you now! Hand it over, Esteban, *amigo.* The damage is done." Esteban passed a small, black velvet case to Miguel, who unfastened the latch, sighing.

Amanda's heart did somersaults as she saw what was inside. A tiny flower, an exact partner to the pendant, gleamed within, pearl petals set about a center of gleaming yellow topaz. A ring, and he'd had it made for her! She looked at him in bewilderment, her eyes huge pools in the candlelight.

"I meant for you to have a memento of Spain, Mandy! Esteban took this to the goldsmith's yesterday morning, and he finished it just this afternoon. I wanted to give it to you when you left, but your damned curiosity! . . . No doubt you would have believed I meant to steal your pendant if I hadn't confessed!"

Her look alone told him she loved his gift, for she was for once, speechless! He gently tugged the velvet box from her hands.

"No, you're not having it until Captain Alexandre comes to fetch you. Now sleep! Bonita, stay with her," he ordered. "Pepe, guard the door and I'll relieve you in a few hours."

She tried to sleep, but couldn't, even after Bonita had tried bathing her temples with cold water and gently massaging her tense body.

The memory of that upturned white face, leering at her as she poised to leap into Miguel's arms, haunted her. And she had loved Paul, or had been blind or stupid enough to think she had! Thank God, she'd suffered no more than a sore throat and a thorough scare to remind her of the inferno in that room!

The afternoon came, and she must have finally slept, because Miguel was pounding at the door, urging her to get dressed for the *corrida*. She did so eagerly, anxious for any entertainment that would take her mind off the night before. She did not ask him from where he had borrowed the gown he thrust into Bonita's arms or the matching *mantilla,* though she did wonder.

It was too big in the bosom, but apart from that it fitted well, although definitely not a style she would have chosen herself, with its masses of ruffles and lace all over the skirt. The plunging neckline exposed so much of her breasts she scarcely dared to breathe.

Bonita fastened the lacy *mantilla* with a comb, and a matching shawl was draped about Amanda's shoulders, the exotic feeling of its long fringes pleasing her enormously.

"*Gracias,* Bonita, I will see you in the morning. Do not wait up."

She left the room on Miguel's arm.

A rented open carriage took them to the arena. They sat in a special box reserved for those who had money to pay for the privilege. Below and to every side were the people of Barcelona, chattering and excited, dressed in their finest clothes. Some were swigging wine from *botas,* and its sour tang mixed with that of the flowers the women wore. A feeling of *fiesta* was everywhere! Amanda scanned the faces of the crowd for Paul or his men, relieved to see no one familiar. She settled back in her seat, a little less apprehensive.

Soon a trumpet blast sounded. A hush grew over the enormous crowd as the governor of Barcelona entered, which changed to a roar of applause as the signal was given, and a strange procession entered through huge gates.

First, Miguel explained, came the three *matadores,* all noblemen, magificent in richly embroidered jackets that sparkled in the light. Their hats were black and had a strange baggy appearance, while across their arms lay the folded, magenta-colored capes. Their bearing was haughty, as if they were oblivious to the crowd's thundering applause.

Behind followed their assistants, the *cuadrillas,* dressed similarly but without such richness. *Banderilleros* and *picadores* followed in their turn, the latter mounted on gaily caparisoned horses, bearing lances. The peculiar procession bowed in the direction of the governor and then to the private boxes, and Amanda blushed as one particularly handsome *matador* let his eyes linger on her a little longer than chance would allow.

"Who is that one, the *matador* there?" she asked Miguel, curious, peering down into the dusty ring.

"Oh, him!" Miguel snorted in disgust. "That is Don Roberto del Mar. He has a villa just outside the city. We are invited to his home after the *corrida* to see some

Andalusian gypsy dancers. But I do not care to—"

"Oh, please, Miguel, I would so enjoy it! May we?"

Her eyes shone with excitement and the pleading expression won him over. He took advantage of the shadows and the long shawl, and brazenly stroked her breasts beneath the cloth of her gown. "Very well, *pequeña,* if you are sure you do not wish to—sleep—early tonight?"

She knew by the sensual dreaminess in his black eyes that sleep had not entered his mind, and with her fan she tapped him sharply on his wandering hand.

"Shame, Miguel, such ardor on the part of an escort is unseemly!" She said crossly.

He grinned at her, and they turned back to the bullfight, which was about to start.

The first of the bulls was let into the ring. A magnificent animal, he trotted to the center and stood there, snorting and pawing at the dust.

Then the *matador,* Don Roberto, re-entered. Clasping the magenta cape in both hands and to his left side, he shook it slightly to attract the animal. The moving cloth angered the beast, and, with a bellow of rage, the bull lowered its head, the huge curved horns thrust dangerously to the fore, and began its charge.

As the bull reached the *matador*'s cape the man, feet motionless, swung his body in a graceful, sweeping motion, the cape cutting a breathtaking arc through the air. The bull thundered harmlessly past the *matador*'s left flank, only a hair's breadth away! The crowd roared its approval of the beautiful movement with a cry of "*Olé*!"

After several well-executed passes, the *matador* retired to the barrier of the ring, and the *picador* took his place, astride a gallant, if ancient, horse, which was padded for protection.

The bull, incensed from the maddening, taunting passes of Don Roberto, charged at the strange horse and rider. The *picador* rose in the gaudy saddle, and, with deadly accuracy, thrust the tip of a lengthy lance into the bull's neck, where it stayed, dancing grotesquely for several moments, until the bull broke free, blood dripping from the ghastly wound. The animal bellowed, reeling in pain and bewilderment.

Amanda, her hand clutched to her mouth in horror, stared on, unable to draw herself away.

Then the *banderilleros* positioned their weakening darts in the bull's huge shoulder muscles, the bull stamping with pain and rage in an effort to dislodge them.

Don Roberto returned, bearing his cape.

Now was the final part of the spectacle, and a breathless hush settled over the crowd. Miguel called it *la fuenta,* when Don Roberto would show to the full his grace and courage and superb skill.

The black bull's hide was streaked with blood, the *banderilleros'* darts still piercing his mighty shoulders. His courage, nevertheless, was enormous. Weakened, he lowered his head for the final charge that would pierce him into eternity on the blade of the *matador*'s sword.

Amanda felt nausea fill her, and turned her eyes from the sight of the gallant bull, now kneeling, blood frothing from his mouth.

He tried vainly to struggle to his feet, not realizing he was already dead, or that the wild shouts of *"olé!"* filling the air were his epitaph.

She clutched blindly for the door, tears of disgust in her eyes, but Miguel was there, conversing with one of the *cuadrillas*.

He bent over her, seeing her face so distraught.

"What is wrong?"

"I—I wish to leave!"

"But there are two more bulls! That last one, he was a *toro bravo,* no? A bull of courage and fire!"

"Yes! And look what happened to that magnificent '*toro bravo*'!" The mules were dragging the carcass out to be butchered.

Miguel shrugged. "He was bred for this moment, *querida,*" he said gently. "Do not be upset, it is—"

"It is barbaric, inhuman! How could anyone condone the slow torture of—"

"Silence! You wanted to see it and now you have! Do not attempt to judge things you do not understand!" Irritated, he leaned back in his chair, scowling.

"I wish to return to the inn!"

"We promised to dine at Don Roberto's villa. You will not disgrace me by shunning his invitation!"

"But you said yourself you did not wish to attend!"

"I have just given our acceptance to Don Roberto's assistant. We are committed, and I wish to hear no more."

Fuming, Amanda sat through the rest of the hateful afternoon.

Don Roberto's villa, a squat building, almost forbidding, beneath the cypresses, was set on a slight incline overlooking the sea.

Along the driveway, oaks trailed vines in shadowy splendor, the shadows broken where light from the windows fingered its way between them. A three-quarter moon shone above the tiled roof, and, beyond in the gardens, water fountains caught the silvery light and sparkled like diamonds.

The don's manservant led them through long corridors and out onto a pretty courtyard, bordered on four sides by the house and walkways with arches. Into the flagged courtyard were set squares of grass, where beautifully pruned orange trees grew, their branches bearing brightly colored lanterns this night. There were stone benches to rest upon, and this Amanda did. She was still tense and upset by the scene she had endured, and angered by Miguel's lack of understanding and his brooding silence.

Several guests were already sipping glasses of wine or sherry, standing and chatting in the light of the lanterns.

"So, Don Miguel! It is good to see you again!"

"So sorry to hear of your mother's death. She was truly a gracious lady! . . ."

"Señorita Amanda, so pleased to meet you! Why, your Spanish is most excellent—Doña Francesca taught you? Ah, such patience . . ."

"I hear this troupe is excellent—Andalusians usually are."

Miguel and Amanda gave every appearance of being a most compatible couple, moving with ease among the guests and accepting their comments with apparent delight. But it was only a front. Soon Don Roberto joined them.

"So, this lovely creature is your guest in *España!* How lucky! You are most charming, *señorita.*" He kissed her hand.

Amanda smiled becomingly, and thanked him. "Why, *gracias,* Don Roberto! You are a most gracious host!"

He nodded, and bowed. "Excuse me, I must see to my staff." He paused. "But rest assured I will most certainly talk with you later!"

He left them, but not before giving Amanda a brilliant smile. She smiled inwardly at Miguel's obvious jealousy. No wonder, for Don Roberto was most attractive in a devilish way! His long black sideburns led to a perfectly trimmed, pointed beard, and his eyes were hooded and brooding, adding to his satanic appearance.

Don Roberto's manservant tinkled a little bell, and coughed discreetly.

"Ladies and gentlemen, this way, *por favor.* Dinner is served."

The rest of the gathering followed him. Miguel drew Amanda aside behind an orange tree and hissed angrily. "Kindly refrain from flirting with that man! He is a known womanizer, and if you value your reputation you will not flirt with him. He does not play games."

"Don't tell me what to do, Miguel! Don Roberto is merely a charming host, nothing more. And my reputation is *my* business!"

"On the contrary, *querida,* as long as you are with me, it is also mine! You will not speak to or be seen with him alone, is that clear?"

"Perfectly!" She retorted hotly, and thrust past him to join the others in the dining room.

Dinner was disaster of sorts. Amanda found herself seated on Don Roberto's right, with Miguel to her left.

An aging *comtessa* was on his right, resplendant with gigantic breasts and a slight shadow of a moustache on her upper lip. Miguel was most displeased, for the lady immediately engaged him in an endless discussion from which he could not escape to supervise Amanda's behavior with the *matador.* Meanwhile, Amanda sparkled and conversed wittily with their host, and as the meal continued Miguel became ever angrier.

Amanda was delighted with the decor of the room. The walls were hung with delicate Flemish tapestries, and rose brocade curtains were held closed against the night air. The table sparkled with silver and crystal, enhanced to perfection by snowy linens. She was enjoying herself tremendously, and any doubts she had of her attractiveness were soon dispelled by the devilish Roberto's flowery compliments.

Later, after the men had smoked their cigars and drunk their brandy, the women rejoined them and they were led out again into the courtyard.

Miguel was seething, and Amanda felt her own anger grow at his boorish behavior. In retaliation, she fluttered her eyelashes at Don Roberto in flagrant disobedience of Miguel's wishes, and when their host left them to converse with other guests, he took her arm roughly and drew her aside yet again.

"How dare you act so immodestly! Either restrain yourself, or we will leave at once!" he stormed.

"Don't be so stuffy, Miguelito!" she replied airily. "I am only trying to be polite. Why, even *you* must admit, the don has great courage?"

"*Sí,* but he also uses his performances to dazzle foolish women such as yourself! His exploits are known from here to Madrid! I am warning you, as my guest, you will behave in accordance with my wishes!"

There was the rattle of a tambourine and the troupe entered.

Amanda could not believe that these dark-skinned beauties were Spanish, for they reminded her of Moorish women she had seen in pictures.

They wore their hair, a glossy blue-black, parted severely in the center, and twisted into a knot above the nape. A comb held the knot in place, and some of the girls wore flowers in their hair, or large gold hoops in their ears. Their dresses were of various colors—bright yellow, scarlet, blue, white—with full layered sleeves to the elbow like bells, and tight over the hips, falling to layer upon layer of ruffles at the hem. In their hands, looped over the fingers and held in the palm by a cord, were wooden castanets. A middle-aged man accompanied them, carrying a guitar.

The dancers struck their poses, and, with the first hesitant chord, remained immobile. Then, as the music grew in power, they suddenly and in perfect unison began their dance. They brought their arms over their heads in graceful arcs, and the chattering *castanets* clacked the story of love gained, love threatened, love lost. Their faces were haughty as they moved around the courtyard like vibrant, exotic blossoms, filled with fire and passion, while the guitar, the blond wood burnished with torchlight, became an instrument of delight in the man's long skilled fingers. Finally, he slapped the wood of it twice, and the guests cried *"olé!"* and clapped with great enthusiasm.

Twice more they performed similar dances, the second time each accompanied by a young man. Amanda thrilled to it! The power of their dance and the throbbing music stirred her blood, made her feel restless and wild inside in a manner she could not explain.

Then Don Roberto stood where the dancers had been.

"Señores, I have a little surprise for you. Tonight, for your pleasure, I bring you Spain's most accomplished dancer, the lovely Señorita Carlotta Maria Vasquez, who I am sure you know better as Caro, Queen of Flamenco!"

With a flourish, Don Roberto beckoned to the shadows, and a stunningly lovely woman ran out into the light, and took up her position. Amanda noticed with surprise that Miguel's hand was gripping her waist almost cruelly, and his face was intent on the dancer.

Miguel had been surprised totally to hear that Caro was to dance. He knew that Don Roberta had known of their relationship before, and he wondered if the man had purposely said nothing—just to enjoy the look of shock on his face! Sure enough, Roberto was looking sideways at him when he glanced in his direction, a wicked half smile on his face. No doubt he is relishing the predicament I am in, Miguel thought. Somehow, he'd have to find a way to tell Caro about Amanda. When he'd borrowed the gown, there had been no time to explain anything. The last thing he needed tonight was the two of them at each other's throats!

Caro began to dance. If the other dancers had been good, she was perfection. As the music began, a mere trickle of sound like a meandering stream, she moved her upper body slowly, sensuously. Her feet were quite motionless, her arms held above her forming patterns in the light. The music was hurrying now, and she matched it note for note, dipping and stamping, her *castanets'* staccato notes accenting the wild pounding of her feet.

Miguel touched Amanda's shoulder. "Excuse me," he said stiffly, "I will be just a moment . . ."

She nodded, and turned quickly back to the dancer. She did not have to be an expert on the *flamenco* to know that what she was witnessing was very, very good.

Don Roberto sidled up to her, and stood at her side. "Señorita, are you enjoying the dancing?" He watched her face carefully. "This one, she is magnificent, *sî?"*

She nodded a little nervously, for she knew Miguel would be furious to see her talking alone with him. They were several feet away from the other guests.

"It is Caro's custom to perform only a single dance each night, so enjoy, señorita. She is almost finished!"

Don Roberto leaned a little closer. God, the *inglesa* was ravishing!

Amanda watched as the woman flung her head and arms up in a last triumphant gesture. The guests surged forward to congratulate her. She watched them idly for a few minutes until she saw the dancer slip way from her admirers into the shadows, where a tall, handsome figure drew her deeper into the gloom. Miguel! She gasped and stiffened, filled with dread and—jealousy? No!

"Is something wrong, señorita? Are you feeling ill?"

"No—no, I am quite well." She turned to Don

Roberto, a dangerously brilliant smile on her lips. Her eyes were hard to conceal to fury within her. "Don Roberto, you must tell me more of the life of a *matador*. Is it not very dangerous?"

He took her arm, and led her through the courtyard and into the gardens beyond.

Chapter Thirty-Seven

It was beautiful in the moonlight. Several water fountains sent silver jets shooting up into the night. The air was heavy with the scent of roses. Still conversing softly, Don Roberto led her far from the courtyard, down little paths that twisted and turned between the shrubs and flowers. The laughter and conversation of his guests, and the notes of a softly playing guitar, reached them only dimly now. Below was the sea, and far to the east the lights of Barcelona twinkled like fireflies.

"Your view is enchanting, Don Roberto!" She turned to him, a delighted smile on her face.

"And so are you, Amanda," he said, softly. His face held a look that frightened her. He took a step toward her, and she realized that the look was one of lust. "I have heard much of the English women, señorita, that they are most passionate and far less protected than our own señoritas. . . ."

"Not all, señor! I believe I should return to Don Miguel, he will be wondering what has become of me."

A feeling of panic grew inside her as he stepped toward her. His eyes seemed hooded, mysterious, and left her in no doubt as to his intentions.

"He will wonder nothing—no doubt he is availing himself of Carlotta's charms in some part of the villa."

"Really, señor? Nevertheless, please escort me back to the courtyard."

"No, señorita I will not." Roberto smiled, and crossed his arms.

"Very well, I will return alone." She turned to go, but he swiftly reached out and grabbed her arm, spinning her into his embrace.

She flailed at his chest, pinned against his wiry body with a strength that amazed her. Taking a deep breath, she brought her hand hard across his cheek with a resounding slap.

The blow seemed to goad him on rather than deter him! He lunged at her throat, smothering her neck with hot, wet kisses. His breathing was hoarse, and she could feel his hot breath down the neckline of her dress.

"No! Don Roberto, please!" She struggled to force his head from her throat, but with a sharp jerk he threw her beneath him to the ground.

"Relax, *querida,* you will find I am an exciting lover!"

"Get off me, you rogue!" She tried to slide from beneath him, but he held her fast, thrusting his lower body against hers. His manhood was painfully apparent against the soft flesh of her thigh, and she knew that with such passion on him he would not stop until he had taken her.

He leaned up a little, intending to free her breasts from the bodice of her gown with his other hand. In a sharp movement she brought her knee up into his groin with all of her strength. He groaned and fell on her, moaning with pain.

"Bitch! You will not get away now! When I have my breath, you will be taught a lesson you will never forget!"

"And you, del Mar!"

A hand grabbed the man by the collar and lifted him bodily from her. Then Miguel's fist cracked into his jaw, sending the man reeling to the earth. There was blood in his beard. Miguel towered over him.

Don Roberto got up quickly, although slightly dazed. His reflexes were honed to perfection after years of a *matador*'s rigorous training.

The two men circled each other warily, arms outstretched on either side. Then Roberto sank forward, dealing Miguel a crushing punch to the eye. Miguel parried with a lightning blow to the belly, and the man keeled forward, the air knocked from him.

As he rose, he grabbed Miguel's knees, bringing him crashing to the ground. For a few moments they thrashed wildly at each other. Then Roberto locked Miguel in a neck-choking grip. Amanda could see the vein starting to bulge in Miguel's head, and was about to help him when he suddenly twisted from the deadly grasp, and cracked a hard punch into Roberto's windpipe. The man screamed. Miguel hung over him, breathing hard. His eye was swelling already, a purplish welt formed high on the cheekbone. Roberto staggered to his feet, clutching his throat and coughing. His face above the beard was cut and bloody, his eyes blazing with hatred.

He lunged at Miguel with the speed that had won him so much acclaim in the bullring, but the last blow had marred his judgment for Miguel stepped nimbly aside, clasped both fists together and brought them down like a hammer across Roberto's skull! He fell to the ground with a thud, rolled over, and lay quite still.

Breathing hard, Miguel checked to be sure the man lived, and satisfied that he did, he grasped Amanda roughly by the elbow and propelled her forcibly back to the villa.

"Miguelito, darling!"

As they entered the courtyard Caro slid away from her group of admirers and wrapped her arms around Miguel's neck. She pulled back, eyeing Miguel's bruised, disheveled appearance with amusement.

"Ah, so! A lover's quarrel! How very sweet, no?" she purred. Her eyes hardened, her lips curved in a malicious smile. "Poor baby!" she crooned sarcastically to Miguel. "Does it hurt *much?*" She ran her finger spitefully over the purple welt on his cheekbone, drawing a wince from Miguel, before whirling on Amanda. "And this must be the little English mouse!" She straightened the bodice of Amanda's gown and scrutinized her with eyes that were dangerously bright. "My gown does little for you, my dear, does it?" she said disparagingly.

"I did not realize it was yours, Señorita Vasquez. However, you are right. You are much larger than I. I'm afraid the English women are not blessed with, shall we say, the *formidable* bosoms of their Spanish sisters!" Amanda smiled a sugary smile.

Caro's face flushed darkly, not deceived by her expression. "Eh, *muchacha,* do you mean—?"

"Come, ladies, enough of this! Caro, Amanda and I are leaving. I will see you—soon!" Miguel tweaked

Caro's cheek and she pouted, and flashed him a sultry smile.

"Very well, Miguelito, *querido mio. Hasta luego, entonces!*"

She blew him a kiss, flashed a look of triumph at Amanda, and glided away.

Chapter Thirty-Eight

When they reached their rooms, Amanda hurried to dip a cloth in water and bathe Miguel's face. It was a mess, the area around his eye purple and swollen, the welt below it now angry red.

Inside, she was furious. The taunts of the *matador* had hit home, and she wondered furiously as she dabbed at the wounds, just what sort of relationship Miguel had with this Caro, and if on all his trips into Barcelona, they carried on as lovers. The thought of this made her angry somehow, and her nursing of his wounds was far from tender!

Finally, he could stand it no more and thrust her from him. His face was set in an angry glare, with not the slightest hint of warmth to soften the hardness.

"That is enough! Now, do you wish to explain your behavior, madam?"

His look was accusing. In his mind she had been tried, found guilty, and only the hanging remained.

"I have nothing to explain—it is you who should explain, if anyone!"

"I? Did I stroll in del Mar's gardens and offer myself to him?"

"I did no such thing!"

"Ha! This is not borne out by your behavior earlier this evening, señorita! Fluttering your lashes, feeding that pompous idiot's vanity with your flattering! And after I had expressly warned you of his reputation!"

"So! You are now the self-appointed keeper of my virtue. Sir, your hospitality does not buy me, only my loyalty, contrary to what you think!"

"Apparently not even that, madam!"

"How dare you! I fought with that—man—with all the strength I could summon!"

"Well, that must have been a disappointment to him! He obviously felt you were loose enough to wander the gardens alone—"

"Loose! Ha! And yet your rendezvous with the *flamenco* dancer in the shadows—that is permissible!"

"I 'rendezvoused,' as you put it, with no one." His look was a little guilty now. "Caro is merely an old friend and I wished to speak with her."

"Could you not have 'spoken' to her in my hearing—or have you been lovers for years? Yes, I believe you have—and you wanted to bed her tonight, too, you—you tomcat!" She was quivering with anger and hurt, the color staining her cheeks crimson. She brushed her hair furiously.

He was taken aback temporarily, for she had come close, at least in part, to the truth. "I have bedded no one but you, since the first time I took you, madam!"

"You lie!" She screamed at him, jumping to her feet.

"I do not, madam," he insisted coldly.

She stood, her hands on her hips like a fishwife squabbling in the market. "And before—you were lovers, were you not?" She trembled as she waited for his reply, her expression accusing.

"Yes!" he roared finally, pacing up and down the narrow room. "Before our meeting, yes! But that is none of your concern!" He strode out of the room, and slammed the door loudly behind him.

Alone, she paced the floor, wringing her hands. She was still shaking with rage, her lips set stiffly, her knuckles white. How dare he accuse her! Why, if she had not seen him in the shadows with his mistress, never would she have flirted with Don what's-his-name. Well, she had wanted to make him angry, and she had succeeded!

She thought that, even now, he might be making love to that over-bosomed Spanish wench! She picked up the porcelain water pitcher and hurled it with all her strength at the closed door. But the wonderful crashing sound and fragments of china did little for her anger. In the end, she broke down, flung herself onto the bed, and sobbed until she fell asleep.

Miguel strode the now-quiet streets like a man possessed, furious at Don Roberto, and even more so at Amanda. *Díos,* had he not warned her? Ah, but she was hot-tempered and stubborn! Across the street he noticed a swinging tavern sign, a black bird almost seeming to fly upon it as it moved. The Raven's Wing! It was the tavern Esteban had told him of, where Paul's men went to carouse and womanize.

It was a rowdy place, for as he watched, two men came rolling out of the doorway into the gutter, screaming curses and thrashing in the filth. From within came coarse laughter and the sounds of voices roaring a bawdy ditty. It would not do to enter dressed as he was, for he would surely be marked as well-to-do, and his purse lifted—or worse. He ducked into an alleyway and removed his coat and stock, then hurriedly rumpled his hair and scuffed his boots with dust. Satisfied he had the appearance of a down-at-heels merchant, he hooked the coat over his shoulder, and swaggered through the tavern doors.

The noise and smells that assailed him were considerable. Unwashed bodies reeking of sweat, sour wine and ale mingled with the pungent odor of pipe smoke, garlic, and sausage spices. Sailors sprawled on the sawdusted floor, dead drunk, oblivious to the kicks dealt them or the dregs emptied over them.

A girl was dancing to a concertina's wail on one of the tables, eager men kneeling to peek up her skirts or reaching out to grasp her shapely ankles. She slapped one across the head with her foot and spat angry words at him, to the effect that he had paid only to look, and if he wished to touch—well, perhaps later, upstairs, and very cheap, too!

Miguel elbowed his way to the bar and ordered a tankard of ale in a loud, hearty voice that suggested he had already had more than a little. His bruises added to his raffish appearance. A tankard was banged down before him, slopping foam over the counter. He grasped it and flung a coin to the wench, then picked his way between the carousers to a seat a little out of the thick of things.

The girl was bending over now, her blouse gaping to reveal, much to the men's delight, both juicy breasts almost totally exposed. With whoops and cheers and many coarse jests as to the quality of the 'merchandise' the men tossed coins down the open garment, the girl giggling as the money filled her bodice.

Miguel nursed his ale between his hands, eyes half

closed and to all appearances quietly drunk. In reality he scanned the tavern for the men who had waylaid him—and for Manuel's possible murderer. There were none that fitted the description Esteban had given him. A lank-haired man in the corner looked right from behind, but when he roared for beer his accent was a rolling Dutch, and Miguel quickly discarded him.

For over an hour he sat there before an idea came to him. The wench was sprawled across a burly sailor's knees now, kissing her, his hand lost beneath the folds of her skirts.

Miguel lurched over to the couple and grabbed the girl's arm, pulling her from the sailor's grasp.

"My turn, *amigo!*" he drawled, slurring the words as if drunk.

He tugged the girl to him and made to kiss her. The sailor grabbed him from behind.

"Hey, *amigo,* I paid her for the night!" He shoved the girl away and grabbed Miguel by the throat in a huge, hairy hand. His stubbly face was nasty.

Miguel gasped in pretended fear. *"Sí, señor,* I am sorry! Perhaps this—?" He allowed his glance to lead the man's eyes down to his hand, and showed him the glint of gold in it.

The sailor's eyes grew greedy and he stared undecided, first at the girl and then at the money. Cursing, he relaxed his grip, and stormed about the tavern clutching his considerable bribe.

The girl led Miguel up a gloomy, dank stairway and into a room, carefully locking the door behind her. She lost no time in removing every vestige of the clothing she wore and stood, totally naked and smiling, before him.

"I am very glad, señor, that you won me! You are much more handsome than that other lout!" she smiled impishly.

Miguel straightened up and grinned. "You are handsome also, Señorita—?"

"Guadalupe. Call me Lupe!"

"Sí, Señorita Lupe! Now, you are most attractive, but I regret I want only to ask you some questions!"

Lupe pouted, and sat down on the bed, totally unembarrassed by her nudity. Suddenly, she brightened.

"Yes, I will answer the questions for the money—I will give you the other, free!" she offered eagerly.

Miguel laughed and shook his head. "Sorry, *muchacha,* not tonight."

"You're not drunk are you?" she decided, after staring at him intently.

"No, I am not. But that is our secret!" He tossed her the grubby blouse and she shrugged it on sulkily, while he crossed to the window and peered into the alley below. It was pitch black.

"I want to know if you have seen some men. In your profession, I thought perhaps . . . ?"

"Yes, I see very many men! There are not many who only wish to ask me questions, though!" Her wide mouth flashed him a saucy grin. "These men, what do they look like?"

"Well," he sat down beside her, "one is an Englishman, very skinny, unkempt."

"And with a great stink about him. *Sí,* I have met him. He is a *peeg.* Look what he did to me!" She rolled back her sleeves to reveal huge bruises on her upper arms. "Did he do that to your face, señor?"

"Hm? These? Oh, no! Tell me, what did this Englishman talk about? Did he say anything about another Englishman, maybe his employer?"

"Believe me, señor, he did not talk very much! I had hardly laid down when—"

"Yes, your charms are most delectable! But do you remember anything?" He waited impatiently.

She pressed a finger to her lips in thought. "Well, he did not say very much. But there was one thing, when he was removing his breeches he did say something very strange, and I did not understand what he meant."

Miguel grasped her shoulder, excitedly. "Yes! What was it?"

"He said he would imagine old 'peg leg' didn't get much of a tumble anymore, and that seemed to please him, señor, for he laughed very much."

"Then he *is* still in Barcelona." Miguel leaned back, satisfied. "Peg leg" was obviously the crude name the Englishman had given his crippled employer. So, now he would have to flush them out!

He described the third who had waylaid him, but this time Lupe shook her head sorrowfully.

"No, señor, I am sorry, so many men fit that description! Why don't you stay a while below in the tavern? He comes here often, the smelly one." She finished dressing, caching the coin he gave her beneath a loose floorboard in the room. "I must go back now, señor. I am a working girl, and the night is still very young." She laughed and winked slyly.

He nodded his thanks. Lupe blew him a mischievous kiss before going back to her work, locking the door once again and thrusting the key into her bodice.

He stood thoughtfully in the dank landing for some

time, finally going back down into the taproom and resuming his vigil. It was almost two hours before Lupe signaled to him over the shoulder of her latest customer.

He looked in the direction in which she pointed. His "friend" from the marketplace had just come in, arm in arm with a fat, greasy-looking man who closely resembled the one he had killed during the attack. He watched, slumped down in his seat, as the two roared for ale and staggered to a corner bench.

Catching Lupe's eyes questioning him, he nodded. Then he pointed to the two men, then to her, and then finally up the stairs.

She caught his meaning immediately, and withdrew from the sailor's embrace. With a lithe, swinging walk she jiggled her way past the two. One of them said something as she passed, and Miguel grinned as she leaned over provocatively to listen, her blouse gaping. The Englishman reached inside and squeezed her breasts, then gathered her into his arm and pulled her onto his lap, fondling her eagerly.

Miguel watched for several minutes as the girl passed from one lap to another. Then, with a look of triumph in his direction, she led the two men up the gloomy stairway. They followed her, grinning in anticipation.

He waited for a while, giving the men a chance to undress. Naked, they would be less anxious to flee! Then he got to his feet and walked slowly up the creaking stairs. The landing had doors leading off it, and from many came the sounds of lusty lovemaking. Lupe's was at the end, directly facing the passageway. He pressed his ear to the door and listened, hearing the ponderous grunts of the fat man and Lupe's giggling.

He pulled the knife from his boot, grasped the doorknob, then flung open the door, stepped inside, and slammed it behind him.

The paunchy man had already mounted her. Miguel was filled with disgust at the sight of his flabby body covering the little doxie. The skinny one, even skinnier now he was naked, sat beside them on the bed, fondling her breasts. Every face but Lupe's turned, open-mouthed in surprise.

Miguel gestured first the fat man away from the girl, then the other. He bent over and picked up all their clothes. They watched fearfully as he swung open the casement and threw the filthy, stinking rags into the alleyway. The Englishman made as if to stop him, but Miguel jerked his knife at him and the man retreated.

"Now, sit!" He pointed to the bed. "Señorita, you go in here, please." Protesting, he shoved Lupe into a cobwebby closet, and made a great show of locking it. He did not want them to get their revenge on the girl. Better they should think her uninvolved!

Silently, he towered over the two men while they wetted their lips and tried not to meet his eyes.

"You, señor—" he gestured to the Englishman—"tear the covers, bind your friend to the bedposts." Fearfully, the man did as he was told. "Now yours. Tie your ankles—tighter! Good! Come here, and bring that rag with you!"

The man, his feet bound, hopped across to de Villarin, who grabbed the rag and lashed the man to the bed by his wrists. Like trussed fowl, naked and ready for the pot, they watched him with fear in their eyes.

"Now, let us have good manners! You have my name, do you not?" They both nodded. "Well, it is only fair that you tell me yours. You first, *ingles!"*

"Charlie, sir, Charlie Watson!"

"And you?"

"Torres. Henrique Torres."

"What do you know of an attack on my life a few weeks ago? There were three men, and one resembled you, Torres. The one that shot at me! I had no choice but to kill him."

"I know nothing of any—"

Miguel held the knife blade across the man's throat, barely touching.

"Yes, yes, I am Joaquin's brother! Do not hurt me, *por favor!"* Beads of sweat broke out on Torres's forehead and upper lip.

"Very good! Now, a second question. Who are you working for?"

Neither man would answer and both refused to meet his eyes.

He leaned across the man who called himself Charlie, and gripped him cruelly by the jaw. "Charlie, I will ask you only once more, you runt! After that I will use my knife to ensure you will never again bed a wench or father a child! Do I make myself quite clear?" He grinned.

Charlie's eyes were round with fear.

Miguel brought his hand down toward the man's groin, and Charlie whimpered in terror.

"No, please gov'na, oi'll tell yer! It's Blake, Paul Blake, the one 'as knocked up yer sister!"

Miguel nodded. "I thought as much! Now, where is

he?" His lips were thin and cruel and he spat the words through gritted teeth. His grip was almost cracking the man's jaw, yet Charlie shook his head. "I said *where is he?*" Miguel's voice was terrifying now.

"I can't—he'd kill me! Honest he would! And if'n *you* kill me, you ain't gonna find 'im. He's well hid, he is!" Charlie added, a little braver as he realized he still held a trump card.

Slowly, Miguel relaxed his grip. "Yes, you have a point there." He stood and walked across to the alley window.

Below was deserted still, but he could hear the chilling howl of mating cats from somewhere near, and very faintly the sounds of merriment from the tavern beneath. He kept his back to his two prisoners, his body tense.

"Who killed the old man?" he asked softly.

There was no word from either man.

"Who killed him?" He repeated, slapping the wicked blade threateningly against his palm. It gleamed in the candlelight.

Two pairs of eyes watched him fearfully and the stench of terror filled the room. But both men remained silent.

"Very well, if we must do things the hard way, we will! I shall carve you into little pieces. Before I am finished you will *beg* for the privilege of telling me the murderer's name." He advanced toward Henrique and the man shook, his naked belly wobbling and glistening with sweat.

"No, señor! *Madre de Díos,* no!"

Miguel ran the stiletto lightly across the man's

stomach. It was paper thin, razor sharp, and left a line of blood where it touched. Henrique was whimpering, pleading with him, but he felt no mercy, for they had shown none to Manuel.

The blood seeped from the light wound and started trickling down the man's belly, like little furrows of rain down a window pane, bright-red and shiny.

Henrique's eyes watched it spill, drip from his body onto the gray sheet and leave a spreading stain. He was praying fervently. Miguel bent down as if to slash him again, and the gross body shivered away from the knife, straining at the bonds that held it.

"Very well, señor, enough! It was another man. He said, he and I, we should take revenge for my brother. Señor Blake, he agreed! He promised us much gold if we killed you. He told us of the villa, everything . . ." The man was babbling almost incoherently now.

"How did you know that I might be riding out that night? How?"

"We didn't! We rode from here to the *pueblo,* and were camped in the *piñons* when the storm started. We—we saw a figure riding down the hillside in the lightning. It looked like you, same spooky horse, the man wearing a rich-looking cloak, señor! So, Gualterio, he said it would be better to get it over with. We—we had planned to follow if you rode out the next day, but this way the storm would give us cover." He was weeping now.

"We sat our mounts beneath the cypresses near the bend in the road. The horse came nearer, nearer. Gualterio, he had his pistol ready, but when the lightning flashed I saw it was an old man, his face dark and wrinkled above the cloak. I grabbed my partner's hand, señor, and told him, 'No, it is not de Villarin, do not shoot!' Gualterio laughed, señor, and said that he needed the practice, anyway! As the old man passed us, Gualterio fired—shot him from behind! The horse kept going to the church. We watched and the priest ran outside. Then, later, when he carried the body inside, we rode off." His look was agonized, and he closed his eyes and shuddered. *"Díos,* forgive us!"

"God may, but I will not!" Miguel thought for a moment, toying with the knife.

His face, its battered appearance giving it an evil cast, was set in a hard mask of hatred. What should he do? To set them free to carry a message to Blake seemed the best plan. It would serve little purpose to hold one as hostage—they were not honorable men and would doubtless allow the man he kept to die! He was forced to hope Paul Blake's desire for revenge was strong enough to overcome his wish to stay in the shadows.

"I will release you," Miguel decided finally, "to carry a message to Blake. Tell him I wish to meet with him, and this—Gualterio. That I demand a chance to resolve this, man to man and to the death! I am staying at—"

"We know the place," Charlie butted in. "We'll tell 'im."

"Good. Have him send word to me there of the time and place. If I do not hear from him, I will not rest until I have torn this city apart and ground all of you into the dust! Is that clear? *Bueno!"*

He leaned over the naked men, whose relief was very obvious, and slashed the bonds from their wrists. They worked feverishly to untie their ankles.

As he reached the door, Henrique pleaded, "Our clothes, señor? What should we do?"

"That, fat one, is your problem!"

He left them hurriedly before they could see the tears in his eyes: tears that he had held in check since they told of the brutal and senseless murder of Manuel.

Chapter Thirty-Nine

Miguel's heart was heavy as he climbed the stairway to his room. Esteban was sitting on the floor, leaning against Amanda's door, and he stood as Miguel reached the landing, his face set in a ferocious scowl.

"Where the devil did you go, *amigo?* Pepe is out combing Barcelona for your worthless hide this very minute," he growled.

"My little *inglesa* and I had a falling out, nothing more. I needed some air and a chance to clear my head. While I was walking, I came upon that tavern you mentioned, the Raven's Wing? I found two of Paul's men there. I told them I wished a meeting with their master."

"They worked you over pretty good, eh?" Esteban grimaced, nodding at his friend's battered face. "I trust you paid them back in kind?"

Miguel grinned wearily. "No, Esteban, they didn't do it! Del Mar tried to force himself on Amanda earlier, at his villa. We had a little show of fisticuffs while I taught him some manners."

"Not so little, by the looks of it! Are you that jealous of her affections?" Esteban queried in a bantering tone.

Miguel bristled visibly. "Was I supposed to let him

rape the woman, then? She *is* under my protection after all. Jealousy be damned!" Esteban did not look convinced, he noticed. "Now, let me tell you what took place." He briefly described the events in the tavern. "We should have word from them soon. In the meantime, get some sleep. I'll take over for you."

Esteban nodded, grinning as Miguel turned the doorknob to Amanda's room. It would not open.

"Here, *amigo,* is the other key." He handed it to him. "She locked it from within while screaming every curse in the book after you! You must have made her very angry, *señor mio.* Something about Caro, was it not?" Esteban finished innocently.

"Mind your own damned business, Esteban, and get some sleep," Miguel growled. He turned the key in the lock and slipped inside the room.

Patches of silver moonlight patterned the walls and floor, falling across Amanda's sleeping form. Her flushed face was tear-streaked, the sweet rise and fall of her breathing as innocent as a child's, he thought, looking down at her.

How could she protest his lovemaking, the little minx, when it was so obvious she enjoyed it as much as he? He'd only to caress her, hold her, and she crumbled as the walls of Jericho had crumbled. Well, she would be free of him soon enough. In a day or so, Alexandre's ship would dock, and on the outgoing voyage Amanda would be returned to her beloved England.

Reluctantly, he admitted to himself he was not eager for her to leave. But he had no claims on her, no means to force her to stay. Damn! The one woman he could have loved, the one woman with fire, courage, spirit to match his own, and she had been the mistress of his sworn enemy! Had she given herself to Paul with all the deep sensuality, the passion he knew she possessed—or with the same show of reluctance as when he took her? Well, either way, it didn't matter. She had definitely not been virgin that first time he'd taken her; he need feel no guilt for taking her innocence too, he rationalized.

The alley was dark and deserted below the casement. He checked the hallway. It, too, was empty. He locked the door from inside, stripped off his clothes and slid into bed next to Amanda.

She barely stirred as he brushed her lips with his own, lifting the heavy tresses of her hair and spilling it through his fingers. His fingertips traced circles on the smooth swell of her shoulder, then across to her throat. He could feel the pulse there, throbbing beneath his touch. He replaced his fingers with his lips, unfastened the ties of her chemise and bared her lovely breasts to his caresses. His mouth played languorously there until the rosy tips puckered, became hard and swollen, and she moaned softly in her sleep. He dropped his head lower, running the tip of his tongue across the flat plateau of her belly, tasting the woman-taste of soap, of salt, and the indefinable fragrance that was her own scent. His hands stroked her thighs, rose higher, plundered the secret portals of her womanhood. A quiver ran through her as even in sleep she responded to his intimate caresses. He laughed softly, breathing into her shell-like ears until her eyes suddenly flew open.

He covered her mouth with his own in time to stem the surprised cry that broke from her lips.

"Hush, *mi estrellita,* it is I, Miguel."

She relaxed somewhat, then tensed again as his hand resumed its exploration of her lush body.

"Why don't you invade your sweet little Caro's bed, not mine," she hissed softly, tearing his hand away. "I'm sure she'd enjoy it much more than I!"

"Perhaps," he agreed. "But I would not!" He leaned over and peered intently into her eyes. "Why, they are brown—not green," he said, in mock surprise.

"I'm not jealous of that over-bosomed wench of yours!" she retorted hotly. "So you are wasting your time."

"Oh, I wouldn't say that, *querida."* Her nipples blossomed under his teasing fingers. "But tell me, if you aren't jealous, why are you getting so angry?"

"I'm not angry," she spat. "I've just decided that I've had enough of you forcing yourself on me."

"Then take my hand away," he taunted.

She reached down, but as she did so he swiftly covered the soft triangle at the junction of her thighs with his own strong hand. His caresses sapped her strength and made her weak, made her breath catch huskily in her throat.

"Once you called me Blake's whore," she cried desperately. "Am I now de Villarin's whore?" Her voice trembled slightly with rage at her own body's betrayal.

A stab of guilt pricked him. "Does it make that much difference, Amanda?" he asked cruelly. Damn, couldn't she sense his need of her, with the confrontation with Blake so near at hand? She'd understood instinctively that night his mother had died.

"Let me set you straight, Miguel, once and for all time. Before you, there was only one man, and he took me only once! Once! That man was not Paul Blake."

Her eyes flashed angrily, and she flung his hands from her body and stepped from the bed. "Not, sir, that it's any of your business!"

"You don't really expect me to believe that! Granted, those strange coincidences may have brought you to Spain, but you admitted yourself that you ran after him to London, that you pleaded with him to marry you! It does not sound to me like the innocent act of a virgin maid—chasing after a man who had ordered her—in no uncertain terms—to get out!" Irritation filled him. God, how he wanted her! The lust was like a fever raging through him, savage and reckless. "I know the passionate nature you try so hard to conceal from me. You ran after him because you wanted him to assuage those passions in the same way he had done so before!"

She turned to him, her naked curves silhouetted by the night, her arms held out on either side as if offering herself.

"This is all men want—this! And you are no better than he, for all your talk of honor. You do not seek to give me love, or ask for mine, only to use me for your pleasure! You know you can take me when you choose. Your strength is greater; you've proved that many times. You can even force my body to respond to your caresses, but you will never, never possess me totally! I will always be only half a woman in your arms, Miguel, in any man's arms, until I am loved, and love in return!"

She tossed back her heavy mane of hair and laughed. Her eyes glittered brightly in the shadows.

"Is half a woman enough for you, Don Miguel?" she jeered.

In answer to her challenge, he gripped her by the hair

and hauled her roughly into his arms. His other arm trapped her around the waist and held her fiercely against the mat of hair upon his chest. He forced back her head and kissed her savagely full upon the lips until her mouth parted and yielded to his questing tongue. He arched her backward into his arms, tumbling with her to the floorboards.

"Tonight, little one, half of you will have to be enough. But, by *Díos,* that half would be enough for any man!" he breathed huskily.

He started to caress her, his mouth and his fingers working their magic, as always, on her senses. He mouthed and lapped at her breasts until her loins pounded for release, until she wanted to scream. Her skin tasted honey-smooth upon his lips and he was lost, reveling in the woman-scent and feel of her beneath his hands. His mouth coursed slowly the length of her lovely legs, lingering to nuzzle the hollows of her knees, journeying upward once again.

There was a desperation in him now. Though he'd said it was enough, it wasn't! He wanted to possess her totally, mind and body, and though the latter responded as always, he could feel no emotion in her but only passion, not caring. God, he wanted her to care for him, not just his body! Could he penetrate her resistance? Could he vanquish her resistance with a passion so great she would cry out, would cling to him, admit she held nothing back, admit—she loved him? What devil in him demanded such a response? What urged him to insist upon it, while he would make no such admission of his own? Could not, in fact. He had never told the women he had bedded that he loved them, and they had not asked him to lie. He did not intend to start now.

Strong hands parted her silky thighs. He dropped his head to them and traced circles on the trembling flesh with his lips. His mouth moved higher. She jerked upward suddenly, moaning. He held her fluttering hands to her side and continued. She writhed beneath his knowing lips, small cries breaking from her. A light film of moisture dewed her throat, trickled down the valley between her breasts. Still his hands and his mouth roamed everywhere. Her skin tingled from his touch as if stroked by lightning. She tossed her head from side to side, begging him with mumbled words to free her, to leave her alone. But her hips arched upward to offer what she had sworn to deny him with a curious frenzy of their own.

He lifted her to the bed and was inside her with a swift and powerful lunge before she touched the sheets. Her nails raked his back, her legs entwined him, held him fast. Her lips returned his kisses with a voracious hunger that thrilled him. Somewhere through the blinding haze of pleasure, she remembered that this could be the last time, the very last time she would ever know this pleasure with him. Overwhelming sadness filled her, why she did not know. But there was no doubt that their bodies could have been made for each other, fashioned by a greater artist than any living, for this one purpose.

Soft, yielding flesh met strength and power and firmness, and the two fused to a greater whole. Silken, fiery tresses tumbled over crisp, black locks; the roughness of his beard, unshaven, rested against the soft, creamy splendor of her own cheeks and it, too, had the power to inflame her by its very maleness. The springy curls upon his chest rubbed roughly against her tender breasts as she lay beneath him, as he took her with mighty, possessive lunges. He forced her to forget the existence of anyone or anything save the two of them upon the sheets, of time, of her vow to withhold all but the physical responses to his loving.

She was filled with a savage pain, a primeval need to have him possess her. The fury and the bitter-sweet ecstasy of his caresses were overwhelming. Now the hardness of him within her and the sheer, wild urgency of his thrusts hurtled her into a spinning maelstrom of dizzying sensation, where touch and taste and scent and giving were all, reality nothing.

It seemed endless, as she wished it could be. The pulsing deep in her belly grew to a throbbing bubble of exquisite feeling that bordered on pain, but was somehow inexplicably mingled with intense pleasure. It poised on the brink of bursting, of flooding her with release, for minutes that seemed like an eternity. She bit wildly at his shoulder, clawed at the smooth, tanned flesh of his back and drew blood, felt the moan surge upward from within her and end as a joyous, gasping sob as the bubble burst. There was a sensation of many-colored lights against her closed eyelids, of being extraordinarily weightless, as if she could fly.

Miguel still moved deeply, tenderly within her. He clasped her chin and forced her to open her eyes. They were dewy and glistening in the moonlight.

"Tell me, *querida,* tell me that you gave me half a woman—and be damned for a liar!" he shouted.

"Yes, you devil, yes! You know I could hold nothing

back—not this time! You tricked me, you forced me, you would stop at nothing to prove me wrong, to satisfy your own enormous lust, damn you!" she panted.

Satisfied with her response, he chuckled softly, renewing his thrusts, gathering her up and holding her close in one arm, while his other hand fondled the crushed weight of her velvety breasts beneath his chest.

She felt a trickle of desire fill her again. Was she insatiable, wanton? Nevertheless, she was soon lost once more in the heady ecstasy of before.

Miguel found violent release at the moment her own needs were satisfied for a second time. She held nothing back, could hold nothing back with the total relinquishing of her body to his will. Tears flowed down her cheeks as she clung to him, crying his name as he fell, panting, to her side.

He held her tightly in his arms, his thoughts in turmoil. He had known that which he'd desired, knew she had given herself to him totally. He'd felt it the first time, and again just seconds ago. Despite her words, she had been completely his, and his own release had been like nothing he'd ever experienced before. It left him feeling awed and—something more. Afraid! But of what? Himself!

"Don't, *querida mia.* Dry your eyes." He dried them for her with his kisses, tasting salt-tears on his lips. "Why are you crying? Did I hurt you?"

He smiled doubtfully. The strange feeling inside him had shaken his composure even more than he thought.

"I'm crying because I love you, you blind fool! And I am equally blind, for I didn't realize it myself until a little while ago! Isn't it amusing, Don Miguel? I have every reason to hate you, do I not?" She laughed, a brittle laugh that bordered on hysteria. "You took me, doubted me, used me—all of it—but *I love you!*" She laughed again, her laughter turning to sobs that racked her body.

His shocked face was pale in the shadows of the room.

Chapter Forty

She was awake when ringing hoofbeats on the cobbles shattered the stillness of the night. Amanda flew across to the casement in time to see Miguel's ghost-gray stallion thunder past below, with his master furiously urging the steed to even greater speed. Sighing, she returned to the bed. The coldness of the space where he had been was what had wakened her. It seemed even colder and emptier now.

Her body felt weak, not so much from the passion they had shared, but from the knowledge of what she had admitted to him. She loved him! Now she understood her reluctance to return to England: She didn't want to leave *him*. You silly little fool, she chided herself silently. You've made the same mistake again, fallen in love with a man who wants only to use you, to use your body for his pleasure! Oh God, she wanted desperately to run away, to hide, to leave Spain this very minute. How could she bear to see the mocking laughter in his eyes in the morning light, to see the triumphant smile on his damned, arrogant face? She sighed again and crawled under the covers, wiping her tears on the corner of the sheet. The sky was growing lighter by the minute. If only the time would fly past to when she was aboard the *L'Aigle d'Or,* and bound for home.

Esteban was pounding furiously on the door, his angry shouts growing louder by the minute.

"Señorita Sommers, open up! Amanda, blasted woman! Damn it, open this door, I say!" The door bulged inward beneath his fists.

She pulled a wrap around her and hurried to let him in, rubbing her eyes sleepily.

Esteban burst in as she opened the door, and looked wildly about him. "So, he has really gone. The blasted fool! Did he say where he was going? No? Damn him and his stupid pride!"

He stormed back and forth, clenching and unclenching his fists. "Didn't I tell him when the time came we would go together? He swore it—and now, this!" He thrust a crumpled sheet of parchment into her hands.

The ink was smudged as if whoever had written the message had been too hurried to blot it dry. She read it swiftly.

"When did this come?" she asked, returning it to him.

"Early this morning, around three of the clock. Miguel was drinking in the taproom below. He'd woken Pepe to guard your door. Then he came and told the lad not to leave his post, that he had to go out for a while. We found this in Miguel's room this morning." He screwed the parchment into a ball and flung it across the room. His tired face was deeply etched with lines of worry, his gray eyes troubled. "Pepe said that he was very drunk, señorita, but that he insisted I should see you to Capitain Alexandre's ship this morning. How long will it take you to get ready?"

"I have very little to pack since the fire. A few minutes, no more. Esteban, please go after him! If he is drunk, there's no telling . . ." Her voice trailed off lamely.

"Sí, but I cannot! He insisted!"

"Nonsense! He's not here now, after all. Pepe is capable of escorting me to the ship—Bonita too, if you insist. I know you want to go after him. Paul Blake and his men will stop at nothing; they've proved that already. I would not believe his promise to meet with Miguel alone, even if it is in writing. Go quickly, Esteban!" she urged, shaking him gently by the shoulders.

Indecision tore at the steward. She could see it in his face.

"You would be safe aboard *L'Aigle d'Or.* Will you promise me that you will not do anything foolish?" he asked with a doubtful expression. "Miguel would never forgive me if—"

"Yes, I promise!" she said impatiently. "Now, go, and God be with you."

She hurried him off, finally, then leaned against the door, breathing deeply. She silently prayed that he would be in time to help Miguel. The crumpled note caught her eye. She stooped and picked it up, scanning the spidery scrawl. It was Paul's handwriting, sure enough. The letters blurred as her eyes swam with tears. A message—or an invitation to a funeral?

She dressed quickly, as she had promised, in Caro's yellow gown. She had nothing else save for her night chemise and a few shifts she had borrowed from Bonita. She lifted the pearl-and-topaz pendant from the dusty dressing table and looked at it for a long while, remembering the matching ring Miguel had promised her. Her memento of Spain, he'd said. It seemed a very long time since that night. But there would be no need of trinkets to remember him: the pain of her unreturned love for him would more than serve that purpose.

Amanda fastened the chain about her neck as Bonita came in.

"Are you ready, señorita?"

"*Sí*, thank you. Could you pin up my hair, please? It's so hot this morning!" So hot, in fact, that she felt weak.

Bonita nodded and began scooping the heavy strands into a knot at Amanda's nape.

They were both busy with their own thoughts and fears, and little was said.

The sun was up now, spilling brilliant light into the room. Noisy doves cooed in the rain gutters. Amanda patted the perspiration from her face with shaking hands, then glanced about the room. Yes, she had everything.

"You can tell Pepe I am ready to leave now."

"Will you breakfast here, señorita, or below in the tavern?"

"Oh, I feel too queasy to eat anything, thank you, Bonita. The heat is so oppressive." She swayed slightly, clutching a chairback for support. The excitement, it had all been too much.

Bonita looked at her strangely. "Are you unwell? Are you sure? Let me see if I can find something cooler for you to wear, that gown is far too hot for daytime, no, señorita?"

Amanda nodded gratefully. "Would you? Thank you!" She sat down suddenly.

Bonita left the room, worriedly clucking like a mother hen over her chick.

Amanda sat there for several minutes, then decided to lie down until the dizziness passed. Caro's gown was sodden with perspiration and stuck to her spine. She passed a limp hand across her brow. If only she could erase the image from her mind, of Miguel's face, white with shock, when she blurted out that she loved him!

Time passed. It seemed to be taking Bonita ages to find a gown. Could something be wrong? Perhaps they had word of Miguel!

She stood, half afraid, half eager, as the door opened a crack, recoiling in horror as Charlie Watson slid through and quickly closed it behind him. He was grinning, showing rotten, yellowed teeth, and she could smell the stink of his unwashed body from across the room.

He stifled her cry with a warning finger to his lips. "Don't try it, luv! There's two o'me mates got that tasty little maid o'yers next door, and yer groom too. If'n ye make a fuss, they've had it, see?" He drew his finger across his throat in a gesture that left no doubt in her mind to his meaning.

"What do you want with me?" she asked, surprised at the calmness of her voice.

"It's not wot *I* want, see, luv, so much as wot Mister Bleedin' Paul Blake wants. And wot 'e wants is you! Now, are ye comin' peaceful, like, or does we have ter persuade ye?" He leered evilly.

"I'll come quietly, but only if you swear you will not hurt my maid and Pepe."

"Right you are, then! We'll just fix it so's they can't start nothin' for a while, tie 'em up. That do ye?" He leered.

She nodded and licked her dry lips, dreading the answer to her next question. "One more thing. Don Miguel—is he—is he—?" The words wouldn't come.

"Dead? No, not yet he ain't," Charlie gloated. "But he walked into our little trap like a bleedin' lamb to the slaughter, he did. Drunk as a lord he was, too, but he got in a few good 'uns before he went down." He fingered his jaw ruefully, and she noticed a darker shadow through the stubble. "I'm reely lookin' forward to finishin' him off, I is!" he added with relish.

Miguel reined in his horse and looked about him. The arena was directly in front, the smell of the bulls pungent and heavy in the night air. The row upon row of benches seemed eerie, as if ghostly spectators sat, hushed, upon them, waiting for the spectacle to begin.

The fog in his head still lingered, dulling his senses. He wheeled the stallion violently about, imagining he saw someone skulking in the shadows. A cat slithered past him, amber eyes glowing, and was swallowed up by the gloom of an alley.

The stallion whickered, stamping nervously in the dust. Miguel patted its head jerkily and the horse calmed beneath him. He kneed its flanks and urged the animal forward through the arch.

Now he sat in the center of the bullring. Fingering his pistol beneath his shirt, he scanned about him for some sign of movement. The place reeked of death from the afternoon's *corridas,* and the sickly sweet scent of crushed flowers. The silence unnerved him. *Díos!* He'd been a fool to ride out here alone! For a second he considered galloping off at full speed. There would be other times to face Paul Blake. But, no, he wanted it done with—finished! There was something more to his life now than vengeance!

A shadow separated itself from the pitch black of the arches leading beneath the arena with an uneven gait, the footsteps dragging in the sand. He knew before the man spoke that it was Blake.

"So, de Villarin, at last we meet again."

A torch flared up with a sputter behind him, casting grotesque shadows on the ground. Miguel watched silently as Paul limped toward him, noting the crooked rise and fall of his shoulders as he did so.

"You're not alone." It was a statement rather than a question, for the bearer of the torch would, of course, be one of Paul's men. Miguel slithered from his horse and swayed sideways, holding onto his saddle for support.

The liquor on his breath reached Paul, who burst into vicious laughter.

"Drunk, de Villarin? Who'd have thought it? The brave, noble lord needed Dutch courage to keep our appointment! My, how you have changed!" he sneered derisively.

"And you, Blake, have changed little. You're still a coward and a liar!"

"Come, come, let's be gentlemen, señor! This is neither the time nor the place for name calling. Didn't we have a more important reason for this little *tête-à-tête?*" His tone mocked Miguel and his condition. "Gualterio!"

A tall figure appeared beside Blake. The torchlight

revealed the hawklike features of the man, twisted into a malevolent grin. Miguel's sharp intake of breath hissed through his teeth. Manuel's murderer! Rage filled him, sobering him somewhat. He forced himself under control, the effort sending a giant tremor through his body. He steadied himself, as a third man, this one short and squat, joined the other two opposite him. Henrique Torres. So it was three against one. The odds didn't scare him, not with the anger and bloodlust coursing through him like strong wine.

"Did you search the alley?"

"Sí." Henrique nodded. "He came alone."

Paul's voice grew louder.

"I've given much thought to this meeting, Don Miguel. It hardly seems sporting for you to take me on in this condition, do you think?" he gestured to the wooden peg that protruded from the knee of his breeches. "These men shall be my seconds. All of them! But, first, answer me one question." He paused. "How were you and that lovely bitch, Amanda, able to be certain that I would fall into your little trap? That first meeting in the tavern with her—was that planned, or did you decide to use it later, at the Comptons' ball? Did they help to conspire to my downfall, hmmm?"

"You talk in riddles, Blake! There was no plot against you. I came to England to avenge my sister, nothing more," Miguel growled.

"You lie, de Villarin!" Paul screamed. "But no matter, you succeeded, however you went about it. There's nothing left, nothing, not even Blakespoint—and for that you will die." He jerked his head at Gualterio and the man advanced on Miguel.

Miguel tore off his jerkin and shirt and tossed them

to the dust, the pistol still inside, and faced Manuel's murderer. The light of the torch lit the sweat on the rippling sinews of his bared chest with a golden sheen.

Gualterio feinted a lunge forward, backed off laughing as Miguel dived at the empty space.

Miguel shook his head, ridding his senses of the last vestiges of liquor. They circled each other warily, Miguel's fists raised ready to attack or defend. Through his concentration, he heard Paul's voice.

"We shall see, de Villarin, if you are as agile when Gualterio has finished with you. Then, you and I, we will finish this man to man."

Miguel let out a great bellow of laughter. "No, Blake, not as man to man—you're too yellow!"

The lapse in his attention was put to good use by his opponent. Suddenly the man hurtled onto Miguel, felling him and pinning his shoulders to the dirt. The breath blasted out of Miguel as he hit the ground. He clawed upward, anchoring his hands about Gualterio's throat and squeezing hard. The fingers at his own throat slackened their grip. He swung his fist upward beneath his captor's chin, the crack as his blow connected on bone sounding sharply in the silence.

Gualterio's eyes blazed, and he returned the punches, first to one side of the don's face, then to the other. Miguel strained upward, the cords in his shoulders and neck bulging as he forced the bigger man from his vantage point above him. Then he rolled over, leaped full weight on the swarthy Spaniard who was now beneath him, his fists hammering into his face, his gut. His knuckles felt good as they pounded against the other man's flesh, and with every blow his rage was renewed.

Then a hand grabbed him by the shoulder and spun him around into yet another meaty fist, as Henrique Torres joined the fray. The squat man lacked the speed of Miguel's lightning moves, but made up for it with blows that had the force of piledrivers. His fists slammed hard into Miguel's belly, and the don doubled over, then hurtled backward as another paw met him on the way down.

Miguel staggered to his feet, breathing hard. There was blood in his mouth and running down from a split in his brow. He flicked his head and came at Torres.

Gualterio had dragged himself to standing again, and stood a little to Miguel's left. Torres was directly in front. Paul Blake lounged against the barrier of the arena beneath the torch, his face shining with excitement.

Miguel lunged between his two attackers with a roar that echoed through the empty rows of seats. The two men dived at him, collided with each other as Miguel stepped nimbly backward. He spun about, gripped them both by their collars and smashed their heads together with a crunch that was fully audible. The two sank soundlessly to the ground.

"Now it is you and I, Blake!" He swung around to face Paul, breathing heavily and wiping bleeding knuckles on his breeches.

"Not quite, Don Miguel," Paul sneered.

Charlie Watson stepped into the light. He was laughing, his outstretched hands revealing the glint of a dagger in one.

"I'll take you too, you bastard—and then Blake, you shall die!" Miguel swore.

Chapter Forty-One

The musty cloth, grain-seeped and moldy, stifled her breathing and tickled her nose. The burlap sack over her head terrified her, for the darkness and closeness of the blindfold rendered her powerless, leaving her in a void with no sense of direction.

The horse over which she had been thrown stumbled, and she sensed the earth close beneath her head before Charlie jerked her roughly back up across his saddle. They galloped on.

Though it seemed to Amanda that the ride would last forever, it was, in reality, a short one. Charlie reined in the horse and dismounted, heaved her over his shoulders and carried her inside some sort of building, she sensed, for the air upon her bare arms changed. The cool breeze of before was replaced by a still, close atmosphere.

Charlie stood her none too gently down and tugged the sack hood from her head. She sucked in a huge breath and looked wildly about her, her eyes wide with fear. A warehouse. Stacked crates and bulging sacks were all about them in the gloom.

"What say you now, Amanda? Do you still pretend love for me?"

Amanda eyed Paul mutely. Since their last confrontaion at the Figurehead, he looked almost himself, save for a slightly puckered scar set high on his cheek. His hair was the same bright-blond that she remembered, his attractiveness almost unimpaired were it not for the cruel twist to his mouth and the naked cruelty in his eyes. She felt nothing for him, he who had tried to burn her alive!

"I pretended nothing, Paul," she answered quietly. "I truly believed that I loved you, and that you returned that love."

"Liar!" Paul shrieked, his pale face mottled purple with anger. So, she, too, would deny it! "Would you have me believe you and your lover, de Villarin, did not connive and plot to disgrace me publicly, to ruin me, to cripple me—and all because of that brat I fathered on his slut of a sister!" His eyes glowed. "Aye, you planned it well, and I, like an innocent fool, thought to use *you!*"

He crossed the sawdusted earthen floor in two steps, brought back his hand and slapped her hard across the face with a force that dashed her to the ground. Amanda cringed, waiting for a second blow, the first still burning her cheekbone and filling her vision with stars.

"Get up!"

Dazedly she did so, rocking on her heels.

"I have a treat for you, Amanda. Something of a spectacle, shall we say? I have decided to allow you to witness your lover's disposal, and then, dear heart, it shall be your turn!"

She cried out as Miguel was dragged in, scarce able to stand. He sagged forward in Gualterio and Torres's arms, as if already dead, his face and hair streamed with water. They'd doused him to bring him around. She would have run to him if Paul had not grabbed her by the arm.

"You scum!" she screamed. "Look at you—four against one!" Disgust was written in her eyes, in the contemptuous curl to her lips, the flaring of her nostrils.

"Well, de Villarin, who shall be first? Your illustrious self—or your whore?" Blake jerked Miguel's head up by a fistful of hair, and held it erect, his eyes blazing into the don's. "Would you watch so docilely while my men straddle her, one by one, before your eyes?" Paul smiled nastily.

Miguel's expression gave away nothing. Suddenly, he spat full in Blake's face!

"That is what I think of you, and of your threats, Blake. I spit on them!" His black eyes smoldered hatred.

Blake nodded to the two men that held Miguel. Gualterio restrained him while Torres slammed a fist into Miguel's belly. Miguel doubled over, stooped, then in a last burst of energy, spiraled upward. But his fists flailed empty air as they held him powerless once more.

Amanda writhed in Charlie's grip, his fingers like steel about her wrists, though he was a small man. The feeling of futility, of the powerlessness of so few against so many, made desperation conquer hope; nevertheless, she fought wildly to free herself. Watson's clenched fist swung backward, ready to strike her.

"Enough, Blake!" Miguel roared. "Leave her alone. She is nothing, a mere pawn!" His voice registered resignation. "I used her, just as you did, though for different reasons. I'd hoped to revenge Maria-Elena's death, as you said. I must admit, you are cleverer than I gave you credit! You saw through our plot to destroy you. But there's no point in killing the girl. Let her go, she means nothing to me, less than nothing! Did you think I'd care what you or your men did to the wench? For all her breeding she's a slut, a *puta*—but one worthy of her hire, no? She enticed you, did she not, with those wanton lips, that body? Give her to your men, Blake, and get it over with."

Amanda turned from him, disbelief, horror in her eyes and in her heart. How could he do this to her, offer her to these vermin? How could he admit to a plot that she knew had never existed? Was he mad! Was he so despicable he would allow them to rape her without protest? Did he hope to barter her body for his own, miserable skin? *She'd sooner die first!*

Uncontrollable fury filled her, burned in her and through her like quicklime. Let them kill him; she'd dance on his grave!

Paul Blake pondered his words, somewhat taken aback. His eyes never left Miguel's face as he strode clumsily across the room to Amanda, his glance flickering coldly over her blanched face and then back to Miguel. Without warning he hooked his fingers in the neckline of her gown and jerked once, then a second time, rending the gown in two from neck to waist.

Amanda felt no shame, only paralyzing fear. Both perfect breasts jutted proudly from the torn cloth, drawing lewd and greedy leers from Paul's foul crew. Their master's thumbs dragged lightly across the rose-tipped white spheres, but his eyes never left the don's face.

Amanda drew a deep, shuddering sob, as she, too, saw the almost bored expression on her lover's face, the total lack of outrage that even a perfect stranger would have felt to see a woman used so. Her heart was twisted with a knife of pain, the like of which she had never felt before. The hands with which she plucked away Paul's fingers were cold as ice, and clammy too. She gathered the torn gown over her bared breasts.

"You waste your time!" she cried brokenly. "He has no heart, and therefore cannot feel. What he says is true, I swear before God that it is so! He used me as his whore, there are no ties between us." Her voice was bitter as gall.

A flicker of disappointment crossed Blake's eager face. It was swiftly replaced by an expression of impatience. His revenge was so near, the taste of it sweeter than honey on his lips. Whatever their bond, shortly it would be severed as surely as their throats. And with his own, last vessel anchored in the harbor, his escape was assured! All that remained was to savor his victory—and their debasement.

Esteban flung the groom aside and cinched the saddle tight himself. He leaped into the saddle and kneed the horse forward onto the plaza.

There were few people about at this hour, most of the citizens of Barcelona still at the enjoyable task of breaking the night's fast. The mellow morning light bore the fragrance of coffee, and carillons pealed from churches and the cathedral to summon the city to matins, their sweet notes echoing through the winding, narrow streets.

Esteban heard none of these as he careened onward to the bullring. There was little hope in him that he would find Miguel there, but he had to start somewhere. The awful feeling that he might never find the don in this rabbit warren of a city was forced from his mind. He cursed Pepe again for not coming sooner to tell him of the don's departure, but the lad stood in awe of his master's ferocious temper, and had not dared to disobey his orders. They had lost almost five hours because of that fear, five hours that could have given Blake and his men time to travel many miles in any of a hundred directions!

As he had expected, there was no sign of Miguel or Blake and his men. Instead, a young *matador* was practicing passes at an ancient bull in the arena, while several older men coached him from the sides. They answered his barrage of questions with indolent smiles and more than one indifferent shrug. *Sí,* there had been someone there during the night, but no, señor, they knew nothing. A gold coin appeared in Esteban's hand. Its effect was magical and miraculous, both loosening the tongues of the men and improving their memories dramatically. Now they nodded eagerly. Had not the sand been stained with fresh blood, its smoothness churned as if many men had struggled there? And did not Armando find a fine, silk shirt and jerkin strewn in the dust? *Sí,* now they remembered.

"You may keep the articles, but let me see them," ordered Esteban.

The apprentice *matador* exchanged wary glances with his friends.

"Perhaps—?" His teeth flashed white as he grinned and pocketed the second coin that Esteban angrily produced. Armando strode across to the barrier and leaped nimbly over it.

Esteban knew at a glance that the garments Armando returned with were Miguel's. Esteban snatched them up and examined them for bloodstains. There were none. The young fool had either stripped to the waist to meet his enemy, or, for some reason, they had seen fit to do it for him. He looked up, and caught Armando signaling secretly to an old man. The *matador* grinned.

"There's more? Tell me, and be quick!" the steward demanded.

Armando shook his head and smiled lazily, rubbing his fingers together to indicate that he would, but only for a price.

Esteban picked up Armando by the collar and slammed him against the barrier. The youth's teeth clicked together loudly as his head snapped back.

"No more, leech! Quickly, what else did you wish to tell me?" His tone held a threat.

Frantically, the lad motioned Esteban back, and delved into his shirt front. He drew out Miguel's pistol from his chest.

Esteban took it and sniffed the weapon's barrel. It had not been fired in some time. He stuffed it into his belt and remounted his horse.

As he rode back to the inn, his heart was heavy. Of one thing he was sure. Blake and his men had Miguel—alive or dead—they had him! For he knew nothing on earth would have prevented the don from returning to the inn—and his Amanda—save capture or death.

Chapter Forty-Two

"Señor! The Señorita—she is gone!"

To Esteban, it was the morning Amanda had climbed from the villa's casement over again. The neatly made bed. The empty room. He ran a desperate hand through his brown hair. Mother of God! If Miguel showed up now, there'd be the devil to pay. He decided he'd rather risk Miguel's fury and pay the devil!

Bonita was babbling on, totally incoherent now, her brown eyes swollen hugely with tears and her buxom figure heaving with shock. Her fingers clawed repeatedly at the red weals of a rope burn about her wrists.

Esteban took her by the shoulders and would have shaken her if Pepe had not swiftly intervened. The lad held Bonita against his chest and soothed her with caresses to her hair and her shoulders. The steward was in no mood for the delighted grin of triumph the amorous groom shot him over Bonita's shoulder. It worked however. Soon the maid was drawing deep, shuddering breaths, the violent color fleeing her cheeks.

"I'm sorry, señor. But it was most frightening! I left

the señorita to fetch her another gown. The other, it was too warm, and she was feeling faint and—"

"It was no trick? You are sure?"

"No. Her face, it was very pale, sir. I did not like the look of her at all. And so quiet she was, this morning. *Aiee,* those devils, they have taken her!" More pats and squeezes from Pepe before she carried on. "I went to my room and, as I stepped within the door, this massive hand covered my mouth and hairy arms like an ox lifted me around the ribs. I kicked, señor, I tried to escape that beast! *Díos mio,* but they—he and the skinny *ingles*—they trussed me up and I could do nothing, señor, nothing to warn the señorita." She covered her face with her hands and wept.

Pepe told a similar tale, ending with how they had carried him down the corridor and dumped him roughly next to Bonita on the floorboards. Rags had been forced into their mouths as gags. "And if Bonita had not kicked her bound feet at the dresser, and if the ewer had not crashed to the floor, the innkeeper's daughter would not have found us, Señor Soreno," finished Pepe, with a proud, flashing grin at the blushing maid.

Esteban muttered an oath and paced the taproom furiously. In God's name, where should he start? Where would they have taken them? He tried to put himself in Blake's boots, but this logic failed. The warped fury of the Englishman's reasoning defied imagining.

"Señor Soreno, there's a gentleman to see you." The tavern keeper nodded across the taproom.

Esteban didn't look up. Instead, he downed the dregs of his tankard and scowled angrily at Señor Cristobal.

"I will see no one!" he growled.

"But, señor, he says it is *muy importante,"* insisted the man earnestly.

Esteban looked across. The rotund visitor was none other than the Jew, Goldstein, whom he had contracted to make the ring for Miguel.

"What brings you here, señor?" inquired Esteban. "Did I not pay you for your labors?"

The dark-robed man hurried forward with anxious eyes, nodding earnestly. *"Sí,* Señor Soreno, and handsomely too! But there's another matter I think you would be interested in—"

"Get on with it. I'm in no mood for guessing games, Goldstein."

"A minute more, señor, of your valuable time."

His hand burrowed into an enormous pocket in the dark robe and withdrew a scarlet kerchief carefully folded over its contents. He almost dropped the item in his nervousness, his dark and doleful eyes sorrowful at his clumsy self. The unfolded kerchief revealed a glittering array of pieces of mangled gold, several pearls and a large, exquisite topaz shimmering on the scarlet cloth.

"Where did you get this?" breathed Esteban, his voice so low the goldsmith had to strain to hear him.

"When I was leaving my warehouse this morning, señor, down by the quayside—I had been making inventory. Not only do I deal in gold, you understand, but also in silks, satins, perhaps a—"

"Yes, yes, get on with it!"

"Well, I stooped to lift the bar for the gate, and these caught my eyes, glittering in the sun. Naturally, I bent to pick them up. Then I recovered the pearls and jewel in the dust. A goldsmith, you understand, remembers the marks etched into certain fine pieces. When I returned to my shop, I took my eyeglass, señor, and realized it was the same piece I had copied for the ring, for Don Miguel. Of course, I knew he would wish it returned, and so I came here with great speed. It appears to have been crushed by a hoof or a wagonwheel or similar. Would you have me repair it, señor?"

Esteban heard only dimly his last words. "Hmmm? Oh, *sí,* certainly. We will talk of it later, Señor Goldstein. Now tell me again, exactly where is your warehouse?"

His thoughts raced, putting a workable plan into formation.

When Goldstein left, haughtily refusing the coin Esteban would have forced on him, the steward had a good notion of where to find Miguel and Amanda.

"Señor, there are only two of us! If they are where you believe, they would pick us off like flies!" protested Pepe.

Esteban calmly silenced the lad and handed him a velvet purse heavy with coins. "Go to the arena, Pepe, and ask for Armando. Tell him the señor he spoke with this morning requires his services. Show him this coin, and bid him bring as many of his fellows as wish to share the purse, and with all possible haste. Come with them. I will meet you at the *Calle de los Indios.* You know it? I thought so. Be off now, and hurry!"

He sat back to wait and to prime and clean his brace of pistols, while his mind sifted through strategies and methods of rescuing his don and the girl, before Blake could panic and finish them first, if they were not already dead.

He made his way to Señor Goldstein's warehouse and looked about him. There were a great many such wooden buildings lining the harbor, deserted now that the city was at *siesta.* He tied his mount to a tree and circled each warehouse warily. The task was lengthier than he had expected, and it was close to an hour before he saw what he was looking for.

This warehouse was set off a little to the side of the others. Close by, in the shade of a tree, were tied five horses. Miguel's stallion was one of them. He ducked into the shadow of the building and edged around it to the back. Like all the warehouses, a winch with rope attached hung from above a door, leading to the upper storage area.

He clambered up the rope, arm over arm, and swung himself quietly in through the opening.

The gloom was impenetrable until his eyes adjusted from the glare of the sun outside. Dust clouds rose from the nigh-empty boards as he edged his way over to a heavy trapdoor. Scarcely breathing, he lifted the metal ring, praying the hinges would not groan. His luck held, and he peered through the aperture.

Almost directly below he saw Miguel, sprawled in the dirt, while Paul's men towered over him. He was motionless. Esteban could not tell if he was alive or dead. Blake sat against one wall, lifting a liquor jug to his lips and then to the girl's, holding her by the throat and forcing the wine between her teeth. She was struggling to resist him.

So, at least the señorita was still alive. He inched backward, satisfied. They obviously suspected nothing in the way of pursuit, and he thanked God for Goldstein.

The winch shrieked slightly as he swung to the ground. Then he darted back between the clustered buildings to his horse, and thence to the *Calle de los Indios.* If Pepe had done his job, there would be enough men to rush Blake and his crew from above and below at the same time.

With a pistol ball in his heart, Paul Blake would have no chance to finish Miguel. And if the don was already dead, he, Esteban, would have avenged the deed. He prayed fervently to every saint he could recall that the latter would not be the case.

Chapter Forty-Three

"'Twas but a rat, *amigo!*" Paul drawled lazily, tilting the jug again. He giggled as Amanda tried to pry his grip from her waist, licking his chops wolfishly at the view her rucked-up skirt afforded him of her legs.

Gualterio peered into the gloom of the upper-story of the warehouse, not satisfied by Paul Blake's nonchalant explanation of the noise he had heard. Nothing. He clambered down the ladder, letting the trapdoor thunder shut above him.

Cocking his pistol, he strode outside into the dazzling sunlight. As his eyes adjusted to the brilliance he caught a glimpse of a man scurrying furtively into an alley between two warehouses.

For all his girth, he sprinted after Esteban Soreno with the grace and lightness of a cat. He knew it was that bastard-of-a-don's-steward, by the fairness of the man's complexion and by the green embroidered vest he wore. *Jésus y Maria!* The fool had not seen him! He raised his pistol, aimed, let it drop back to his side. The distance was too great and he had no wish to fire unless assured of a kill. There might be others with him.

His cruel face broke into an ugly smile as he returned to the warehouse. Blake had promised him a turn at the wench, and Gualterio had decided that the time for his turn had come. He'd best hurry. He had no desire to bed a dead woman. It was more to his liking when they fought and scratched in terror. Then their wild lunges added considerable enjoyment to the taking.

He burst back into the warehouse as Blake was flinging the wench's skirts above her head, kneeling between her rigid thighs. Torres held her wrists, and the *inglesa*'s face was a mask of utter terror—just as he liked them!

"How so coy, Amanda, my pet?" Paul grunted through clenched teeth. "Remember that time in England, when we went riding together? You did not resist me then! Was it that you were paid to be warm and willing, eh? Was that why? Well, willing or not, this time I'll have you, slut!"

Her eyes were bottomless pools, swimming in unshed tears. The fat, swarthy lout squatted above her. His hands, though sweating with excitement and eagerness as he awaited his turn, were nonetheless unmovable, she fast discovered.

"Señor Blake, there is not time now! We must leave. Miguel de Villarin's steward—it was him I heard above, climbing down the pulley. He's gone for help, señor!" Gualterio cried.

"No!" snarled Paul. "I will have her first! The bitch has scorned me since first we met. You'll not deprive me, nay, never!" He fumbled to unfasten his breeches, unbridled lust in the blazing blue eyes.

"You are a fool, señor! We can take her with us, if we hurry. Then you may enjoy her at your leisure, for the voyage is a long one, no? Think of it, señor, to have her not once, but many, many times, before you end her worthless life!" Gualterio's voice was wheedling and ingratiating as he knew Paul expected. The eyes above the hawklike, swarthy features were sly as a weasel. He, Gualterio, would also enjoy her favors many times!

Paul's expression changed. He stood, a crafty smile spreading from ear to ear until it seemed to Amanda she was looking at the face of the Devil incarnate.

"You are right, friend. He will return with others and we shall be trapped like rats in a sinking ship. Yes! Take her to the *Pride of Suffolk*. I will follow you."

Gualterio hoisted Amanda over his shoulders, digging cruel talons into the soft flesh of her buttocks. Her eyes clouded with pain as she passed Paul Blake.

He reached out and chucked her beneath the chin. "Just a little while, my dearest, and we shall continue our sport."

She jerked her head away as Gualterio made a speedy exit, her body flopping like a broken doll on his shoulder.

Paul waited until the hoofbeats of Gualterio's horse were no longer audible. Then he aimed a vicious kick at Miguel's unconscious form, forcing a groan from the don as his boot chopped into the don's kidneys.

"Dog! Fate has seen fit once again to deny me the pleasure of finishing you myself. Henrique, you take care of him. Here's gold for your trouble. A pistol ball through the belly or a knife across his damned throat, I care not—*but make him suffer,* you understand!"

Henrique nodded eagerly. He would not hurry, there would be time to flee. He grinned and opened his shirt, nodding at the hairline-thin scar that traversed his bulging belly. "I will, señor! Trust me. No man leaves his mark on Henrique Torres, not without paying twofold for his stupidity!"

Paul nodded, well satisfied, then he limped hurriedly from the building without a backward glance. The area surrounding the warehouse dozed in the late afternoon sun. The distant sound of many drumming hoofbeats in the dirt reached his ears.

Paul lumbered into the saddle and, with his whip, slashed the skittish mare across the head. The animal bolted forward and careened toward the quay.

Chapter Forty-Four

The horse slowed to a walk and finally halted. Gualterio clambered down and dragged Amanda after him, hefting a kick at her thighs when she stumbled. She was sobbing raggedly.

They were at the quayside, Amanda saw, though the place seemed deserted. Tall-masted ships loomed alongside, rocking gently at their moorings. The disappearing sun cast monstrous shadows onto the quay.

The Spaniard grabbed her wrist and twisted it up and behind her. "Get going, and no tricks or I'll break your arm, by *Díos!*"

He thrust her before him up a slimy gangplank that stretched from the quay to the rail of an enormous, ill-kept ship. Its paint was peeling and the sides needed careening. There was water below the narrow plank, and she wondered fleetingly if she could hope to leap into it. A sharp, agonizing jerk on her arm assured her it was impossible, and Gualterio shoved her aboard the vessel.

She heard the gangplank draw up behind them, and when her eyes were accustomed to the gloom, realized he was taking her along a lower-deck passageway with many cabins, little better than stalls, on either side. The stench was unbelievable; the usual mildew and briny odors of a ship mixed with smells far less pleasant, like sweat and something more she could not define. She held back a violent urge to vomit, and then, after numerous jerks on her arm, Gualterio finally stopped at a cabin. He flung her through the door and left without locking it.

She gingerly tested her arm and found, thankfully, that though it was painful, it was not broken.

Inside it was almost pitch black. As she crossed to the porthole, something bristly brushed against her face! She shrieked, her nerves shattered after her ordeal, then sobbed and laughed hysterically to find on feeling the object, that it was only a hammock! Few people were on the quay below at this time and they did not respond to her frantic cries for help. She turned away, the spark of hope that had filled her dying miserably.

Dear God! There were rats in the cabin! She could hear them squeaking and scampering barely five feet away, their eyes catching the feeble light and glinting like glass. An ache in her belly grew stronger now; indeed, she ached all over. She hugged herself and shivered in the damp air, wondering if Miguel was badly hurt or perhaps dead. What did they intend for her?

The sound of men singing in unison to keep time and the shriek of chain against metal as the capstan was turned to raise the anchor broke violently in on her thoughts. Oh no! They were setting sail!

She determined to try to make a run for it. The door

had not been locked. It was worth anything to attempt it!

Fumbling through the darkness, she found the latch and stepped out into the passageway. The cabin opposite was open, and a stub of candle lit the gloom. As she crept cautiously along the slimy passageway a woman came to that cabin door and called to her, leaning, arms crossed, against the jamb.

"Hello, dearie. Takin' a little stroll around this lovely ship, are ye?" She laughed loudly.

Amanda pretended she had not heard, and continued on.

But at the end of the passageway Charlie Watson stepped out of the shadows and blocked the way.

"And where are you off to, m'lady? Lookin' for me, were ye?" He laughed, darted out his hand, and pinched her cruelly on the cheek.

She turned and fled back down the passageway. So, there was to be no escape! Dejected, she retraced her steps. The woman was still leaning against her door.

"Nasty piece of work, that Charlie, cut yer throat soon as look at yer, he would! What's wrong with ye? Cat got yer tongue?"

Amanda lifted her head dejectedly. "No, I'm sorry, it's just—never mind! Why are you aboard?" She sighed deeply, not really interested.

"Me! Well, dearie, I had a little run-in with the law. Had to kill one of me customers, I did. Bloody gentry, a bleedin' pervert, he was, I'm tellin' ye! So I did him in, cracked his noggin with a warming pan! Only trouble was, his brother happened to be a magistrate and they were after lookin' for me, with hangin' on their minds. I decided to hop it to the colonies, afore I'd dance on the end of a rope! Are ye in the business, then?" Her eyes traveled up and down Amanda's disheveled figure.

"Business?"

"Ye know, girlie, t'business!" She made a crude gesture with her fingers, rocking with laughter at Amanda's shocked expression. "Suppose not, eh?"

Amanda shook her head. "Where are we bound?"

"Ye mean, ye don't know? Cor, why'd ye come aboard then?" The woman peered at her curiously.

"Some men brought me here. They mean to kill me." At the very least, she thought grimly.

"So, ye're in trouble. Gawd, at least I's left mine behind! Ye're in a pretty pickle, though." She thoughtfully scratched her armpit. "Wot's yer name?"

Amanda told her and the woman nodded genteelly, patting her dyed red hair as if it were an elegant coiffure.

"Pleased ter meet ye! Mine's Nellie, Nellie Flagg. Ye're bound for New Orleans, missie, like it or not." She grinned and smacked her lips. "Some say 'tis well on it's way to being the wickedest place on this earth. City of Sin, they do call it!" She added with relish.

"I doubt I'll ever live to see it." Amanda stated flatly.

Nellie startled at the deadness of her voice, and, after darting a quick glance up and down the gloomy passageway, nimbly hurried across to the girl.

"Eh, luv, don't talk like that! Pretty thing like ye, they'll not *kill* yer, though I dare say wi' yer breedin', ye might wish they had arter they done wiv ye! Anyways, what could ye' a done that'd make them so riled up?" Nellie sniffed. "Ye don't look like butter'd melt in yer mouth, ye don't."

"Someday, perhaps, I will tell you. But not now, I couldn't bear it!" No, she didn't even want to think of it, any of it. "But I will say this, Mistress Flagg, you need not fear me, I have done nothing to make you fear me."

Nellie gaped at the earnest, innocent young face with the wide, sable eyes, and exploded into guffaws of raucous laughter, finally flinging her arms about Amanda's shoulders and squeezing her tightly.

"Lawd, but ye're a one! Me afeared o'ye? Nay, love, Nellie Flagg don't fear no one 'ceptin' God, and the Devil—least of all a scrap like ye!" She rocked with laughter again.

Amanda smiled in spite of her worry and her fear. She couldn't help it. Though she was petite herself, Nellie was a full three inches or so shorter! But on closer inspection, Amanda believed Nellie. She looked quite able to take care of herself, for her arms, exposed below the masses of grubby white lace, were weather-beaten and wiry. Nellie's face indicated a strength of character that would border on stubbornness, if her firm chin and jawline were anything to go by. There was an air of faded beauty about her, as if once she had cut a fine figure of a woman. All that was left now were deep lines etched into skin tanned brown as a berry, startlingly brown next to her pale blue eyes and rouged cheeks—these, and unquenchable optimism and good humor. Amanda decided she liked her, but hoped never to cross her!

God! Suddenly Amanda doubled over as a vicious cramp knotted her belly. The cabin blurred. The dizzy feeling she'd experienced that morning returned and, with it, the nausea.

If Nellie had not darted out an arm to catch her, she would have fallen to the deck.

"Eh, Luv, what's up?" Clucking, Nellie peered about, her expression concerned. "Naught else for it. Ye come across ter my cabin. Lyin' down in a bleedin' hammock ain't going t'help yer none."

She led her to her own cabin and spread a straw pallet in one corner, motioning Amanda to lie down.

Amanda had no choice but to do so. Her own cabin was even sorrier than this.

Nellie unfastened the torn gown as Amanda drew her legs up to her belly in another spasm of pain. Sweat broke out on her forehead. Had she somehow been poisoned, was that it? Perhaps the wine Paul had forced on her. . . .

The woman's hands traveled knowingly over Amanda's restless body, gently holding her down while she inspected her breasts.

"How many months, luv?" she inquired finally, eyes bright as a curious monkey.

Amanda's white face showed confusion. "Months of what?" she gasped through yet another cramp.

Nellie sighed patiently. "How many months gone are ye, yer know, with child?" These gentlewomen never did call a spade a spade!

"With child? But I'm not!" Her legs flailed as she tried to stand up, but Nellie held her down and raised her skirts to her waist.

"Aye, luv, if'n ye knows it or not, yer carryin'. And wot's more, ye're likely to drop the babe. Ye're bleedin', see?" She tore a strip from Amanda's shift, as it seemed the cleanest cloth in the entire cabin and wiped the girl. "Aye, but ye're an innocent! Not wed, are ye? Thought as not; ye've no ring. But believe Nellie, luv, yer in the family way, right enough, though 'tis hard t'tell how far gone with yer tiny little scraps. Could be only two months, maybe even four. But one look at those bosoms and I knowed yer condition! See, the circle around here, didn't ye notice how dark 'tis now? And, see, these little blue veins? Did ye not notice yer monthly curse hadn't come around, luv?" Nellie picked up the girl's limp hand and squeezed it. "Don't take on, there's a dear. If'n ye wishes, a good walk up and down should be enough to drop the babe early—ye're startin' already by the looks o'it."

"No!" Amanda exploded, her mind in utter chaos.

The idea of being with child, Miguel's child, had barely sunk into her brain, but she knew she could never willingly try to miscarry. "No," she said again, in a softer tone. "I can't do that. A baby!" The idea thrilled and horrified her at the same time. Dear God, what was to become of her? She made to get up, but Nellie again forced her down.

"Nay, love, if'n ye mean t'keep it, ye'll have ter stay off yer feet. Even then, I don't know as how we can stop it—but I'll do all I can ter help ye. I've been midwife plenty o'times afore this, never fear. God willin', by the time we reach this New Orleans, ye'll be as big as a pig's bladder stuffed with sausage, ye will!"

The image Nellie conjured brought unwilling laughter to Amanda despite the pain. She laughed until tears finally fell.

Nellie sat by, saying nothing. She knew when to keep her mouth shut and when to open it.

Amanda tried to put some order to her thoughts. Nellie was right. She'd not even noticed her time of month had failed to come around, not with everything else that had happened. Rapidly, she calculated.

If her figuring was correct, Miguel had got her with child the very first time he'd taken her—over two months ago, it was! Miguel's baby. Her baby. But never *their* baby. Would Paul let her live to bear it? Oh, God no! They couldn't kill her, not with this new life unfolding inside her, this tiny, precious life! And if she lived, she would never need another soul in this world, save her and the child, would never know again the desolation that had driven her to Paul's arms. She had to live!

"Nellie," she whispered. "Nellie, you have to help me! They'll come here, they'll do terrible things to me, unspeakable things. I'll lose the baby! Nellie, please help me!" She clutched desperately at the woman's arm.

"'Course I will, ducks. Wot did ye have in mind?"

"I don't know! I can't think straight, not with this pain. They mustn't hurt me, Nellie, not now, not with the baby within me. Think! Oh, God!" She clutched her belly and doubled over once again, her face twisted in an agonized white mask.

Nellie kneaded Amanda's back and wiped her streaming face, filled with a maternal urge she'd never felt before. Poor little blighter, n'more than a child, she weren't and her in a right mess too! Gawd in Heaven, wot could they do? She patted Amanda's shoulder with an unaccustomed gentleness.

None of the gents had ever seen this Nellie, nay, and weren't likely to, neither! Flat on her back with her skirts shoved up, that's how they saw Nellie, then a few grunts, a poke or two, and another coin held fast in her hands, to add to the hoard she'd used for her passage on this very ship. That's how it'd been, and would be, 'til she were rich as Midas! Aye, Nellie planned to be rich, someday. Then she'd thumb her nose at those who'd scoffed at her, used her, she would. Piss on 'em, all!

"I've a notion, ducks, but don't know as how it'd work," Nellie said hesitantly.

The girl was quietened down some now, but her beauty in the aftermath of her pain caught Nellie's breath. She scarce seemed real, she didn't.

"I'll try anything! Quick, tell me, do, Mistress Flagg. Paul Blake will be here any second, I know it!"

The pain had subsided to a dull ache in the pit of her belly, but with its lessening came the terror of Paul and his men once again, so intense her mouth was dry as sawdust, her bowels churning like butter.

"Well, 'ow's 'bout this?" Nellie leaned over and softly told Amanda her plan.

Amanda paused for only a second, then nodded. "I have nothing to lose by it. Go on then!"

She grinned weakly, a trace of her fiery spirit returning as Nellie winked broadly and laid her finger alongside her nose.

"Then I'll be off, love—ter have ye fished from the drink!"

Nellie's cackle faded as she hurried down the passageway.

Chapter Forty-Five

Amanda rose shakily, clutching her belly, and staggered after Nellie. She paused just before the spot where Charlie Watson had halted her the first time. Nellie's strident voice carried clearly.

"Oh, my, but ain't ye a loverly lad! I was always one for a strapping young cock, I was. Give us a kiss, luv!"

Amanda fought down the wildest urge to giggle hysterically as she peeped around the corner.

Charlie had been perched on a stool at the junction where the fore-and-aft gangway crossed the port and starboard gangway. Now he was flattened on his back under a mass of yellowed, grubby petticoats, as two pairs of booted feet flailed wildly—Nellie's and his own. His head was held between her hands and she was planting smacking kisses on every inch of flesh visible.

"You bleedin' old bag! Get orf me, ye'll gimme the pox, you old bawd!" he snarled.

Oblivious, Nellie kissed on, promising Charlie unmentionable pleasure for the mere price of a farthing or two. It struck Amanda briefly that Nellie seemed to be doing an overly good job of distracting him, but then she had no time to think more of that as she crept past the thrashing pair.

She had less than a vague notion of where the ship's stores would be, unless they were located as were the storerooms aboard the *Princess* and the *Sea Dragon*. But luckily Nellie, who'd seen them replenishing the victuals in Spain, had noted its whereabouts well. No doubt, Amanda realized now, with an eye to warding off Nellie's own personal starvation on the voyage, should it become necessary!

Amanda scurried the length of the passage, ducked into an alcove made by a massive beam where it met a dividing wooden wall, and watched as a seaman carrying a huge sack of something exited from the door and started on up to the galley. She ducked swiftly inside.

The ship's stores were an orderly clutter of astounding quantities of foods, all of them drygoods in bulging sacks, such as grain, flour, and similar. Barrels of salted pork flanked one side. Another huge area that led off the room was given over to nothing but precious vegetables in barrels, stack upon stack of them. Coiled lines were looped upon hooks in the wall and all number of pieces of tackle for the rigging. Spare lanterns filled one shelf, a few new buckets and boxes of candles still another. It was all neatly stacked row upon row, and the perfect place to stowaway.

Amanda nudged behind a mountain of bulging sacks, and burrowed between them.

Unless there was an enormous, sudden need for oats, she should be well hidden for another month, perhaps two. She curled on her side and, as Nellie had ordered, tried desperately to sleep.

Nellie flung an oath at her unwilling swain and

hitched up her skirts to go abovedecks, still cursing hotly as she went.

There were over a hundred men, women, and children on deck, all milling about as Captain Johnson Heath was reading off a list of orders to the immigrants.

Nellie didn't bother to heed what he was saying, for she had no intention of following any orders, whoever was giving them. But she grinned gleefully at the first-rate confusion about her. There was a right good chance her hasty plan would work, for no one seemed to know what was happening.

That dark Spanish bastard was picking his fingernails no more than five feet from her. Him it was, she'd seen bring the little lady down to the cabin. Charlie-boy joined him, and, after a scathing glance in her direction, the two conversed softly and burst into spiteful laughter. Well, laugh they might, she vowed, but they'd come sniffing at her skirts soon enough when they found the wench had flown the coop!

Nellie sidled down the deck, hugging close to the rail and looked about her. Good, no one was watching! The Spanish coast was already only a gray hump on the horizon, and nightfall fast drawing in.

She took a deep breath and let out a shriek loud enough to wake the dead, hands clutching her throat in a paroxysm of pretended horror.

"Oh, Gawd, the little leddy! Help! Oh, someone, help!"

At first no one heard her in the hub-bub.

She renewed her efforts, doubling the pitch of her shrieks. "Oh, mercy, what's to become of 'er? Help! Help!"

A burly sailor craned over the rail at her side, scanning the water.

"Where is she, then?" he quizzed in a deep voice.

Nellie waved her hand vaguely in a gesture that encompassed all waters from east to west, which mollified the man. She appeared close to swooning. "I can't bear it, I can't! So young to take 'er life!"

She sagged full weight into the man's arms.

"Man overboard!" he bellowed, trying to disentangle himself of Nellie.

Immediately, as Nellie had known they would, all on deck rushed to the rail to see the excitement, Gualterio and Charlie among them.

"Oh, it were dreadful! We'd best turn back, Cap'n, sir, we can't leave 'er in the drink!" Nellie cried.

Captain Heath appeared rather the worse for liquor, and glared at her crossly.

"Now, my good woman, calm yourself, do." He belched loudly as he turned to the rows of waiting passengers. "Are any among you missing family members?"

They all shook their heads.

"O'Riley, fetch my glass," he ordered.

But, of course, he could see no one and said so.

Nellie wrung her hands and squeezed more tears from her eyes. "But I see'd her!" she wailed. "A li'l scrap of a wench, she were, pretty as a bloomin' picture, climbing up onto that rail a'fore she leaped to 'er death! Her loverly gown were blowin' in the breeze—like yeller angel wings, it were. Oh, Cap'n, sir, we must save 'er from 'erself!"

The captain appeared dumbfounded. But Gualterio and Charlie Watson exchanged nervous glances, then tore across the decks like madmen, tripping and stumbling as they went.

"We cannot go back, madam," the captain said stiffly, belching again. "My deepest regrets but—" He wandered off, leaving Nellie still sprawled in the squatting sailor's arms.

"Oh, I'll never forget it, never, I won't, 'til my dyin' day I'll see 'er standin' there!" She batted her eyelids at the highly uncomfortable tar. "I needs a strong pair o'arms to carry me down t'me cabin, I does. A lady 'as ter rest after such a shockin' ordeal, she do." A crafty smile lit her face. "Are ye married, then, luv?" she crooned.

The sailor heaved a sigh, like a condemned man resigning himself to the gallows, and picked up the scrawny Nellie, who languished in his arms for all the world like a rescued princess.

Nellie's tactics changed drastically as he made to carry her through her cabin door, for from the cabin opposite—Amanda's cabin, came the harsh sounds of a furious argument.

"Put me down, 'ere, luv, there's a dear," Nellie commanded.

"But you promised me a bit!" stammered the sailor, color crimsoning his face.

"A bit o'wot?" snapped Nellie, tossing her head indignantly. "Cor, bleedin' cheek! Ye deserves to be 'orsewhipped, ye does—takin' advantage of a woman wot's not herself. Get off, wiv yer, ye filthy bugger!"

Gaping and more than a little puzzled, the sailor did as bidden. Nellie slipped inside her cabin and closed the door, except for a crack, which she left open and pressed her ears to.

"You fools! Damn your stupid skins! Why did you leave the girl alone?" the voice railed, almost hysterical in its rage.

"Señor, we had set sail. I did not believe she would take her life!" That was Gualterio, sounding less than his cocky self, Nellie noticed with a grin. He'd been gloating, before.

"Oh, gov'na, wot do it matter? We'd'a had ter finish 'er off soon enough, right?" Charlie-boy's voice wheedled.

Keep it up ducks, Nellie thought.

"As for you, you stupid lout, how'd she get past you, I'd like to know?"

"Some dirty old hag took a fancy t'me, she did, and she started—"

"Shut up! Didn't I tell you not to let *anything* distract you? God, I could slit both your throats, I could," stormed the first voice. "Heath, turn this vessel about, I order you."

"I will not," the captain replied in a drunken tone that sounded as if he could turn nasty.

"Aye, you will, Heath—as long as I own the *Pride of Suffolk*, you will follow any order I choose to give!"

"Nay, Blake," sneered Heath, "for as of two hours ago, she's *my* ship, not yours, d'you recall? I have the paper you signed t'prove it! I offered only a berth for you and your men, naught else—save the monies I paid ye for the *Pride*. I'll not turn about for some slut you've taken a fancy to, be damned if I will! It's cutting it fine enough as 'tis, to make the voyage with winter drawing near; the turn'd bring us another half day off schedule!"

Nellie saw the captain storm from the cabin without a backward glance. Gualterio left then, and Charlie, too, both wearing somewhat cowed and gloomy faces.

A few minutes later, the other blond-haired man hitched his way into the passage, pausing, unseeing, directly in front of Nellie's peephole.

He cursed vividly, his expression so twisted and malignant that even Nellie could not help but suck in a horrified gasp and barely repress a shudder of revulsion.

"By the devil, I hope you drown slow, Amanda Sommers. That your lovely body bloats and the fish feast on your innards! Yes," he breathed, "I hope you die a thousand deaths before you find release in one!"

He chuckled harshly and tapped down the gloomy passageway, dragging the wooden peg as he went.

Chapter Forty-Six

"Mandy! Mandy, luv? Where are ye, ducks? It's me, Nellie." She stumbled, cracked her shins, and cursed lustily.

"Over here—no, left a little. I can't get up, my feet have pins and needles. The Cook, he was in here for ages, taking inventory. I didn't dare move, and now I can't anyway," Amanda whispered.

"Ah, there ye are. How're ye doin'? All right are ye?"

Amanda nodded and took the stale bread and greasy pork from Nellie's outstretched hands, fumbling in the gloom. In truth she felt far from fine, but Nellie was doing her utmost. There was no sense in worrying her further.

"How are you, Nellie? They don't suspect anything?"

"Nah! Think ye gorn to a watery grave, they do! And me, I'm right as rain—makin' a fair penny, too, I might add, what with all these lusty sailor boys and Spanish seniories beatin' a path t'me cot! Believe me, it were worth the extra t'have me own cabin." She shuddered. "Them poor folk what's plannin' on settlin' in New Orleans be crammed in that foul hold like bloomin' peas in a pod! I heard tell from Georgie—t'bosun, y'know—that the *Pride o'Suffolk* saw service as a blackbirder afore this. Cor, stink something awful it do—and he did say as how the smell ain't ever wholly gotten rid of," she added darkly.

"Blackbirder?"

"Aye, luv, or slaver, call it what ye will. Did ye know it were one o'*his* ships afore, yer Mister Blake's? Proper bastard he is, let me tell ye! But that Cap'n Heath do fair keep him in his place, he do. He! He! Serves him right!"

Amanda shivered. The slaves must have cowered, terrified, in the darkness, not knowing to where or what they were bound much as she was doing now. It came as no surprise to hear one, at least, of Paul's ships had been involved in that filthy trade. Nothing he'd done could shock her now, however low or foul it seemed.

Nellie withdrew a hip flask of brandy from her garter and took a deep swig. She smacked her lips, wiped the rim on her palm, and handed it to Amanda. She drank several sips, choked, gulped down several more. It would warm her through the bitter cold of the night ahead more thoroughly than Nellie's tattered cloak could do. It also helped to numb her mind against the terror the rats and her own imagination instilled in her.

"Right ye are, then. Anything else yer wantin', love? No? Then I do be off. We've need o'all the coin I can scrape t'gether, if'n we's not t'starve in New Orleans. God bless ye, ducks. See ye t'morrow."

Amanda bade her a reluctant farewell, and Nell crept quietly away.

Alone again. Amanda shuddered, hugging herself

tightly. Could she stand another minute, another second of this black and solitary hellhole? Three weeks, now, it was, three weeks of unending darkness and terror, broken only by Nellie's brief visits with food, water, and a stinking bucket for a chamberpot.

Three weeks during which she'd come no closer to discovering the answer to her question: How could she have fallen in love with Miguel de Villarin? Did one even need reasons for loving someone? Was it enough that a mere smile could soar you to the heights of desire? That a touch could sear your flesh as surely as a brand? Aye, he'd had the power to do all that, and more.

And yet, the hatred she felt for him still burned as fiercely as the loving him did. Had he taken the memory of her saying she loved him, laughing, to his grave? She would not think of him dead by Paul's hands. No!

Whatever he'd done or said, she could not bear to think of him dead! Instead, she would remember only his body on hers, tanned and beautiful in its symmetry. His eyes had been dark and sensual, drowning her in endless depths of passion. Oh, dear God, what could she do? Even the memory of his lovemaking stirred her! She felt her nipples harden with expectancy and longing; felt her loins turn liquid with the memory of his caresses there, teasing her womanhood until she'd nigh fainted with delight. And his lips, his traitorous, glorious lips! How she ached, lusted to feel them upon her flesh, melting the icy clutch of fear about her heart as fire melts ice, traveling upward along the column of her neck to outline her ears and breathing in them huskily in a way that sent tingles coursing her spine. "Don't!" she whispered weakly. "Don't torture yourself! Forget him!" she urged. Mayhap she could in mind, but never, never in body!

She flung her arms about a stubby sack of oats and ground her teeth into her lips to staunch her sobs.

Her life stagnated. Day and night ran together in monotony, and she neither knew nor cared which was which, for in the darkness of the storeroom there was no day.

Periodically, a sailor or a cook would enter, find what he required, and leave hurriedly, cursing the rats that had gnawed their way into a sack of flour he needed.

Amanda cringed in her hiding space, holding her breath until he left, each time praying this once, please God, he would forget his lantern. But he never did. All seamen dreaded fire aboard ship, and lantern and candle alike were guarded carefully and with respect. Woebetide the careless lout who left one unattended!

Nellie relayed the details of what was happening on ship to her daily. One of the crew had been flogged for falling asleep on watch, she said, and Captain Heath had been sotted as usual and lashed him to death.

Amanda grew squeamish when Nellie described the man's raw and bloodied back in gory detail. A fleeting image of Garcia with his cat-o'nine tails filled her, but she hurriedly wrenched her thoughts away as Nellie talked on.

Fights were breaking out daily now as the vessel neared the halfway point of her voyage, Nellie said, and tempers were becoming strained by a large number of people forced to live in such proximity to one another. The immigrants squabbled and came to blows as they lined up on deck for their water rations at the enormous scuttlebutt on the forecastle, outraged at the pitiful amount dealt them. Though the biscuits were fast becoming riddled with weevils, these, too, became the subject of endless arguments as the *Pride of Suffolk* sailed on.

Once, when the ship fell silent and Amanda was certain night had come, she sneaked out into the passageway and stood at the foot of the stairs, inhaling the fresh night air as deeply as if it were the very elixir of life, drinking in the serene beauty of a night sky spangled with myriad stars, as if it were food for her soul. Emboldened, it soon became a nightly pleasure.

Then one night, footsteps sent her fleeing to her hiding place, barely in time to avoid discovery by Captain Heath as he staggered past, inches from her, down the passageway. She'd dared not risk discovery again.

If she but knew it, it was unlikely even Blake would have recognized her now. Her face was sallow from lack of sunlight, her eyes as black and beringed as spilled pitch on snow. Her clothes and her glorious hair were now hidden under a layer of filth, the latter so badly matted that even a finger could not rake through it as the fourth week grew to six, then seven.

Nellie pleaded with her to return to her own cabin, but she dare not.

"Oh, luv, they ain't even lookin' for ye! Come along o'me, do. Think o'the babe!" In truth, Amanda's demented appearance made her fear for the girl's sanity.

"No! I can't. They'll find me, I know they will! Did you not say they were using my cabin now? How can you ask it of me? The babe is the only reason I've endured this hell for so long." Her voice grew shrill, but Nellie knew it was her fear that made it so, rather than anger at her.

"Hush, now, do. I'll not press ye. But think on it. Them sacks do be dwindling fast. There'll be no hiding here afore long."

Amanda nodded wearily. Nellie was right. What would she do then? As it happened, the decision was not hers to make.

A day passed, the longest in her weeks as a fugitive, for Nellie did not come. Amanda huddled in the darkness, willing her to do so. A second day dragged relentlessly by. No food, no water, no companionship. A dreadful fear gripped her. What if Nellie never came again; what if something had happened to her? What if Blake and his men suspected their ruse, were even now scouring the vessel for her? She felt sick with worry, more so for Nellie than for herself. The bond of friendship they had wrought was a strong one.

By nightfall of the third day she was so thirsty and terribly worried she could stand it no longer. She pulled Nellie's tattered cloak about her and ventured out.

She passed no one on her way, the vessel eerily silent as the grave.

The door to the cabin occupied by Gualterio and Charlie Watson was closed, she saw in the lantern light, as was Nellie's opposite.

She fumbled clumsily with the latch and slipped inside. The darkness of the cabin revealed nothing, but she sensed Nellie's presence. A loud moan sounded from the woman. Amanda's groping fingers found a stub of candle set in a tin platter and a tinderbox. She hurriedly lit the candle.

Nellie sprawled on the straw pallet, her eyes bright and her lips cracked with fever. With a soft cry Amanda knelt at her side.

"Nellie, oh, Nellie dear, what's wrong?"

Nellie's eyes closed, fluttered open again. "I—I tried ter b-bring yer vittles, luv, I truly did! But the sickness come on me sudden, like, and—"

"Sssh, now. Don't worry, I'm going to take care of you." She had no idea how, but she intended to do her damnedest.

Nellie lapsed off to sleep again. Amanda pressed her hand to the other woman's brow. It was burning hot and dry as parchment. She peered into the tin mug. Empty. Water, they must have water if Nellie were to survive. She'd have to go up on deck. It would mean risking discovery, but it was a risk she would have to take. If the situation were reversed, she knew Nellie would not hesitate to do the same. She pulled the cloak tightly about her before slipping quietly from the cabin.

The decks were silent as she crossed them, her footsteps faltering with the unaccustomed exercise. A cold, white moon shone in frosty sky, and her breath made plumes in the chill of the air. She rubbed her palms together for warmth. Her heartbeats boomed louder and louder in her ears as she neared the forecastle and the scuttlebutt. Her courage seemed about to desert her.

Oh, God, no! The sailor guarding the precious water was slumped over the lid of the huge cask, asleep. She shook him gently by the shoulder, then harder as he failed to wake.

"Please, sir, I need water. My mother's sick with fever."

He opened one eye and peered at her balefully. "Ye'll get water—on the morrow, wench, and not before," he growled sleepily.

"Just a cupful, no more. Please!" she begged.

"Nay. T'Captain will have me flogged, he will, if'n I give ye extra." He scratched the stubble on his chin and yawned.

"I'll tell the Captain you were sleeping on watch," she threatened softly, "then you'll be flogged for sure."

A nasty look crept into his eyes. "Oh, ye will, will ye! We'll see who be gettin' flogged when I tells him I caught ye stealing water!"

She stepped backward as he reached to grab her. "Very well," she sighed, "but could you not draw me a bucket of sea water to bathe her with? I'll not tell if you do that much for me." Her voice was pleading.

He hesitated, torn between refusing, and complying for the sake of keeping the wench quiet. "Very well," he agreed finally. "So long as ye don't tell Cap'n Heath I were dozin'?"

She shook her head.

He tied a wooden bucket to a line, lowered it, then brought it up, brimming full, to the deck.

As he bent to untie the line from the bucket's handle, Amanda snatched up the oversized ladle from the water barrel and whacked him hard across the back of the skull.

He fell forward with a grunt and lay still.

She hopped over him and took up a second bucket, wresting the cover from the scuttlebutt. She plunged the bucket inside, drew it out full and replaced the lid on the cask.

In her weakened state, the heavy buckets seemed even heavier. She staggered across the deck, bowed under their weight, slowly so as not to spill one precious drop of either.

She had to make two trips down the stairway, but finally she was heaving her burdens the length of the passageway leading to Nellie's cabin.

Muffled moans and the ranting of some poor soul in delirium startled her as she passed one of the cabins. Only then did she realize that the fever and sickness held the entire ship in thrall.

Nellie lay exactly as when she had left her. Amanda scooped a little fresh water into the mug and held it up to her cracked lips. She allowed Nellie only a few drops. Too much might start her belly heaving after so long without and do more harm than good.

Then she peeled off Nellie's grubby lavender gown, tore yet another strip from her own ragged shift, and started to bathe the woman from head to toe with the icy salt water. When she had done, she lightly patted her dry and wrapped her in the cloak.

Every so often she held the mug to Nellie's lips and forced more drops of water down the parched throat.

She bathed her twice more that night, her own body weak and trembling from lack of food.

Shortly before morning, the fever broke. Nellie's breathing was regular, her forehead cool. When gray morning light misted the porthole, Amanda finally allowed herself to sleep.

Chapter Forty-Seven

Nellie's bout with the fever was soon over, thanks to Amanda's careful ministering. Not so lucky was the plight of the immigrants, crammed together in the fetid hold.

The fever had raged like fire throughout the vessel, and few were spared the awful vomiting and bloody flux that debilitated even the strongest aboard. Amanda, whether by sheer good fortune or the fact that she had been isolated at the height of the epidemic, was one of the lucky few.

As soon as Nellie was able to do so, she took her place in line for food and water once again on deck.

Amanda could have cried for relief. The days that she had been forced to fetch the victuals for them had been times of sheer terror as she waited her turn; terror lest the sailor she had crowned, or Paul or his men, should see her and start an outcry.

Nellie rapped three times on the cabin door and slipped quickly inside as Amanda opened it.

"Nellie! What on earth happened?"

"Bleedin' witch! I showed her what for, I did!" Nellie brandished two portions of biscuits and stew on a platter. Her scratched and bleeding face was triumphant, her red hair even wilder in disarray than normal. The sleeve of the lavender gown was almost completely torn off, exposing a pasty-white, grubby shoulder.

Amanda laughed despite her dismay. Nellie bristled like a fierce little terrier in a bear pit. "Who did you give 'what for'?"

"That ugly Spanish witch with the warts—her wot lost her husband t'the fever. I tried to give 'er a coin in place o'her man's grub—arter all, 'e don't be needin' it where 'e's gorn, do 'e?"

"And she refused you?"

"Aye, but not fer long!" Nellie answered with a grin of utter relish. Her cheeky face darkened. "It do be awful though. So many dead—they're throwing them over by the hour, without canvas nor shroud! Poor wee babes, little nippers n'more than five or six years old, along o'their mothers, some of 'em. Them's what's left be too weak t'shed tears. They only watch it all, dry-eyed." Nellie sniffed back a tear of her own, then brightened resolutely. "Still, I heard tell we be approachin' a warmer clime soon. Praise be t'God, I hope it'll not be long." She scratched her armpit thoughtfully.

Amanda mutely echoed her prayer, and the two of them fell to eating the sorry meal. Halfway through, Amanda dropped her spoon with a clatter, a look of utter disbelief on her face. She set the trencher down, and pressed her palms to her belly, face shining.

"Nellie, the babe moved! Oh, it's beautiful!" From deep within her belly came a quiver, an awakening of the new, exquisite life cradled within. Again, a fluttering as soft and delicate as dainty wings, or the trembling of a dewdrop poised on a petal's tip before falling. She hugged her belly, fighting the urge to sing for sheer joy, to whirl about the cabin in mad delight. Her baby, living, moving inside her! It was real—she was not alone anymore!

Nellie watched her, the hard lines of her face softening to a gentle smile of shared pleasure.

"Aye, luv, he's movin', God bless the little mite! And we should be safe long afore he makes his entrance into this world."

Safe? Amanda wondered. Would she ever truly be safe as long as Paul Blake lived and remained driven by his lust for revenge?

Several squalls lashed down upon the ship during the latter part of the voyage, and then the *Pride of Suffolk* tossed like a leaking keg upon the foaming swells.

Amanda, never a good sailor in rough weather, and the rest of the passengers hung out of the portholes retching miserably, praying that the pitching vessel would finally level itself. The decks were awash and water streamed from the bilges. The holds split, and no amount of pitch used to patch them could save the flooded food supplies. Their rations were decreased so drastically that the very young or the old died daily and were cast overboard, while only those stronger souls who could withstand the deprivation coming so soon after the fever, survived to stagger around once the storms subsided. Indeed, conditions became so terrible, the number of deaths so great, that finally the newer deaths were met with a stony indifference more shocking than the wails of sorrow that had met the first losses.

When they reached the Caribbean, the storms took a different tack. These brought winds of such hurricane-like intensity that sailors were simply blown from their precarious perches like feathers before some gigantic bellows. The days in between were balmy, the heat and stillness of air and ocean oppressive and uncanny after the previous violence. Then the storms would rise again, whipping the water until the waves towered above the ship like vengeful gods, before crashing down upon the vessel and shattering all that lay in their wake. They would cease as suddenly as they commenced.

Around the Bahamas, Captain Heath posted extra lookouts, only too well aware of the threat that pirates in these waters presented.

Amanda lived in horror of a second capture, and kept her own vigil by the port window, scanning the ocean. Sometimes she saw small fleet vessels come over the horizon by twilight, these vessels dousing their lanterns on seeing the bigger ship, and staying off in the distance before resuming their course. She knew that these had to be smuggling vessels, evading taxes and slipping their cargoes ashore under cover of darkness.

The heat was stifling, far more humid than Spain had ever been, and though she had cursed the thinness of the yellow gown on bitterly cold Atlantic nights, now she was grateful for its relative coolness. Nellie and Amanda, disguised in a stifling cloak, stood at the rail and watched the coastline appear, fanning themselves. Nellie, who had withstood the rigors of the journey so remarkably well, was now all a-fluster with excitement to see her new homeland, and babbled on incessantly as they grew closer, primping and preening herself for the moment they would disembark.

Amanda was suddenly unwilling to leave the familiar, if awful, confines of the ship. Would the new land bring her happiness and peace of mind—or fresh dangers she could only imagine?

Chapter Forty-Eight

At last they dropped anchor up the mouth of the Mississippi River.

Amanda felt a surge of disappointment, for through the early-morning mist, the sinful New Orleans she had heard so much about was a dimly seen cluster of wooden buildings, with not much to recommend them.

As they had planned, Amanda and Nellie slipped in with the crowd of immigrants as they surged forward for places on the waiting longboats.

Her heart hammered wildly as Captain Johnson Heath himself reached out an arm to assist her down the ladder to the boat. She mumbled, *"Gracias,"* as she clambered down, relief flooding her as nothing further happened.

Nellie insisted garrulously on coming in the same longboat, and, despite Heath's obvious distaste, she clutched his arm for support and shinned down, lugging her small trunk over the side with amazing speed.

The longboat had them on the wharf in no time. Nellie and Amanda drew apart from the immigrants, who stood silently gaping at the town with an air of disappointment.

"Where do we go, Nellie?" asked Amanda eagerly, her eyes wide at the throngs of people milling noisily all about them.

Hawkers with baskets or carts yelled their wares in good-natured discord. The odor of fish and overripe fruits, of grain and spices hung in air that was thick and rich as clotted cream. No one paid the slightest attention to the grubby, dishevelled pair, and Amanda was glad to be able to walk freely finally on the boards that served as pavements along the edges of the muddy street.

"Oops! Don't know where yet, luv, but we'd best duck in 'ere. His Lordship do be a'comin' down the street!"

Amanda cocked an eye in the direction in which Nellie had nodded.

Sure enough, Paul Blake, resplendent in a sky-blue coat and striped satin vest, lounged carelessly in the back of a clumsy *calèche,* a sort of wagon-cum-carriage. Gualterio and Charlie Watson, sullen-faced, trudged behind him in the mud.

Paul's lips moved furiously, she saw, a curious expression on his face, and even from the safety of the alley they had ducked into, she could see the strange, heated glow in his eyes.

Thankfully, the *calèche* rumbled past, its occupants oblivious to the nervous pair in the alley.

Nellie tugged Amanda back into the street, and they walked on. Her legs, after so long at sea, felt strange.

She soon noticed that New Orleans was less primitive than it had seemed at first glance. The streets had been laid out in an orderly manner, each running at right angles to those intersecting them. Down by the levee a fair-sized landing had been built, and this was the site of a great deal of coming and going. They strolled along the Mississippi banks, watching the burly flatboatmen unload cargoes and passengers from their rugged craft.

One elegantly dressed Frenchman was explaining patiently to a woman, obviously his nervous wife, that if they wished to travel anywhere on the Mississippi, the flatboat was the only means of doing so, for the sandbars, overhung by trees and deep shadow, were treacherous to larger craft. This made sense to Amanda, for the squat boats would draw little water. They certainly seemed to transport the most diverse kinds of people, for there were priests, nuns with clicking rosary beads, and farmers, as well as gentry, waiting to board them. Great wooden wagons drawn by oxen stood at the levee to receive cargoes which would, in turn, be loaded onto some sea-going ship.

"Cor, look at that hunk o'man! Wouldn't mind tryin' him, I wouldn't. Proper savage he looks!" Nellie chuckled. She nudged Amanda's arm and pointed rudely, batting her lashes and pursing her lips in a pretend kiss as the brawny bear of a man returned her look.

Amanda stared, too, equally fascinated, but for a different reason. She'd never seen anything like him! The hat he wore seemed more like some sort of animal than an article of clothing, for it was made entirely of fur, the tail left hanging in the back. His jerkin was of soft skin, the edges fringed, and the whole ornamented with what looked like pine needles, dyed and arranged in attractive designs. Leggings of skin and shoes of the same soft hide were laced with thongs of leather.

As they watched, two other men, similarly dressed, joined the first, carrying bales of skin that made them stagger from the weight. Their hair hung down past their shoulders in matted wads and their shaggy beards, long and unkempt, gave them all the appeal of cavemen, Amanda thought, casting a sidelong glance at the fascinated Nellie. They had powder horns slung across their chests and long-barreled weapons clamped under their armpits, while a pistol was stuffed carelessly into each rawhide belt.

A cry of alarm drew their attention away from the fur trappers. The river was high, the current swift, and a flatboat had swirled out into midstream so swiftly that the men aboard had to fight to hang on to their poles as the flatboat spun like a top. The mules aboard snorted and brayed in fear. Amanda and Nellie watched anxiously until the craft was righted again, and then continued their tour along the levee beneath the shady cypress and live-oaks planted there.

A little further on they passed a brickyard, and whistles and catcalls met their passing from the sweaty laborers within. Nellie opened her mouth to blast them with a scathing retort, but Amanda pinched her arm to silence her. She steered Nellie away from the levee and back into the town proper.

A colorful billboard, garishly painted, announced that a quardroon ball would be held within the huge wooden building the following Sunday.

"I had no idea there would be balls and such," mused Amand thoughtfully.

"Aye, I heard o'these—it's when them high-fallutin' young bloods get's t'choose 'oo warms their beds for t'next few months," muttered Nellie darkly. "Like a bleeding cattle market it is, but very posh."

"How do you know so much about it?" Amanda asked curiously, pushing back a heavy strand of damp tangled hair. The mid-day heat was stifling.

"T'bosun. Taught me a lot, 'e did, afore we landed." Nellie winked roguishly.

"I'll wager he did!" Amanda laughed, hugging Nellie about the waist. "Not that you had much left to learn, h'mmm?" she teased.

"Aye, ye're right ye are! Proper educated, I am! And if'n I don't start to look for work, it's likely I'll be forced t'put all me education 'ter work! Look, luv, this's all we've left." She held up a worn coinpurse.

Amanda gasped. "Only a florin left? But Nellie, you said you had made a fair penny on board, I remember you—"

"Hush, now! I knows what I said, but this be all we're left!" Nellie retorted crossly. "Don't make no to-do about it, girlie, there's a dear." She tossed her dyed-red curls, and stomped onward.

Amanda hurried after her, whirling her about by the arm. "You used it all for my rations on ship, didn't you?" she accused, her eyes narrowing as Nellie looked over-innocent. "Tell the truth, Nellie," she threatened.

Nellie sighed heavily. "Aye, I suppose I did. Ain't so many what'd pay fer a tumble with the likes o'me now, there ain't! They likes a fresh, comely young lass, like ye, and I ain't seen nineteen fer a long time. Don't suppose ye'd like me t'teach yer the business, do ye? With yer looks—oh, well, if'n ye're sure." She agreed hurriedly as Amanda's face reddened with indignation.

"We'll find some decent labor. I can work hard, Nell,

I'm no milksop, swooning at the idea of making an honest living. And Nell, thank you, for everything! I'll make it up, somehow, I promise you," she vowed earnestly.

Nellie looked embarrassed, but her rouged cheeks were even redder with pleasure. "No need o'that, love," she said gruffly. "In yer condition, though, I'll be the one wot does the 'ard labor—and no arguin' mind!"

Amanda laughed. She had no intention of letting Nellie make a living for both of them, but that could be sorted out in due course.

They walked on, oblivious of the curious stares they drew, for Nellie pranced proudly on the boards that served as pavements with an air of brassy gentility, despite the tattered ruffles and grimy lace *fichu* of her lavender gown. Amanda's yellow brocade was obviously the worse for wear, too, though they had repaired the ripped bodice as well as it could be repaired. Amanda yearned for a proper bath and to wash her hair, and the luxury of clean clothes. Nellie, never the most fragrant of companions, seemed not in the least anxious for either!

They passed a wig-maker's, then came upon an alley that opened out onto a square. The pungent odors that assailed their nostrils brought saliva to their mouths and groans to their bellies.

One stall holder had a half dozen panniers of oysters and clams, and an open, fat-bellied cauldron of water bubbled next to him. Richly dressed men and women were a bright splash of color circled about the man, exchanging coins for clams served steaming on wooden trenchers in the open air. A little old woman dressed in black made a somber contrast to the exotic, brilliant fruits arrayed behind her back, and at her feet were baskets of roses and other flowers, wilting rapidly in the heat.

"Shall we 'ave somethin', then, luv? Bleedin' starved, I am! There'll be just enough left fer a night's lodgin', I reckon, if'n we don't get piggy?"

Nellie had seen the longing in Amanda's eyes. A woman in her condition deserved a little treat, she did, especially after all the slops they'd had to eat during the three months at sea! Still, unless one looked carefully, it was real hard to tell Amanda was expecting. Lost weight, she had. There were hollows under the girl's eyes that hadn't been there before, the skin stretched so tight over the high cheekbones it seemed transparent. Her skin was very wan too, from lack of sunlight, and added to her tragic beauty, emphasizing the haunting sadness of her enormous sable eyes. A looker, she was, right enough, but she needed filling out, funning to make those eyes sparkle merrily again. Aye, and a man to bring out the fire in her.

"No, let's not. It looks very expensive. I'm starved, too, so let's save the money and buy something more filling."

Reluctantly, Nellie agreed. Amanda felt the now-familiar pain clutch at her. They passed Spanish-style houses with black iron galleries to their upper stories, soft white walls washed with early afternoon sunlight. They provoked the memory of Miguel all too easily, of Villa Hermosa where the babe had been conceived. She had to put him out of her mind, had to, if she was ever to live fully again. But the choking agony that made her heart feel ready to burst from her was not easily exorcised. Nellie grasped her shoulder, sniffing the humid air like a hound scenting game.

"Smells good, dunnit?" she grinned, nodding at the open coffeehouse door.

Amanda smiled agreement. The delicious odor of savory meats, mingled with the rich, spicy fragrance of fresh coffee, smelled appetizing indeed.

"Shall we 'ave luncheon then?" asked Nellie genteelly, inclining her head and patting only one of many stray red ringlets.

"Oh, let's," replied Amanda airily, offering her arm to Nellie in best society fashion.

They entered the café as regally as queens—although the manner in which they devoured their luncheon was anything but regal!

Chapter Forty-Nine

Amanda kneaded her fist into her aching back and stretched, groaning. The hand that she used to wipe her streaming face left a thick smudge of soot on her face, but she never noticed. All she could think of was that if the fire wasn't cleaned out and restarted, Monsieur Robineau's shrew of a wife would lay the broomhandle across her buttocks again.

Oh, yes, it didn't matter to that sharp-nosed old witch that she was heavy with child! Come to think of it, it hadn't seemed to deter her husband overmuch, either! Despite the obviousness of her condition, he still pursued her amorously like a rotund, balding little gnome, pinching her bottom whenever she turned around, peeking up her skirts, or pressing a hurried peck to her cheek, and all the while casting furtive glances over his shoulder to make sure Madame Robineau was nowhere in sight. Still, she rather liked her would-be aging lover, for although amorously inclined, he'd been very good to her and Nell—even given her a beautiful carved cradle, which, though not new, was still a lovely, thoughtful gift. Yes, the past three months had been happy ones, for the most part.

In that time, though she'd worked as she had never

worked before, a certain amount of contentment had come over her. Her labors served to channel the grief over Miguel's betrayal of her and to take her mind from it.

Indeed, with all the work to be done, there was little time for thought at all! The food, though plain fare, was plentiful, and had filled out the hollows of her cheeks and body again. The burnished mane of her hair had regained its former luster, although, under Madame Solange's orders, it was now concealed under a prim white mob cap. In all, she glowed with vitality and the new life blossoming within her, cheeks flushed, eyes sparkling. The babe grew lustily, energetic kicks showing even beneath the starched white apron fastened around her bulging middle. She looked forward to the babe's birth, eagerly imagining how it would be to hold her child in her arms.

She hummed a lullaby to herself as she got the fire started, and tossed a handful of coffee grains into the huge pot bubbling on the iron over the fire. The baby kicked, and she wondered for the millionth time if it would be boy or girl, toying with names for him or her, discarding them as quickly as she decided on them.

She couldn't believe the good fortune she and Nellie had found. If good old Nell hadn't started that row with the serving wench who'd tried to shortchange them of their florin that first night, they would never have witnessed the lightfingered chit's dismissal, never have found work so quickly. Monsieur Robineau had been desperate, having lost another girl that same day to one of the brothels on Royal Street, and on hearing they were seeking employment, had hired them on the spot.

Amanda had not lasted long in the position of serving girl, for once her dejected appearance had been banished by a hot bath and a few days of good food, the young bloods of the town who frequented the café had come around her like bees to a flower, and caused more uproar than was good for business, much to Madame Solange's disgust. Amanda had been exiled to clean the anonymous confines of the Robineaus' living quarters and to helping in the kitchen, and secretly she'd been rather relieved.

Nellie, though, seemed to be in her element, dispensing wit and raucous good humor along with the coffee and food. Amanda suspected that, secretly, Nellie might be dispensing her favors too, after hours, but tactfully refrained from inquiring too closely. That sort of busybodying was best left to experts such as Solange Robineau. Still, even that woman had been shrewd enough to see that Amanda was a willing and hard worker, and had agreed to let her stay on despite her condition, and, if things worked out, after the baby's birth, too.

Amanda smiled. She'd be able to have the cradle right here in the kitchen next to her while she worked, and still make enough for their living.

They'd seen Paul or his ugly henchmen twice in those three months, but though she'd been terrified, she and Nell had been able to scurry off without being seen themselves. When the baby would be old enough to travel, they planned to leave New Orleans and go somewhere else, perhaps La Fayette or Baton Rouge, where they would be safer.

"You are always at ze daydreams, Madame Sommairs. *Vite, vite, le café!* Maison Robineau is open—

and the coffee still not ready! Ah, *mon Dieu,"* she snapped, "I am of a mind to give the thrashing to you!"

Amanda almost dropped the coffeepot in shock. Madame Robineau was enormous, but able to creep up on one with the stealth of a cat.

"Oui, madame, it is ready. I will start the *bouillabaise* at once!" She gasped as she lifted the heavy pot to the back of the black range where it would keep warm.

"Bien, see that you do—and make sure I do not catch you shirking again! Believe me, I would not 'esitate to see you off!" She stormed from the kitchen, black taffeta skirts swishing over bell-like hips.

Amanda sighed, and started scaling the fish the boy had brought, fresh from the harbor, that very morning. It was a job she loathed, for the nausea she'd experienced those first few months still bothered her from time to time. The smell of fish always made her want to gag. She couldn't even stand the way the thing's eyes seemed to stare at her reproachfully, as if she was the sole cause of its demise. She covered the eyes with a thick slice of onion, fileted the fish deftly with a knife.

"'Ard at it, are ye, luv? Oh, 'tis wicked how that woman do take on, an' you so big an' all! Here, ducks, I'll finish it for ye. Take the weight off o'yer feet, do."

"No, Nell! The customers will be screaming for coffee soon. Here, take it out to them. The croissants will be ready in a few minutes." She opened the door to the range and peeked inside, the wave of heat bringing an even rosier flush to her cheeks.

"Let 'em scream! Bin up since cock's crow, we 'ave, working our bottoms off, while those bunch o'young rakes were at their pleasures on Royal Street, no doubt.

No, I'll do that fish for yer, 'cos there'll be no stoppin' that French cow from seein' us orf if you upchucks in her bleedin' kitchen."

Nellie firmly pushed Amanda into a chair and took the knife from her. She hacked up the fish into large chunks, then scraped its head, eyes, guts, blood and all, into the pot, grinning broadly. "There we goes, best bloomin' boolabaisey in all of New Orleans!" She smiled wickedly.

Amanda smiled, too. Nellie, thank God, never changed! In her prim gray frock and snowy apron and cap, she still contrived to look like a bawd masquerading as a nun. Her red hair was fast growing out, to be replaced by a soft, warm brown color that would eventually be far more flattering to her coloring than the former, virulent red. Despite Madame Robineau's stern caution, however, Nellie still sported rouge and little black velvet hearts upon her cheeks. She was always an incorrigible cheeky, cockney sparrow—always Nellie Flagg.

"Phew, it's so hot! That attic of ours will be like an oven tonight," Amanda observed, casting a glance out of the door at the unclouded blue sky.

"Aye, ducks. Reckon the 'ot weather'll bring out the beast in yer Mister Robineau too!" Nellie teased, "fair taken wiv you, he is." She paused. "Don'tcha want t'get wed, t'find some nice young fella t'take care o'ye and the nipper?" Nellie's voice grew wistful.

"No, I don't," Amanda retorted hotly. "I'll not fall so easily into *that* trap again—it's far too painful when one allows the heart to dominate the head. No, thank you, Nell, never again!"

"Aw, come off it! Ye're too young t'think that way.

'Never again' indeed! What about the babe? Don't he deserve no Pa t'dandle him on his knee? Proper selfish, ye are," Nellie scolded, but her smile belied her words.

Amanda removed the croissants from the oven and set them to cool. The next batch had risen already, and she slid them in through the little black door to bake.

"I'll see yer later," Nellie called. She left bearing the coffeepot.

Soon there would be silverware and pots to wash in the tub, then luncheon to prepare. Cook would not return soon enough from Baton Rouge, as far as Amanda was concerned. Mignon Boucher was a hard taskmaster, but a fair one, even though she kept herself to herself.

Amanda climbed onto a low stool to fetch an onion off the string hanging from the beam. She let out a shriek as a hand cupped her buttocks lovingly, and would have fallen if that same hand had not steadied her.

"Monsieur Robineau, please! I asked you not to do that!" she cried exasperated.

"Ah, *cherie,* I cannot resist! Ze curves of your most charming *derrière* are purest poetry, a feast for these poor hands!" He sighed deeply, rolling blue-gray eyes heavenward. "You are cruel and 'eartless to be angry wiz me, to deny me. Come, a little kiss, I beg you!" he wheedled, taking a few, surprisingly agile steps to her side.

"Not one! Monsieur, your wife!"

"Ah, Solange! She does not understand me—always she 'as ze 'eadache!" His hands clasped her about the waist, and he pecked little birdlike kisses on her cheeks, her throat, the bare flesh above her bodice.

She struggled, laughing aloud as his lips were impeded suddenly, by her jutting belly, from traveling any lower.

He released her, sighing. "Mmm. After this—" he pointed to her bulging stomach —"I shall not take 'no' for an answer, *petite ange*. Believe me, I am a devil once roused!"

He puffed up proudly, smoothed back an imaginary mane of hair on his shining, bald head, and gave her a look that was meant to create images of smoldering passion, but merely conveyed the impression that he suffered badly from indigestion.

"Oh, poor monsieur! Come, I will give you a kiss—but only one, mind!"

She stepped lightly to where he stood, trembling in anticipation, eyes closed and lips puckered. Raising herself on her toes, she kissed his shining dome briefly, before polishing it with the dustcloth in her hand. "There, you have your kiss, monsieur! Now, leave me be, before Madame Robineau takes the broom to me again!"

Sadly disappointed, Robineau did as she suggested, muttering woefully as he went.

Mignon Boucher returned to her position as cook at Maison Robineau three days later, and Amanda heaved a sigh of gratitude at the efficient, calm manner in which she did so.

"*Merde!* That Solange—nevaire have I seen such a cold one! Come, give me that great pot! The *bébé* will be 'ere zis evening if you insist on carrying it! 'Ow could she allow it? *Mon Dieu,* she works you like a slave, *petite mè*re. Bed wiz you—and this very minute. I am in charge here. You will do as *I* say, Amanda!"

Mignon scolded.

Amanda was only too glad to do as she was told. In truth, it was all getting to be too much, all the lifting and carrying. Thank God for Mignon, and Nellie, and for Monsieur Robineau, too. God bless him, she adored the cradle he had given her.

Later, in the attic room that she and Nellie shared, she rocked the carved rosewood cradle gently, imagining how it would be with the baby, her baby, lying there inside it. She drew the candle stub closer, and leaned to the meager light to sew a final seam on the latest of several tiny gowns she had made. There, it was finished. She lay back and closed her eyes, pressing her fingertips lightly to her swollen belly.

As if in answer, the child stirred. Amanda smiled, caressing with circular, massaging movements the spot where she'd felt the tiny hand or foot. What did it matter that the attic was stifling, the sloping roof so low it forced one to stoop when crossing the room? Who cared if the cot was lumpy or the floorboards bare, with the treasure she had within her? The days and the hours seemed to stomp by on clogged feet of late, instead of on wings as the first eight months had. The time could not pass soon enough for her!

Outside, far below, the streets of New Orleans were dark, lit only by a slave or a serving man carrying torch or lantern for his master to light the way. The sounds of bands of carousers, voices raised in bawdy chorus, carried but faintly, as did the clop of hooves and the rumble of wheels on the dirt street.

The air was sultry, filled with night smells: cape jasmine and gardenias; earth wet with evening dew; the vague, spicy scent of bay rum and sweet wines; and the less pleasant, faint tang of the river. Sweet or pungent, they combined in a heady, exciting odor, filled with life and vigor.

An enormous, peach-colored moon rose and hung lanternlike directly outside the tiny window in the purple-black sky. She watched it, mesmerized, until sleep's velvet wings enfolded her.

Chapter Fifty

The heavy wicker basket went flying as she fell heavily into the mud, scattering fruits and vegetables alike in all directions. A burly arm raised her up, another man scrambled to retrieve her purchases, some of them burst and squashed, from the ground.

She brushed aside their concerned offers of help, stammering her thanks as she half staggered, half walked hurriedly around the corner and through the wrought-iron open gate of one of the Spanish-style houses.

Amanda did not know whose house it was, nor did she care. Her heart was racing, her breath ragged and hoarse, prickles of fear coursing the length of her spine and rendering her knees weak and trembling. Had he seen her? *Oh, please, God, he had not!* She waited, blood singing in her ears, for a full ten minutes, her thoughts chaotic. Even if Paul appeared, she doubted she would have the presence of mind or the strength of body to flee him.

If he *had* seen her, it could only have been a glimpse at most—she'd tried to stroll inconspicuously past the market stalls and to the corner, but on reaching it, common sense had taken flight and she had panicked, started to run and fallen.

"Eh! *Muchacha,* be off with you!" The housekeeper of the house had spotted her, and now brandished a mop in her direction.

She cautiously crept from the sanctuary of the garden and back out onto the street. It was filled with housewives and servants alike, hurrying to purchase their pick of the produce in the market square. Beautiful, coffee-colored mulatto and quadroon women glided elegantly along the wooden boards with panniers of laundry balanced on heads bound gaily in brightly colored *tignons* or kerchiefs, defying gravity with their precarious loads.

An overseer, bearing an evil-looking bullwhip, snarled and chivvied his chained group of slaves through the mud. Their eyes were white with terror at the sights and sounds about them, the glistening black of their fear-sweated bodies raw with sores.

She stumbled through the droves of people on the way back to Maison Robineau, scarce seeing any of them, but instinctively alert for that one face she dreaded seeing most.

An ache had started in her belly. It grew in intensity, gripped her, and subsided quickly. Had she hurt herself in the fall? She bit her lip and cursed Paul Blake with a hatred born of fear for the babe's well-being.

The kitchen of Maison Robineau stood apart from the main building of the coffeehouse as did all the kitchens in the town, a sensible means of containing any would-be fires to one small area. She barely made it through the doorway when another cramp racked her. She doubled over, barely managing to set the basket down. Her fingers grasped her belly, felt it surge outward beneath them, peak, and relax. Sweat dewed her brow and her upper lip. In seconds the pain passed. Drawing a deep breath, she picked up the basket and carried it inside.

Mignon pushed a black wisp of hair from her eyes and turned, smiling, as Amanda went in.

"Why, zat was fast! 'Ave they nothing worth purchasing today at ze market? Poof! *Cherie,* why did you buy this?" She held up a trodden, mangled loaf of bread with a reproachful frown.

"I—I'm sorry. I fell, and it rolled into the gutter. I'll make it good, I promise," she whispered.

"Non, non. It will do, I shall turn it into ze English bread-and-butter pudding—*mais, ma petite,* are you well? The fall, were you hurt? *Hélas,* what a fool I am, you look terrible!" She enveloped Amanda in a hug, held her at arm's length, and peered at her searchingly with concerned hazel eyes. "Your time—it is 'ere, *oui?"*

"I'm not sure—perhaps it's only the shock, of falling, you know. I went flat on my face and belly. I think just the breath was knocked from me—oh!"

Amanda gasped as another pain gripped her. Her hands clutched convulsively at the folds of her dark-blue frock, the knuckles bleached white from the intensity of her grip. Mignon laid her hand across the girl's stomach.

"Oui, it is time. Come, we will take you up to your room. Go carefully now, *cherie,* we will stop if you have another pain. It is your first, there will be plenty of time to get you comfortable, *oui?"*

Mignon helped her to undress and don a clean shift. She pulled back the shabby coverlet on the cot, hurried away, and returned minutes later with a clean sheet, which she spread beneath the girl and made her lie upon it on her side.

"Zere you are! Oh, *petite,* is it not exciting? Soon it will be over, and the little one will be lying beside you!" She pulled Amanda's hair back with a piece of her own ribbon and tied it at the nape. "Do not be afraid; the pain, soon it is forgotten, you understand, and then, only ze joy!"

Amanda nodded doubtfully. Now that the time had come, she was torn between wishing she could be anywhere—doing anything but this one thing—and with excitement that she would finally hold the baby in her arms. At the back of her mind was also the nagging question of whether Paul had or had not seen her. She knew it was him, wearing the same sky-blue satin coat and striped vest he had worn the day they'd disembarked from the *Pride of Suffolk*. She'd caught only a second's glimpse of his profile, but that had been enough to send her swiftly in the opposite direction, swallowed up by the crowd. No, he'd not seen her, she was certain of it!

Another contraction pushed all other thoughts from her mind, for this one was long and hard. She ground her nails into the sheet-covered pallet and tried unsuccessfully to stifle a moan by gritting her teeth. It passed gradually, like a wave rippling over an enormous rock, then ebbing away, only to rush in and to ebb yet again. Her hair was dripping wet.

The afternoon sunshine mellowed to the liquid golden light of early evening. Mignon returned to her kitchen, and Nellie replaced her at Amanda's side.

"Not much more now, luv. The pain do be coming long and 'ard. Rest easy between times, it'll save yer strength, right?"

She wrung out the cloth once again, and wiped Amanda's streaming face and neck with tender, calloused hands.

Every few minutes Amanda's features screwed up in concentration and pain, suffused with color, as she strained at the knotted ends of torn sheet tied to the bedposts. Her features relaxed and her body slackened as it ended.

"I'm so scared, Nell—no, not of the babe's coming—of him! What if Paul *did* see me, what then?" Her eyes were wide pools of fear, her breathing panting and short.

Nellie moved about the room lighting the candles Monsieur Robineau had brought. The attic room was near bright as day when she blew out the taper, and she clicked her teeth reprovingly.

"Now, ye do be a good girl! If'n he *did* see yer—I'm not sayin' as how he did, mind—he'll not know where t'find ye now, will 'e? New Orleans do be a regular rabbit warren. And by the time he searches 'ere—if 'e do—we'll be gone and the nipper with us," Nellie reassured her, patting her arm.

"I suppose you're right. Oooh! Nellie, I have to push, I have to!" she shrieked suddenly.

Nellie positioned her legs and aided her rigid arms to find the knotted sheets.

"Aaagh!" Was that awful sound from her own mouth? She arched upward, straining at the hand knots, holding her breath instinctively to aid the downward thrust of her body.

"'Ere 'e comes, luv, ye're almost there, ye are! Push again, I see's 'is little 'ead! Hold it. Now, again, 'ard!"

Amanda held her breath once more and pushed and pushed again. A searing pain and, finally, exquisite relief. There was utter silence. Then a loud and lusty wail, a deafening, glorious wail of new life rent the silence of the night asunder.

"'Tis a boy, me luv, and a lovely lad 'e is, too!" Nellie crowed proudly.

Amanda's face shone as bright as the myriad candles. The new emotions coursing through her were strange and wondrous. Such joy, a marvelous exultation of heart and body! She held out her arms.

Nell tied and severed the cord, then wiped the baby's face, bundled him in a tiny blanket, and handed him to his mother.

Amanda never noticed nor felt the final stages of birth, her rapt attention riveted on the perfect infant in her arms. A beautifully molded head, covered in jet-black damp curls, rested in the crook of her arm, and a tiny rosebud of a mouth searched, and finally found a miniature thumb and sucked lustily, filling the attic room with smacking sounds. She lifted the blanket and counted the little toes, smiling softly as her son's free hand clamped hard over her fingers and held it fast. Love overflowed her heart.

"Oh, but 'e do be a beauty!" Nellie breathed, tears shining in her faded blue eyes. "Good sized too—and likely t'get even bigger right fast if'n that appetite o'is be aught to go by! Put him t'the breast, luv. 'E'll not get much yet, but th' nursin' will satisfy 'im for now."

Nellie held him, rocking him gently while Amanda adjusted her shift. Then the rosebud mouth found the breast, and a deep sigh of satisfaction filled mother and child alike. Nellie pulled the coverlet up over the pair.

"I'll get ye some broth now, and then the two o'ye can rest, right, luv?"

Nellie smiled, for Amanda's face wore the serenest of expressions, and the new mother gave no sign of having heard a word of what she'd said. Nellie took the kettle and cloths and tiptoed from the room.

Chapter Fifty-One

Monsieur Robineau gazed deeply into her eyes, plucked her hand from the folds of her gown, and kissed each fingertip lovingly.

"Ah, *ma cherie,* you grow lovelier with each passing day! Your eyes, zey are pools of mystery. I long to lose myself in their depths. And your breasts, *mon Dieu,* zey are as full and ripe as ze fairest of peaches!" He stretched out his hand to touch those forbidden fruits, the expression on his face as excited as a schoolboy scrumping apples in an orchard.

Amanda rapped him sharply across the knuckles with the handle of the feather duster, and he withdrew his hand instantly, sucking on the stinging joints, his sad, reproachful eyes reproving her.

"Shame on you, monsieur, to press your attentions on me—and my child asleep in this very room, too! Now, if you would have me work for my keep, you must leave me be."

"But I love you! Run away with me, *petite* Amanda, I beg you! Nevaire will you work again! I will shower you with jewels, with satin gowns, anything you want, for you and your *petit fils!* I will love him as my own," he vowed hotly.

"Henri? Where are you? Ah, *sacre bleu* that man, he is as lazy as a slug!" Solange's strident voice carried clearly from the main building.

Henri Robineau leaped back, guilt on his face.

"Coming, my angel," he stammered, before beating a hasty exit.

Amanda laughed and, bending, blew the gaily colored pinwheel she had fastened to the side of the cradle. Its scarlet-and-blue sails whirled madly, bringing a delighted smile to two-month-old Michael Robert's face. His clenched chubby fists waved excitedly. His rounded, dimpled legs fought free of the restraining blanket and kicked vigorously. When the motion ceased, he turned his head and regarded his mother solemnly from wide, long-lashed dark eyes.

"Again? Very well, my sweet. I shall blow it once more, and then I must get back to my work. Would you have us thrown onto the streets, hmmm, would you?" She tickled Michael's rosy cheek and was rewarded with a beaming smile and a crow of delight. "So you would like that, eh? Well, there would be no fine cradle for you then, young man, and no pretty baubles to play with, either!" She blew the pinwheel again and set the cradle to rocking.

Michael was such a good baby—well, most of the time—she thought grimly, for he seemed bent on inheriting the fiery temper of both his parents. Michael Robert. She'd called him Michael after Miguel, for it was the English version of the Spanish name, and she had known from the first time she had held him there would be no forgetting his father, not with the soft, blue-black curls that clung to his head, nor with the firm line of his jaw and chin, albeit they were softened now with necklaces of baby fat. She fancied when Michael grew older, there would be times when her heart would ache at the memories his likeness to Miguel recalled. Robert had been her second choice. Her father would have been so honored, so very proud to have his grandson bear his name.

The pile of potatoes to be peeled dwindled rapidly under her flying fingers. Nellie came in once to admire and play with her "nephew," whom she loved with fierce possessiveness. Michael would do no wrong in Nellie's eyes, and it seemed the infant tyrant felt the same about her, for all crying would cease when Aunt Nellie scooped him into her arms and rocked him, much to his mother's annoyance.

Mignon breezed into the kitchen, a huge-brimmed straw hat perched jauntily on her head, green ribbons trailing from the crown and spilling onto the green-sprigged white dress she wore. Her face was flushed with excitement and, though no longer a young woman, this morning Mignon *was* young, and beautiful, too.

"You look enchanting, Mademoiselle Boucher." Amanda smiled. "Am I to believe you went dressed so merely to purchase supplies for Maison Robineau—or was there some ulterior motive?" she inquired innocently.

Mignon blushed, removing the pin from her hat and laying it down on the scrubbed white table. "But of course, there was an ulterior motive, *cherie!*" She laughed gaily. "And what a motive! Tall, blond, shoulders this wide! Ah, he is *magnifique,* my Jean-Louis!"

Amanda, who had seen Jean-Louis often, laughingly

nodded agreement. Mignon's face told her the morning had been even more interesting than a casual meeting with her sweetheart. "Out with it, Mignon. I can tell, you are keeping something back," she teased.

"Ah, oui, I am indeed. Look at me—do I look different? Do I—" she paused—"look like a woman who has just received the most wonderful proposal?"

"I hope it was of marriage!" Amanda inquired, serious-faced, but then she couldn't keep from smiling. She flung her arms about Mignon and hugged her. "Congratulations! When is the wedding to be? I'm so happy for you!"

"Well, Jean-Louis wants it to be very soon, for he has been offered work in Baton Rouge. But I told him I must give ze notice to Madame Robineau first, so perhaps one week, not more than two." She grinned.

"An April wedding! Oh, but Nell and I will be gone by then! I'd so love to be here to see you wed. Be happy, you and Jean-Louis. Perhaps we can return here—later." Her face darkened.

"I still see no reason why you and Nell must leave? I know you like it 'ere, *cherie*. No, no, I do not wish to know why, I respect your privacy. But tell me one thing, is it something to do with *petit Bon-Bon*'s papa?"

Amanda smiled at the pet-name Mignon had decided to bestow on Michael. She nodded, serious again. "Yes, indirectly. He's—gone, now though. It—it is another man I am afraid of."

"Ah, I see. If there is anything I can do, you will let Mignon know, *oui?"*

"Thank you, I will, I promise. And now you had best change to your apron and your so elegant gray frock, or you will feel the bite of Madame's tongue, I fear!"

"Poof! That woman, she has the tongue like ze snake, *non?* But I am not afraid of ze old witch." Mignon asserted firmly, "I will tear out her eyes if she so much as snap ze finger at me, so!" Mignon snapped her own fingers, and retrieved her hat, then sailed out of the kitchen.

Amanda sighed after her, a little envious of the charming gown she'd sported. Anything would be preferable to the three she had, all previously owned by the former serving wench, all old and in severe gray, black and serviceable dark blue. It would be wonderful to dress up in gay, vivid satins, to dance and drink wines, to have fun again. The last dancing she'd done had been in Barcelona with Miguel in the plaza, and, before, that terrible time aboard the *Sea Dragon,* the time she'd been so close to losing her mind from sheer terror! And before that, yes, it had been at the Comptons' anniversary ball. Almost two years had flown, somewhere, since then, she realized with a shock!

An indignant wail rose from the cradle, of hunger mixed with rage, at the full three minutes she had taken to heed his cry. "Hush, Michael, my love, Mama's here." She picked him up and set him to nurse.

Maison Robineau was filled to capacity. Flatboatman, French and Spanish gentlefolk, Swedish laborers, German artisans, all jostled for places at the booths to sup their evening fare and partake of steaming cups of coffee and good conversation.

Nellie was close to being rushed off her feet, her face ruddy with hurrying from kitchen to coffeehouse and back again, arms aching from the heavy wooden tray piled high with steaming platters, bowls of food, or dirty dishes. Her feet hurt, her head ached, and her mood was as strained as her nerves.

Furious, she dumped the latest load into the washtub and whirled around to face Madame Robineau.

"I tells you again, I gotta 'ave 'elp! Wouldn't 'urt *you* none t'give me a hand or two. Bleedin' impatient lot they are t'night, believe me!" She scowled crossly.

"Watch your tongue, Mademoiselle Flagg!" Solange snapped back. "Do you forget who is in charge? *Mon Dieu,* you will be out of 'ere tomorrow, if you do not mend your ways!"

"'Appen I might—o'me own accord, not yours!" Nellie retorted, hands on hips. She had henneaed her hair again, and it was as brazen as the bold expression on her face. "Where would ye be then, Madame Fancy Knickers!"

Amanda choked back a shocked giggle, darting a furtive glance over at Mignon, who suddenly seemed over-concerned about the *beignets* she was frying and was checking them again with twitching lips.

Madame Robineau's face turned beet-red. "You old 'ag! 'Ow dare you speak to me so! Monsieur Robineau will 'ear of this when 'e returns, believe me! Madame Sommaires, you will help 'er tonight. *Allez, vite, vite."* She shot the unperturbed Nellie a violent, scathing glance, and flounced haughtily from the kitchen, muttering curses in rapid French.

Nellie stuck out her tongue at the enormous, retreating backside, and hurled her own expletives after it, which, however, were not unintelligible, and caused Mignon and Amanda to cover their ears in shock. She glared at Amanda.

"Wot you gigglin' at? Get yer dainty backside off o'that there chair and take this bleedin' tray out t'them bunch o'animals. Don't know 'ow I does it, I don't." Nellie grumbled as she left, the air blue behind her.

Amanda raised her eyebrows at Mignon, and the cook shrugged, grimacing.

"I'll go now, then, and help her. We have everything under control in here, at least, do we not?"

"Oui, certainement. Go, I'll finish up, *cherie."*

"Oh, and could you keep watch over Michael for me? He should sleep until midnight, for I fed him a few minutes ago, but just in case he cries?"

"You know better than to ask, *petite maman!* Ah, look at little *Bon-Bon,* an angel, 'e is!" She peeked into the cradle, pulling the coverlet up around the baby gently, so as not to wake him.

Michael was in good hands. Amanda brushed a kiss to his brow, and left, bearing a tray of dishes that were steaming with the fruits of Mignon's labors.

The coffeeshop was indeed crowded, but Amanda found it invigorating.

The booths seated six or so, and every one was filled to capacity. The patrons' faces were flushed from the heat in the crowded room, from good humor or from spirits or combinations of all three. Clouds of smoke from cigars and pipes rose in plumes to the ceiling and clung there in a blue haze, mingling with the gray smoke from the candles of the three very austere chandeliers.

A group of poets and artists, she guessed, took up two entire booths in one corner, in heated discussion over some new literary work she'd never even heard of. She took their orders along with their flowery compliments, and refilled their coffeecups. Surprisingly, she was enjoying all the noise and color and even the work.

Lately, the novelty of cleaning the upper story where the Robineaus lived had palled. It was a lonely, thankless task, relieved only by the times when she was summoned to aid Mignon in the kitchen.

A Frenchman, obviously wealthy, for he wore the finest of embroidered coats and his hands flashed with many jeweled rings, beckoned to her. As he whispered his request, he slipped a coin into the gaping neckline of her bodice and winced lecherously.

"I will not!" Amanda fumed, color staining her cheeks.

He laughed delightedly at her horror and repeated his request. She slapped the heavy tray down on the table, fully conscious as she did so that his fingers were beneath it. As she swung away bearing the cups to be washed, he let out a yowl of pain.

"Your foot? Oh, pardon me, monsieur!" Grinning, she served the next table. That would teach him to make indecent proposals to her!

"Eh, you bloomin' nitwit! That gent's drippin' with loot! Yer could'a made a fortune if'n yer weren't so flippin' pure!" Nellie hissed in passing.

"Pure I'm not, Nellie, but I doubt they'd even heard of what *he* wanted in Sodom or Gomorrah!"

"Mayhap they 'adn't—but I'd wager *I* 'ave," Nellie mused thoughtfully, fingering the black velvet patch on her cheek. "We could o'set up 'ouse in that there Baton Rouge in grand style, with just *one* o'them rings 'e's sportin', we could."

"Oh, stop grumbling, do, Nellie! Something will

come up. Look, that nice young German fellow is beckoning you!"

Diverted, her ill-tempered friend sidled off coyly, and Amanda was able to see to the patrons at her share of the tables without further distraction.

By ten of the clock, her thighs and buttocks were bruised black and blue from the numerous pinchings she'd received, mostly anonymous, as she went about her duties. Many of the voices were growing shrill now, as the coffee, brandy-laced and potent, went to the patrons' heads.

Amanda leaned against the long serving hatch and surveyed the room, for once able to stop for a few minutes and rest. Her cheeks were flushed, strands of chestnut hair slipping out of the prim white mob cap she wore and adding tantalizingly to the allure of her wantonly full lower lip and the dark mystery of her thick-fringed eyes. She surveyed the room.

The crowd had thinned somewhat with the lateness of the hour, but Maison Robineau was still far from empty. It seemed everyone had what they needed. This would be a good moment to look in on Michael.

She found him fast asleep as she had left him, his lips, even in slumber, sucking dreamily. Mignon sat next to him, dozing in a chair, a pair of knitting needles and yarn held loosely in slack fingers, Michael's wooden rattle in her lap.

Amanda dipped the ladle into the water barrel and drank her fill, wiping her mouth on her wrist as she hurried back into Maison Robineau.

That was strange? The hum of conversation in the coffeehouse had died to silence. She quickened her pace, lifted the hinged counter that separated the serving area from the patrons, and slipped in.

All eyes were turned to the wealthy Frenchman who had propositioned her earlier. He and his companions were obviously the worse for liquor, and now stood, somewhat unsteadily, in a circle about Nellie.

"You are a thief! Give it back to me, I say, or I will get it myself, you thieving English bawd!" fumed the Frenchman.

"I don't 'ave yer bleedin' ring, I'm telling yer! Only wanted t'clean your table orf, I did. Proper nerve, you got, callin' me a thief! I got a mind t'scratch yer bleedin' face, I have!" Nellie screeched indignantly, her voice hoarse with fury. She reminded Amanda of a fighting cock, hackles up, her red feathers bristling.

"Here, *mon ami,* search her! I'm afraid I will catch the pox if I do!" He shoved Nellie hard across the circle of men to the other side, dabbing delicately at his nose with a lacy kerchief.

"Me, too, Claude. Here, Philippe, you do it!" The second man whirled Nellie around again and flung her forcefully clear across the room to yet another dandy in lavender satin. Philippe declined, also, and he in turn spun Nellie about to another fellow.

Drunkenly they reveled in their childish game. Nellie sprawled from one to the other, her head and shins cracking against the tables as they tripped her, laughing uproariously at their sport.

Amanda could stand it no more. She burst into the circle, eyes flashing murderously, hands on hips, aggressive and furious.

"How dare you? You call yourselves gentlemen? Hah! I've seen swine with more gentility! Leave her be!" she stormed.

A glint of new interest lit Claude Ferenette's eyes. "And what business is it of yours, little *poulaine*. Go back to your pots!"

Nellie, somewhat dazed and her composure for once thoroughly shaken, staggered toward Amanda, faded blue eyes unfocusing.

Ferenette shoved her viciously to the floor with a snarl of rage. He lifted his boot to kick her. Before he could do so, Amanda swung her hand back and around, her open palm landing with a resounding crack full on Ferenette's cheek.

The circle of men and patrons alike heaved an enormous gasp in perfect unison. Ferenette took a step toward her.

Amanda's eyes glittered dangerously, every muscle in her body poised and ready. She knew exactly what she would do if he came one step closer.

"No one strikes Claude Ferenette, *mademoiselle*. You will regret your rashness, I promise you!" he hissed, taking the final step to stand only two feet in front of a seething Amanda.

"And no one, Monsieur Cochon, treats *my* friends so lowly. Run, Nell, run!"

As she screamed the last words, she heaved her booted foot up and jabbed it hard into Ferenette's groin. He howled and doubled over. She whirled about, petticoats swirling, and raced after Nell, down the corridor to the doorway that led to the kitchen.

"Didn't know y'could fight dirty, I didn't," panted Nellie admiringly as they fled. "Fixed him proper, y'did!"

"I've learned to fight fire with fire, Nell! Let's fetch Michael and get out of this place!"

Nellie nodded as she followed Amanda through the doorway. Sounds of uproar in the coffeehouse reached them. A brawl must have started, from the crashing and yelling going on.

The cool of the night was like sherbert after the heat of the coffeehouse.

"No one's after us, Nell. Let's take a breather." She stood still and drew a deep, refreshing breath, then started to laugh. "Oh, Nell! If only you'd known me before! I was such a *proper* young lady—*aaagh!*"

A strangled scream tore from her throat as a pair of scrawny hands came out of the darkness and fastened about her throat. A knee nudged her viciously in the tail bone and propelled her forward.

She tried desperately to unfasten those choking hands from her throat. The pressure of her windpipe was unbearable. Dear God! He was strangling her! Dimly, she heard Nellie screeching something. The sound was blotted out by the buzz of her own blood humming in her ears.

She screamed soundlessly, her world reeling, filled with many-colored explosions of light. Her lungs were exploding. There was no air, no air! Her fingers lost their strength and fluttered aimlessly. Panic. Darkness.

Chapter Fifty-Two

Coming out of the unconsciousness was like swimming through a syrupy black fog. But she made it.

There was a draft blowing on her. Amanda shivered and opened her eyes, blinking against the dazzling light. Someone was bending over her. Enormous. Grinning. Coal black.

The image blurred, righted itself.

A huge black woman, head swathed in a yellow-and-brown-striped *tignon,* was hovering over her, so close she could smell the chewing tobacco on her breath and see the open pores of her skin. Golden hoops dangled from her elongated earlobes—no, not gold, for the metal was tarnished. It was uncanny how she could observe so much, and still be so very dazed and frightened!

The draft came from a palmetto frond the woman was waving over her face. Amanda brushed it away, irritated. What was happening? Where was she? And, furthermore, who had brought her here and why?

The black woman's face retreated, still wearing that infuriating grin. Details of her surroundings impressed Amanda now. Gilded plaster cupids romped on the headboard of the bed upon which she lay. Somehow, their expressions were obscene rather than angelic. Pink hangings curtained the bed, drawn back with the same, bilious-pink tassels. Hand-painted French wallpaper of a repeating gilt pattern covered the walls, half-naked shepherdesses and centaurs romping lewdly in the innocence of a pastoral setting.

Her eyes came to rest on another woman. Tall and svelte, this one bore the exotic beauty of the quadroon. Her skin was *café-au-lait*. Wide, feline eyes, thickly lashed, stared back at Amanda above a nose that showed none of the broadness of an African lineage, although it was apparent in the full, sensual lips below. These lips curled up at the edges in a smirk. Not a nice smile at all, Amanda thought distantly.

"Well, well! So you've decided to return to the land of the living, eh? I'm so glad, Amanda—I thought you had cheated me yet again!"

Paul's voice. She felt no surprise that it should be him, almost as if a part of her had known all along it would be he who had kidnapped her.

Blake snickered. "You seem in quite excellent health, my dear. You look positively voluptuous. Gained a little weight haven't you? But don't worry, Amanda, it is most advantageously distributed!"

She made to cover her eyes with her hands, to blot out his beautiful, evil face with the puckered scar, to hide from the brilliant, cornflower eyes that held a suggestion of madness in their brilliance. Her wrists brushed against her breast. Naked. They'd taken her clothes!

She fought the urge to cover herself, to conceal her body from their eyes, for, no, she would not give them the satisfaction of seeing her afraid, to know her shamed! A slight tremor ran through her.

Paul crossed the room, swaying unevenly, and loomed over her. His finger traced a line down from the bruises on her throat to outline her breast. Her flesh crawled with loathing.

"Well, Yvette, what do you think? Was I right? Can you use her?"

The beautiful quadroon came and stood beside him. They both inspected her casually, as if she were some specimen under a magnifying glass.

It took all of Amanda's will power to lie there, unmoving. Her natural modesty urged her to cover her breasts and pubis with her hands. She gripped the coverlet beneath her fiercely to prevent herself from doing so.

"Oui, certainement!" Yvette pronounced finally. "I believe she could be an asset indeed, with a little teaching, however. At the moment, she is far too passive. A log!" She smiled scornfully.

"Rest assured, Yvette, she has a passionate nature beneath that cold facade she is presenting now. Remember, Amanda, that time in the woods, hmmm?" He casually brushed his hand across the swell of her hips.

A muscle in her thigh twitched violently, much to the pair's amusement.

"Ah, I see! The slut will do well, I believe. And you will have the satisfaction of seeing her degraded while I, *cheri,* will see my house grow richer by the night! She's young, fresh—the men will be eager to try her—and willing to pay well for it, too."

"You *must* be careful, though, Yvette, and guard her well. She'll try to escape, I *know* it! She must not, not until—well, you know when!" Paul's voice had grown belligerent, but dropped to almost a whisper at the last.

Yvette nodded in understanding. "She is very beautiful, Paul. Are you sure that revenge on the Spaniard is all you seek? Love and hatred—they go hand in hand you know. Are you quite certain you want only to use her?" she accused.

"Good God! Haven't I proved I love only you?"

Paul's face was suffused with violent color. He gripped Yvette by the upper arms and crushed her to him. It was as if the rigid girl upon the bed did not exist. He tried to force his lips on Yvette's, but she averted her face.

"You are hurting me, Paul," she said softly, a mocking, disdainful expression on her face.

Immediately his hands dropped to his sides.

He quivered. "Damn you! What must I do to make you mine again, you cold-hearted whore! Before—before that thing we did, you were willing enough then! Ah, yes, you panted after me like a bitch in heat! It's been four years, four *long* years of wanting you, needing you—!"

"Shut up, you fool!" She nodded angrily toward Amanda. "Do you think she is deaf? Give me my papers, Paul, then I will be yours!"

"No, Yvette. I have no funds. You would take your freedom and run! I will recoup my losses, you'll see! Then, my tigress, we will live like Solomon and Sheba! I will take you anywhere, anywhere you wish to go! Please, my dearest, don't turn me away—I want you! *I love you!*"

He knelt at her feet, clutching at her skirts, clutching her about the knees like a weeping child. She shook him off as if ridding herself of some detestable vermin.

"Get up!" she ordered coldly, "and try to act like a man, Paul, instead of a sniveling brat!"

Paul did as bidden, his cheeks wet with tears and his chest still heaving.

Yvette crossed to the door, her turquoise silk skirts rustling. She turned, one hand upon the doorknob, and faced him.

"You are a fool to have come back! They are many who once suspected us. With your return, their suspicions will resurface, suspicions best forgotten! But, remember, Paul—my destiny is your own, *cheri.* If I am taken, I will make very sure that you are, too! Stay low. I have no wish to feel a noose about my neck. Have you?"

She left the sinister question hanging in the air as she softly closed the door.

Amanda sat up, drawing the coverlet over her. A chill grew in her belly and spread even to her fingers and toes. She watched Paul's inward fight to master his emotions with growing apprehension.

When he turned to her, the breath caught in her throat. His face was a horrifying mask of evil: his mouth, a twisted slit, his eyes aglitter with a terrible, malevolent light. She realized only then the extent of his madness.

Paul limped across the room and threw her backward over the bed with a snarl of rage. She had no time to evade him. His teeth split her lips as he brutally covered her mouth with his own, but when he tried to enter her, he fell back sobbing as his manhood failed him. He rose with vacant eyes and stood for several minutes, looking down at her, but not seeing her.

Amanda thought he'd forgotten her existence, but she was wrong. Paul shoved her cruelly aside and flung the coverlet over her quivering body.

"Cover yourself, bitch! You disgust me, you understand? Disgust me! And your beloved Miguel will feel likewise when I have him watch you 'perform.'"

Paul lifted a strand of her hair, knotted his fingers in it cruelly, and yanked her face to his. "What are you, a cat, that you have so many lives? That—or a witch? How did you and that old bawd conspire to hide you from me on the *Pride?* Tell me!" He shook her until her teeth rattled, but she would say nothing. "No matter, I have you now! And when I am ready, you will die, once and for all, Amanda! Never again will you rise like a phoenix from the ashes of my ruin to plot against me, you and your lover. Think of it often as you lie here, wonder if each day that dawns will be your last, or the next or the next. . . ." He grinned happily. "Sweet dreams, my phoenix!"

She lay motionless for a long time after he had left. Too much had happened too fast for her mind to register it all. One thing that *had* registered was that Paul had spoken of Miguel as if he still lived. Was it fact—or merely another indication of the confused state of Blake's mind? Who could tell?

Her throat hurt miserably, her lips throbbed from his brutal rape of them. Her lungs felt crushed and burning, and it pained her to swallow. She fought back the tears. Crying would solve nothing. Michael—she had to be strong, for his sake. Strong enough to plot and scheme, and, when the chance presented itself, escape. Poor baby, he would be hungry by now.

As if her body had received some mysterious signal, she felt a tingling sensation in her breasts. They were full, ready to suckle. Would she ever see Michael again? The thought, the uncertainty, was agony! She would welcome death if the answer was no. Nellie would take care of him as if he were her own, she had no doubt of that. He was in good hands and with someone who loved him. But she was his mother! Whatever they did to her, she must not let them suspect she had borne Miguel's child, giving Paul Blake yet another innocent victim on whom to vent his revenge.

Heavy footsteps padded to her side. A hand shook her shoulder.

"Missy? You go't wash up, chile. Madame Yvette done told me t'help you. Get up, now."

She sat up obediently, the enormous black woman grinning still, as she did when Amanda had first awakened.

"You kin call me Salome, chile. Pull that there rope if'n you needs anything. Oh, my, honey, this house ain't seen nothin' like you for a long time! He! He! He!" She chuckled, her heavy breasts and belly wobbling under yards and yards of rustling bronze taffeta, setting the hoops in her ears to swinging.

She appraised Amanda's nude loveliness as she poured hot water into the porcelain basin, her eyes narrowing as her gaze rested finally on the girl's blue-veined breasts.

"You nursin' a chile, missy?" she asked suspiciously, pausing in her preparations.

Amanda shook her head slightly. It would not do to deny the woman too vigorously. It might serve to make her believe her suspicions were correct.

"No, I'm not. Now, let's get on with it, shall we?" she snapped, eyes cold.

Salome rolled her eyes heavenward and grinned. "You look like honey, but you shoh got mustard, chile! Now fasten up that hair, do, so I kin git to yer back."

After the thorough scrubbing Salome had given her, Amanda felt a little better, at least partially rid of the soiled feeling Paul's touch had left. She felt more sure of herself, too, now she knew where she was.

The formidable Salome had seemed quite willing to answer her questions, even eager to do so. She was, she'd known already, in a bordello. What she had not known, having no idea of how long she had blacked out, was that it was situated in New Orleans still, on Royal Street, only a few hundred yards from the log stockade that surrounded the town, a protection against the "painted savages," Salome had said.

Madame Yvette owned and ran the converted boarding house, and Salome seemed rather proud that the establishment boasted the cleanest, most accomplished girls in the entire town. Curious about the conversation she had overheard, Amanda asked how a woman with Yvette's black blood, however diluted, could have succeeded in setting herself up as a free woman so well, but this Salome would not or could not answer.

"I has my freedom and a roof over my head, chile, and I ain't fool enough to go nosin' inter Madame's business. No, suh!"

After that, she'd obviously been afraid she'd talked too much, and left Amanda alone again.

Amanda figured it was not long until dawn. The sky was growing lighter in the distance, as she pulled aside the dusty, cream-colored velvet drapes, and peered out of the window.

Two *calèches,* their hoods drawn up, waited in the drizzling rain. Their drivers squatted in the dirt, whiling away the time waiting for their masters by throwing dice in the pool of light cast by a red-shaded lantern.

A pair of sailors lurched down the street singing bawdily, arm in arm. They staggered up the stairs to the front door with eager whoops and much coarse laughter. Amanda let the curtain fall and turned back into the room.

The window offered no escape, for six iron bars, each close to an inch in diameter, ran vertically from top to bottom of it. There was nothing left in the room that could conceivably be pressed into service as a weapon. Even the mirror over the dressing table had been removed, for the wallpaper where it had been was a lighter, oval-shaped patch. Had they feared she'd smash it, use the shards to stab them—or herself? Probably the latter. The bed coverings were gone too, save for the brocade coverlet, which, she smiled grimly, would be hellishly hard to tear into a noose, even granting she *was* suicidally inclined. Yes, they'd obviously planned her capture well, thought of every conceivable manner in which she could escape them, even death.

What they had *not* bargained for was the fiercest

reason a woman had to survive, save the love she bore for her man, and that was the all-consuming instinct of a mother.

"I'll be coming back for you, Michael, my sweet one," she murmured softly, determination filling her.

Somewhere, somehow they would slip in their vigilance, and she would be gone!

"Oui, Salome?" Yvette asked impatiently.

"Ah knowed you're busy, Yvette, but Ah reckon you ain't too busy t'hear what Ah has t'say. You—"

"Get on with it, blast you!" growled Paul impatiently. "And then get out!"

He downed the glass of port he held in one short movement. Yvette sipped a glass of brandy, and even from across the room, Salome could smell the liquor on her breath.

With barely concealed loathing, the black woman eyed Paul, sprawled in a chair with his good leg propped up on the desk. His satin coat fronts were stained and crusted with the red wine and food drippings; his stock rumpled and seamed with dirt. He looked foul, and smelled worse.

Salome sniffed disdainfully. "All Ah wanted to say, suh, was that I'm nigh shoh dat gal is nursin' a chile. Her bosoms, dey ain't those o'no li'l gal, or my name ain't Salome!" she declared. "Ah reckon we'd best find out foh shoh, 'cos she ain't never gonna stay here, willin', if her and a li'l one be separated!" Salome finished, her breasts heaving. "It sure would be nice t'have a chile around!"

Just like the old days, when she'd helped the missus

in her birthin's on the plantation.

"What!" Paul's head snapped up as if jerked by a string. He hitched hastily across to Salome. "Are you sure, woman?" he asked, excitement building in his face.

"Shoh as can be, short of knowin'," Salome affirmed. "I got a feelin' 'bout that girl. Could be trouble, I reckon. But if she—"

"Yes, yes! Get out of here!" Paul snapped impatiently.

Crushed, Salome waddled out, shaking her head in disgust.

"Did you hear that?" Paul cried gleefully. "A child! So the bitch was bred when we left Spain, and the illustrious don has a bastard!"

"But you can't be sure," Yvette insisted.

"Perhaps not—but I am going to find out, one way or another," Paul declared. "Send Isaiah to that foul den where Gualterio and Charlie are carousing. Have him get them back here by dusk." His eyes glowed.

"Where was it they traced the girl to?" he asked thoughtfully.

"Maison Robineau, a café just off the Vieux Carré," Yvette supplied.

"Hmmm. Then that will be our starting place!"

"And in the meantime, Paul? How can we force the girl to do our bidding? Salome is right—she could mean trouble! The slut will be worthless if she's marked. And I have plans, big plans, for her, *cheri,*" Yvette mused.

Paul pondered this, then a slow, ugly grin creased his face.

"If she resists, tell her we have her child! If she *did*

whelp the don's bastard, she will comply. And if not, we have lost nothing! There are certain types of men who would not object to their woman being, shall we say, unwilling?"

He grinned evilly again, and Yvette's own expression was the perfect partner to his.

Chapter Fifty-Three

Amanda swayed slightly, the reality of her predicament hitting her full force when she saw the upturned faces of the men below, each one filled with lust.

This was like some terrible nightmare, a nightmare without end! First the bathing in the tub, amidst spiteful pinches and jeers from the girls of the house, supervised by the gloating presence of their madam, Yvette. Then the prolonged agony of a ritual dressing, as if she were a bride preparing for her wedding night. But what a bride!

A whalebone corset of vivid emerald-and-black satin stripes pushed up her breasts until they rested in the black lace cups like apples on a platter, ready for serving. A narrow velvet ribbon of black encircled her throat and black, flower-patterned lacy stockings covered her legs to the thighs, held up by frilly green garters of satin and more black lace. Her feet were encased in high-heeled slippers with ridiculous green bows. Over this was a sheer, green silk wrapper, left untied to allow a tantalizing glimpse of the 'merchandise' beneath, and the chestnut mane of her hair flowed over it all to her waist.

Yvette stood at her back, the expression on her face one of ill-concealed pleasure at the girl's obvious humiliation.

Amanda hesitated, trying to postpone taking that first step down the curving staircase, anything to put off the degradation of the auctioning of her body for the night, and the terror that would follow.

The smoky blue haze of the men's cigars made her feel as if she were looking into the very pit of Hades, and Madame Yvette, her willing Cerberus. A murmur grew below as she lingered.

"Get down there, *cherie,* your public awaits you!" Yvette hissed, giving her a shove in the small of the back.

"No! I won't do it! You can't make me!" Amanda vowed fiercely, gripping the balustrade to prevent herself from falling. The staircase yawned beneath her feet, the road to ruin and death like the thirteen steps the condemned took to the gallows at Tyburn.

"Oh, but I can, *ma petite!*" Yvette said through clenched teeth, covering her anger from the awaiting throng with a false smile. "You see, we have your baby! A beautiful child, *cherie*. I trust you would have it remain so?"

Amanda stifled an agonized cry. No, not that, not that! How could they have taken him?

"You will not hurt him if I do as you wish? Promise me that much!" she implored, totally defeated.

"I do not believe you are in any position to bargain, *mademoiselle*. But I promise you this—if you do *not* do as I say, it will be the worse for the child, *oui?*" So Salome's guess was correct!

Amanda nodded mutely, drew a deep, shuddering breath, and wetted her lips nervously with her tongue. She started down. It was easier after the first step. The seductive, lingering descent that Yvette had insisted upon helped to steady her trembling limbs.

She held her head high and focused her vision over the heads of the men, on a little enameled clock set on the salon mantelpiece opposite. The brittle smile of enticement upon her lips was frozen in place by sheer terror.

The men sighed as she made the last turn of the curved stairway, and reached them. The silence was so great a pin could have been heard if one had dropped.

Overstuffed chairs, two black horsehair chaises, and a dozen high backed chairs had been arranged to seat the men and to leave a clear space in which to parade the women. But even so many chairs were not enough.

Men lounged in rows behind those seated, crammed even to the closed doors. The odor of musky, masculine bodies, of sweat and liquor and arousal, permeated the air and mingled with the smoke.

Yvette herself came down the stairs now, and took Amanda by the elbow.

"Is she not *charmante,* my good sirs!" She led the girl into the center of the carpeted space. "Just arrived in New Orleans, and, gentlemen, at your service—if you have the price for this fresh English rose!" She laughed gaily, giving the men a broad wink. "Turn," she hissed softly to Amanda.

Amanda turned, and the green satin folds of the wrapper swirled about her, leaving a glimpse of white thigh where they gaped, provocatively contrasted with the filmy black hose. The men ogled and gaped, then let out whistles and hoots of appreciation, feet stamping on the polished wood floor until Amanda could feel the vibration beneath her feet.

"More, *mes amis?*" Yvette asked temptingly. Her dark eyes, eyes very like the white girl's eyes, glowed with pleasure at the wild and furious roars of assent.

"Remove the wrap! Now, hurry up!" Yvette ordered.

Amanda slowly pulled the wrapper back to reveal her bare shoulders. It fell with a silken hiss, lay in a soft, billowing pile at her feet.

The men's reactions were frenzied. In the lamplight her hair glowed with a rich reddish luster, as if touched by fire. Her eyes were unnaturally bright, made so by the unshed tears behind them. They seemed to sparkle darkly against the creamy pallor of her skin, pale except for where the rouge blushed high on her cheekbones. Her lips were parted slightly to help conceal the raggedness of her breathing, but to the men they were only further proof of her seductive nature.

A fat, swarthy gentleman licked his lips eagerly and roared a price that made Amanda vaguely astonished. Another upped his bid by half as much again.

Yvette frowned reproachfully. "*Mais, messieurs,* she is worth *ten times* as much! She will be yours not for a minute, not for an hour, but for a *night* of unimaginable delight! Look at those lovely breasts—do you not yearn to cup them in your hands? And such legs! Ah, who among you, my young stallions, would not die for a night enjoying the pleasures between those thighs!" Yvette was expert saleswoman's craft, and seemed to be overly enjoying herself.

Amanda could have died of mortification as one young blade with a sadistic curl to his lips reached out a hand and viciously pinched her buttocks.

Yvette sternly rebuked him. "My apologies, *Monsieur,* but not unless you pay the price. . . ."

The men were bidding frantically now, and Amanda knew from the excitement in Yvette's dusky face, in the tenseness of her body beneath the russet silk of her gown, that the prices were rising beyond even her wildest imagination.

Amanda paraded long-legged, thanks to the high-heeled black slippers, around the perimeter of the circle as ordered.

A fistfight broke out as one man attacked another who had outbidden him. The pair were quickly ejected by a powerful black man at a mere nod from the madam.

By now the bidding had gone beyond the means of most of the men. Only two remained: a gangling, pale fellow with lank, black hair, and a paunchy, elderly man on the other with an old-fashioned, powdered white half-wig. Then there were more bids, more flowery extolling of her bodily virtues, worded craftily to inflame the lust and the licentious imagination.

Amanda's cheeks flamed crimson, both from outrage and from shame. Her stomach churned with dread. Please God, don't let them hurt my baby, she prayed silently. She could withstand anything, *anything,* if only they wouldn't hurt Michael.

"Sold!" crowed Yvette triumphantly, her beautiful face twisted in a gloating smile. She extended her hand, glittering with rings, to the winner. "Monsieur Kirkland, you are a lucky man, indeed! Now, if you will come with me for a few moments, and then afterward. . . ."

It was over, Amanda realized numbly—or just beginning. Madame Yvette led the winner, the tall, melancholy man with the lank black hair, into her study.

Amanda dazedly followed a beaming Salome back up the staircase. A disappointed groan from the assembled men followed her departure.

She had to squeeze her way past two more of the girls, eagerly awaiting their own practiced descent. Madame Yvette's monthly "auctions" gave the girls a chance to make a little extra coin than the meager amount usually dealt them, after food and lodging had been deducted. Though young, their faces were already etched with hard lines of their profession.

They laughed at her openly, arms crossed over voluptuously bared breasts hardly contained by garments similar to Amanda's, their disgust obvious.

Gina Amora smirked spitefully. "All that coin for a night with *her?* Bah! Those men, they are *loco,* no?" She winked at Jeanne. "One would think she had something different down there!" Gina pointed suggestively.

"Perhaps she 'as, *oui?* Perhaps hers is made of gold!" Jeanne jeered, hands on hips, grinning.

The two doubled over in raucous laughter as Amanda retreated down the corridor.

"Guard your gold well, *pequeña!* There are no locks between your thighs!" taunted the Spanish girl, tossing a luxurious mane of black hair over her shoulders, dark eyes vicious in their mockery.

"If there were, *cherie,"* Jeanne whispered loudly, "Monsieur Kirkland has a more than adequate key!"

Her sally found its mark. The two doxies were rewarded by the sight of Amanda's face turning crimson as she stepped inside her doorway.

But despite appearances, it was not embarrassment that caused the color in Amanda's cheeks. Rage, hot and utterly futile, coursed through her. She swung around violently as Salome closed the door behind them, her hands on her hips, two vivid spots of color in her cheeks.

"What sort of place is this new land, where women are bought and sold like—like cows?" She stormed, pacing angrily. "If it were not for my baby—!"

"Sure, chile," Salome interrupted, "it'd be a different story, then! But as things are, you ain't *got* no choice, honey! You done made some bad enemies in that Mistah Blake and Madame. Crazy as a loon *he* is, make no mistake. Ain't no one gonna help you run away, not in this place! You done gotten all the gals riled up, 'cos not one of them done fetched such a price, no, not since *I* bin here! That's good, for you, honey, 'cos they ain't gonna get rid o'you until the men stops handin' over all dat money! With your looks, could be a *long* time, chile!" Salome grinned, teeth flashing white against the black of her skin, "cain't say the same foh that ugly friend o'yours." She laughed, the sound rumbling deep within her like the rumbling of a volcano.

Amanda grasped her fiercely by the upper arms. "Tell me, quickly, what friend? A short woman, bright-red hair, is that—?"

"Ah ain't saying nuthin'! You done make me open

my big mouth again. You'd best—"

"No!" Amanda hissed through gritted teeth. Her fingernails bit into the woman's flabby arms. "Tell me—or else!"

Salome looked flustered. "Yes'm, dat's de one, but don't tell Madame I done told you?" Fear in her eyes.

"I won't. Is—is my baby with her, with my friend? Is he? Salome, tell me or—I'll hurt you before anyone can get in here to help you, I swear it!"

Her eyes searched the black woman's face, hope filling her. At least she would know Michael was with Nellie.

"You've no need to break my arms, chile!" Salome whined. "Ain't no child in dere. Only dat red-haired, screechin' ole witch they brung in here same time as you. Lord, she can cuss out t'devil!" Salome shuddered, massaging her throbbing arms, as Amanda's fingers slackened their grip.

"You'd best get a hold on yo'self, now, y'hear? Dat Mistah Kirkland don't like t' be kept waitin', no sir!" Salome rolled out of the room, obviously nettled at what she considered Amanda's irrational behavior.

Amanda tore off the black slippers and hurled them across the room. They bounced off the metal bars of the window and landed on the floor with a dull thud. Frustration, fear, anger filled her. She would tear this damned room apart, vent these useless, hopeless emotions somehow!

During her absence, the bed had been made up. By God, she'd tear it to shreds, every last sheet and pillowcase!

She grasped the coverlet and flung it off, quivering with fury and bent only on destruction.

"Well! I see you're anxious! That's enchanting, sweet, because so am I!"

The cultured, plummy voice with its pronounced English accent whirled her about.

Roger Kirkland lounged against the closed door, his clothes scattered at his feet. He was completely naked, and very obviously aroused.

Chapter Fifty-Four

Kirkland padded barefoot across to the lamp and blew it out, leaving only its partner alight. Their shadows made monstrous giants on the walls.

The man's face gleamed palely in the dim light. His thin lips split in a smile. "Well, m'dear?"

"Well what?" Amanda queried defensively, wiping sticky palms on her satin corset.

"Come, I've paid the price! Now for your part of the bargain! You know, if you weren't British, I never would have gone so high, love! It struck me well, t'hear the sounds of love in the accent of my mother country." He stood behind her, massaging her shoulders.

For all his great height and slender build, she could sense the wiry strength in those hands. She broke nervously from his embrace. "Indeed, sir? Then what do you here, so far from it!"

"Ah, I sense a temper! No doubt it goes with the hair, eh? A little vixen, that's what you are! But in answer to your question, as a soldier of fortune I go wherever I'm paid to go. Presently, I find it profitable to stay here." He leered at her again, slate-gray eyes feasting on the rounded curves of her body. "In more ways than one!"

"A mercenary! How despicable!" she snapped,

hoping to anger him.

He looked at her, amused. "Hardly any more so than yourself, my dear!" His long arms entrapped her waist. "Enough talking," he commanded.

He drew her into his embrace and dropped his head to her throat, his mouth working feverishly there. His manhood was a hard and questing shaft against her waist. Despite her fear, she felt a stir of response within her own treacherous body.

His lips plundered her mouth, cruel in his passion. He lifted her unresponsive arm and curled it around his neck, his tongue forcing deep between her teeth and finding her own. Her other hand he clasped over his manhood, urging her to caress him there with fevered little grunts of encouragement as he continued to kiss her mouth.

Still she did nothing. She *could not* fight him! Her limbs felt turned to stone. What would become of Michael if she resisted?

He pushed her backward a little, tearing his lips reluctantly from her own. His fingers fumbled for the hooks of the gawdy corset, and finally found them.

Her breasts sprang free of the frothy, imprisoning lace, surging against his practiced hands. Hurriedly, he finished the task, casting the garment aside.

Clad only in her lacy stockings, the green satin garters gleaming in the light, she stood waiting before him. He was breathing hoarsely now, his eyes afire with passion.

"By God, two months' pay, and worth every crown!" he breathed, eyeing his prize hungrily.

The lamplight caught her hair, reflecting subtle hues of warm color. It dappled her naked skin, adding a golden sheen to the rounded curves of her shoulders, the proud swell of her breasts. Her hips flared out below the tiny expanse of her waist, surmounted by a gleaming pelt of dark auburn curls at the junction of her thighs. She was Aphrodite come to life, hiding her shame at her birth state in a heavenly aura of silken hair that tumbled over the satin-smooth flesh to her waist.

She couldn't stand this way much longer, his gray eyes devouring her. If only he would hurry up, get it over with! She bent to unfasten the green garter.

"No, don't," he insisted, drawing her hand away. "I'll do it," Roger murmured huskily.

He knelt and unfastened the garter and drew it slowly down the length of her leg. His lips nuzzled the milky skin of her thigh as he peeled the filmy hose down to follow the garter. He was crouching at her feet like a savage worshiping some gorgeous idol! The second stocking he removed in the same, lingering fashion. His tongue circled the mysterious depths of her navel, lapped at her belly, rose upward, and to her breasts. Despite herself, a moan of longing escaped her. Nibbling, teasing, his mouth worked feverishly on the rose-peaked orbs.

Involuntarily, her hands twined in his black hair, her breathing thickened, grew husky in her throat. It had been so long, so long! Her hungry body cried out for his caresses. She found his manhood with her own trembling hand. It throbbed at her touch, surged still further under her faltering strokes.

His expression was ecstatic. He ran his hand down the curves of her body, kneading her buttocks, pressing her against his loins in rhythmic squeezes. Finally, he slid his hand between her thighs and into the warm, secret, wetness of her throbbing womanhood.

She cried out, holding him to her fiercely, thrusting against him in abandon. Pleasure-explosions dazzled her mind, drove her to frenzy as his lips replaced his fingers. It didn't matter that she scarce knew him, that he had bought her for this night. She wanted him as a man, to hold her, and to fill her with himself, to blot out the ugly, hurtful memories and her fears.

She clung to him, whispering Miguel's name as he laid her across the bed and opened her before him. Her womanhood pleaded to be filled, to ease the growing agony of desire.

His inward plunge was like the mighty thrust of a spear, his manhood was so great. She jerked upward on the bed, twined her legs and arms about him, her nails digging furrows in the flesh of his back. She ground her hips against him, frenzied with lust, drew shuddering breaths with every glorious thrust. Faster he moved, his mouth locked to hers, his hands cupping and fondling her breasts with feverish pleasure.

Her release was as sharp, as sudden and as powerful as a pistol ball's explosion. It burst on her, fragmenting thought and leaving her breathless and drained, trembling damply like a leaf.

She looked at Roger Kirkland wide-eyed, astonishment mirrored in the deep darkness of her eyes, bewilderment in her mind. A choking sob spiraled upward from her belly, stemmed by her own clenched fist to her lips.

"Dear God! What have I become!" she whispered brokenly.

Chapter Fifty-Five

There were no more auctions, but the following nights were filled with men, always rich, always eager for her. After that first night, she felt aroused by none of them, felt only disgust and detachment. It wasn't that Roger Kirkland had been more tender or even more accomplished a lover; simply that he had been the first, and at a time when she deeply needed his lovemaking to forget her terror. Though Kirkland had been gentler than most, his parting words had cut her to the quick as he'd tossed an extra sovereign to the floorboards, his face lazy and replete as a cat fed cream.

"A worthy price, my dear, for a night such as that! I'll be back, rest assured. And tell your mistress I will most highly recommend you to my friends!"

He hadn't meant to be cruel. He believed her a doxie, and had treated her accordingly, she thought miserably, the promise of a good recommendation obviously intended as a compliment of sorts. Still, in a sense he'd helped. Madame Yvette had been delighted; Paul had reveled in her degradation; as he'd promised; and they had bothered her little.

The loathsome pair, Amanda discovered, had witnessed at least part of that torrid night by means of a cleverly concealed peephole that extended through a wall in her room to that adjoining. The thought of the two of them, watching and laughing, filled her with revulsion. On succeeding nights she'd attempted to cover the spyhole, on locating its presence, carefully concealed to appear as a flower on the patterned wallpaper. They had not even allowed her the dignity of privacy, though, for each time she'd attempted to block the aperture, Salome had been sent in to uncover it once more. She felt like an animal, like the animals in the zoological gardens at Regent's Park she'd visited as a child. Caged, naked, fed, watered, and mated in public, as if she had no feelings whatsoever.

Salome escorted her downstairs for her meals now, and she ate at a table flanked on all sides by gaudily dressed women and girls, who watched her every move with spiteful eyes.

She had been "accidentally" stabbed in the back of the hand with a fork, had pepper showered "mistakenly" in her eyes, suffered all manner of minor hurts from their jealousy. She sensed their hatred in the air as they sat at breakfast beneath the elegant crystal chandelier just as strongly this morning.

One of the girls, a popular French girl named Danielle, had been ousted from the house that morning by Madame and her serving man, Isaiah, who also acted as bouncer when the men got out of hand. Amanda knew the girl had been gotten rid of because of her quick tongue, or the way she could incite the other girls to rebel, to speak up against the madam. She had been, to Yvette's way of thinking, a troublemaker.

"You see! It is your fault, *inglesa!* Poor Danielle,

there is only one place she can go, now that Madame has spread the rumor she is poxed!" spat Gina, dark eyes sparking hatred at Amanda.

"Oui," agreed Jeanne fiercely. "To Natchez—Under-the-Hill, upriver. Those stinking stews—the women there die fast, you know. Nothing but shacks, not even a cot on which to sell themselves! Filth, squalor, rats, drunken men with twisted, vile perversions. And diseases such as you've never dreamed of, *petite princesse!"* she hissed.

Amanda sighed, honestly confused. "But what has that to do with me?" she asked.

"Danielle was Madame's most popular girl—before you came! Now she doesn't need her, for they only want to bed *you,* no?" Gina spat. "Danielle was trying to make that quadroon bitch give us more of the money she gets. Do you understand now?" The Spanish doxie sat down, scowling.

"But it wasn't my idea! You know yourself I was dragged here, forced into this life! Believe me," she said vehemently, "I have no wish to stay!"

Gina said nothing, her black eyes flickering at Amanda from beneath dark lashes with the cunning of a weasel. Finally, she spoke. "If you mean what you say, *pequeña,* we might be prepared to help." She shrugged. "It cannot bring Danielle back, but it would give us the chance to bargain again, with you gone! Are you sure you want to try it?"

"Yes," Amanda whispered eagerly. She would not have believed that help could also come from enemy quarters! "One thing, I have a child, a baby. They have him too! Do any of—?"

"No, we've not seen any child. However, *pequeña*—" she grinned—"your friend is very much in residence. *Aiee,* what a harridan she is! She's in the small room, at the end of the hall, and she claws and spits like a cornered alleycat!"

"I—I'd like to see her. Do you think that would be possible?" Amanda looked from Gina to Jeanne anxiously.

Jeanne seemed doubtful. "Madame Yvette, she watches her like ze hawk! We—Gina and I—heard her and Monsieur Blake arguing. He wanted to—to kill her, get rid of her, he said! But Madame Yvette said no, that it was too risky now. That later on would be soon enough, and that no harm could come of the delay as long as the two of you weren't allowed to escape. They are waiting for someone, *oui?* This person's arrival, it appears, will give Monsieur Blake great satisfaction, but they mentioned no names."

Miguel? Amanda wondered. Surely not! But if he *were* alive, it was a logical act, to follow Paul Blake to New Orleans. After all, had he not sworn to have revenge for his sister, for Manuel, the old gardener, both dead directly or indirectly, because of Paul? So what did they intend to do with her? What reason did they have to keep her alive? Did they hope to use her as bait, to lure him into some kind of trap? But that was ridiculous! Hadn't Paul heard, as plainly as she, Miguel's denouncement of her? Did it have something to do with Michael, and the fact that he was Miguel's son? None of it made sense!

"But, go on, how can you help me to get away?" she continued cautiously.

Gina shrugged. "That, I do not know—yet!" She lowered her voice. "Enough for now, Madame's here. Later, we'll talk more, *sí?*"

Amanda nodded, returning her attention to the food, toying with it listlessly. The mealtimes did little more than act as markers, dividing the days into segments that drew her ever closer to the nights.

That night, bathed and ready for her work, angry screeches reached her. She ran to the door, pressing her ear intently to the wood. Nellie! She'd know that wonderful, raucous stream of curses anywhere.

"Bleedin' heathen, wot you plannin' on doin' then, boilin' me up fer yer blasted supper, ye cannibal, ye? Gawd, them bloomin' crabs gets themselves *cooked* in colder water 'n wot ye got in there! Take yer bleedin' 'ands off! Ow! *Oww!*"

Amanda couldn't resist a smile. Nellie sounded totally undaunted by her imprisonment and as bossy as ever!

"Ain't nat'rel it ain't! Don't see no horses takin' no bloomin' baths ye don't! Good splash o'parfumey's all a body needs, ye know."

Nellie screeched again and the sounds of a hearty struggle carried even through the closed door. Then more silence. After several moments, Nellie's voice bellowed again, somewhat subdued compared to her former tirade.

"Wot the bloomin' blazes was yer mother thinkin' of ter call yer Salome, ye old cow?" A throaty belly laugh here. "Must ha' been blind, she must—woulda taken all seven o'them veils o'that Bible Salome t'go around ye *once,* it would! He! He! *Heeee!*" Nellie's laughter died into a shocked gurgle.

Amanda surmised the furious Salome must have ducked Nellie into the tub to shut her up, for she heard no more.

She fastened the green wrapper about her waist and paced restlessly. Though the days flew past, as time has a way of doing when one wished it to tarry, the nights seemed inexorably slow.

The house sounded busy tonight. The heavy tread of feet on the staircase was nigh constant, as was the slamming of the front door and the roars of laughter that reached her from the crowded salon. Her attempts at composure were useless. Try as she might, she would *never* be able to reconcile herself to the relinquishing of her body to a stranger each night.

When the door finally opened and the rustle of taffeta skirts signaled Madame Yvette's entrance, she could not bring herself to look up.

"Voilà, monsieur! This is the young lady you requested. Is she not *charmante?"*

The man mumbled agreement. Still, Amanda could not bear to look at him. Head bowed, hair falling like a curtain about her face, she continued to perch timidly on the bed.

Yvette started out of the room. *"Bonne nuit, mes enfants!"*

Amanda mechanically untied the wrapper and cast it aside once more. She lay naked upon the bed, her face turned to the wall, refusing to acknowledge the presence of her lover of the night by so much as a glance. The grinning centaurs on the hand-painted wallpaper seemed to mock her.

"Well, pretty bird, shall we see if you deserve Roger's flowery praises?" The voice was young, teasing in tone.

Amanda went rigid, shock and disbelief filling her. She sat up slowly, turning her head until she could look at the man fully.

For a second, disappointment filled her. No, not *him,* she'd been a fool to think it could have been! The lamplight showed a stranger, bearded, stooping slightly to peel off a pair of elegant tan breeches.

He sensed her eyes upon him and looked up, grinning. The grin faded. Instead his mouth dropped open, an exact replica of her own astonished face as she saw the glint of green eyes above the beard.

"It *is* you! Dear God, James, you're alive!" She leaped from the bed and hurtled into his arms.

He whirled her into the air, hugging and kissing her heartily. "Mother of God, Amanda, yes, it *is* you! And as you can see, I'm most assuredly alive—or am I dead and this, heaven? This isn't happening; it must be a dream!" He took her hands between his own and kissed them, looking incredulously into her face.

Amanda was speechless, shaking her head repeatedly from side to side as if unable to believe her own eyes. Finally, she murmured weakly, "How—?"

"It's a long story! Suffice it for now to say I escaped! And you—how did you reach New Orleans and—and *this* place?" He drew her down next to him on the bed, cradling her in his arms.

Amanda cast a fearful eye at the spot where the peephole was. "We cannot talk. You see, they watch me. Yvette and Paul Blake. Through a peephole, up there. They must not suspect—!"

"Ah! So Blake's back, is he? I should have guessed. Then you are not here, of your own accord? How foolish, I should have known better than to ask! Shall I cover it?" The roguish grin amid the reddish brown of his beard was so dear, so familiar it made her want to cry.

"It won't work. I've tried before, and each time the maid was sent in to uncover it," she whispered.

"Then, shall we give them what they wish to see?" Without waiting for her answer, James pressed his hungry lips on hers, grasping her to him with a fierceness that made her feel he would snap her in two, like a twig.

She yielded to his embrace, giving herself into his arms with a gentle submissiveness she had allowed no other man to enjoy. Her desire was to please him and she needed only the faintest of urgings on his part to follow his directions.

He began to make love to her with practiced lips and hands, moving over her body in a manner calculated to excite, to inflame. Her body responded, but her head refused to!

She desperately tried to force herself into a more passionate mood. What was wrong with her? Damn! Had she not believed him dead? Was this not something she had dreamed of? His lips roamed the peaks and valleys of her breasts, but still she felt nothing, nothing! She pretended pleasure, smiled encouragement into his eager emerald eyes, moaned a moan of feigned desire. Her arms pulled him close, and burrowing her face into the soft skin where his neck met his shoulders, she held on to him tightly, tears of disappointment welling against her closed eyelids.

"Amanda?" James's questioning face peered into hers. "What's wrong? You're not with me, are you, love?"

She shook her head, unable to meet his eyes. "No, James. I'm sorry, I tried, I really did! Perhaps, perhaps it's the shock, of finding you alive, after believing you lost for so long." She sighed deeply. "So much has happened to me, James, you have no idea how much." She lifted her eyes to his. Was she mistaken, or was there anger there, in his expression? Surely, he could not be angry with her, not now?

"You don't have to explain, Amanda. I understand." His tone sounded overly light. "But I must admit, I'm a little surprised at your—coldness. Kirkland implied otherwise." He shrugged on his breeches and fastened them, watching her as he did so.

"Kirkland! So, you couldn't wait to trot down to Royal Street and try your prowess with the new 'piece' at Madame Yvette's, is that it? Well, I'm sorry if I did not reach your expectations, Captain!" She furiously pulled on the green wrapper and tied the sash tightly about her waist. "It is not easy to lose oneself in the heats of passion, when fearing for the life of one's child!"

"A child? Yours? Good God! Not mine, too?" The idea seemed to horrify him.

"No, not yours, James! I told you, did I not, that much has happened since the *Sea Dragon* exploded that night? I was rescued by a Spanish fisherman. Fernando, his name was, Fernando de Villarin."

"The name strikes a bell. It is his child, then?"

"No, his brother's. Don *Miguel* de Villarin! He took me in as a guest at his villa—that is, until he realized who I was! Then he kept me prisoner there. He believed Paul Blake had sent me, or that I had come myself, to avenge Paul's crippling." She quickly told him everything, finishing with her abduction from Maison Robineau.

"Ah, I see. Then we must get you away from here—this very night!" He hurriedly pulled on his shirt, raking his reddish-brown hair into a semblance of order with his fingers. "Now, how to go about it? Do you have anyone here that would help us?"

"There's Nellie, a dear friend. She's in the room at the end of the hall. They took her the same time they captured me. I won't leave her behind, James! Some of the girls, they said they'd help, but I'm not sure if we can trust them. They want only to be rid of me. But, James, I cannot escape. You see, Michael, my baby—they are holding him, too! They have threatened to kill him, if I do not do as they say, or if I attempt to escape!"

James frowned thoughtfully. "Very well, love, not tonight. Let me see what I can do. Kirkland will help—if the price is right!" he added grimly.

He thrust his arms into the sleeves of his coat and came across the room to her, placing a hand on each of her shoulders.

"Don't fret, my love, we'll have you and your babe safe very soon, I promise you." He kissed her lightly on the nose. He did not say it, but he had grave doubts that the child was yet alive. "Be ready for my return. I don't know how or when yet, but whatever occurs, you follow my lead. Until then?"

Amanda nodded. "Godspeed, James. I still can't believe you are alive!"

"Well, I am, very much so! I'll prove it to you soon, when I can get you alone with naught to draw your thoughts from our pleasures!"

He winked wickedly and left her.

"Are you sure this fool—Robineau?—are you sure he spoke the truth?" Paul cried angrily.

"Sí, señor! The husband, he seemed fond of the girl, unwilling to talk to us at first. But the wife—*Aiee, Díos,* what a viper! She was glad the slut had disappeared, and only too willing to tell us—Señorita Sommers' 'dear friends'—what place she hoped the wench had gone to!" the hook-nosed Spaniard grinned. "I told Henri Robineau she'd been taken ill, and had sent us for the child, to care for it until she recovered."

"Good. And he fell for it?" Paul queried.

"Sí, finally. He said that this woman, Mignon Boucher woman, up an' marries her betrothed, something about him having been offered work in Baton Rouge or such, and they left for upriver straight after, taking the brat—Michael, its name is—with them. They left word that if the Sommers bitch came back, that they could find them there, *sí?"*

"Damn!" Paul breathed softly. He rubbed his forehead jerkily, deep in thought. "Charlie, you and Gualterio here, go up to Baton Rouge, leave this afternoon. I don't care what you have to do, but *bring de Villarin's bastard to me!"*

"Us, señor? Oh, no, señor! We are not wet nurses. I'll have none of it!" Gualterio spat across the room in disgust, wiping the flecks of spittle from his lips with the back of his hand.

Yvette gave him a caustic glare, which he ignored as he stomped to the door.

"Wait!" Paul screamed. "Blast you, haven't I paid you for your trouble thus far? Yes, and bloody well, too! I'll send that cow, Salome, with you to tend the brat. Now, get!"

"No, señor." Gualterio's face was a swarthy mask, unrelenting. "Not unless you are prepared to pay us more."

"Damn you for leeches! Very well. Here's half—" he flung a handful of sovereigns across the room—"and there'll be the same again, when you return with the brat."

Charlie Watson scratched his armpit and gave Gualterio a sly glance. He nodded almost imperceptibly. Gualterio bent down and picked up the scattered coins, a smug expression on his evil face.

"*Sí,* Señor Blake, we will be back."

"You damned well better be!" Paul snarled at their backs as they left.

He limped across to Yvette and kissed her bared shoulder above the flame-colored silk of her gown. She flinched and drew away. Paul noticed her distaste, and a shadow crossed his face.

"This is why you refuse my advances now, isn't it? This!" he said hoarsely, stabbing at the wooden peg with his finger. "No, my love, don't deny it, I'm no fool! Well, my sweet, the bastard that did this will pay, with his life, and then, then I will take you away with me, anywhere you wish to go. Anywhere!"

"Revenge? *Merde!* Your lust for revenge has addled your wits, you fool! What do you hope to achieve by bringing the child here?" Yvette said sulkily.

"When de Villarin learns we have his son, he'll give himself into my hands like a lamb to the slaughter, that's why! That we have his slut of a mistress will sweeten the bait even further. What did he do the very hour he disembarked from his ship here? Post a reward, that's what, and a sizable one too! And for knowledge of whose whereabouts? Hers—not mine! So you see, he lied that last time. There *is* something between them!"

Yvette brightened. "Ah, now I see it. Then you will take both his money and your revenge at the same time. *Oui,* I like it!" She sidled toward him and perched on his lap. "Then, *cheri,* you will give me my bill of sale, and we will run away, just the two of us, *non?*" she purred.

"Oh, yes! Do you still think me a fool, eh?" Paul grinned wolfishly.

In answer, Yvette pulled the *tignon* from her head and shook out her hair, a gleam in her slanted eyes. She reached behind her to unfasten the hooks of her gown.

Paul's breathing quiekened to a hoarse, ragged sound as she quickly undressed and stood naked before him. She put her hands on her hips and laughed throatily.

A strange cry, half human, half animal, gurgled from Paul's parted lips.

"Yvette! Oh, God, it's been so long!" His cornflower-blue eyes shone feverishly. He limped across the room, clutched her to him and kissed her hungrily.

"You will not forget? My papers?" she queried softly

in his ear.

"No, no! Everything I have, it will be yours," he agreed hastily, thrusting her down to the carpet beneath them.

As they fell, Yvette's lips drew back over her teeth in a gloating, triumphant smile.

Chapter Fifty-Six

"Shall we go, then, sweet?"

Even in the gloom, Amanda caught the white flash of James's teeth as he grinned. He took her nervous hand in the cup of his own strong one, and drew her after him to the door. He opened it a crack and paused, listening intently.

Amanda's mouth felt dry. She swallowed. Her stomach's nervous groan sounded deafening in the silence. She huddled closer to James, drawing strength from the nearness of his body, its heat relieving the fear-chill of her own.

"Relax a bit, love, or when the time comes you'll not be able to move," James whispered, drawing her close.

"I'm trying to. It's just that—James, they seemed so convincing, so awfully sure of themselves! It's hard to adjust to what you said. Part of me won't believe it. I still fear for him!" She shivered, blinking back the tears.

James shook her slightly.

"Trust me, Amanda! Your Monsieur Robineau was most concerned about you. He did not seem disposed to lying. This Mignon, she and her fiancé fled with Michael after you were abducted. As soon as we are out of danger, we'll find them, I swear it! Meanwhile, he could not be in better hands—did you not say so yourself?"

Amanda nodded, anger flooding her anew. They had tricked her, damn them, tricked her into submitting to their whims, using her fears for Michael to obtain her compliance! Now she understood the white fury of Miguel's vengeful quest in her own veins.

Salome must have told her mistress that she believed their new girl had recently borne a child. A little careful questioning at Maison Robineau would have revealed the truth. They knew she had no way of knowing what had become of Michael, and had used that knowledge to cow her into submission! Her hatred of them was like bile in her throat. She would see them punished, yes, by God, if it was the last thing she did on this earth!

"It's starting, Amanda. Are you ready?"

"Yes!" she hissed, aware of his surprise at her vehemence by a slight flinching of his body next to hers.

A loud shriek penetrated the silence, followed by a torrent of Spanish curses that needed no translation delivered in a pitch bordering on ear-splitting. Gina!

James opened the door a little wider. Now they had a clear view of what was going on in the upper hallway.

In the lamplight Amanda saw Gina, the Spanish *puta,* and Jeanne, the French one, facing each other about ten feet apart. Both were scantily clad, and stood belligerently, hands on hips, glaring at each other. Roger Kirkland, an amused grin on his face, leaned against an open doorway further down the hall. He wore only his breeches, and by the scratches on his chest and shoulders, Amanda surmised the reason for the delay. His determination to get his money's worth before the enactment of the little charade they were now witnessing!

Then suddenly, Jeanne flew forward, grasped a huge hank of Gina's long black hair, and yanked cruelly. Howling, Gina lashed out and raked her nails across the French girl's cheek, drawing blood. At the same time, she gripped Jeanne's wrist with her other hand and twisted it, frantically trying to break the grip on her hair. Jeanne refused to let go.

"Alleycat! Bitch! Whore!" Jeanne hauled Gina down to her knees by the hair and leaped on her.

They rolled over and over, grunts and shrieks and gasps of pain muffled by the rucked-up scarlet and black ruffles of their petticoats.

James chuckled, obviously enjoying the spectacle of the catfight. He seemed in no hurry to be off.

Amanda nudged him sharply with her elbow. "Why are we waiting? Let's go!"

"Patience, my dear. There's another we have to divert first, before we can risk it. Isaiah. He is no small matter to contend with, eh?"

She muttered impatient agreement. Isaiah, Yvette's "peacemaker" for the house, was built like an enormous black wall, well over six feet in his stockings and nigh two hundred and fifty pounds of ebony muscles. Oh, yes, she could see the wisdom of waiting!

Gina and Jeanne were both standing now, bosoms heaving with exertion. The French girl's rouge was smeared and this, mixed with the trickles of blood from the scratches on her cheek, made her look like a clown. Gina sported a fast-blackening eye and a split lip. The expression on her face was murderous. Amanda realized that the pretense had gone beyond that for the two doxies.

Gina tossed the mane of black hair back from her eyes and leaped at Jeanne, taking the lacy straps of the girl's corselet in her hands and ripping them from the garment. Jeanne's teeth clamped into the Spanish girl's shoulder. Gina's fists pummeled at Jeanne's now-naked back, to no avail. A spiteful pinch to Jeanne's bared breast finally broke the bite on her shoulder. Tears of pain and rage streamed down both their faces. Jeanne's blond hair stuck out in wild tangles about her enraged face. She let out a whoop suddenly and leaped on Gina's back, wrapping her legs about the other girl's waist and pulling at her hair with her free hands. Gina whirled about, frantically attempting to unseat her gleeful rider, who now goaded her with taunts in bawdy, gutter French.

Heavy footsteps thundered up the stairs. Isaiah charged at the women like an enraged bull. His presence seemed to act as a reminder to the girls of the real reason for their fight. As one they turned on him, and as he disappeared beneath their tangle of thrashing limbs and lacy frills, James suddenly dragged Amanda through the door and down the hallway.

"Wait! What about Nellie and Roger? We can't leave—" she whispered anxiously.

"Hurry up! They'll be along, never fear," James promised, hurrying her down the staircase so fast her feet barely touched ground.

Twice she tripped over her cloak, but finally, bunching it up about her hips, they reached the foot of the stairs.

From an open doorway ahead to their left came the

tinkling sound of glasses and the muted hum of male voices. The sweet smell of brandy and other spirits and the fragrance of cigar smoke permeated the air.

A scream from above them carried clearly, and following it, a crashing, splintering sound as wood shattered. Just in time, James dragged Amanda into the alcove beneath the stairs. Another second would have been too late, for Madame Yvette came flying from the room and tore up the stairs in the direction of the disturbance.

They slipped the length of the hallway, poised for immediate, swift flight if it should become necessary. It wasn't however, for they passed the crowded salon without being discovered, and were soon out of the rear door of the house and hurrying through the balmy, jasmine-scented night to the waiting horses.

With a gasp of surprise and pleasure, Amanda realized that Nellie was there and already mounted, albeit awkwardly, behind Roger Kirkland. Their joyful reunion was stillborn, as James all but threw Amanda across his mount and leaped into the saddle behind her.

Kirkland led the way at a brisk trot, surprisingly easy in the saddle despite his rangy build. Nell shot Amanda a wicked smile as they passed a well-lit tavern, and snuggled against Kirkland's back as if the two were lovers. It was not for some time that Amanda realized what Nellie's nimble fingers were about beneath Kirkland's concealing cloak, and her fears that Roger had been injured in the escape were dispersed when she realized the cause of the strange laboring of his breathing!

She leaned against James's chest and sighed with relief. His lips brushed her hair in a caress as he lent to whisper in her ear.

"I have something to ask you, love, later, when we're alone," he murmured.

She nodded silently, feeling she knew the question he would ask. But what answer would she give? It would require much consideration, affect not only her own life, but that of her child. She could not be hasty with her reply.

The New Orleans she had loved for its boisterousness by day was more subdued by night, but far from sleeping. Their night ride drew no curious stares, in fact, scant attention at all.

A lopsided moon floated high above, trailing streamers of gray cloud. A soft breeze rustled the foliage and bore fresh scents with it, a sweet relief after the overpowdered, overperfumed atmosphere she had grown accustomed to while at the brothel. She drank in the air, reveling in her newfound freedom after the long confinement. And, as if there could be more, at the back of it all was her longing, her eagerness, to cradle Michael in her arms once more. She squeezed her eyes shut, remembering for the thousandth, the millionth time, that precious face, lips curved in a gurgle of delight. He would have grown these past three weeks, certainly. Would he have forgotten her? A babe's memory at such a tender age was a fragile thing, she realized sadly.

The horses stopped. Kirkland stood in his stirrups and pulled hard on a ring set in the arched gateway of the Spanish-style house before them.

A manservant eyed the women with unabashed curiosity as he led the horses away.

Kirkland ushered them across a small courtyard and

into the house, where his housekeeper awaited, bleary-eyed and still in her nightcap and gown, for her master's instructions.

"Well, my dear ladies," Kirkland said finally, peeling off his riding gauntlets with great finesse, "my woman is heating water for your baths. Please, make yourselves at home, and feel free to ask for anything you might require. If my humble abode does not have what you need, I will be honored to acquire it for you on the 'morrow."

He bowed slightly, and, Amanda thought, not without more than a hint of sarcasm. Still, she was too grateful to her rescuers to remark on it. She let his actions pass as if unnoticed.

"And now, the gallant knight will claim the favors of his lady fair! Come, Princess Nell!" Kirkland made to swoop the giggling Nellie off her feet, but she good-humoredly shoved him back.

"'Old yer bleedin' 'orses, luv, there's a dear. Cor, ye're a one, ye are!" She shook her red curls coquettishly and took Amanda by the hand. "Gawd, luv, am I glad ter see ye! These young gents'll look out for us now, so's ye've no need to worry none. The King o'England over 'ere promised me that much, 'e did—" she nudged Amanda—"and a lot o'other things too, that a lady can't mention, if'n she's proper! See ye in the morning, luv. Pleasant dreams!" She eyed James saucily and offered her ample *derrière* to Kirkland, who swept her up as he'd first intended, and carried her up the staircase.

James offered Amanda his arm, and side by side they climbed the stairway to her room. He and Kirkland had obviously planned well for their rescue bid. An expensive, coffee-colored lace nightgown was spread out across the bed. A tub and toilette articles had been made ready and next to them, a low stool held several fluffy towels.

She turned to bid James a goodnight, and to thank him for all he had done. As she did so, his arms closed around her and he drew her against his chest. His lips hungrily found the soft, bared flesh above her breasts, and he untied the cloak and let it fall, covering her with kisses as far as the gaudy garment she wore would allow. Feverishly, his hands fumbled for the hooks to free her body from its imprisoning covering.

She stiffened. His breath was hot upon her breasts and his desire evident in the hurried motions of his hands and in the hardness of him against her thigh. A wave of panic swept over her.

"Don't! Please!" she cried finally, pushing him away and gathering the cloak about her once more. "Just—don't."

"But why not? I want you, Amanda, God knows, I do! And it's not as if you're vir—." He stopped short, realizing too late the folly of what he had been about to say. "I'm sorry. I didn't mean it that way," he finished lamely. "Come, let me tell you what I promised to tell you." He took her hand in his own.

The expression on his face reminded Amanda of her father, in some peculiar way, boyish, eager and, perhaps, somewhat selfish.

"I want to ask you—"

"No," Amanda said softly, placing a finger gently against his lips. "Not now, James. Later, when the time is right—ask me then."

He read the seriousness of her expression and stood

up. The sulky droop of his lips deepened as she refused his kiss. He left her hurriedly then, and Amanda could not help but sigh with relief that he had done so without an unpleasant scene.

She was sure he intended to ask her to become his wife. Sadly, she realized she would have to tell him no, for his touch inflamed no passion in her, stirred no love other than that for a brother or a very dear friend, and that she hoped, he would always be.

Chapter Fifty-Seven

Breakfast the next morning had a festive air, despite the previous evening having ended, Amanda thought, on a decidedly dismal note.

James had recovered from his attack of the sulks and was as charming as ever. Roger Kirkland and Nellie had obviously spent a pleasant night together and were flirting outrageously.

Nellie, Amanda thought, had never looked better. The blue gown the men had selected for her flattered her coloring, and Amanda was sure her friend had never sported anything nearly as fine before, for she primped and preened even at the table, using the silver coffeepot as an impromptu mirror.

Her own gown, she knew, could only have been selected by James, for it was an excellent imitation of the one she had worn when carried aboard the *Gypsy Princess* by his men, yellow, and sprigged all over the bodice and skirt with dainty white flowers. She'd looped her hair into a heavy coil and fastened it at her nape with a tortoise-shell comb. She felt marvelous and looked, she knew by the expression in both men's eyes, equally so.

"And what will you fair flowers do today?" asked

Roger finally, dabbing at his mouth with a monogrammed napkin. The monogram, Amanda observed, was not his own.

"Whatever you decide, don't let it take you outside these walls, ladies—not until I've had the warrant sworn out against Blake and his quadroon, anyway. I'll not rest easy for your safety until that pair are under lock and key! A charge of abduction should hold up, with Roger here and myself as witnesses," James said with satisfaction.

"Hmmm. Though abduction is the least of their crimes, eh, Mallory?" Roger added grimly.

James nodded. "By God, yes! When we—met—aboard ship, Amanda, I knew only rumors of Blake's doings here in New Orleans. After I found you at that sporting house it reawakened my curiosity. I decided to delve into his past. There was nothing ever proved, you understand, but then, again, nothing was ever disproved either!" He paused to draw on his pipe, and scratched his newly shaven face thoughtfully. "After everything you've told me about the little larks he got up to in Spain, I'm inclined to feel the rumors are true."

"Stop hedging, James, do, and get on with it," Amanda demanded. "And then I want to hear how you cheated death on the *Sea Dragon.* It still seems incredible that you could have escaped that inferno alive!" She shuddered, the memory vividly flooding back.

"Very well, first Blake. Now, there used to be a big plantation down Bayou Tranquil, owned by a Frenchman, Guy St. Vincent, and his wife, Simone. They were a young couple, had more money than they knew what to do with, and used it to entertain, somewhat lavishly,

I discovered. Well, Paul Blake was out to make his fortune, and he'd met the St. Vincents and done some business with them, and, in due course, they invited them to stay at their home, Belle Rêve." Three pairs of eyes were fixed intently on him. James took a leisurely sip of coffee, enjoying their suspense, before continuing.

"At Belle Rêve, Paul was treated as an honored guest. He was, apparently, capable of great charm, and the St. Vincents grew rather fond of him."

Amanda nodded. The story of Villa Hermosa seemed to have been a repeated one. James continued.

"As wealthy sugar-plantation owners, Guy and Simone naturally had an extensive number of slaves. Among them was a beautiful quadroon ladies' maid—"

"Yvette!" Amanda exclaimed.

"Correct. Soon, Paul Blake had taken her to his bed and convinced himself that he loved her. She appears to have made him believe she felt likewise. Paul demanded that Guy St. Vincent sell the quadroon to him, so that he and the girl could go away together. Simone refused. Yvette had been trained in Paris and had some education. Simone did not want to give up her talented maid. She refused to sell Yvette to this arrogant English merchant! The records show no more facts. This much is all we know for sure, testimony given by the one surviving slave that would give evidence at the inquiry."

"Fair gives me the creeps, it do!" Nellie shuddered.

Though brilliant morning light flooded the room, it seemed chilly suddenly, as if a cloud had covered the sun. Amanda murmured agreement.

"And—what happened?" she asked in a whisper. "You said 'surviving' slave?"

James nodded. "The rest were too scared to talk. Shortly after Madame St. Vincent's refusal to give up Yvette, the Frenchwoman became ill. With every passing day, she grew weaker. Now, this is conjecture on my part, but I believe Guy St. Vincent decided to ride into town for a physician. He never arrived here—and he never returned to Belle Rêve! The slave who gave testimony had been with Monsieur and Madame St. Vincent since he was a boy. He was afraid for his mistress's life. Blake and Yvette ruled the house, the plantation, openly mocking his mistress as she grew daily nearer to death and unable to run her household.

"The slave, Abram, ran away—not to freedom, but to the next plantation, where friends of his master and mistress lived. He told them what had taken place at Belle Rêve, but before they could return with him, a hurricane blew up, destroying almost every plantation hereabouts. By the time anyone could reach Belle Rêve, it was total disaster. Most of the slaves were dead, the few survivors of the hurricane too shocked or too scared to point the finger at Blake and his mistress. The house itself was a tottering ruin, the fields destroyed. No trace of Madade Simone or her husband was ever recovered. Strangely, the hurricane seemed to have also 'blown' away all of the St. Vincents' silverware and Madame's jewelry!"

"And Paul and Yvette?" Amanda queried.

"Aha, my dear, that *I* shall recount!" interrupted Roger firmly. "The evil pair were able to produce witnesses who saw them in New Orleans the evening before the hurricane. They both swore, on oath, that they had left Madame St. Vincent alive, that they had come to town to fetch her a physician when Guy had not returned. There was no way to prove what everyone in the area believed—that the pair had brutally murdered and robbed the Frenchman and his wife!"

"But if'n that were true, why didn't that brace o'devils run orf together, like wot they planned?" asked Nellie, puzzled.

"Because, my peach, your friend, Yvette, is greedy! She wanted Paul no more than she wanted to hang! So, I heard she sent him away, with a promise to go with him only when he had sufficient money to keep her in luxury befitting a queen. She used him, and the fool still can't see it! She does well on Royal Street. It offers her all she really wants, short of freedom. A position of power over the poor white fools who lust after her fancy women, and some independence, which she will gain completely the day Paul hands her her freedom papers. But meanwhile she'll feed on any wealth Paul might bring her like a leech on blood!" Kirkland ended.

"I see it now. He thought if he married Maria-Elena de Villarin, he would have access to the de Villarin assets. When he realized Miguel was opposed violently to the match and that he'd withhold all monies, he left the girl! That—bastard!" Amanda exploded suddenly.

"Which brings us to his attempt to wed you, my sweet?" James inquired. "You had no money," he pondered thoughtfully.

"No, true enough. But I think I mentioned that time I went to see him at the inn, he told me he'd wanted only to use my name and to have an heir by me. I was so stupid, so naive! I thought he was just saying those terrible things to protect me, that he didn't want to bind me to him in marriage after he was crippled! I must have been blind. But I suppose it was that I didn't *want* to believe him. Truth is so painful!"

Nellie nodded agreement. Her cheery face was, for the moment, solemn.

"It's turned out for t'best, luv, ain't it? Ye be rid o'him now. An in time ye'll forget the shame o'wot was forced on ye at Royal Street, truly ye will, love." Nellie squeezed Amanda's hand and peered at her earnestly.

There was concern in her blue eyes, and a great deal of love, Amanda observed.

"You needn't worry, Nell. You see, I feel no shame for anything that has happened to me! I reacted to each situation to the best of my abilities. I would ask no more of another, so I cannot expect more of myself, can I? But I don't think I could bear to live here, or, for that matter, return to England. As soon as I have Michael back, I think I'd like to go east, perhaps to Boston."

She noticed James and Roger exchange grins. Was the moment of the grand proposal near at hand? James cleared his throat nervously and seemed about to speak, but, at that moment, the maid entered and started to clear the breakfast dishes. The four about the table awaited her exit in uncomfortable silence.

Whatever James had intended, the moment was lost. Nellie tried to regain the camaraderie that had existed before the maid's untimely entrance by urging James to tell of his narrow escape from death at the pirates' hands, and the subsequent explosion.

"There's no mystery or miracle to it! After Amanda and my men had slipped over the side, I crept for'ard to the magazine and helped myself to a keg of powder. The crew was so sotted with rum I believe King George himself could have walked aboard naked and still not have been noticed!"

His green eyes sparkled with excitement as he relived the moment. Amanda felt a pang of regret that he could not be the one for her. Truly, he was so very handsome! His deep auburn, waving hair made a striking contrast to the weathered tan of his merry face, as it tumbled in unruly fashion to his shoulders. In any physical emergency she knew, he could always be depended upon, for, like a boy, he reveled in danger. But he could not offer her the deep strength of character, the resolution of purpose she needed in a man. She had said rashly that she was her own strength, that she needed no one but Michael. Was that really so? Hadn't her willingness to rush blindly into marriage with Paul proved it was not?

"—and so I laid a trail with the powder from the magazine to the rail, figuring I would have time to jump overboard and swim for it before all hell broke loose! Well, anyway, that rat, Abner, was still tied to the mainmast and he spotted me! I suppose he thought he could buy some time for himself if he set up the alarm, so he started yelling and carrying on like a banshee. Then another cry started from the stern side. Someone had discovered Garcia's body in his cabin."

Amanda bit her lip, the old guilt filling her. She would never be able to reconcile taking another's life, for whatever reason, as long as she lived!

"I decided to go ahead. I tore a strip from my shirt and lit it from a lantern, tossed it into the powder trail and leaped for the side—the wrong side, as it turned out. You know the rest. Twin explosions, and the *Dragon* was no more. The swells from the explosion carried me far from where you had gone into the water. I believed you lost, Amanda! Dawn found me swimming among shattered remains of the ship. I dragged myself ashore near Barcelona, and an old woman was kind enough to take me into her cottage until I'd recuperated. The sword wound Bloody Harry had dealt me when he took the ship had festered, and it was sometime before it healed completely. Half of my illness was, I know, due to my grief at losing you, sweet, and the other, guilt at having been unable, I thought, to prevent your death. Not to mention a sizable crack to my skull from a blasted timber!" He parted his hair and bent his head to reveal a white scar about four inches long.

The two women made appropriate noises to show their concern, and James straightened and grinned.

"Many of the villagers living by the coast had seen the offshore explosion, but none knew of any survivors. Finally, I gave up. When I had recovered, I worked my way back here on a merchant ship, and it was aboard her I met up with our mutual friend here, Mr. Kirkland." He slapped Roger heartily across the back. "Eh, Roger?"

Kirkland nodded. "The rest you know."

Amanda agreed. "I cannot tell you how I appreciate your assistance! I wish there were some way I could repay you."

Roger pushed a strand of black hair from his eyes and grinned lecherously. "Perhaps it could be arranged, m'dear!" His grin faded as James cast him a warning glare. "Then again, perhaps not," he added hurriedly, squeezing Nellie about the waist as she, too, glared at him, this look, a jealous one.

James pushed back his chair and feigned a groan.

"A magnificent breakfast, Kirkland. And now, I will be off! I have much to do. There's the warrant to be sworn, a baby to find and the small matter of finishing the papers for the purchase of my new vessel. Don't be foolhardy and venture outside, Amanda. I will return as soon as I have Michael."

He retrieved his tricorn from the serving table, and strode from the room.

Chapter Fifty-Eight

Roger Kirkland made his exit shortly after James, mumbling vaguely about some business he had to attend to. Nellie and Amanda eyed each other knowingly after he had left.

"Business! Gamblin' more like," Nellie sniffed disdainfully.

Amanda smiled. "I think you're probably right, Nell."

"Probably! I *knows* I am! How did ye think 'e got this 'ere place? Not by the sweat 'o 'is brow, not bloomin' likely! Won it, 'e did, lock, stock, an' barrel. Under all that honey, 'e do be cold fish, I reckon. At times . . ."

Amanda nodded, stood, and went out through the double-arched salon doorway and into the courtyard beyond. She sat on the bench and raised her face to catch the sunshine. Nellie sat beside her and did likewise.

"Then, you have no designs on Mr. Kirkland, I take it?" Amanda asked, a teasing not in her voice.

"Lawd, no," Nellie declared. "My designs lies in other, more profitin' directions!" She grinned broadly.

Amanda's brow creased in a puzzled frown. "Then who is he, if not Roger?"

Nellie sighed impatiently. "It's not an ''oo,' it's a 'it.' And I'll say no more until certain things 'appen—if'n they do. No, luv, don't ye try t' worm it out o'me, 'cos I ain't sayin' nothin' yet!"

Amanda, who had indeed been about to quiz her friend, closed her mouth and peered earnestly at Nell, but Nell carefully averted her face, seeking for some means to change the subject.

"I do believe yer James is fixin' to propose t'ye, Mandy! Offered Roger a tidy sum for this bleedin' great house, 'e did, and Roger shook on it, too. It'd be grand for the three o'ye, wouldn't it?"

Amanda laughed. "And now who's quizzing who, Nellie Flagg? Hmmm, the proposal I had been expecting, but that James is planning on purchasing this house is news to me! It will be for naught, Nell. I realized last night that I could never marry James."

She picked a twig from the branch of the orange and commenced peeling the bark from it with her finger-nails, deep in thought.

"And why won't ye marry him, loverly lookin' lad that 'e is?" Nellie demanded.

"Because it wouldn't be fair to him, Nell, don't you see? I cannot love him as anything more than a brother, and James is too much of a man to accept anything but my love as a woman, not a sister. In time, his love would turn to hate, I know it. Last night he tried to kiss me. He was furious when I refused him! He believes, I think, that marriage could change that—make me love him, but it wouldn't. I'm not even sure that he hasn't convinced himself that he loves me out of guilt, and feels that marriage would be a suitable way to make everything up to me!"

Nell pondered this for several moments. "'Tis yer life, luv, and yers to do with as ye see fit. But what of Michael's pa? If 'e comes for ye, will ye refuse 'im too?"

"Of course!" Amanda insisted, adding, "though the chances of him doing so are about as good as my becoming Queen of England! No, as I told you, Nell, he cares less than nothing for me. He would have handed me over to Paul and his men on a silver platter to save his own skin! He said that I meant nothing to him, that he had used me." She smiled a bitter smile. "On second thought, perhaps I *would* marry him—if only to make his life hell on this earth!"

"Bold words, luvie, but ye' don't 'ave it in ye, t'bear grudges. Under all that hot-blooded temper ye've a soft 'eart, and a forgivin' one."

"Nay, not soft—stupid! Now, don't let's talk of this anymore. I do declare, Nell, there's a definite streak of the matchmaker in you!"

"Where ye're concerned 'tis more than a streak, ducks—a bloody great stripe, more like! Gawd, these slippers are fair killin' me!" She kicked off the offending shoes, hoisted her skirts and looked down at her throbbing feet, encased in their fine hose. Amanda made no comment. Nellie glanced sideways to her.

Amanda leaned back on the bench, her unbound hair spread out in the sunshine which, it appeared, would soon be replaced by a glowering gray cloud. Her eyes were closed, a half smile on her lips, but Nellie knew that she wasn't asleep.

Carefully, Nellie tiptoed across to the orange tree, grinning as she saw that, as she had expected, the leaves were still soaked with dew. Taking careful aim she pulled back on one thickly leafed branch, then let it spring back, showering Amanda with a considerable amount of water.

With a yell Amanda leaped up, shock replaced by merriment as she spied several wind-blown, tiny oranges on the flagstones. Pelting them at a now-screeching Nellie, she raced after her into the house.

"I'll not forgive you, Nell Flagg, for my daydream was of Michael, and you banished it."

She sat down suddenly at the foot of the stairs, her knees buckling.

"You!" she hissed through clenched teeth. "Get out of this house!" Her hands shook uncontrollably in the folds of her gown as she stood up.

Yvette smiled slightly. "Ever the brave one, *petite* Amanda, *non?* What I have to say will not take long, however, and it will profit you to hear me out!"

"I care nothing for profit," Amanda replied coldly. "Leave this instant, or I will send for the authorities."

"They've already been sent for, luv, a minute ago," interrupted Nellie. She spoke the lie quietly. "If ye doubt me, madam, I suggests ye wait! That maid do be fair nimble on 'er feet—shouldn't take her long t'reach the magistrate's house, it shouldn't." She descended the stairs and stood behind Amanda.

Yvette appeared unperturbed, except for a tightening of her jaw and a cold glint in her brown eyes. She crossed the room with a faint rustle of taffeta skirts, and stood directly in front of Amanda.

"Then hear this! If you wish to see your child again, alive, you will bring Miguel de Villarin to Belle Rêve—ah, I see you have heard of the place—along with the reward money, within forty-eight hours. If not, your son will die!"

Amanda faced her unmoved. "Do you think me a fool to fall for that ruse twice over! Oh, no, Yvette, my son is safe. I have no fears for him!" She glared fiercely at Yvette.

The quadroon shrugged, a sly smile creeping over her face.

"Are you quire certain of that, *cherie?* Then, if so, how did I come by this?"

She reached into a petit-point bag that hung from her wrist, and withdrew a baby's wooden rattle, Michael's rattle, which she shook softly, her eyes never for a second leaving Amanda's face. Amanda paled. Every instinct in her screamed for her to fling herself on Yvette, to tear at her and claw at her eyes, to do something!

"A child's toy! It could be purchased anywhere for a few francs. If you wish me to do your bidding, you must give me better proof that you have him and that he's still alive." Her voice broke as she said the last words, and she clutched a chairback for support.

"Oh, come! I saw your face when I took out the rattle! It *is* your *petit* Michael's, as you well know. He is such a pretty child—those dark curls, and what lovely brown eyes!—small wonder that Mignon Boucher was so loathe to part with him, *non?* But, naturally, when she understood that it was the baby's father himself who had come for the boy—!" Yvette paused.

"Miguel?" Amanda queried, confused.

"Non, non, of course not," Yvette said impatiently. "Gualterio played the so-amorous Papa, who could not wait to reunite with his little boy."

Amanda felt her stomach heave. The mere thought of Michael in Gualterio's brutish hands was terrifying. But Mignon was not to blame. She had known nothing of the situation, save that Amanda was fleeing from someone. It would not have been difficult to convince her, to fabricate some tale to put her mind at rest. . . .

"As for proof that he yet lives, I can offer none save my word! I'm afraid, *cherie,* that you will have to take it or leave it." She yawned. "Salome cares for him well, and will continue to do so—until the deadline for Miguel's delivery into Paul's hands is up. Then you and the child will be allowed to go free. You have forty-eight hours, no more. Use them wisely, *oui?"*

Yvette exited swiftly.

After the front door had slammed behind her, the maid hurried in with an anxious expression on her face.

"I am sorry, Señorita Sommers, but she would not allow me to announce her! She simply marched in and—"

"It's all right, Celestina. You may go," Amanda said wearily, running her fingers through her hair.

"But, Señorita, she said to give you this," Celestina added, handing over a small scrap of paper and the wooden rattle.

Amanda read the paper hurriedly. Miguel's name. The address of his hotel. Nothing more. So, he *had* come after Blake and had not been killed.

It was a strange feeling, to know for certain that he was alive, and one that she could not name.

A throbbing pain started in her temples. She clutched the rattle to her breast, an ache filling her heart that far surpassed the one in her head. Dear God, what was she to do?

Chapter Fifty-Nine

"Now, come on, luv, don't be a bloody fool! Wait until James comes back, do. 'E'll know what t'do," Nellie pleaded.

"I don't have the time, Nell, so please stop it," Amanda demanded sharply. "It could be days before he returns, and I can't risk waiting. You can tell him for me what has happened. Then, if we have not returned by, oh, let's say, Thursday, you can send the authorities after us. But not until then, promise me, Nell?"

Nell set her lips defiantly and ignored the plea. "Well, why don't we send for Roger? 'E'd 'elp, I'm sure of it," she persisted.

"No, no one! Yvette said that if I wanted to see Michael alive, that we were to come alone, Miguel and I. I cannot chance it," Amanda said firmly.

"Now, look, luv, I didn't want t' say it, but someone 'as to! The little luv could be dead already, probably is, knowin' that Paul and 'is evil lot! So why risk gettin' yerself harmed too? Once 'e has ye in his clutches, 'e'll let none of'ye free—or out o'there alive!"

"That's a chance I have to take, Nell—and you know it, as long as there's any hope that Michael can be saved." There was a determination and a note of desperation in her voice that Nellie had never heard before. "Now, enough of your delaying tactics. How do I look?"

Nellie eyed Amanda's elegantly upswept hair and scrutinized her gloomily from head to toe. The rich, ruby red of the satin gown made her glow like a jewel, its voluminous folds accenting her tiny waist, the whiteness of her cleavage, and highlighting the copper sheen in her hair.

"You look loverly—fit t'kill," Nellie pronounced in a doom-filled voice. "But why all o'this fol-de-rol?"

Amanda patted a stray ringlet into place with a dampened finger, eyeing herself critically in the mirror.

"Because, Nellie, I have to look like Miguel's mistress! Do you think he'll let me lead him meekly into Paul's clutches like a lamb to the slaughter? No! I must force him to go with me—and this getup is part of the plan. I'll explain it all to you later, God willing. There's no time now, it's almost dusk." She drew on a burgundy-colored velvet cloak and fastened the jeweled clasp at her throat. Then she opened the drawer of the chiffonier and withdrew a handsome silver-chased pistol.

Nellie appeared aghast. "Gawd! Please, luv, don't take that along, it's askin' fer trouble."

"Well, I can't force Miguel to do my bidding with words alone. This—" she added grimly, brandishing the pistol—"will speak volumes as to the seriousness of my intentions!"

She stuffed the pistol into an evening bag, where it bulged noticeably.

"You may tell Roger I have taken this when he returns. Did you have Celestina order the coach to the front door?"

"Aye. It should be waitin' for ye," Nellie said resignedly. "Mandy, let me come along! I could help ye, I know I could."

"Dear Nellie, I know you would, but I *must* do this alone. Thank you, for everything."

"Tsk! Lot o'good it did, hidin' ye on that there ship, when ye're bound and determined to go an' kill yerself now! One thing: don't it bother ye, to hand over another human being into that Blake's clutches? I wouldn't o'thought it of ye, no matter what, reely I wouldn't." Nell shivered.

Amanda seemed unsoftened by her friend's words. She set her jaw squarely and pulled on elbow-length evening gloves, picked up the bag with its bulging load, and went to Nell's side.

"The life of my son could be in my hands alone, Nell. De Villarin, by his own admission, used me. I have no qualms about doing the same to him! Take care." She hugged Nellie in farewell and briskly left.

Driving rain greeted her as she slipped from the front door. The groom handed her up into the coach and she settled back, clutching the pistol's unfamiliar bulk somewhat nervously.

It was, the groom had said, no more than a quarter hour's drive. She peered through the curtained windows, seeing the streets awash and even muddier than usual, an occasional lamplight illuminating huge puddles. As they slithered around one particularly sharp corner, she lurched from her seat, and was thrown clear across the coach to the other side. The pistol thudded to the floor. She retrieved it gingerly for it was primed and loaded, she knew. She had no more powder, nor any idea of how to reload the weapon even if she had. If Miguel became balky, one shot would have to serve to persuade him. Dead or alive, she would get him to Belle Rêve!

All too soon the coach halted in front of the brightly lit hotel, and the coachman handed her down.

She pulled the hood of her cloak well over her head against the rain, hoisted her skirts to scamper through the mud, and hurried inside.

The elegant foyer blazed light from several chandeliers. Overstuffed chairs ranged along one wall, with potted palms at intervals between them. There were a great many people coming and going, but a brief glance reassured her that Miguel was not one of them.

She swept across to the desk and allowed the hood of her cloak to fall back.

The desk clerk's polite smile broadened to a genuine smile of appreciation.

"*Bon soir, mademoiselle.* A room? We have two excellent ones available?"

"No, thank you. I believe you have a Don Miguel de Villarin registered here, do you not?" she inquired sweetly.

The clerk had no need to consult his register. He beamed. "But, of course! The don is one of our most honored guests, mademoiselle!"

She nodded. "I was hoping, perhaps, that he is in, monsieur. We are old friends, you understand, and if you would be so good as to give me his room number—"

His smile turned apologetic. "My regrets, but the gentleman went out a short while ago. If you would care to wait—?" He indicated the chairs across the foyer.

"Oh, dear, I *had* thought to find him in!" She feigned disappointment, then brightened and flashed the clerk a dazzling, conspiratorial smile, inwardly thanking the gods for her luck.

"I have it! Perhaps you might give me the spare key to the don's room, monsieur? Would it not be enchanting to surprise him?" She fluttered her lashes coyly.

The little man appeared genuinely distressed. "Ah, *mais, non, mademoiselle,* I am sorry, but it would be out of the question. The hotel policy forbids the issuing of—"

"But, monsieur, the don and I are such very *good* friends!" Amanda winked naughtily and slid a gold coin across to the clerk's side of the desk.

"Then perhaps, under the circumstances, we could help you." He pocketed the coin hurriedly and slid the key to her, after a furtive glance about him. "The number is seventy-six. Up the staircase and to your right, mademoiselle."

She thanked him prettily, and followed his directions.

Miguel's suite was at the end of a long corridor.

Unlocking the door, she slipped inside, then locked it carefully behind her and withdrew the key.

The draperies and casement were closed against the rain. The suite was cozy in reds and browns. Amanda unfastened her cloak and draped it over a chair in the corner, away from the door. The room bore the faint odor of sandalwood, and the memories it evoked almost swayed her from her purpose. His clothes hung neatly in the armoire. His toilette articles and a few odd pieces of jewelry, a cravat pin and a pair of gold buckles, were set tidily on the secretary. There was nothing to do but wait. She removed the pistol from the velvet bag, and perched on the bed to do so.

Over ten months had passed since she saw him last. Would he have changed? She wondered idly. What would be his reaction when he learned of her child, their child? Her mind teemed with questions. She had no idea how she could force him to accompany her, except by threatening him with the pistol. If he resisted in any way, she didn't know *what* she would do! I'll cross that bridge when I come to it, she resolved. Each time that resolution weakened in the two hours of waiting, the memory of Michael's baby face flashed into her mind and strengthened it.

The sound of a key scraping in the lock finally came. She almost froze. Not a second too soon, she flung herself behind the door, the pistol clasped firmly in both hands.

Miguel stepped inside, carefully closing the door and locking it behind him, before turning around. When he did, they were face to face. There was not so much as a flicker of surprise in his expression as their eyes met.

"A terrible night, no?" he remarked casually, unfastening his sodden cape and hanging it on the hook behind the door. He peeled off an equally rain-soaked coat and did likewise. His movements were calm, unhurried, infuriating.

Amanda's grasp on the pistol faltered for a second, but she regained her grip and her composure.

"Miguel, I—"

"Some sherry, perhaps?"

As if he had noticed neither her attempt at speech

nor the weapon in her hands, he unstoppered the decanter and deftly poured two glasses, one of which he carried across the room and offered to her. She shook her head ever so slightly, irritation welling. Damn! He hadn't changed, not one whit! He was still as arrogant as ever. She opened her mouth to speak again, but he swiftly turned back to his own glass.

"My regrets, *querida,* but there is nothing else. I could summon the bell captain, if you—"

"Damn you, stop it!" Amanda fumed. Her eyes showed increasing bewilderment as Miguel cooly stripped off his white shirt, tossed it carelessly to the floor, and commenced tugging off his boots. The task completed, he pulled back the coverlet, and slid inside the bed, totally ignoring her.

Nonplussed, she wondered nervously what to do next, but it was nervousness coupled with frustration. Two paces found her at his bedside, and in a single, angry movement she flung back the covers with one hand, the other training the pistol at his head.

"Sit up and listen to me," she demanded imperiously, "or I'll blast your head off! I might even blast it off should you sit up, for I admit, Miguel, I have no skill as a marksman, and even less in knowing how this thing works," she added, waving the pistol dangerously to and fro.

As she had hoped, Miguel did as ordered, a hardness to his jawline now and in his eyes.

"I'll listen, *querida,* if and when you put that down." His glare was steady and unwavering.

"Very well," she agreed finally. "But if you make one move to take it from me, or to disobey any orders I might give you, I will use it!"

Miguel nodded. "I agree. Now, what is it you have to say that necessitates such dramatics?" A trace of a grin tugged at his lips.

"It concerns the life of someone very precious to me, Miguel. His name is Michael, and he is being held captive in a plantation house down Bayou Tranquil, by Paul and his henchmen."

Miguel's expression appeared bored. "And of what concern is that to me?" he inquired offhandedly. "It is your captive lover's problem, not mine!"

Was there a slight jealous edge to his voice? It seemed she had ruffled his feathers.

She took a deep breath before announcing stiffly, "No lover, Miguel. Michael is my son. *Our* son."

Chapter Sixty

"Our son!" he roared, leaping from the bed and grasping her so tightly by the shoulders that the pistol thudded harmlessly to the floor. He kicked it quickly under the bed with the back of his heel. "Our son!" he repeated, incredulity in his tone. Still he held her so tightly she was half-lifted from the floor. There was pleasure, great pleasure in his voice. His expression changed, concern swiftly taking the place of joy. "Are you sure?"

Indignantly, her head snapped back and she glared daggers at him. "How dare you! Michael is almost four months old! If you choose, you may count—"

"Not that, you little idiot! Are you sure that Paul has him?" At her weak nod, the fire seemed to fizzle out of him like a doused candle. He released her and offered again the glass of sherry he had poured earlier. "Drink it all," he ordered, "and then tell me everything."

She meekly did as bidden. "After Paul and his men left you in Henrique's hands, they took me aboard a ship, bound for here. A woman, Nellie Flagg, who is now a dear friend, helped me to escape them by pretending I had jumped overboard. In fact, I stowed away, hidden in the ship's storeroom." Remembering, she shuddered.

Miguel nodded. "That explains the conflicting stories I encountered while trying to discover your whereabouts! Go on!"

"Well, during the voyage I became aware that I was carrying your child. We—Nell and I—managed to leave the ship without our ruse being discovered. We were able to find work at Maison Robineau, a coffeehouse, and they agreed to let me stay on even after Michael was born. Monsieur Robineau was very kind." She sipped the sherry thoughtfully with a furtive glance at Miguel's face. His expression was unfathomable.

"Anyway, everything seemed to be going well. We planned to leave New Orleans as soon as Michael was old enough to travel because Paul and his men were much in evidence in the town. I was frightened they would find me and realize I had not drowned, as they thought. Well, it appears that they *did* spot me, for one night about three weeks ago, Nell and I were waylaid. I passed out. When I came to, I was in what I believe is termed, in politer circles, a sporting house. Brothel. Call it what you will!" she said defensively. "They—they must have ferreted out the fact that I had borne a child, and have realized it could be none other than your child. They told me they had him, that if I did not do as they said that they would kill him. And I believed them!" She finished miserably. "Then I discovered that James was very much alive, and he did some inquiring—"

"Slow down, *querida*. Now, who is James?"

"He is the captain whose ship was captured by the pirate, Bloody Harry, remember?—and whom I believed dead after the *Sea Dragon* exploded."

Her face crumpled and, for a moment, he thought she would cry. But she carried on, though in a very low voice.

"He and a friend helped Nell and me to escape. He'd discovered from the Robineaus that Mignon, who was the cook at the coffeehouse and who, incidentally was very fond of Michael, had fled with him to Baton Rouge. You see, she knew that I was hiding from someone, but I had given her no details."

Miguel seemed confused. "But if she has our child?"

Amanda shook her head vehemently. "She *had* him! Today, Yvette, Paul's—"

"Ah! Her, I have heard all about!" Miguel interrupted grimly, "you need explain nothing of their relationship!"

"Well, Yvette came to the house where I was staying and said that this time Paul really *did* have Michael, that Gualterio had convinced Mignon he was the baby's father come to fetch his son and reunite his family! James had left that very morning to find Michael for me, little knowing he was too late! Yvette said I had forty-eight hours to bring you to Paul at Belle Rêve, and that if I did, Michael and I would go free!" Amanda faced him defiantly. "I will find some way to do so!" she vowed hotly.

Miguel nodded. "Did she offer any proof that what she said is true this time?"

"Only her word! And she had a little wooden rattle that Mignon had given Michael. I dare not chance that she is lying again!"

"Then you *shall* deliver me into their hands," Miguel pronounced softly, deep in thought. "I expected a showdown of some kind, the minute I found out about the warrant posted for their arrest. I have been searching for you for over ten months, Amanda, for Henrique Torres would not tell where Paul had taken you. I traveled to England, thinking to find you there, by some miracle. Nothing! New Orleans was my last chance, but every lead led to a blind alley! I met a Captain Heath in one tavern, and it was he who told me a young girl fitting your description had leaped from his vessel shortly after leaving Spain. Then I heard some outlandish tale that a fiery-tempered Englishwoman had, with her 'accomplice,' stolen a ring from a Monsieur Ferenette. I knew then that it could only have been you! No other would have dared do as he described you did to him, *pequeña!*" He smiled admiringly, dark eyes merry.

"Of course!" she muttered, bridling, "you *would* believe me a thief! There is nothing too low for you to think me guilty of."

"Sssh!" He laughed, replacing his hand on hers for a second time, the first touch having been angrily rebuffed.

"You rightly call yourself thief, my darling, because you have stolen something of mine, whether you know it or not!" he teased.

"I have nothing of yours, you arrogant—!"

"Now, now, no more of your tantrums, *por favor!* I meant, quite simply, that you have stolen—my heart! In other words, you foolish wench, I love you."

His tone was soft and bantering, and, for a second, his words did not register. When they did, her color heightened.

"Don't toy with me, Miguel!" she snapped. "I have a

long memory, and have yet to forget your crowing to Paul about how you had used me!" Her body quivered with anger, long repressed, from head to toe. God, how she yearned to slap his damned face!

Miguel sighed, shaking his head in disbelief. "I thought you an intelligent woman, Amanda, but you're acting like an empty-headed imbecile! Tell me, how else was I to save you? We were outnumbered more than two to one in that warehouse! At the time I saw no way out for you, as long as that lunatic, Blake, believed you were dear to me! He was ready to kill us both, *sí,* and would have! I intended to convince him of your innocence of any plot, to make him believe that you were only a pawn. Apparently, I succeeded only too well, for I convinced you, too! Come, Amanda, why would I admit to a plot to entrap him into marrying you? It doesn't make sense! So that I could publicly disgrace and maim him? Rot! There are other, easier ways. We both *know* that such a plot existed only in his warped mind!"

"Perhaps it is as devious as your own, Miguel!" Amanda retorted. "I heard you urge his men to—to—rape me! You only insist otherwise now because of Michael! Is that what it is?" she demanded. "Do you think you'd be able to take Michael from me, if we somehow escaped Paul? No, Miguel, he is *my* son, yours only by accident of birth!"

She made a sudden dive to retrieve the pistol from under the bed.

Miguel's hand was the swifter, and he wrenched her about and forced her onto the bed, holding her wrists to keep her from struggling.

"Listen, Amanda, and listen well, or I shall be forced

to make love to you to prove my point, and we both know how much you detest my lovemaking, *sí?"* he added, grinning.

"Remember, that last night, when you confessed you loved me?"

She glowered at him, unblinking, her breathing labored from his weight as he held her down.

"Well, at first it bothered me. I had enjoyed our fights, our passions," he grinned, "especially our passions! But your—admission—made me feel guilty. Yes, I, Don Miguel de Villarin, felt guilty. I retreated to the taproom, and over a tankard or two of ale, I realized that much of the guilt stemmed from the knowledge that I had treated you unfairly, that in many ways I had been responsible for all that had happened to you after I shot Blake. I handled it badly, I admit it now. I knew then that I loved you—no, stop that wriggling, *Madre de Díos,* woman!—that I loved you, and could offer you nothing, as long as this business with Blake was unresolved.

"When his message came, I believed I could finally end the whole thing, one way or another, and that if I triumphed, be free—to ask you to be my wife!"

Amanda's mouth dropped open in astonishment. Miguel took advantage of her shock and gathered her into his arms, pressing his lips over hers in a long and breathtaking kiss that sent tingles through her.

Her senses did battle within her. She desperately wanted to believe him! Instinct told her he was telling the truth, but could she trust those instincts that had failed her before? There was no doubt that her body responded to his kisses, like a finely tuned instrument, bursting into rippling song at his very touch. She moaned softly as he broke the kiss, her lips yearning for more.

"No, *querida mia,* I am a rogue reformed!" he said, laughing at her disappointed expression. "There will be no more than the chastest of kisses—until you swear that you are mine!" He slapped her bottom and yanked her to her feet. "Let's not waste time, Amanda. We must be ready to leave soon if we are to reach Belle Rêve in time." He gravely handed her the fallen pistol. "Would you agree to a truce? Together we have a chance to free our son, that's what's important now. We can settle our differences later, when all of this is behind us. Agreed?"

He did not say that they may not be around to settle any differences, but it was there, in his voice, nevertheless. Miguel was right: together, their chances for success were doubled, the odds a little better.

"Agreed." She nodded.

He took her hand in his and lifted it to his lips, giving the chastest of kisses to seal the pact.

Chapter Sixty-One

The track they followed was deeply rutted, the ruts filled with water from the previous night's rain. Dragonflies dipped and hummed over the puddles, and the clover sagged with the furry weight of the busy bees. The woods were rich in cool green shadows, the feeble sunlight falling through the leaves upon their faces with green and golden light, and wild violets nestled secretly in the deep, wet darkness of the tree trunk's shade.

Soon they came out of the woods, and the track led them alongside fields that stretched for miles with the light green of rustling sugarcane. Slaves, stripped to the waist, toiled at weeding the young stalks, their bodies bent and shiny with sweat. Their women labored beside them, the brightly striped *tignons* on their heads making brilliant splashes of color against the green. Some carried wide-eyed brown babies strapped in slings upon their backs, and the infants surveyed the world around them solemnly, tiny fists thrust into little mouths.

Amanda could hardly bear to look at them. Her heart felt like a heavy weight, a stone in her breast, and the creaking wooden *calèche* made her think of the open carts that carried the condemned to Tyburn: Such morbid thoughts when surrounded by so much beauty.

Miguel glanced sideways at Amanda from the driver's seat, his grim-faced expression softening as he saw her misery. But though he much preferred her crimson-cheeked and furious, he could think of no way to cajole her out of a depression that he was feeling himself.

"These oxen handle the rough roads far better than any horse, don't they?" she remarked suddenly.

The casual comment cheered him out of all proportion in its content. She was trying, at least, to put on a brave face.

He nodded, smiling. *"Sí!* They are not the most elegant of beasts, but hardy, worthy creatures. Thanks to them we are making good time." Damn, why could he think of nothing more intelligent to say!

"How much farther to Bayou Tranquil?"

"I would say less than five miles. Thank *Díos* the rain has stopped! It should be easier going, now the weather's let up."

Amanda murmured agreement. Never would she forget that morning when they had rumbled through the gateway in the wooden palisades that surrounded New Orleans. The dawn sky had been so low-hung that she believed she could have reached up and touched it, like the bulging insides of a circus tent. The atmosphere itself had seemed crackling with electricity—or was it her? It was as she imagined the sky would be when the end of the world came—sullen, brooding, charged with explosive tension, and it gave one a jittery, sick feeling deep in the belly.

The fields of tall grasses, made gay with glowing wildflowers still dew-drenched in the morning light, gave way in turn to swampland, where wild pigeons fluttered and bullfrogs squatted and croaked in the reeds. Above the trees rose a plume of wood smoke, and Amanda knew that the first part of their journey was all but over.

Out of habit, she set to smoothing out the folds of her gown, forgetting she now wore none, but was instead clothed in a pair of Miguel's old breeches, cut off to fit her legs, and a still older shirt they had purchased for one franc, an outrageous sum, from the rogue who had rented out the *calèche*. It hadn't occurred to her that the red satin gown was totally unsuited to such an expedition when she left Roger's house, and she had to admit her present clothing was much more comfortable, even if it did bring back memories of a time before when she had masqueraded as a boy.

The *calèche* rolled up to the log-built trading post. Miguel hauled hard on the reins, jumped down, and lifted Amanda from her seat.

Inside the trading post some Indians eyed her curiously, grinning and pointing at Amanda's clothing. One reached out and fingered the heavy braids she had woven her hair into, and said something to the trader in a harsh, guttural tongue.

"He says your hair is like the leaves of fall, missy, touched with the Fire God's hands," the trader said, and laughed. "Mebbe he has an eye on yer scalp! He! He!"

Amanda smiled at the Choctaw brave, doubtful that

her friendly thanks for his compliment would be well received.

Everyone had called the Indians savages or blood-thirsty murderers in New Orleans. The few Choctaws she had seen in the town had been, for the most part, old men, or women with children, and they had appeared neither savage nor blood-thirsty. This man wore his black hair long and flowing to his waist. His skin was a rich bronze, and his piercing black eyes were scrutinizing her no less thoroughly than she inspected him. His forehead was exaggeratedly flat, a result of his head having been bound while he was yet a babe, as was their custom, Mignon had said. About his throat hung a rawhide necklace, strung with animal teeth and shells, and from the rear of his loincloth draped a horsetail that covered him. But behind the frightening mask he was still just a man, and one whose eyes twinkled merrily at her curious perusal of him.

"Would you tell him I thank him for his compliment?" she asked the trader, who nodded and did so.

The brave grinned and extended his hand to Amanda, and after shaking hers in a friendly manner, he went out with his supplies.

While Miguel and the trader talked, Amanda explored the interior of the trading post. She loved the way it smelled of cut wood and creosote, and its safe, warm, darkness, like a womb. She fondled the silky beaver pelts stacked on the countertop that the Indian had traded for his supplies, examined the brightly striped woven blankets piled in another corner, going from item to item, touching, turning over this and that, her hands restless with tension.

"Are you ready, *querida?*" Miguel strode across to her, his eyes searching.

She heaved a sigh. "Yes, I suppose so. As ready as I will ever be!" A wan smile crossed her face.

He gave one of her braids a playful tug. The desire to touch her, to hold her, was overwhelming. He fought it down and turned brusquely away, heading out of the post and across a well-worn grassy area to the bayou's edge and the wooden jetty there.

Bayou Tranquil. A just name, Amanda thought as she stood beside Miguel, looking out over the water.

Live oaks hung with moss cast soft shadows on the gently rippling surface. The sky above was almost white, the sun vainly trying to pierce through it, but succeeding only in glimmering hazily behind the mist.

The stillness was so uncanny that when the soft tread of moccasined footsteps padded behind her she swung violently around.

"Oh!" Relief flooded her. It was just the Choctaw brave they had met inside the post. Behind him came the stocky trader.

"Is it settled, señor?" Miguel asked.

"It is. The canoe's yours." The trader affirmed.

"His price?"

The trader spoke in halting Choctaw to the brave.

The Indian spoke, pointing to the silver St. Christopher's medallion about Miguel's neck.

Miguel gave it to him, and they clasped hands to seal the bargain. With a salute to Amanda, the brave and the trader left them.

Amanda passed their few provisions down into the canoe and then Miguel lifted her in behind him. He pushed hard on the jetty, sending the long canoe a few feet out into the water. Then he took up the paddle and dipped it in and out of the water with hardly a splash.

The canoe slipped swiftly into midstream. When Amanda looked back, the trading post could no longer be seen.

Chapter Sixty-Two

"Let me paddle, Miguel! You rest, now. That way we can make better time."

Miguel shook his head, but he did ship the paddle and relax, letting the canoe drift aimlessly for several minutes before continuing. The back of his shirt was sodden with sweat and beads of it covered his face and chest, for he had not slackened their speed in the three hours since they left the trading post.

He peeled off the shirt suddenly and flung it into the prow. He took the kerchief she offered and mopped his drenched face and neck.

"Señor Burro!" She laughed softly.

"What?" he asked, scowling as he turned to face her.

"I called you Señor Burro. It seems apt. You *are* as stubborn as a donkey, are you not?" she teased.

Dear God, but he was handsome, even with that look as dark as thunderclouds on his face! He returned to his paddling, and she idly watched the way his muscles flexed beneath the golden-tanned skin of his biceps. Between his shoulder blades were the three crossed knife scars he had told her of last night.

Esteban and his hired rescue party had been just

minutes late, and Henrique Torres had already begun to carry out his master's last wish, that Miguel should suffer before he died, when they burst into the warehouse. Miguel added ruefully that Esteban had been grimly satisfied to see his don suffer a little, as repayment for his stupidity!

She half reached out to touch the scars, caught herself doing so in midair and guiltily dropped her hand to her lap. No! She must not allow herself to be wooed into caring again, she mustn't! The hurt was too great, when one cared and wasn't cared for in return. It would be so very easy to say, 'Yes, Miguel, I love you! I am yours!' just to have him hold her close and banish the fear inside her. But he had said he loved her! A part of her clung desperately to those words, believing them, while another, less reckless self, argued coolly that Paul had said them, too.

The bayou here was as wide as many rivers, sometimes with little islands of trees growing strangely from its center. The green water was covered in a scum of tiny weeds. She saw something slither through the scum, and realized with a shudder that it was a snake!

The banks were thick with lush foliage, fan-shaped palmetto fingers reaching skyward between the cypresses. A pair of egrets waited motionlessly on a rotted log for an early supper.

In the fading afternoon light, the phantomlike shrouds of moss that trailed from the cypresses looked like funeral weeds, and now the croaking of the frogs seemed ominous and threatening. Was it her imagination—or did each chorus throb louder and louder? The air had the smell of decay—dank, rotten, and clammy through the cloth of her shirt. She shivered. The very silence seemed to breathe with a brooding, supernatural life of its own. Glancing at Miguel, she wondered if he experienced the same choking dread that the stillness bred in her. He must have sensed something for he turned, laid the paddle in the bottom of the canoe, and flexed his aching arms.

"Here, wrap this around you," he ordered, handing her one of the striped blankets. *"Díos!* I would give a king's ransom for a bowl of Rita's soup!" He grabbed at an overhanging branch and hauled the canoe against the bank.

"Hold on to this, *querida.* We'll have to stop for the night. Without a moon it will soon be too dark to continue, no?"

She nodded and grasped the branch with both hands while he jumped out onto the bank. Amanda clambered after him. Together they heaved the canoe onto land. Grabbing their provisions, he took her hand in his own large one and hauled her after him through the thick foliage.

Here and there an exotic flower glowed amid the green like a brightly feathered bird. Dead leaves and twigs snagged at her hair, and by the time he had found them a suitable camp, several scratches had bloodied her face. He spread another blanket on the damp ground and motioned her to sit.

"And here, m'lady, is your boudoir for tonight. Does m'lady approve?" he bantered, grinning.

The pallor of her face scared him. With relief he saw a tinge of crimson seep into the white.

"I am not *your* lady!" She retorted with a trace of her old spirit, adding woefully, "Do we have to stay here?" The memory of that snake slithering through the water was just too recent for comfort!

"Regrettably, yes." He uncorked a bottle of wine with his teeth and handed it to her.

Amanda took a swig. It warmed her a little, though she knew her coldness was born of fear. She pulled the blanket tightly about her and retreated into its warmth while eating a strip or two of the dried meats from their provisions. He had a fire started now, and he rocked back on his heels and surveyed first it and then her.

"A poor excuse for a fire, no? You have only to say the word, and I will warm you myself, *querida.*" His eyes were sensual.

"I'm quite warm enough, thank you," she lied haughtily.

Miguel shook his head. "Mandy, you are a liar to the end! But *Gracias a Díos,* you said 'no'! I had feared you might say yes and I have no wish to make love to an old Indian squaw!" He waited her reaction.

Her head jerked up, ready to retort in kind, but she caught the smile twitching at the corner of his lips and self-consciously laughed too.

"Do I really look that bad?" she asked at length.

"Worse, *mi estrellita!*" he replied.

They were unable to draw their glances away. The silence was uncomfortable as they gazed into each other's eyes, but Miguel finally broke the spell. He scrabbled across to her side, an expression she knew well on his face. His eyes smoldered with desire beneath sleepy, sensual lids and his voice was thick with emotion.

"Damn me for a fool for making that promise! *Querida,* you can have no *idea* how I long to make wild, savage love to you!"

His words sent a delicious tingle through her. That is what you think, Don Miguel, she thought. She refused to meet his eyes. Her heart fluttered like a bird in her breast. His fingertips brushed the fine hairs at the nape of her neck as he began to unfasten her braids.

Whether the touch had been accidental or intentional she knew not, but she flinched as if scalded. Did he mean to take her? Her heart raced with excitement, and she wondered guiltily if he could hear it.

Now he was combing her long tresses with his hands, stroking the heavy chestnut mane and spilling it through his fingers.

She itched to reach out and draw his head down to hers, to place his tanned, strong hands upon her breasts and glory in his caresses.

"Good-night, *pequeña.*"

His hot breath in her ear inflamed her further, but, damn him, he crawled away from her, and rolled in the blanket!

She envied the exhaustion that made sleep come easily for him. After her lustful thoughts had abated, there were only her fears for Michael to keep her company that night, and terror made a chilling bedfellow.

"Amanda! Amanda!"

Miguel's loud bellow reached her from the depths of sleep.

She poked her head out from the damp blanket like a turtle from its shell.

"Is it light already?" she grumbled, retreating again from the rain beneath the blanket.

"Amanda, wake up! We'll have to leave now, while it's still dark. The weather is getting worse. It will take us longer to reach Belle Rêve."

"Oh!" Fully awake now, she stood, stamping the pins and needles from her feet. In seconds, her hair hung in streaming rat tails and her clothes were drenched. A chill in the pitch-black night now added to their discomfort.

Miguel led the way back through the undergrowth to the canoe, holding the storm lantern over his head to light her path. The dense foliage was even more oppressive now. It seemed to be closing in on her. Breathlessly, she ducked under a last branch and reached Miguel.

He had fashioned a handle for the lantern from a long, sturdy branch, which had a deep fork at its tip. He seated her in the curved prow of the canoe and handed her the pole with the lantern hooked in its cleft. This would guide the way, but as the pole extended just a few feet over the prow, the lantern illuminated only a small area of black water; it was far from being very efficient.

"Tell me if you see anything in our path," Miguel ordered, shoving the canoe out into the water and leaping in behind her.

She scanned the bayou carefully, wishing the puddle of light were larger. By the time obstacles could be seen in their path, it took all of Miguel's strength to steer the canoe around them. There was no current to aid his paddling, only black glistening water on every side and a black void beyond. She wished that he would allow her to take some of the burden of paddling.

"Go right, right, ooh, quick!" Amanda squealed suddenly. With relief she felt the canoe veer rightward.

The lantern's light had revealed cypress knees, squatting like obscene, twisted dwarfs in their path, and the small craft had but narrowly avoided crashing into them.

In places she sensed that the trees met in a tunnel over the bayou, for moss hung down to the water's surface and brushed against their faces like cobwebs in the dark. It was all she could do not to scream, for her nerves had reached a point where she felt anything would unhinge her.

Still it rained. She threw off the Indian blanket, which had long since been soaked through, as were her shirt and breeches. Her arm ached from holding the lantern pole, her back groaned from the cramped position she had maintained.

"Miguel, can I rest my arm, just for a few minutes?" Relief flooded her as she saw him nod.

She wedged the lantern's makeshift handle under the seat, and stretched, then tried to squeeze the water from her streaming hair. There was a little wind now. Perhaps it would blow away the rain, she thought? She would not allow herself to think of Michael. If she did, she knew she would fall apart.

Miguel, watching her, marveled at her calmness. Though they had made little progress that night, he knew Belle Rêve was not far off. She must know it, too, yet she showed no outward sign of fear.

With her hair hanging in a wet curtain about her face she looked as she had that first day by the pool above Blanes. Her eyes shone wide and luminous in the lantern light, the lashes tipped with raindrops, and despite all that had occurred, her beauty, like that of a child, was still fresh and innocent. Reluctantly, he tore his glance away from her, and diverted himself by trailing his blistered hands in the bayou.

The rain eased somewhat over the next hour, though the wind did not. It lifted, shaking the cypresses playfully and causing the trailing, gray moss to dance and cavort like ghastly fairies. A sickly moon appeared, fleeing before a retinue of tattered clouds. Amanda shivered and huddled deeper into the false security of the fragile canoe.

The feeling of impending doom grew. She wondered desperately how she could ever hope to rescue little Michael, when all of her felt frozen rigid with fear. Her teeth began to chatter. She hugged herself tightly, clamping her jaw hard as a soft, strangled sob escaped, to quell the sound.

"Don't, Amanda," Miguel commanded.

His voice was comforting, oh, God, yes, so comforting. There was anguish in his eyes.

She nodded mutely, drawing a deep breath to calm herself. And then suddenly, wonderfully, he was pressing her down, down into the canoe.

His lips were sweet and filled with urgency as they covered her own, his arms, a haven for her trembling body. His touch beguiled and tantalized her senses, dispelling fear and melting through its icy grip about her heart.

Softly he loved her, prolonging what could be their last time together, willing himself to linger. His caresses seemed to promise an eternity could pass and they would not forget this night, could not forget it. No words were said, for none were needed. Desire—savage and hungry and bittersweet, born of their need for each other—said it all.

Miguel's lips upon her breasts created ripples of delight that eddied ever wider through her, and the feel of his body, pressed tightly to hers, excited a silent cry of yearning deep within. Yes! Love me, Miguel, take me, I am yours! she pleaded soundlessly.

As if he heard her innermost pleas, he entered her. She was like a flower that opened its petals to welcome the sun as he did so. He was drowning inside her, lost in a sea of the senses, and *Díos,* how he wanted to drown! The perfume of her hair was like fresh grasses in his nostrils, her lips were clover on his own. How could he have denied that he loved her? If it was destined they should die, then let it be now, now while he cradled her in his arms!

Afterward, he still held her tightly, as if loath to be parted from her by so much as an inch or a second in time.

When he finally spoke, his voice was thick with emotion.

"I love you, Amanda, more than I believed it possible to love a woman! Without you, there is no life for me. I vow, before God, that never will we part again; *nothing* will part us!"

"Not even—death?" she whispered.

"Not even death!" he swore hotly.

A tear trickled down her cheek, and with it came an overwhelming stab of regret. They had wasted so much time! Would there be a tomorrow for the two of them? Or would Death's spidery fingers spin a final web of Destiny about them?

Chapter Sixty-Three

When dawn came it found them exhausted, trying to paddle the light canoe against a blustering wind that whipped the bayou until it resembled a sea, sending miniature waves scudding against the banks.

"It's no use, Amanda!" Miguel cried, shaking his head. "We'll have to leave the canoe and go the rest of the way on foot, *sí?"*

She shouted agreement, her words lost in the wind.

Together they managed to battle the craft to the banks, then wedged it between some bushes.

"Here's your pistol, *pequeña."* Miguel grinned. "You're sure you won't change your mind and hand me over to them, aren't you?" He feigned doubt.

"Quite sure," she replied softly, taking it from him.

Miguel held her briefly, brushing a kiss to her lips. "Then, let's go."

They kept close to the bayou, squelching through the muddy banks and forcing their way around the tangle of bushes and trees. Amanda stumbled after Miguel, branches snagging in her hair as it flapped about her in the wind.

Miguel crouched down suddenly, and she followed suit.

"What is it?" she whispered.

"Look—through there—do you see it?" He pointed.

A few yards farther down the bayou a post stuck up out of the ferns, a weather-beaten sign hanging from it drunkenly by one nail. It creaked back and forth in the wind. Though the paint was faded by time and weather, Amanda could still make out the words: Belle Rêve. Beautiful Dream.

"The house must be around here somewhere. Keep low," Miguel murmured.

They moved like Indians through the undergrowth.

And suddenly there it was, set back from the muddy levee by only a few dozen yards. Somehow, she had not expected the house here, so close to the bayou. Much of the roof had been torn away, as if gouged out by some huge animal's claws, while the rest sagged inward. The once-white walls were faded and lichened a dismal gray-green. The ornate columns were rotted and overgrown with vines gone rampant, while the upper veranda sagged crazily under the weight of the vegetation. The shutters that still remained banged open and shut with a forlorn, hollow sound, while the glassless windows stared blindly out across the bayou like stark, sightless eyes.

Amanda felt a hysterical urge to giggle, for never had she seen a dwelling that resembled a beautiful dream less: it was the house of a nightmare!

The live oaks that straddled the bayou fronting the mansion had massive width to their branches. Here the cypress roots hung down exposed, as if a giant knife had hacked away the natural levee to reveal these grizzled cords. It was an eerie house, she sensed, a house of evil memories, and she shivered and felt suddenly cold.

They retreated back into the bushes. Amanda could feel the tension building inside her. Now that they were here, she wanted it over, done with!

"What do we do now, my love?" she asked breathlessly.

Miguel eyed her eager face and prepared himself for the argument that would undoubtedly follow.

"You, my fiery wench, will do nothing!" he announced sternly.

"Oh, no, Miguel! We agreed we'd do this together! I'll not stand and watch like a—a docile cow, while you do it alone!" she fumed.

"Now, listen. I will *not* let you take the risk!" He ran his hand through his black hair wearily. "You're a woman, and—"

"And nothing, you arrogant, overbearing bastard!" she flared angrily. "My being a woman has nothing to do with it! God knows, haven't I proved myself this past year?" she demanded. "I've survived everything that has happened to me as well—and better!—than most men could have. He's my son too, Miguel. I won't stand by and watch and have no part in freeing him! You're outnumbered, anyway. Now, *you* listen!" She raised the pistol. "I'm coming with you!"

Miguel heaved a defeated sigh. "Very well. But I promise you, Señorita Sommers, that *I* will give the orders when we are wed! And," he added sternly, but with a wicked gleam in his eyes, "your pretty rear will feel my hand upon it, if you defy my orders then!"

Amanda grinned cheekily. "I won't doubt that I'll feel your hand there, m'lord—but I wager it will not be for a thrashing!"

Miguel shook his head in exasperation. "Don't count on it, *querida,* don't count on it! Are you ready? Then, come. It's time I saw my son!"

Miguel swung himself quietly over the upper-story veranda, testing the rotted boards beneath his feet.

A shutter battered loudly behind him and he swung around, pistol in hand, before he realized the sound's source. Cursing himself for a fool, he pushed open the broken door and went inside.

The bedchamber looked little like it must have when the St. Vincents still lived there.

A four-poster bed, its pallet rat-bitten and mildewed, dominated the room. The commode and several carved chairs and a footstool lay overturned on the grimy floor. He poked the footstool with his boot. It crumbled where he touched. Cobwebs festooned the corners and the once-elegant brocade draperies were discolored and rotted, and hung in moldy shreds.

He slipped out to the landing, listening intently, but heard nothing except the keening of the wind in and about the house.

The stairs creaked as he went down, and several of the treads were missing. The balustrade rocked beneath his hand and he held his breath until it ceased, pistol cocked and ready.

In the hallway, the low hum of voices reached him. He sprinted toward the sound.

The door to the drawing room was closed, but Blake's voice carried clearly now, and that of the woman with him.

"You fool! She'll never bring your damned de

Villarin here! Let's go, before it's too late."

"No, Yvette. We'll stay here, you and I, my sweet, as you once promised. Or have you forgotten?" he sneered.

"I beg you, Paul, give me my freedom papers, *cheri!* I'll meet you, *oui,* that is good—I will meet you in Baton Rouge and we will flee together. But let me go, now!"

"You're a liar, Yvette!" Paul sneered. "You would run and keep on running! Yes, I know now why you swore you loved me. The papers—that is all you *ever* wanted!" Paul giggled. "But they are in a safe place, my lovely Yvette, where you will never, never find them! So you see, *with* me you could live comfortably, but *without* me you will have to run, run from the hunt like a pretty little doe for your life. A runaway slave."

"*Non,* it's not true! I—I love you, Paul, I've always loved you. Didn't I go to the English bitch and tell her your terms for letting the brat go? That damned *capitaine* had warrants posted for our arrest all over town. But I took the risk of being caught because I wanted to please you, *cherie!*" Her voice was desperate and shrill.

"Hmmm. Perhaps you did it for me—and perhaps not," Paul answered petulantly.

Miguel tensed outside the door as the conversation ceased within. He heard the dragging of Blake's crippled leg upon the boards, then the crack of fist meeting flesh. The quadroon shrieked.

"No, Paul, please, don't, *cheri!* You're confused, you're tired! *Oui,* why don't you sleep until the girl comes with the don. I—I will watch for them."

"You only watch out for yourself, Yvette. While I sleep, you would kill me, I know it!"

"How could I," Yvette insisted, "when you keep my papers from me? Didn't I try to stop Gualterio and Watson from running off? You know I did! Doesn't that prove anything? Aah! No, Paul, *mon Dieu,* no! Don't hurt me!"

Miguel drew away from the door and slipped back down the hallway, a grim smile of satisfaction on his face. So, there were only the two of them, down here. Salome and his son must be in some other part of the house, if the baby still lived. He would catch up with Gualterio—Manuel's murderer—later!

The rooms leading off the hallway held nothing but decaying furniture. He headed back toward the stairway. As he mounted the first tread, a low wail reached him.

Miguel's reaction to his son's cry was a surprise even to himself. He halted dead in his tracks, unable to move. A great wave of joy rushing over him. Alive!

A door opened above him. He retraced his footsteps hurriedly, ducking inside the first room he came to. From his hiding place he watched as a huge black woman lumbered down the stairs. He sucked in a breath of excitement as she turned, and he saw his son for the first time, carried on her shoulder, his tiny hands reaching up to trap the woman's dangling earrings. Emotion flooded him.

Miguel took two steps before he realized he had moved. No! He couldn't, damn it, not yet! If he attempted to take the child, the woman's cries would bring Paul and Yvette running, and there was a chance that little Michael might be injured in the fighting. No, he'd have to wait! If Salome went back upstairs with Michael, he'd try to get the boy out first, then handle Blake.

But for that, he realized ruefully, he would have to get Amanda. She had been right, he admitted. He needed her.

Chapter Sixty-Four

Amanda paced furiously in the root cellar, fuming at Miguel's trickery. Barricading her in, indeed! She'd take him by the throat and choke him, bare-handed, when he returned!

He had seemed intent on learning the lay of the land when they circled the house, but she knew now that he'd really been looking for a place to lock her in. Damn, damn, damn him! And what did he expect her to do, if he never came back? Burrow out like a—a mole?

Little trickles of water were seeping under the rough plank door. It must be raining again, she realized. The wind whistled through the gaps in the planks. She peered out between the chinks: a white sky and a distorted view of Belle Rêve. There was no sign of Miguel, or anyone else. The minutes seemed hours, she thought miserably. Oh, Michael, Papa's coming! Please God, let him be alive!

Miguel shinned down the rickety columns and raced behind the mansion, past the ruined kitchens and crumbling slaves' huts to the cellar. He lifted the wooden slats and flung open the door.

"He's alive, Mandy, alive and thriving!" he yelled.

"Come on!"

There was no time for further words. He clutched her hand, and they tore back to the main house.

The wind was howling like a banshee now, threatening to wrest them from the ground and the rain, a wild and stinging whip against their faces. Suddenly, there was a great, ripping sound behind them. As they whirled about, a tree uprooted and crashed to the ground. One of the shutters tore from its hinges and whirled away like a playing card.

"Hurry, Amanda, up you go! Salome and our son are in the third room down the landing, *querida.* I'll distract Paul and Yvette to the front."

He hoisted her up the column. The furious wind tugged the shirt half free of her breeches and it flapped madly, as did her hair. Miguel's heart was in his mouth as he watched her make the short climb, for he feared the wind would pluck her from her hold. Sighing relief, he saw her clamber over the rickety railing and disappear into the bedchamber.

"Blake! Come and get me, you bastard!" he roared as he exploded through the front door, brandishing the pistol. His black eyes blazed, his mouth was set in a thin, hard line. The diversion worked.

The drawing-room door flew open and Blake stood there facing him, Yvette at his back.

"Damn you, de Villarin!" Paul's hand jerked up.

Miguel saw the flash as Paul fired, and threw himself aside. The ball gouged a trough in the plastered wall behind where he had stood, the pungent odor of powder filling the air.

Miguel squeezed the trigger on his own pistol. Nothing! It was jammed! He flung it aside, took a run and a flying leap down the hall, crashing Blake to the ground.

They fought like devils down the length of the hallway and halfway up the stairs. The rickety balustrade gave beneath their weight and they toppled down, Paul landing heavily on Miguel.

The strength of Blake's arms seemed superhuman to Miguel, and try as he might he could not break his grip! The madman's blue eyes blazed into his. The face seemed barely human, twisted into a snarling mask of evil. Paul held his advantage, his fingers like a vise about Miguel's throat, squeezing the life from him.

"Get the child, Yvette," Paul shrieked. "Get it! Kill it!" Still his fingers squeezed and squeezed, until the veins in the don's forehead bulged.

"No!" Miguel roared, summoning all his strength as Yvette fled past them to do her master's bidding. He arched his back and Paul's grip shifted.

"Yes! Yes!" Blake screamed, battering Miguel's head against the floorboards. "You have taken everything from me; now I will deprive *you* of your son!"

Miguel heaved upward, muscles shuddering with strain, thrusting his arms up between Paul's and forcing them apart to break his grip.

"You brought it on yourself, Blake!" Miguel spat through gritted teeth, as he bore Paul's arms down to his side. "With your greed and your lust! And for what? A woman who cares *nothing* for you! And for that, my sister died!"

Paul slammed his fist upward suddenly, the power of the blow sending Miguel reeling. He dragged himself to his feet and towered over de Villarin.

"If you had not sworn to cut her off without a penny,

she'd still be living!" Paul cried, his chest heaving, his pale face mottled purple with rage.

"Better dead than condemned to a living death as your wife!"

Miguel pulled back his knee as Paul leaped on him, jackknifing his boot into Blake's gut.

Paul ricocheted against the wall, his crippled leg bent under him. The blazing blue of his eyes grew feverish with cunning as he searched wildly about him. Miguel's pistol lay not two feet away! He scrabbled across the floor like a crab and picked it up, hurled it viciously at the don.

It caught Miguel full between the eyes, stunning him.

Amanda heard Paul's screamed command as she exited the bedchamber. It chilled her to the quick.

Yvette reached the landing and sped down the hallway, to the room where Salome watched fearfully from the opened door. The brat was wailing now. If she could but do Paul's bidding, this one last time, *oui,* then, then he would free her! She had to get the child!

"Give him to me!" the quadroon screamed at Salome, arms outstretched.

Salome hesitated, and, in that second, Amanda flung herself from the bedchamber onto the madam with all the fury of a hell-born wildcat!

"Kill my child, will you Yvette? No, never!" Amanda screamed as she knotted her fingers in the quadroon's ebony hair and hauled back hard. The woman shrieked in pain, clutching desperately at her scalp.

Yvette's eyes had narrowed until they were but slits, her mouth an open gash of color, but Amanda felt no pity. Bloodlust surged through her veins. She was invincible!

Suddenly Yvette brought back her elbow with a vicious jerk into Amanda's belly, and she reeled backward, the breath knocked from her in a sickening rush. The force of the blow sent her sprawling to her back on the rotted carpet of the landing.

The quadroon laughed throatily, her eyes glittering with excitement as she stood, hands on hips, staring scornfully down at the girl. She brought back her foot, aiming a kick at Amanda's ribs.

Instantly Amanda's arm snaked out, grasped the quadroon's ankle and pulled hard. Thrown off balance, Yvette toppled headlong over Amanda with a muffled oath.

Hurriedly, Amanda shoved the taller woman from her and scrambled to her feet. A painful cramp knotted her side, and her breath came in short, gasping pants. She stood quite still for several seconds, trying desperately to catch her wind.

Yvette rolled sideways, stood finally, and feinted a lunge to Amanda's left.

Amanda sprang to block her path, fearing the quadroon meant to rush her, to pass her at speed in a desperate attempt to reach the room where Salome and Michael were.

As she threw herself forward, Yvette leaped nimbly to one side, shoving Amanda hard in the small of her back as she did so!

The impetus hurtled Amanda full force against the staircase bannister, and would have thrown her clear over it and to the hallway below, had she not had the presence of mind to fling herself about to face Yvette and break the momentum.

The woman was on her instantly, forcing back her

face with a splayed hand until Amanda's hair hung free over the empty space. Below came furious crashing and falling sounds as Miguel fought his own desperate battle with Paul.

Amanda gripped fiercely at the flimsy wooden bannister at her back. Yvette's dusky face was but inches from her own, the full, scarlet lips split in a smile of victory.

"Nothing can help you now, *cherie!*" she crowed, suddenly removing her palm from Amanda's face and, instead, thrusting her full weight against her, her nails biting like talons into the girl's shoulders beneath the rough cloth of her shirt.

The bannister gave an ominous cracking sound behind her. Now! She must do something now, or it would be too late! Grunting with effort, she thrust forward, trying frantically to topple the woman backward. At the same time, her hand crept up, unnoticed, from its grip on the bannister, up, up the length of Yvette's body, until suddenly, she hooked her finger in the woman's hooped earring and yanked with all the force she could muster!

Yvette screeched and let go, raising her hand to her torn and bleeding earlobe. While she was distracted by her wound, Amanda, freed from her, lashed out with her feet, cracking the madam hard across the shins. This was no time for fair play, she thought grimly, for life was the victor's prize, and death, the vanquished's!

Nimbly, she grabbed Yvette's wrist, forcing it up and behind her back until the quadroon screamed with pain. Using the twisted arm as an agonizing lever, Amanda forced the woman down the landing.

"The authorities will be delighted when I hand you

over, Yvette," she panted. "Get in here!" She forced the woman before her into the dusty bedchamber, intending somehow to lock her in.

Suddenly, the madam sidestepped from Amanda's grip, and tugged her to the floor. They thrashed wildly there for several minutes, until, finally, Amanda gained the upper hand. She straddled the quadroon, fighting to draw a deep breath, convinced that now she was the victor, for the woman lay curiously still. The confidence faltered. Confused, Amanda saw a slow, sly grin crease Yvette's face, and simultaneously she felt the nose of Roger's pistol—forgotten in her fury—at her back! She clutched at her shirt front. Gone!

"You fool!" Yvette sneered, crawling out from under Amanda, the weapon still trained on her back. "You'll never live to hand me over!"

"Will you kill me too, then?" Amanda countered, playing for time. "Will you murder me as you murdered Simone and Guy St. Vincent!" If only she had a weapon.

"Oh, I didn't kill them, *cherie!*" Yvette declared. "It was Paul. I merely told him how! He loves me, you see, and they would not sell me to him. A little poison every day for Madame Simone, a nasty, messy accident for Monsieur Guy—it was simple! And if that crazy fool had but given me my papers, I would have been safe, and rid of him by now!" she finished, her eyes glittering.

"Then you never loved him! You promised you would go away with him when he returned rich, when the people of New Orleans had forgotten their suspicions. But you lied to him, didn't you?" Amanda sought desperately to prolong the strange conversation, for but a foot away lay an upturned footstool, so near—and yet so agonizingly far!

"Yes! He set me up on Royal Street and promised to return a wealthy man. As soon as he freed me, I would have taken his money and left!"

Amanda smiled. "You're a clever woman, Yvette, but not clever enough!"

She dived for the stool, picked it up and hefted it at Yvette.

The quadroon stepped backward to avoid it, one, two steps. They carried her out of the French windows and onto the sagging veranda.

Damn! Amanda cursed hotly, for the pistol was still clasped in Yvette's hands! Frantically she swung around, searching for a vase, a chair, anything!

Yvette's smile broadened. She leaned confidently against the railing, a triumphant smile upon her face.

And then, as Amanda watched, Yvette's expression changed to a mask of terror as the railing gave way behind her. Her scream sounded even above the howling wind. She disappeared from view.

Salome charged past Amanda to the gaping hole and looked down, shaking her head in disbelief. She let out a deep wail of anguish, her enormous body rocking with grief.

Amanda turned and raced across the landing to the other room. She stopped at the doorway, suddenly afraid to go in.

But, no, he was there in a little wicker basket and very much alive, chubby legs thrashing, arms flailing, his mouth wide open and screaming lustily for food! She picked him up, her eyes streaming with tears of joy, and pressed him fiercely to her breast.

"Michael, oh Michael, Mama's here, Mama's here!" She laid her cheek against the soft, downy one of her son and tightly squeezed her eyes shut. "Dear God, thank you!" she breathed.

Miguel shook the fog from his head, tasting blood as it trickled down from the gash between his eyes. He hauled himself upright by the sagging balustrade.

Paul Blake was standing too, blond hair disheveled above wild, tormented eyes.

He came at Miguel suddenly with a tremendous roar that was almost inhuman, meeting Miguel's fist as he charged. The crack of knuckles against jaw was as sharp as a pistol shot. Paul folded to the ground.

Miguel whirled about and leaped up the stairs, his only thoughts for Amanda and their child.

The wind was maniacal, screaming in through the ravaged roof and with it, now, came the rain.

Amanda met him as he reached the landing, Michael in her arms. Her face blanched white as they heard a cracking sound behind them.

"Miguel!" she cried. "The house!"

"Sí!" Miguel agreed grimly, hurrying her down the stairs. "It'll be about our ears any minute, *querida!"*

He looked back up the staircase warily, fearing pursuit.

"Yvette's dead, Miguel. The railing—it gave way!" She sobbed.

"Paul's still alive, but unconscious. I'll get you and our son to safety, and then I will deal with Blake!" he swore harshly, hurrying her down.

"That's what you think, de Villarin!"

Paul blocked the doorway, a dagger in his hand.

"Now, where's Yvette?" he demanded. He wore a dazed expression.

Miguel fought the urge to throw himself on the man, and stepped in front of Amanda.

"She's dead, Blake, as surely as if you killed her with you own hands!" he said in a soft voice.

"Dead?" Paul asked wonderingly. "No! It's a trick—she can't be dead!" He took a faltering step toward them. "What have you *done* with her?" His voice rose to a shriek.

"What Miguel says is true, Paul! She toppled from the veranda railing," Amanda vowed, her eyes never leaving the gleaming blade in his fist. Her heart hammered, and she quietened the whimpering baby with trembling hands.

Paul stared at them blindly, turned, and flung open the door. With a last, disbelieving smile, he limped out into the savage storm.

"Come on!" Miguel urged Amanda, taking Michael in his arms.

"Where—?" she cried, the wind stealing her breath away as they stepped outside.

"To the root cellar! It's our only chance!"

Together they fought their way to the rear of the house, battling the wind's ferocious onslaught at every step. It was nigh impossible to stand.

Beneath the veranda, Paul Blake kneeled over Yvette's twisted body. His mouth worked, but his words were inaudible. Fear froze Amanda in her tracks.

"Don't stop, *pequeña!*" Miguel roared. "We're almost there!" He dragged her the last few yards, Michael bundled under his other arm.

She took the baby from him, while he clambered up the earthen bank to wrest open the cellar door. Flinging the hair from her eyes, she peered through the whirling rain for Paul's figure. She could see no sign of him! Then she realized why.

Where Paul had been crouched now lay a massive, uprooted live oak.

Epilogue

Amanda slipped out of bed and pulled a wrapper around her.

In the courtyard, birds were singing in the sunshine, and above their chirruping came the furious din of a baby's hungry cries.

Taking a last peek to make sure Miguel was really asleep, she left him to his snoring and hurried to the adjoining bedroom.

Michael's cries had stopped before she entered the room, and she knew that Nellie had reached him first.

Sure enough, Nell sat in a chair, the baby happy in her lap and babbling as she spooned him his porridge.

"Thank you, Nell! You're so good with him—and he loves you! Are you sure you won't come back to Spain with us?" she wheedled, while kissing Michael's forehead.

"I'm sure, ducks, though Gawd knows, I'll miss the two o'ye!" Nellie pronounced firmly. "Never was a body so 'appy as this one, when I seed the three o'ye in that there canoe! Thought ye be dead at yer Mister Blake's 'ands, I did, or blowed away by that bleedin' hurricane, at the least!" She shuddered.

"Believe me, Nell, we were equally glad to see you,

and Roger and his men! Well, that's all behind us now, thank God!" Amanda's face darkened somewhat. "Paul deserved to die, but I'm glad it wasn't at Miguel's hand! I—I think Paul would have wanted it that way—to be with Yvette 'til the last!"

Nellie nodded sagely. "Aye, luv, God moves in mysterious ways! And where is the King o'Spain? Still at 'is bed?"

"Yes." Amanda smiled. "He—he was exhausted." She blushed crimson.

Nellie's red curls jiggled as she burst into guffaws of raucous laughter.

"I'll wager 'e was, ducks, if'n that look 'e gave yer as ye climbed the stairs last night was anything to go by—fair gobbled ye up with 'is eyes, 'e did!"

Amanda's blush deepened. "Any word from Roger?" she asked, trying to change the subject.

"Aye. 'E sent word this mornin' that Charlie-boy and that Gualterio was caught last night by 'im an 'is men, trying to buy passage on a merchantman. So yer see, yer free at last!"

"Hmmm," Amanda said doubtfully. "Except for James. He knows none of what has happened yet!"

"Oh, don't ye fret, Mandy. It'll work out, mark me words! 'E'll go back to 'is bloomin' ships for consolation—in 'is blood it is, the sea." She chuckled and winked at Amanda, blue eyes twinkling. "Much as my profession's in mine! I'll be rich as Midas, ducks, ye'll see, if'n that place on Royal Street be 'alf the gold mine I thinks it—oh! Me and me bloomin' great mouth!" She covered that mouth with one hand, looking decidedly guilty and not a little flustered. "Are ye done then, Michael, my sweetin'? Off to Mama then!"

Nellie suddenly handed a sticky Michael to his mother and beat a hasty exit to the door.

"Just a minute, Nellie Flagg!" Amanda said sternly, lips twitching.

"Wot?" Nellie inquired innocently, her eyes refusing to meet Amanda's.

"Am I to understand you mean to take over that—that *place?*"

"Ye've got it, luv!" Nellie replied defiantly. "And don't ye try t'talk me out o' it, neither!"

"I wasn't going to, Mistress Flagg, for it would not sway you if I did! I only wanted to say, if you ever change your mind, about coming to Spain, you'll always have a special place with us there, and in our hearts." She grinned. "After all, Nellie, 'tis your life, t'do with as ye see fit!" she finished, mimicking Nellie's broad accent to perfection.

Nellie shook her head in exasperation, and left Amanda and Michael alone.

She wiped his porridge-covered chin and laid him down on the bed to play. He'd grown in the few weeks they had been separated, but the resemblance to Miguel showed in his stubborn little chin and wide, brown eyes.

Michael crowed with delight as she leaned over him, letting a coppery strand of her hair dangle in his reach. He batted at it, arms and legs flailing with glee as he trapped the silken tress and drew it eagerly to his mouth.

"No, my pet, that's not to eat!" she laughed, disentangling her hair.

She rocked him until he fell asleep, then returned him to his basket.

Miguel was still asleep in their room, his face burrowed under a pillow. Amanda donned her yellow-sprigged gown and sallied below.

Roger's cook had outdone herself with the morning fare. Steaming coffee, mounded platters of buttered sweet rolls, fragrant, savory omelettes stuffed with mushrooms, grilled kidneys—the table was set for a feast!

"Good 'morrow, Roger!" she cried gaily. "I'm ravenous!"

"It's not surprising, m'dear, after your ordeal. Coffee?" he inquired.

"Yes, please!"

"I'll take a cup, too," James called from the doorway.

He strode across the salon to join them.

Amanda smiled her welcome, at a loss for words. When she could finally speak, James spoke at the same time, and their voices trailed away, embarrassed.

"You first!" James declared gallantly.

"No—no, you, please." What on earth was she to tell him? That by the end of the week, she would be another man's bride? No, that would never do! She must be kind, but firm; regretful, but not *too* regretful. Above all things, she didn't want to hurt him!

"Well, Amanda, I just came to tell you that you would do me great honor by consenting—are you unwell?" He stopped, eyeing Amanda's sudden pallor and shortness of breath.

"No, no, James, it—it was the coffee," she lied breathlessly, fanning her mouth with her hands, "too hot!"

"Hmmm. Now where was I? Ah, yes, you would do

me great honor by consenting to allow me to name my new vessel after you, the *Fair Amanda.* How does it ring?" he asked her, grinning at her confusion. His sea-green eyes were merry.

"It sounds—wonderful!" she admitted lamely, a tinge of disappointment in her voice.

"Don't look so glum, madam! Anyone would think from your face that you had expected a proposal!"

She startled, caught the gleam in his eyes and broke into relieved laughter.

"You rogue!" she exclaimed in mock severity. "You know, don't you—about Miguel, and that Michael is safe?"

"Guilty, Amanda! Your garrulous friend waylaid me, dragged me into the study, and sat upon me until I'd listened to it all! Am I invited to the wedding?"

"Why, yes, I suppose so," she answered doubtfully. "You don't seem too disappointed that you're not to be the groom?" In truth, she felt a little hurt!

Roger coughed discreetly and left the room, and Amanda shot him a grateful smile. James picked up her hand and held it tenderly.

"I am, my love, in many ways. I care deeply for you, you understand? But marriage!" He shuddered. "It struck me well at first, but then I thought on it as I rode the flatboat up to Baton Rouge. A wife, a child, a home! Amanda, I'm not ready yet to settle down. Can you forgive me?"

"Yes!" Amanda cried, a little too eagerly for James's liking. "And thank you for everything."

"Then, forgiven, I will claim a kiss from the bride!"

He lifted her clear off the floor and gave her a smacking kiss full upon the lips.

* * *

"Happy, *pequeña?*" Miguel asked.

"Very!" Amanda replied, sighing as he put his arms about her waist and drew her close.

He rested his chin on the top of her head thoughtfully. "When I found you gone after Esteban freed me from the warehouse, I went crazy, thinking I had lost you!"

"We were both blind! But I'm yours, Miguel, for always!" she vowed. "There will be no one else."

"I should hope not, Doña Amanda. I am a most jealous husband!" Miguel grinned, his black eyes gleaming devilishly. "Though I feared it might be necessary to call out your Captain Mallory at our wedding! Young rogue! He claimed his bride's kiss many times over, I thought," he added in mock severity.

"Oh, Miguel, there was never anything between us, save that one time, and—"

"Sssh, my love, I was but teasing you! Whatever happened before is done, finished with! I care only for tomorrow, all of our tomorrows, together, *sí?* Is our son sleeping?" he added, pride in his voice.

She glanced across the cabin. "Yes. The ship's motion is like a cradle; he's fast asleep." Amanda smiled tenderly.

Miguel released her, and she leaned against the port window, staring dreamily at the rosy sky, shot with fiery orange and amber light from the setting sun.

The trough cut by the ship was flecked with molten gold, as gold as the topaz ring upon her wedding finger, she thought, pressing it to her lips.

Miguel turned her to him, and she saw that he was

naked, all curling black hair and tanned flesh, and dark eyes that smoldered with desire for her.

He reached down and plucked the pins, one by one, from her hair, until it fell to her waist, a tumbling river of burnished silk in the sunset. Her lips were moist and slightly parted below sable eyes that glowed with love.

"'We have wasted so much time,' you said, *mi estrellita,* did you not?" he asked, a slow smile spreading from his eyes to his lips. "Well, I intend to make it up to you!" he murmured huskily.

"And how, m'lord, do you intend to do that?" Amanda demanded, teasing.

She unfastened her gown, letting it fall in a silken mass about her feet, and stepped toward him, as naked as he.

"Come, *querida,* and I will show you," Miguel promised, leading her to the bed.

"On the contrary, Miguelito, my love! Tonight, *I* will show you!"

Amanda leaned up on one elbow and blew out the candle.